Unanimous praise for bestselling author Susan Johnson

"Johnson uses her fertile imagination to blend a strong heroine, unbridled sex, and . . . history into unadulterated fun." —*Publishers Weekly*

"Her romances have strong, intelligent heroines, hard, iron-willed men, plenty of sexual tension and sensuality and lots of accurate history. Anyone who can put all that in a book is one of the best!" —*Romantic Times*

"The author's style is a pleasure to read and the love scenes many and lusty!" —*Los Angeles Herald Examiner*

"She writes an extremely gripping story . . . with her knowledge of the period and her exquisite sensual scenes, she is an exceptional writer!" —*Affaire de Coeur*

BOOKS BY SUSAN JOHNSON

Seized by Love
Love Storm
Sweet Love, Survive
Blaze
The Play
Silver Flame
Hot Streak (writing as Jill Barkin)
Golden Paradise
Forbidden
Sinful
Outlaw

SEIZED By LOVE

Susan Johnson

BANTAM BOOKS
NEW YORK TORONTO LONDON SYDNEY AUCKLAND

SEIZED BY LOVE

A Bantam Fanfare Book / published in association with Doubleday
Publishing History
Playboy Press edition published in 1978
Doubleday Loveswept edition / October 1993
Bantam Fanfare edition / May 1994

FANFARE and the portrayal of a boxed "ff" are trademarks of
Bantam Books,
a division of Bantam Doubleday Dell Publishing Group, Inc.

ISBN 0-553-56327-0

Published simultaneously in the United States and Canada

Bantam Books are published by Bantam Books, a division of Bantam
Doubleday Dell Publishing Group, Inc. Its trademark, consisting of the words
"Bantam Books" and the portrayal of a rooster, is Registered in U.S. Patent
and Trademark Office and in other countries. Marca Registrada. Bantam
Books, 1540 Broadway, New York, New York 10036.

PRINTED IN THE UNITED STATES OF AMERICA

OPM   0 9 8 7 6 5 4 3 2 1

Then talk not of inconstancy,
False hearts and broken vows;
If I, by miracle, can be
This live long minute true to thee,
'Tis all that Heav'n allows.

JOHN WILMOT,
SECOND EARL OF ROCHESTER
CIRCA 1670

Dear Reader,

When I wrote my first book, SEIZED BY LOVE, in 1978, I was thoroughly enamored with Georgette Heyer's Regency romances. Having recently discovered her, I'd managed to find copies of all her romances in a matter of a few months and read them in a pleasurable rush. But I was utterly frustrated in one sense because these fascinating characters never went beyond the genteel bounds of a kiss or two. What this world needs, I said to myself, is a Regency with sex. And that's what I set out to do when I wrote SEIZED BY LOVE. In my usual cavalier way, I ignored the fact that SEIZED BY LOVE wasn't set in England, nor did the events take place in the Regency period. It was stylistically a Regency, my paean to Georgette.

Now, I hadn't read SEIZED BY LOVE since I'd written it all those years ago, and when I looked at it recently with the thought of doing some minor revisions, I was astonished to discover how typical it was of the bodice-ripper era of romances. There's an actual bodice-ripper scene in the story. Wow, I thought, did I write that? I'd forgotten. But in the end I altered it very little because SEIZED BY LOVE is a book I couldn't write today. So much has changed. Women's and men's roles in our culture have substantially altered in the years since SEIZED BY LOVE was first published: steps toward equality in the workplace, in the family; legislation to insure civil liberties; new options for career choices have all contributed to both the perception and reality of today's woman and man. And those transformations—radical, subtle or mood permutations—are reflected in current romances.

But so many readers have written to request reprints of the Kuzan family series, I was very pleased when Bantam decided to reissue them. SEIZED BY LOVE is my only tribute to Georgette Heyer; books two and three in the series (LOVESTORM and SWEET LOVE, SURVIVE) are further evolutions in my story-telling techniques. As a painter originally, I'm familiar with stylistic and creative changes. Think of these books as my "early Russian style" in contrast to the new Susan Johnsons.

I hope you enjoy this introduction to the Kuzans. Nineteenth-century Russia was a land of beauty and harsh contradictions, its aristocracy capable of savagery and the most refined sensibilities, the landscape vast, varied, dramatically majestic. Nikki and Alisa's story is one small part of that enormous canvas. LOVESTORM and SWEET LOVE, SURVIVE travel to more distant locales in the Empire of the Tsars and continue the story through two more generations.

Best wishes,

Susan Johnson

Susan Johnson must know a witch—one of those good, yet powerful witches who can create magic for her . . . I'm not often asked to review books for *Affaire*, and I must say to review a classic like SEIZED BY LOVE was indeed an honor.

Written in 1978, SEIZED BY LOVE is the first of the Russian series written by Susan Johnson. It was our first hint that Susan Johnson was special. Let's start with her annotated footnotes, an exceptional tactic because for the first time, an author realized and addressed the intellect and interest romance readers have in history, and she educated us. Secondly, she threw convention to the wind and set her story in Russia. And, just think, 15 years ago, it was almost unheard of for a heroine in a romance not to be a virgin; the hero never admitted to having children, except with a deceased wife. More than those things, though, Sue Johnson took sex scenes to a new level, still unreachable by most.

Meet Alisa and Nikolai, the two unconventional stars of the tale. Alisa is prim and proper and is in an untenable marriage with an old, abusive husband. Nikolai, privileged, spoiled, and bored to tears is idling his time away at his country estate when a friend challenges him to seduce the unapproachable Alisa.

Alisa turns out to be much more than a single-minded, virtuous country maid. In fact, she's almost too much for Nikolai who not only doesn't want to marry now, he wants to marry a stupid woman who is a good breeder.

Is SEIZED BY LOVE a classic?

You bet! Because it withstands the test of time. It's true the market has undergone some changes since it was written, and authors have shied away from manipulating their characters in the same manner Ms. Johnson does Nikolai and Alisa. Yet, SEIZED BY LOVE rises above those changes and tells a wonderful tale.

Pass the Magic Wand over here, please, Sue. Better yet, keep writing!

—Louise B. Snead, Publisher
Affaire de Coeur

Contents

I.	The Wager	1
II.	The Seduction	28
III.	The Unbidden Spectators	52
IV.	The Reconciliation	60
V.	The Blissful Interlude	65
VI.	The Dénouement	75
VII.	The Necessary Option	80
VIII.	The Recalcitrant Mistress	97
IX.	The Beguiling Belle	160
X.	The Angry Lover	167
XI.	The Stalemate	196
XII.	The Chase	217
XIII.	The Halcyon Days	222
XIV.	The Reluctant Bridegroom	227
XV.	The Volte-face	257

Chapter One
THE WAGER

Karelia Province
Grand Duchy of Finland
April 1874

The last goblet had, long before, been flung aside in toast and joined the brilliant display of broken crystal gracing the stone hearth. There, the litter of crystalline shards reflected and transformed the firelight into a dazzling, fluttering phosphorescence. A few surviving candles guttered low in their branches while the shattered stumps of others bore mute evidence of Prince Nikolai's capricious fancy for a contest of marksmanship several hours earlier.

Now, on a low stage at one end of the large room, a weary group of musicians continued playing wild, haunting Gypsy music, while nervously watching the brooding face of their master, the young prince. They hoped to successfully anticipate or assuage Prince Kuzan's mercurial moods and thus avoid, at least this night, any more dangerous whims.

At times like these, when the tedium of the world was too much with him, the Prince retired to his hunting lodge to brood upon the melancholy inequities.

Nikki's hunting lodge was a timber and stone villa constructed by local artisans in the early years of the seventeenth century. A Swedish noble had this retreat built for himself, situating it prettily on a rocky rise in a pine forest. The terraced gardens, in the Italian manner, were added by a later heir after a tour of Italy. With the advent of the romantic English garden, yet another descendant landscaped acres and acres of forest, transforming the wilderness with an extravagant hand and the toil of hundreds of laborers over ten years into charming green alleys, wide vistas of rolling terrain, crowning the elaborate scheme dramatically with a Greek temple perched on a distant grassy knoll. The local stonemasons had erected a reasonable facsimile in rough-hewn granite, a rustic but altogether lovely interpretation symptomatic of the then-fashionable rage devoted to whimsical follies.

Although the high Renaissance had already come and gone when the main structure had been built, none of the lighter attributes characteristic of Renaissance architecture had filtered up north. The villa itself retained an overwhelming medieval character; stone turrets crowned with peaked tile roofs punctuated the walls, bottle mullioned windows caught and reflected the northern sun, enormous stonework on the ground floor supported the heavy timber walls of the second story. In a lavish display of his wealth, the Swedish aristocrat had the walls pierced wherever possible with windows, lighting the interior with dazzling color through the multicolored panes.

Tonight Prince Nikolai Mikhailovich Kuzan had been entertaining a small party of fellow officers from his Guards Regiment. After participating in the April sixth fête-day of the Chevaliers Gardes with its day-long riding exhibition and religious celebrations, they had felt the need for a holiday and Nikki had invited them to his lodge for a fortnight of hunting. However, in the eight days elapsed, the quarry had been confined exclusively to the two-legged female variety, since Nikolai had thoughtfully imported a bevy of Gypsy wenches to provide diversion.

Now, as morning approached, men and women lay entwined in each other's arms about the room, some on pillows scattered on the Tabriz carpet, others on the colorful divans. One couple, in what to a less dissipated audience would be a tasteless lack of decorum, was busy on top of the dining table; all were in diverse states of drunken abandon and dishabille.

Tanya, a beautiful young Gypsy girl, was swaying in a provocative, sensual dance before Nikki's sprawled form. One of his hands lightly held a small flask of brandy on his powerful chest. The other hand, lying carelessly on the chair arm, would occasionally move listlessly to the nearby table and turn over another card in the game of solitaire he was indifferently and infrequently pursuing while regarding Tanya, who skillfully undulated to the wild, frenzied tempo. Through narrowed tawny eyes, Nikki watched her tantalize him. Her graceful young body, half revealed in a scanty blouse and silken skirt, twirled close, then retreated, displaying a wanton invitation from brilliant dark eyes. The firelight caught the coruscation of golden highlights from the heavy hoops in her ears and from the multitude of sparkling necklaces twined round her slender neck and swaying against her trembling half-naked breasts.

Behind the curtain leading to the kitchen corridor, the youngest footman whispered to an old retainer familiar with the idiosyncrasies of his new employer. "Is the Prince always so surly and moody?"

Igor admitted that the Prince was not in the best of spirits. "The Kuzans have a devilish temperament, sometimes little better than savages," the old servant explained without malice, having happily served the household for decades. "They like fast horses, bad women, and good wine. Between father and son, they have developed one of the finest studs in the Empire, crossing English mares with bloodstock from the Orlov-Rostopchin and the Provalsky stud. They also breed Stryelet stock, which are even more rare. Their horses are world-renowned. The young Prince doesn't do so badly in the breeding department either." The old man chuckled. "Like father, like son, they say," he added softly, remembering the reckless pace the old Prince Mikhail had set in his youth before marriage to a young Gypsy girl had tamed his ways.

"More brandy!" The roar from the hall beyond echoed as Prince Kuzan impatiently banged on the table. The old man lifted his eyebrows and shrugged in cheerful resignation. Both servants hurried to obey the command.

Tanya's hips still moved to the hypnotic tempo. Her dance was intended to arouse, to primitively and seductively provoke the animal mating instinct.

It did and he was.

With a casual wave of his lace-covered hand, Nikolai abruptly dismissed the musicians and picked up his fresh bottle of brandy. Then he lunged to his feet and, as the music slowed to a stop, lifted her and disappeared into a curtained alcove.

The musicians discreetly stepped over the drunken bodies, avoiding, when possible, the broken glassware and china littering the floor. As they edged cautiously through the elaborately carved double doors, never certain of their safe departure from the eccentric young Prince and his raucous group of intimates until well out of sight and sound, their exit was hastened by a wine bottle thrown violently against the doorjamb, crashing into a thousand fragments and narrowly missing the last violinist. Some drunken music-lover, no doubt, annoyed at the termination of the pleasant background accompaniment to his lovemaking.

Scurrying through the narrow, dimly lit hallway and foyer out into the relative security and peace of the deep porch of the hunting lodge, the musicians exhaled a collective sigh of relief.

"Heaven help the servants in the morning who have to attend young Prince Kuzan. There's going to be hell to pay for his pounding head and thick tongue. Praise God, we won't see him again until evening, when the worst of his headache is gone." The leader of the musicians sighed.

"Maybe the pain of a throbbing head might make him more docile or at least more silent. I've never seen Nikolai so sullen as tonight. He must be tiring of his newest Gypsy bed warmer," the second violinist said wearily.

"Well, thank sweet Jesus, we'll be out of his range at least until tonight. Maybe Tanya will be able to soothe the dark mood he's in. Let's go to sleep, although the night is practically over," the youngest member of the troupe suggested.

In the alcove, Nikki casually dumped the girl onto the couch, thus freeing his hand to tip the brandy bottle to his mouth. The liquor flowed warmly down his throat. Thank God for brandy, he thought. It made life more bearable as it blurred the morbid edges of reality.

Sinking down heavily next to the recumbent girl, Nikki set the brandy bottle carefully on the floor and began to pull off his hunting boots. Tanya softly crept up into one corner of the large pillow-strewn couch and leaned back against the tapestry-hung wall, watching him with her dark eyes.

"I'm not in the mood," she said, pouting.

Nikki barely glanced at the sultry woman nestled against the wall, and continued without a pause to divest himself of his garments.

"You'd better get in the mood," he growled.

A thrill coursed through the black-haired beauty and passion blazed into her dark eyes. Tanya, although only seventeen, had long ago learned to accommodate men's varying tastes in bed, but she preferred violence with passion; hostility intoxicated her.

"I won't. I'm tired," her petulant tone persisted as she swung her long, shapely legs over the edge of the bed and began to rise.

The Prince's bare, powerfully muscled arm shot out and grabbed a handful of her satiny black curls, yanking her back onto the bed, pulling her down until she looked up into his golden eyes snapping with irritation.

"Bitch!" he whispered, well aware of Tanya's sexual preferences by now. But, having watched her enticing dances all evening, he wasn't in a temper to be toyed with.

"You're always playing games, aren't you? However, tonight, my sweet little whore, you find me in a suitably black humor to accommodate your preferences. If it's violence you want, I can be obliging."

Tanya's hand lashed out, long nails poised to rake Nikki's face. He caught her hand in midair, his reflexes still relatively sure despite the large amount of alcohol consumed. He crushed her wrist in a savage grip and she winced in pain—or was it pleasure? He couldn't tell.

As he held her, Tanya's little pink tongue appeared and ran provocatively over her full red lower lip, her dark eyes began to moisten, her breathing became ragged.

"Ah, my dear, you *do like* pain. I should introduce you to Prince Gorcheviv. He has a penchant for whips."

The Gypsy girl's half-closed lids lifted and she moaned sensuously.

"Damn!" He surveyed her through half-narrowed eyes. "How can I force a woman as aroused as you?"

Roughly he pushed her down into the pillows, spreading

her legs with his knees, pulling her nipples up and away from her necklaces into hard points of desire. Her body writhed beneath his coercion and her teeth bit into her full lower lip to keep from crying out in joy. She held her arms out wide, reaching for something to cling to as he pushed her skirt above her waist. Then, forcing her wider, he fiercely drove into her melting body, each violent thrust releasing a part of his frustration, each powerful surge a mindless hope for temporary oblivion. She began whimpering as he moved faster into her, his unbridled penetration and withdrawal savage, brutal. He didn't notice his back was running with blood where Tanya had run her sharp nails over the hard muscles that now moved rhythmically above her.

Much later, Nikolai abruptly woke from his sleep. The slightest sound was enough to instantly arouse him after many campaigns on the eastern frontiers, where the merest noise could be warning of danger from a stealthy Kirgiz intent on dealing a slashing *hallal*. Without moving, he slowly opened his eyes and through heavy black lashes swept a glance about the alcove. Tanya was searching through his clothes, which lay discarded on the floor. Looking for roubles, no doubt, he thought, dropping back to sleep. Prince Kuzan was extremely charitable to his light o'loves, showering them with gifts, jewelry, furs, as well as money, with a careless generosity. Greedy little bitch, he later reflected sleepily but not unkindly, for, after all, Tanya had to think of her future; her youthful charms would quickly fade.

By midafternoon Nikolai's fractious, irascible temper and pounding head were somewhat subdued; his two cohorts in arms, Major Cernov and Captain Illyich, and his young cousin Aleksei relaxed in the solace of a small clearing in the birchwoods. There they lay warmed by the April sun, calmed by the peacefulness of their surroundings, free from the chattering, volatile young Gypsy girls who had been discourteously dispatched and told to remain out of sight until called for.

Nikki lay sprawled at ease on the soft green grass, casually attired in superbly fitted cavalry boots, buckskins, and an embroidered moujik shirt open at the throat. His hands were clasped behind his neck as he squinted slightly into the bright sun of a gentle spring day—a poetic, storybook day redolent of bursting buds, fresh turned earth, and fertility.

Nikolai Mikhailovich Kuzan was a giant of a man. His mother's long-ago heritage from the Caucasus highlands was proclaimed in his swarthy complexion, heavy dark hair, prominent cheekbones, and aquiline profile. From his father's White Russian roots he had inherited not only his tremendous physique but also his enchanting tawny, liquid eyes, the pupils so large and dark as to appear black; magnificent, beautiful eyes brooding beneath heavy brows. The same kind of eyes that gazed out from opulent, exotically gorgeous Byzantine icons for eight hundred years; arrestingly splendid eyes that could be piercingly alert, indolently shuttered, or benignly calm. His harsh-featured face was softened by those redeeming eyes and by a sensitive mouth, now pursed in discontent.

Nikki tensed, stretched his lean frame like a great cat, then relaxed once again; the quiet sounds of the forest washed over him—new young birch leaves rustling in the breeze, a soft whisper from the bubbling stream lapping at the shore near the boundary of the clearing, the unceasing chatter of the birds overhead. The tranquillity of the woodland eased his tired body but failed to more than superficially alleviate the restless dissatisfaction of his spirit. Nikki was bored. Boredom—that constant and irksome companion that trailed him with a dogged persistence. Nikki had been leading the arduous and difficult life of leisure now for many years. Chronic leisure with its deadly, restless tedium was inexorably closing in on him.

He propped himself up on one elbow and from under slack lids surveyed his companions lounging carelessly around the remains of the repast the servants had brought out from the lodge. The ice had almost melted in the silver wine cooler and the half-empty bottles were sweating in the heat of the spring sun. The remains of the sumptuous *déjeuner sur l'herbe* lay scattered across the damask cloth and two wolfhounds were diligently eating them. Cernov and Illyich were carelessly tossing dice on a silver tray on the grass between them, while Aleksei was engrossed in a novel by Turgenev.

Nikki listened with his usual tolerant aloofness to the friendly bickering going on during the dicing.

"Tonight I want Cecelia; you had her the last two nights and I think it's my turn," Cernov said in a faintly bearish tone.

"Can I help it if she prefers me?" Illyich smiled complacently.

"I don't care. It's my turn tonight," Cernov insisted.

"What can possibly be the difference?" Nikki inquired in a low, husky drawl. "The wenches are all agreeable in every way if one does not mind being bored in short order."

"Oh, no. I fancy Cecelia's long legs and slender grace to those more voluptuous charms of Olga," Cernov responded ardently, recalling Cecelia's dancing performance the previous night.

"Come now, Gregor," Prince Kuzan remarked with the disenchantment of his thirty-three years, "one woman is as good as another." Then he lay back in the warm sun and shut his eyes.

"Speak for yourself, Nikki. I find Cecelia much more attractive, and I intend to have my turn," Cernov stated with a slightly aggressive emphasis.

Nikki's golden eyes fixed a look of mild contempt on the good-natured but now thoroughly heated Cernov.

"As you wish, of course, Gregor," Nikki replied soothingly. "Illyich, you understand, as host, I must attempt to placate all my guests. Perhaps tonight I could persuade you to take Tanya instead of Cecelia," he suggested politely, as though he were offering courteously the less blemished of two pears to a dinner guest.

"With pleasure!" Astrakan Illyich responded avidly. Tanya had been Nikki's mistress for three months now, and no one dared approach her, but if Nikki were graciously relinquishing the girl, Illyich would be a fool to refuse the offer.

Nikki calmly continued. "It is my firmest conviction that in order to survive, it is necessary to be amused, that one of the requisites in life is to stave off as long as possible the unpardonable sin—monotony. Tanya has become monotonous, so she's yours if you wish, Astrakan," he finished with finality.

Nikki tolerated a certain amount of boredom, but he had his limits, and Tanya had become tedious. He would give her a suitable parting gift after they returned to Petersburg. Nikki was known to be benevolent to his mistresses and she'd find a new protector soon enough if Illyich didn't wish to keep her, he assured himself.

Prince Kuzan was one of those aristocrats who filled their leisure with a dilettante's interest in literature, art, and even science. He spent the required time in social intercourse, gambling, clubbing, and country sports, but, above all, practiced an adroit venal gallantry as he dallied with the most exquisite of time-killers, *amour*.

He deliberately flaunted those principles that supposedly assured the continuance of the patrician order of society and publicly repudiated the cult of Victorian temperance and earnestness that was gripping even the volatile Russian mentality in the seventies.

In the crème de la crème, the genteel and refined upper reaches of Petersburg society, Nikki had been the despair of all the hopeful and enterprising mamas these fifteen years past, and now, at thirty-three, had been reluctantly abandoned by all but the most tenacious and optimistic matchmakers. The only child of a rich and powerful Prince, young Nikolai was himself rich beyond avarice, too handsome by half, a master of charm if the occasion warranted it and his fickle temperament acquiesced, well-liked and generous to a fault with his friends, doted on by his parents, and consequently marked by the complete absence of moral prejudices. He looked out on the world with the serenity that birth and wealth made possible, a spoiled child of fortune who accurately assessed the world as his pleasure garden, for nothing had yet occurred to disturb this comfortable and perfectly orthodox belief.

"Nikki! You can't simply give Tanya away! We no longer have serfs!" young Aleksei responded with the youthful, passionate chivalry of his nineteen years.

"Don't fear, Sasha, I don't intend to brutally turn her out in the cold. Tanya shall be well taken care of," Nikki said softly to soothe his young cousin.

Perhaps Aleksei was too young to be exposed to this licentious, whoring life he led, Nikki reflected uncomfortably. Maybe I should send him home. Aleksei's mother, indulgent in all things to her youngest son, had hesitated at Aleksei's pleas for an extended holiday with his favorite cousin, Nikki. Perhaps she was right. He himself had been thoroughly schooled in the notorious depravities of life before he was nineteen, but maybe this new generation was different. The rumblings of discontent and revolution, the promise of the industrial age, were beginning to be felt more insistently throughout the land. Maybe this seriousness of purpose was typical of Aleksei's generation. Although the revolutions of 1848, which had toppled thrones and melted governments away overnight, had barely touched Russia, and where they had, in outlying provinces, been ruthlessly suppressed, even the autocratic Russian monarchy had found it reasonable and prudent to free the serfs in 1861.

Nikki had been indulgently raised in an aristocratic society without purpose. Had society changed that much in fifteen years, or was Aleksei by nature simply less quixotic, less reckless? he wondered.

"Ah, chivalrous youth," Nikki teased Aleksei, "so quick to come to the defense of some poor damsel in distress, so ready to jump to the obvious generalizations and conclusions, always striving for the whole truth, as your present author so clearly points out."

"You've read Turgenev?" Aleksei asked incredulously, holding up the book, having never seen his older cousin so much as page through a magazine in his presence.

"Yes, I have, young sprout. I *can* read, you know." Nikki's leisure offered considerable free time. After all, one can spend only so many hours of the day and night in gambling and copulating, he thought, laughing to himself.

"It doesn't hurt to search for the truth," Aleksei protested. "It's better than just drinking, gambling, and whoring, which is all you ever do." He stopped abruptly, afraid he'd overstepped the bonds of friendship. His adoration of his older cousin was remarkably close to hero worship.

Nikki didn't take offense, ever ready to indulge his young cousin's moods, but said softly and thoughtfully,

"You young people crave primary colors, crave certainty, must have absolute answers to the 'accursed questions.' When you're older, you'll discover absolutes are often so elusive, they defy the most optimistic determination. Don't worry about Tanya, though, I'll not let harm come to her."

Nikki sighed to himself and marveled at the fresh vitality and naïveté of Aleksei's youth. Had he indeed ever been that young? He knew the sobering answer to that question and tried to shrug off the depression that always accompanied the contemplation of his past seventeen idle, world-weary years.

Nikki had never been able to deal in absolutes, right or wrong. He had, from a very early age, been plagued by doubts. He saw human beings in the glaring nakedness of their frailty.

The excellence of his education could be blamed, at least partially, for this slough of harsh reality. The diverse succession of scholars lured to "Le Repose" to instill in the only child and heir the fruits of their learned disciplines had found ready and fertile soil in the mind of the precocious young Prince. The monumental amount of knowledge of past civilizations he'd absorbed early on had reinforced his pernicious inclination to see each generation's touted achievements as puny human efforts in the ongoing scheme of things.

This lack of illusion left Nikki at times feeling helpless, if not, in fact, cynically melancholy. He often chose to dispel these bouts of depression by engaging in drunken, mindless orgies of pleasure. These week-long escapes into inebriated madness would for the brief interval anesthetize the worm of discontent. But his discontent was never explained, only assuaged or suppressed by the frenzied activity, the bottle of wine, a woman's touch.

Illyich broke into this morbid reverie with his usual jovial bonhomie.

"Aleksei, rest easy. I'll take excellent care of the beautiful Tanya," he assured the young boy.

"If she doesn't take care of you first," Nikki observed sardonically, raising one mocking eyebrow. "I hope you can afford to mount her. Like all women she's never satisfied, although, in contrast to the rapacious Countess Amalienborg, the price for Tanya's pleasure is cheap," remarked Nikki, remembering Sophie's insatiable demands for jewelry and furs.

"Have you no romance in that black soul of yours, Nikki?" Cernov inquired.

"Very little," Nikki replied dryly. His was a cynicism born of disenchantment, born of a constant struggle to keep a deepening melancholy at bay. "Most of the women in my reprehensible and checkered experience are ultimately vastly more interested in my considerable fortune than my romantic inclinations. And rich or poor, young or old, they are all willing—too willing. I've been whoring up and down this country for years and done my share of tasting the debauchery Europe has to offer as well, and I have yet to discover a woman who is any different. They are all yielding, all willing, all delightful, but inevitably all boring." To Nikki there was a deadly sameness to the affairs that all began so promisingly and then became so monotonous.

"Daily living is becoming so damnably dull, I'm beginning to consider the life of an ascetic as an alternative to this routine," Nikki complained.

Cernov clucked his tongue sympathetically and laughed. "My heart really bleeds for people like you, Nikki. If you do, you'll leave many unhappy and unfulfilled women behind in Petersburg. There have been allusions to your giving the Duc du Richelieu's reputation a run for the money in the boudoirs, as well as pressing the Elector of Saxony's record in the nursery.[1] Maybe Illyich and I could attempt to console those languishing doves in your absence."

"If we waited a fortnight or so, the ladies would be extremely eager for our—ah—solicitous ministrations, I should think," Illyich concluded playfully.

"Do you care about anything at all, Nikki?" Astrakan asked, half jesting, half seriously.

"Not a damn thing to care about, seems to me." The Prince yawned.

"Not even women?" Cernov asked.

"Least of all women, Gregor," the lazy drawl avowed. "On a scale of one to ten, I would be forced to reply—is there a number lower than zero?"

"Admit it, Nikki," Illyich continued more earnestly, "you'd be more bored after a week without women than you are this way. At least there's a variety to the boredom."

"You're right, of course," Nikki agreed reluctantly. "If only they weren't all so yielding; it takes away the piquancy of the chase. There's simply no challenge anymore. I can have any woman I please." The Prince closed his eyes.

"Oh-ho! Such illusions, such a lack of modesty." Cernov laughed.

"Three to one you can't," Illyich interjected quickly, the obsessive gambler in his nature unable to pass up an opportunity for a wager. He would quite happily lay odds even on his mother's demise.

"Can't what?" Nikki asked, not altogether sure what Illyich was betting against, but always ready to gamble too. His eyes sparkled with interest.

"Can't have any woman you want."

The Prince sat up. "You're on. But kindly soul that I am, I'll give you even odds. And let's say fifty thousand roubles just to make it amusing."

"Done!" Illyich laughed with pleasure. "A limit on the

time allowed, say, three days. That should be enough time, and I choose the woman, of course."

"Of course," Nikki replied affably. A small flutter of anticipation coursed through him, and a glint of amusement lit up his eyes as thoughts of the chase ran through his mind. Anything—any brief bagatelle to release him from this glazed lassitude. Yes, a seduction would be more interesting than hunting four-legged game. And in the case of a woman, the chase wasn't everything; one was always assured of additional delights upon completion of the hunt.

One can excuse Nikki, perhaps, for his lack of scruples, his indifference to others' feelings, his selfishness, when one considers that in the society in which he lived, his opportunities for observing noble thoughts and deeds were scarce in comparison with his opportunities for observing the utterly selfish ruthlessness with which pleasure was pursued.

"You're sure it matters not who my choice is?" Illyich inquired. He thought for a few moments, then a faint smile warmed his cheerful countenance as his eyes strayed across the river, over a picturesque but small meadow to a figure of a woman sitting near a grove of birch trees engrossed in her sketchbook and watercolors.

"It makes absolutely no difference," Nikki replied arrogantly. Then he hesitated, rising up on one shoulder. "You wouldn't be thinking of some old dowager, would you? I categorically draw the line at age fifty," he said suspiciously, scrutinizing Illyich.

"No, no," Illyich assured him. "Have no fear, she's suitably ripe."

Nikki sighed, his momentary pang of dismay dispelled.

"Ripe, you say. I look forward to the game," he said as he stretched supine once more on the green grass, conscious for the first time in weeks of a tangible excitement in his loins. With Illyich's money riding on the wager, it wasn't going to be child's play. Illyich bet to win, but Nikki was equally confident of success. He believed in his ability to overcome any woman's reservations, and Illyich's choice of a difficult, wary victim would make the predator's reward that much sweeter.

"Feel free to begin anytime," Illyich remarked as he smirked at Cernov and indicated the object of the wager with a nod of his head in the direction of the river.

Nikki's reverie was interrupted by these words. What did Illyich mean? Surely there was no one in these secluded acres except Gypsy or peasant girls, and neither of those would present him more than a second's hesitation before rolling in the hay. Was Illyich drunk this early in the afternoon?

As he slowly rose from his position of comfort under a flowering wild plum bush, Nikki stretched his long arms and flexed the muscles of his powerful shoulders to shake off some of the torpor of the lazy afternoon. His muscles rippled under the fine linen of his embroidered peasant shirt as he lifted both hands to run his fingers through his long black hair. He wore no beard, as per regulations for the Imperial Guard requiring a clean chin, nor chose to cultivate a mustache; his only concession to the hirsute fashionableness of the day was the growth of sideburns that extended several inches down his jawline.

Nikki strolled leisurely over to where Illyich and Cernov still rolled their dice. "Surely you jest. There can't be a likely female within ten miles of this spot," he said with mild incredulity.

"Beg to differ with you, my fine stud, but do direct your bloodshot eyes across the river and over yon grassy meadow. I believe you will take notice of a blaze of coppery hair with a delectable young body underneath the glorious coif." Illyich couldn't control his mirth any longer, and sputtered and guffawed rollickingly as he looked up into Nikki's horrified face.

"Good God! You can't mean the old merchant's wife. Come now, Illyich, that's even too bad for you. I recognize your necessity to make the assignment formidable, and I didn't anticipate an easy or willing quarry, but let's keep this somewhat within the bounds of propriety."

"Sweet Jesus. You and propriety don't even have a nodding acquaintance," Illyich retorted, still chuckling, immensely pleased with his choice.

"Look," Nikki pleaded in an effort to persuade Illyich of the folly of that particular woman, "why not choose a married Petersburg 'lady' who has already produced the necessary heir but has not hitherto strayed from the path of virtue or perhaps, an untried peasant or Gypsy girl who also values her innocence, even some bourgeois wife conscious of the earnestness of marital duty. Any of these would be difficult enough, but, my God, Valdemar Forseus's wife! She's totally outside the pale, rarely out of his sight, as closely guarded as a harem houri. And in addition, from the few times I've caught a glimpse of her in the Viipuri market square at her husband's side, she looks as cold as an ice maiden.

"Excluding those 'slight' problems"—Nikki's eyebrows emphasized the euphemism—"my father would horsewhip me or have one of his apoplexies if he caught wind of such an escapade. Forseus's land marches with ours along the entire river, and Father insists on friendly relations with the locals, so he's forever lecturing me that one must govern with mildness and justice. He's absolutely adamant about not misusing one's power and influence in autocratic actions. Why do you think I always import my females? It's safer than wenching all around the countryside and leaving by-blows so close to home. Father says the winds of change are bringing a new era, in which noble, bourgeois, and peasant will dwell together in a vast social mutation of some kind. You know he is perpetually concerned with the productivity of his estates, the conditions of his peasants, maintaining the dignity of the workingclass, and establishing a rapport with the hoi polloi. God, the whole idea is unmentionable!

"Besides, have you ever met Forseus? He's not entirely rational, I suspect; his eyes burn with a fever that's unnatural. I shall, with your gracious consent, beg off this particular female if you don't mind, Illyich."

"Nikki, I don't mind one whit. *Au contraire*, an easy profit, I say. That's fifty thousand sweet roubles, and I frankly admit, I don't mind taking it from you, Nikki dear, since you can so readily afford it."

"Damn!" Nikki exploded sullenly. "I didn't renege on the wager. I just think you should choose another woman."

"Sorry, Nikki, you said it was my choice, and there is my choice," Illyich said, and pointed theatrically toward the small figure on the opposite bank, completely oblivious of the attention she was attracting, unaware that her virtue was a subject of interest and debate among complete strangers.

When Nikki recognized that argument was pointless, with his characteristic charm he graciously conceded Illyich's point.

"Daresay, I might as well be off to commence the chase. There's no time like the present, et cetera, et cetera." He smiled, already half amused and anticipating the flirtation. For Nikki, obstacles existed only to be swept aside. He brushed away impediments that would bring lesser men to their knees and more sensible and prudent men to a cautious standstill.

"Nikki, reconsider," his young cousin Aleksei interjected uneasily, "it's not right. Your father, depend on it, would find it totally unacceptable. Suppose he does catch wind of it."

"With any luck, Father won't find out," Nikki responded calmly to his cousin's objections. "The lady scarcely would be inclined to bandy the news about, and we all are capable of holding our tongues."

Once Nikki's mind was made up, he could be unusually obstinate to change and, after all, he did have fifty thousand roubles riding on the outcome. Even though he didn't personally need the money, it would indulge his pet project of embellishing his cavalry troop. The magnificence of his troop outshone all others, and outfitting the men and horses in such extravagant adornments gave him a great deal of pride, but the personal expense was astronomical. He contemplated the new tack that could be purchased with the fifty thousand roubles. Some dark blue leather bridles ornamented with silver had caught his eye just a week or so ago at Neimeyers. Besides, after a few moments Nikki had convinced himself that the confrontation wasn't so insuperable as first imagined. His growing excitement over the unique and piquant diversion was enough to allay any slight misgivings he might still harbor.

Once a decision was made, Nikki faced all prospects undaunted. He looked on the world as available for his pleasure alone, and therefore his inclinations, however extraordinary, must be satisfied.

Nikki stood gazing across the small river with a cold, calculating look. Half musing, half aloud, he quietly murmured, "Now, this calls for a nice judgment, this art of seduction. You must be plain but not too plain, be adept at murmuring fulsomely expressed endearments with a delicate sincerity, and you must smile politely as you pretend to take what is, in fact, willingly given. It goes without saying that one cannot be overhampered by scruples."

"That may all be very fine in the society in which you

move, Nikki," Cernov retorted, "where everyone knows the rules of amorous jousting and seldom departs from the proscribed formula, but in the case of Forseus's wife, I think you'll be dealing with a female unfamiliar with those 'niceties.' "

"I am credibly informed," Illyich stated with cheerful maliciousness, "that she's untainted by scandal."

"So *far*, she's been untainted by scandal," Nikki remarked humorlessly, and with a careless gesture of farewell walked toward the river.

Thus these elegant, bored, restless young blades became involved in this peccadillo to breathe some freshness and vitality into their boredom. The nascent industrial energy of the age had doubled their already princely revenues without efforts of their own. They were, in the words of a contemporary chronicler, "dulled by luxury, enervated by ease, staled by amusement."

As for the object of this chase, the pursued, the diversion to the restless young birds of paradise, Alisa, the young wife of the old merchant Forseus, was an innocent. She wasn't an innocent to deliberate cruelty or coldness of a man (no one who had lived with Valdemar Forseus for six years was unacquainted with evil), but unschooled and innocent in receiving kindly overtures from a man playing the game of seduction. An education from books, however exceptional, lacks the necessary information that real-life experience teaches. In the gilded circles of Petersburg society, amatory dalliance and flirtation had attained the status and perfection of a fine art, and over the years Nikki had refined and polished his practical and aesthetic skill to a virtuoso proficiency.

So here we have the age-old confrontation.

The unsophisticated and untutored young girl encountering the master technician with an artist's touch.

Nikki's career in dalliance had, in fact, begun in earnest when he was barely seventeen, and that first episode had disastrously left its mark.

One afternoon, sixteen long years ago, while squiring *Maman* to one of her numerous visits in the manner of a dutiful son, he'd caught the practiced eye of one of his mother's friends; in fact, had almost heard the audible click in Countess Plentikov's beautiful head when she had, for the first time, seriously noticed that the moody, sulky, darkly romantic boy had turned into a man.

Even at seventeen and not grown to his full height, Nikki was formidable, inches over six feet, lean, with raw-boned, powerful shoulders tapering to a narrow waist and slim hips. The sulky coltishness, restless under the conflicting urges of his adolescence, had suddenly intrigued the Countess. With the eye of a confirmed connoisseur of male flesh, Soronina's glance had appraised the splendid young body as if he were standing at stud.

Countess Soronina had known Nikki from the cradle, and at thirty-six she had two marriageable daughters of her own. She was, however, still an exquisitely beautiful woman, slim, petite, golden-haired; her figure was carefully maintained, the soft, pale complexion still perfect, although its beauty took increasing time to care for.

Like most patricians of their class, the Count and Countess Plentikov had many years before acquired the habit of being unfaithful to each other, but out of tacit agreement and courtesy had overlooked each other's numerous infidelities. Count Plentikov spent more time in the country or on the Continent than he did in Petersburg, and this arrangement was mutually satisfying. Soronina's silver and white boudoir had been the scene of many tumultuous encounters as a succession of men had paid amorous homage to one of the reigning beauties of the day.

Nikki absently listened to the ridiculous flow of trivial remarks and pleasantries that fell from Soronina's full red lips that first warm summer afternoon. He gave the obligatory answers in a desultory fashion, but he preferred to let his eyes play over her bounteous curves while visualizing that soft body under his.

Nikki at seventeen was by no means the consummate lover, but not altogether unskilled either, and Soronina was definitely offering him more than sherry and madeleines as they sat in one corner of the huge drawing room, conversing. His mother would occasionally glance toward them during the course of the visit, knowing full well what Soronina was up to, but resigning herself to the inevitable. For half a lifetime Soronina had been aware of the seductive power of her beauty and had never failed to exert its influence successfully. In this case Nikki was more than willing to be agreeable.

And so began a long summer of sweet delirium for them both. The sweetness overtoppled mind and sense; they had something unique, something to be cherished. She taught him much about women and love and she drew from him bittersweet memories of what raw, uncontrolled youthful passion could be. He was to her simultaneously both anguish and ecstasy, anguish for her youth forever beyond recall, and the ecstasy of blossoming under Nikki's ardent naked desire. There was no permanent cure for the dreaded fears of approaching middle age that plagued Soronina, only temporary relief in the arms of the young Nikki, who made her forget for the moment the threat of the future without her beauty.

Nikki's parents returned to Le Repose after a month, but he stayed behind. He had come into an inheritance from

his grandfather on his sixteenth birthday which allowed
him to further indulge his propensity for independence.
Nikki's mother attempted to persuade her son to return
with them. She felt he was being drawn in too deeply, after
having seen Soronina's overt, frankly loving gaze envelop
her boy one evening at a ball. It was so unlike the frivolous,
shallow Soronina and terrifying in its possible consequences. Much as Princess Kaisa-leena adored Soronina as
a friend, one did not care to contemplate her as a daughter-
in-law. Prince Mikhail kept his peace and forbore issuing
any unwanted words of fatherly advice, hoping that his
reckless son would tire of the affair in due course. If not,
time enough then to intercede.

That summer the affair swiftly reached notoriety as
Nikki, with blazing indiscretion, escorted Countess Plentikov everywhere. He arranged his life to please her because it pleased him also. When they went out he was at
her side, masterful, proprietary.

However, on the rare occasion when he would decide to
leave town for a few days, no amount of coaxing, either
amorous or petulant, would change his mind. Regardless of
their easy intimacy, Soronina lacked her usual control.
Nikki simply went when he wanted to go. He never stayed
long, and when he returned, she would look into those
tawny, brooding eyes and a shiver of pleasure would run
through her.

By the end of August Prince Mikhail stepped in. The
gossip and rumors were becoming serious. Never one to
pander to discretion, Nikki had practically installed himself
in Count Plentikov's town palace during that nobleman's
absence. Dangerous rumors were making the rounds of the
clubs to the effect that the cuckolded husband was about to
ask for satisfaction from the young pup warming his wife's
bed. Because Count Plentikov's reputation as a superb
sportsman was nonpareil, Prince Mikhail didn't wish to

contemplate a duel between such unmatched parties. Nikki didn't have the experience to survive an encounter regardless of his skill with rapier and pistol. His youth was quite dramatically a disadvantage on the dueling field in contrast to its obvious advantage in the bedchamber.

One morning Nikki was bodily removed from Countess Plentikov's city palace by four of Prince Mikhail's body servants as he strolled down the marble stairway toward the breakfast room to join Soronina. All that day Nikki raged and stormed and threatened his father as Prince Mikhail attempted to explain the seriousness of the dilemma. Unfortunately neither party was open to reason.

Late that night Nikki managed to elude his jailers and immediately returned to the Countess, who was distraught over the possible repercussions of this scandal. Having long adhered to the aristocratic principles of unlimited dalliance so long as no hint of it reared its ugly head, she was beside herself now with terrified misgivings. What had come over her this summer to so wildly throw away all restraint and discretion? Nikki's impetuous temperament had overcome her sensible prudence. Dreadful forebodings of being cut from polite society plagued her.

Pacing her bedroom chamber, Nikki pleaded with Soronina to marry him, but she shuddered to think of a May-December marriage between a youth and a woman old enough to be his mother. She could not tolerate the ridicule. Then he begged her on his knees to go to the Continent with him. He had plenty of money, they would have a glorious life together, they would be happy. Again she shuddered—to be a kept woman was beyond her comprehension. Nikki insisted he would then kill her husband in a duel. Again she was appalled at the raw, passionate nature of her young lover. Tears came to her eyes and spilled over onto their entwined hands.

Above all, their love must not be lost, he said. No hazard

was too great. He wildly promised her anything she wanted. He waited for her answer.

But it was impossible. All her life Soronina had unquestioningly accepted the dictates, the refined etiquette, and protocol of exclusive Petersburg society and would no more consider ostracizing herself from the comfortable confines of that world than she would consider becoming a circus performer. She tried to explain to Nikki that one must do what's expected of one's class, understand the necessity for society's conventions, serve as an example.

Even at that young age Nikki was sufficiently his father's son to curl a well-bred lip. When he broke in contemptuously, standing erect, and spat coldly at her to spare him any more of those inconsequential platitudes, Soronina was grief-stricken and the young boy's heart reached out and longed to give her comfort, but he couldn't give her what she wanted: security—safe, comfortable, snug, luxurious security. She cried harder when the door burst open and Nikki's father and servants once more dragged young Prince Kuzan away. She wept bitterly and whispered, "I'll never be the same."

The young Prince was never the same either. What shreds of romantic illusion and idealism and naïve belief in happiness he had managed to retain in the brittle society in which he lived were swept away that night and eventually obliterated during the next two years he spent in Europe.

Prince Mikhail had not taken any chances of losing his only child to some dueling pistol held in the hands of an irate husband. He had kidnapped Nikki to save him. And after his confrontation with Soronina, Nikki was unhappy, disillusioned, and consequently could be persuaded to sojourn away from Petersburg.

"You will forget her, my son," his father had said, and he was partially right. Once in Europe, nothing was too rash to attempt. Morality, never of great concern, was gone from his mind. Unfettered feverish activity prevailed, and before long the pursuit of this wildly dissipated life served to dislodge most of his old romantic memories, but not without its price of self-torture.

Two years later a much wiser, more cynical young man came back to Petersburg, cool, restrained, elegant, guarded. He took his place in society and never again was persuaded to turn from a confrontation. He was, in fact, extremely quick to take offense, indeed, provocative to an unnerving degree, soon bordering on the notorious after his fifth duel in the same number of years. Nikki could even manage to meet Countess Plentikov in public and blandly pass the time with her as if their tempestuous *amour* had never been. It took an effort, for one never quite forgets the sweetness of first love, but he had grown up and civility demanded that much from him. One must set an example, he would mirthlessly remind himself.

But the unhappy affair set the direction of his future liaisons. Never again did he expose his heart, swearing that the ignominy of offering his heart and soul only to find them refused would never be repeated. Women became merely an amusement, a convenient receptacle for his passions when the need came over him, or else a frivolous pursuit to idle away the measured tedium.

Chapter Two
THE SEDUCTION

Lightly jumping across the gurgling expanse of water, Nikki silently walked up behind Alisa. She was seated with her back to the water, a sketchbook on her lap, rapidly capturing the woodland scene in vivid watercolors.

"Nikolai Mikhailovich Kuzan at your service, my lady," he said softly (and unthinkingly in the habitual French spoken by the Russian aristocracy; it was not the language of this area of the duchy).

Alisa jumped up, wildly scattering her sketchbook, paints, and brushes in the process.

"How do you do, sir," she stammered, replying in the same language, but totally flustered by the unexpected handsome stranger looking down at her. She flushed uneasily under his close inspection.

Nikki lifted one eyebrow quizzically, smiled slightly, and

calmly waited for her to introduce herself. The silence lengthened.

Nikki prompted her.

"I believe I've seen you on occasion in Viipuri, but, unfortunately, always at a distance," he said smoothly. "I fear I don't know your—"

"Of course," Alisa blurted out, embarrassed at her lapse in manners but shaken by meeting the piercing scrutiny of those pale golden eyes. "I'm sorry, forgive me, Monsieur. Mrs. Valdemar Forseus at your service, sir," she responded rapidly, and bobbed a quick curtsey.

I certainly hope so, Nikki said to himself. His eyes swiftly swept her bowed figure as she gracefully executed the curtsey.

Nikki's former glimpses of Mrs. Forseus hadn't done her justice. She wasn't simply another wholesome country lass, merely pretty and vivacious. She was breathtakingly beautiful. Her hair at a distance seemed to be copper. It was in fact a scintillatingly luxuriant golden-red; her eyes were large, dark violet, seductively lashed; her lips inviting (still slightly parted in surprise); her creamy complexion was flawless; her figure full-bosomed and slender-hipped. She was a lovely sight, and Nikki viewed her with a slow smile of sheer aesthetic appreciation. On second thought, alas, only partly aesthetic, for she had an opulent, ripe lushness about her that generated a surge of pure lust in Nikki's libertine soul.

Her long-lashed eyes lifted, bright with a startled vivacity, and meeting Nikki's gaze, she encountered a hungry look that made her creamy skin glow again for an instant with rose.

For a man of his experience and jaded appetites, Nikki felt, ridiculously, a crazy, youthful elation as he contemplated the beautiful upturned face, a stirring of desire that comes on one at the sight and scent of a perfect masterpiece of female flesh. This little seduction should prove to be tantalizing, he speculated pleasantly to himself.

"You must be related to the Prince Kuzan who owns the hunting lodge," Alisa remarked a little unsteadily, feeling she must say something to break the spell of those magnetic, unnerving tawny eyes.

"One and the same, Madame," he carelessly retorted in a deep, husky voice. "Allow me to retrieve your sketching materials which I so heedlessly forced you to scatter," Nikki continued agreeably as he dropped to one knee and began gathering her supplies.

"Oh, no, Monsieur, that's not at all necessary," Alisa quickly responded in supreme embarrassment, "I can do it myself." And she, too, knelt down and frantically began picking up the pencils, brushes, and paint containers.

The Prince Kuzan here! It was horrifying! It quite shattered her composure. Rumors and gossip of his eminence and escapades had penetrated even her confined, retired world. She would simply die of mortification if she stammered one more time; she must certainly appear as the most gauche, discomfited girl he had ever met.

At one point their hands accidentally brushed as both reached for the same object. Nikki was amused to see her drop her eyes self-consciously and snatch her hand back as if burned. A true innocent? Nikki reflected. Impossible! She was married to that old misanthrope Forseus. No doubt she was merely an accomplished coquette who could very effectively blush on cue. Whatever the case, he thought, innocent or actress, he'd know the answer before three days were past.

All the artistic paraphernalia properly replaced in Alisa's small basket, Nikki disposed his lean form comfortably on the grass, remarking politely as he scrutinized her landscape sketch, "You're a most accomplished artist, Mrs. Forseus. Are you self-taught or have you studied with someone?"

Alisa didn't answer.

"Please sit down," he requested cordially, and patted the grass as she remained kneeling. "It's such a pleasant spring day, I impulsively decided to taste the pleasures of nature, and upon seeing you painting, intruded on your privacy. Do forgive my impertinence." And he grinned warmly to disperse the lie.

With consummate skill he continued to try to put her at ease. What could she say unless she wished to be rudely uncivil?

"Of course, Prince Kuzan, there's no need to apologize. You're right," she said as she settled less stiffly on the grass, but kept her distance from him, which didn't escape Nikki's notice. "The weather is altogether remarkable for this early in the spring."

"*Have* you studied somewhere?" he repeated politely.

"Oh, no, I've never been beyond Helsinki, but my parents studied in Paris; in fact, they first met while sketching at the Louvre. Both served as my teachers, although Father viewed his painting as a hobby and was rather more interested in gathering information on the historic roots of the Kalevala. He quite devoted his life to the enterprise and had collated thirty-four stanzas of the epic before he and mother died—"

An unmistakable expression of pain passed over her lovely face and her sentence trailed off.

She was from the gentry. That accounted for her delicate beauty and fluent French, he thought.

"My condolences, Madame, the memory must be painful."

Alisa nodded, unable to speak. Recalling her parents' death could still paralyze and stupefy her even after all this time. With a palpable effort she returned to the present and quickly brushed off Prince Kuzan's sympathy and her self-pity. "It all occurred six long years ago; I am quite reconciled to my loss."

Nikki, however, could see she was not, and he experienced an uncharacteristic pang of compassion for the obviously distraught young woman. She at least wasn't acting when it came to her bereavement over the loss of her parents.

"With your training, you no doubt are interested in the new exhibits of the Wanderers," he conversationally stated, hoping to distract and cast aside her painful thoughts. "I saw an extraordinary reception of their work last winter in Petersburg."

The diversion was more successful than he'd anticipated. Mrs. Forseus's eyes, her expression, immediately, patently brightened.

"The Wanderers!" she exclaimed. "Have you *really* seen their work?"

"Yes, I have several catalogues of their exhibitions and a small landscape of Shishkin's."

Her violet eyes widened in fascinated excitement. "You do?" she breathed in wonder, her face overcome with a childlike awe.

Nikki refrained from revealing to her that he was relatively uninterested in the Wanderers, or any other painters, for that matter. He'd been cajoled against his will into attending the exhibitions because his mistress, Countess Amalienborg had seductively insisted, and he was in a receptive enough humor to yield to her extremely pleasurable methods of entreaty. And as for his purchase of the Shishkin landscape, the only reason he'd bought it was to annoy that pompous ass, Count Borcheff, who was bent on having the painting. Nikki had derived inordinate satisfaction from carelessly raising each one of Borcheff's bids until the bombastic Count had been forced to drop out and lose the painting. His personal secretary, Ivan Dolorosky, conscientiously bought the exhibition catalogues as well as every other new book, pamphlet, and article published and added them to Nikki's extensive library. Ivan had been given carte blanche to purchase for the library since the pursuit was so gratifying to the young man. Nikki vaguely recollected Ivan speaking rapturously of the newest Wanderer catalogue; thank heaven, he'd attended, however superficially, to Ivan's enthusiastic monologue.

Alisa conversed freely after Nikki's fortuitous attempt at diverting her morose memories, explaining her admiration for these new painters, who with a technical skill, par excellence, portrayed socially significant subjects, historical scenes, landscapes from life, that were poignantly effective as well as exquisitely rendered.

Alisa glowed with fervor when she spoke of the courage it took for Kramskoy and a group of fellow students to resign from the Academy in a dispute over subject matter. How the "Mutiny of 13" had become the "Peredvizhniki" or "Wanderers," basing their approach on N. Chernyshevski's revolutionary book *Aesthetic Relations of Art and Reality*, which stressed the superiority of reality over its representation in art.

"You see, my parents, too, painted from nature; painted outside and not exclusively in the studio. It was revolutionary in their generation, but they were acquainted with many French painters who vacationed at Barbizon and worked directly out of doors."

"Ah, yes, the vanguard of the—what are they calling those young painters in Paris?—the Impressionists?"

"Yes, that's exactly right!" Alisa replied in delight. Since the death of her parents she'd not had a single opportunity to discuss art with anyone. "And Repin . . ." she breathed ecstatically, "such subject matter; it brings tears to one's eyes."

"His new painting 'Volga Boatmen' was just finished last

year after three years of preparation. Marvelously stunning when I viewed it," Nikki said.

"Oh!" another gasp of excitement, and Alisa chatted away volubly, free from restraint. Nikki had only to murmur appropriate responses intermittently and he was not, after all, completely untutored in the new movements in art. Having lived in Paris for two years, he toured Europe often and extensively, and when lured to the new art exhibits by Countess Amalienborg's desire to be seen at the avant-garde displays, he was not altogether unseeing. Behind Nikki's normal posture of indifference was a keen mind and a perspicuity beyond the common. He observed much without appearing to. As a matter of fact, on the occasion of his purchase of the Shishkin landscape, he'd also impulsively bought an extremely small Savrassov still life which he'd sent to his mother and until the present moment completely forgotten.

"I have some of the catalogues in the library at the hunting lodge and also the Shishkin landscape," he lied. "Perhaps you would like to come over for tea some afternoon and see them," he casually suggested. He would send a message to Ivan this evening in Petersburg and have the catalogues and painting delivered to him post haste, wherever they were.

"No! No!" Alisa exclaimed in highly nervous agitation. "I couldn't—I'm sorry, I'd love to, but—" she stopped in a near state of panic.

Were his intentions that transparent? Nikki wondered uncomfortably, and decided not to press the suggestion. He quickly changed the subject, exerting his charm to calm the unusual display of alarm his invitation had occasioned.

Nikki couldn't have known that fear of her husband's actions rather than Nikki's had prompted her inordinate manifestation of fear. Valdemar Forseus had on two recent instances beaten Alisa, not grievously, but enough to frighten her. After years of almost total indifference, since the birth of their daughter Forseus had once again begun, infrequently, to press her with bizarre and unwelcome demands. Alisa was dreadfully terrified, and more sure every day that soon she would have to take her daughter and leave her husband regardless of the consequences. The last few months had become so increasingly intolerable, she now wondered daily how much longer she could last.

Nikki restricted himself to polite and innocuous inanities for the next fifteen minutes, ultimately succeeding in restoring Alisa's lively spirits and bringing the delightfully ingenuous smile to her lips. Feeling it best to depart now that her cheerful disposition was reestablished, Nikki rose from his relaxed sprawl and, towering magnificently above her, remarked equably, "Perhaps if you're sketching here tomorrow, I could bring my catalogues to show you."

"I don't know. I can't, I mean . . . I don't think so," she stammered falteringly.

"It doesn't signify if you're otherwise engaged," he reassured her. "I'm rather at loose ends at the moment, and if you're not here, the stroll over will, at least, be a pleasant occupation of my time." He smiled faintly. "Charmed to make your acquaintance, Mrs. Forseus. Good day."

"Good day to you, Monsieur," she quietly replied.

And bowing courteously, he strode slowly away.

Alisa was left with multitudinous and conflicting emotions waging war in her mind, a sweet confusion holding sway. He was so handsome, faintly foreign- and exotic-looking. Alisa couldn't drag her memory from the strikingly attractive maleness he exuded. Prince Kuzan was also enchanting company (of course, since Nikki was out to ingratiate himself), so kind to her and wholly conversant in the new art movements, a topic of infinite delight to one who could keep abreast of the new currents only by irregular periodicals that might find their way to Viipuri. Alisa didn't allow herself to dwell on his handsome attractiveness. In the six years since she had been forced into marriage with the sixty-one-year-old Forseus, no man had ever treated her gently. The entire encounter that afternoon was bewildering and left her unusually agitated. She couldn't concentrate on her painting anymore. All thought of color and form had left her mind. She knew she wanted to meet Prince Kuzan tomorrow. But dared she follow her own warm feelings of pleasure he engendered within her this afternoon? If her husband had been home, she would have had no choice. But he wasn't, and these few days of freedom from his tyranny had brought a Prince into her life.

Alisa gathered her supplies and walked home slowly, lost in tumultuous thought, hugging each enchanting memory of the Prince to herself. Arriving home, she devoted herself to her five-year-old daughter, Katelina, who had just awakened from her afternoon nap, and in entertaining her child endeavored to push aside the distracting, disturbing thoughts of Prince Kuzan.

When Nikki returned to the lodge, he was greeted with rapid-fire, coarse, and teasing questions from the importunately inquisitive, now slightly drunken Cernov and Illyich.

"Well, how is the bull of Petersburg doing with Forseus's ice maiden?" Illyich laughed uproariously, more amused than ever at his choice of prey. He felt quite certain of collecting his winnings.

Cernov slyly added, "I see your clothes are as unruffled and immaculate as ever. Didn't get to her this afternoon, eh, Nikki? Losing your touch?"

Nikki good-naturedly accepted the crude jesting interspersed with much helpful and extremely graphic advice.

He was eminently familiar with barracks humor and also entirely satisfied with the course of the afternoon's efforts. He looked forward eagerly to a leisurely, unhurried seduction; the victory would be sweet.

"My friends," Nikki explained with a patient forbearance, "Mrs. Forseus is not a common slut. She is, surprisingly, in spite of having married that peasant-merchant Forseus, of gentle birth and upbringing. She's also a lovely, skitterish young filly unused to the bridle, so I must gentle her slowly before she'll be tame enough to ride. Today was not entirely unsuccessful, so don't count your winnings yet, Illyich."

Nikki had been unprepared to find Alisa so well-bred. Her French was fluent and without accent. She wasn't a peasant after all, although Nikki had no scruples or class distinctions when it came to taking his pleasure. His sexual diversions were international, interdenominational, non-ideological, entered into with a true and open spirit of brotherhood.

That evening Nikki remained aloof from the ordinary orgy of drinking, dancing, and whoring. With barely tolerant amusement and ultimately total indifference he watched the drunken antics of his friends. Finally, to the astonishment of the servants, for the first time in years he retired alone to bed at the relatively early hour of one o'clock. He was even sober. Now they were worried. Was the master ill?

For all his drunken wildness and eccentric behavior, Nikki had an old-fashioned regard for his responsibilities to his peasants and was, in turn, adored by them. He was generous to his servants, a quirk denoted by most as softness or eccentricity. He was genuinely interested in their problems, laughed and joked with them, would partake in their amusements, had learned to ride, hunt, and ski from his father's Finnish Lukashee (trackers).[2] In fact, Nikki's ardor for hunting interfered considerably with his regimental duties, but his superiors favored him and intervened more than once to save him the consequences of overstaying his leave or being absent without consent.

Nikki, oblivious to the servants' whispered solicitude for his health, slept deeply and peacefully throughout the night.

Alisa, for her part, was not so imperturbable. She tossed and turned, in long stretches of wakefulness restlessly wondering if she should meet Prince Kuzan the next day. Still distraught with indecision, she finally fell into an exhausted sleep at four in the morning.

Nikki had dispatched a trooper to Petersburg 100 versts away (66 miles) the evening before, with a message for Ivan, instructing him to gather all the current art catalogues from the library and send them back by return messenger. Ivan was also to ascertain the provenance of the landscape by Shishkin and have that delivered as well to the hunting lodge.

By mid-morning of the second day of the wager, the catalogues were in Nikki's hands and a note from Ivan explained that the painting was being sent by carriage since its size made it impossible to be carried on horseback. Nikki selected four of the newest catalogues he felt would be of most interest to Mrs. Forseus.

Dressing leisurely, he left without waking his friends, who were still sleeping off their fuddled heads, although the day was well advanced beyond noon. He wore the buckskins and peasant shirt he preferred as country dress. Books tucked under his arm, Nikki strolled without haste to the small meadow on the opposite side of the shallow river. There he lay down in the warm sun, arms hooked behind his neck, and waited for Alisa. He'd deliberately arrived very early in order to precede the woman to the assignation. Alisa's quavering trepidation had been extremely evident yesterday, and Nikki was afraid she might quickly reconsider and bolt if he wasn't there first to greet her.

Nikki entertained himself, as he waited, by mentally cataloguing the various and delightful attributes of the beautiful Mrs. Forseus. This pleasant exercise was eventually disturbed by the arrival of the subject of his musings.

The hunt was on once more. The luscious quarry was full in sight. She was even more delicious in the flesh, he noted, as Alisa walked toward him with a long, graceful stride, her slender hips swaying beneath the sheer dimity of her apple-green dress. Nikki closed his eyes briefly and controlled his rising passion. To have that fair creation of womanhood alone in the forest and refrain from making love to her was going to require superhuman discipline.

"Good afternoon, Mrs. Forseus." Nikki greeted her courteously, rising politely from the ground and sweeping her a formal bow. He could see her hesitancy and uncertainty, and hoped by remaining coolly formal to allay any misgivings she might have about having come here to meet him. One more day and they would be experiencing the ultimate familiarity, he thought, so he was willing to bide his time today. He didn't want her to flee in panic, sorry that she'd come. That wasn't out of the question, he realized as she stood trembling before him, holding tightly to her basket of art supplies. Her demeanor reminded him of a very young girl, an unsure adolescent on the threshold of first love.

"Good afternoon, Prince Kuzan," Alisa softly replied in greeting.

"Come, Mrs. Forseus, please call me Nikolai, and may I address you by your Christian name? All this rigid etiquette seems out of place in the natural arena. I brought the catalogues," he quickly added when he noted the alarm with which she viewed him.

The lure of her favorite topic was enough to overcome her apprehensions, and the lovely young woman visibly relaxed as Nikki held the booklets out to her.

"My name is Alisa," she said demurely without lifting her eyes to Nikki's face. She held out her hand for the books, touching them as if they were a precious metal. Then she gracefully seated herself on the ground a safe, respectable distance away.

Nikki didn't make any sudden moves because Alisa exhibited the unmistakable nervousness of a frightened doe. Soon, however, her natural vivacity surfaced as she oohed and aahed over the colored lithographs in the catalogues. Nikki contentedly watched her and ventured a comment or two on some of the artists or explained occasionally just how a certain painting appeared in its large format. He talked to her of his meetings with Kramskoy, Repin, Shishkin, and Savrassov, and Alisa's interest was itself intoxicating; her eyes shone in wonder, her cheeks flushed with fervor. After hearing Nikki had actually been in their company, she was full of eager questions and didn't notice or appear unduly alarmed when he moved closer to point out some special quality or detail in one or two of the catalogue plates.

The afternoon passed thus pleasantly in this discourse on art; she animated, high-spirited, inquiring, he politely courteous and ever restrained while answering her myriad questions.

Apparently by accident, since the maneuver was performed with such discretion, Nikki would occasionally touch Alisa's hand while pointing out a particular object of interest in an illustration, or brush her arm as he leaned across to turn a page; these stratagems were carried off with an unqualified innocence for all their contrived planning.

Alisa vividly responded to Nikki's casual touch; a rosy blush, a start, down-cast eyes. He was pleased to see that she was aware of his presence, and it wasn't coquetry, he decided; she was indeed virtuous. But hers was a virtue that was assailable, it appeared from her agitated reaction to the unexpected contact. If Alisa was susceptible to slight brushes of his fingers, it presaged well for her response to his more ardent and practiced caresses. This was no ice maiden after all.

Alisa herself was overwhelmed by her strange feelings. She'd lain awake the greater part of the night and hadn't been able to stay away today, although she'd consciously made the attempt. These tremulous sensations within her were new and unfamiliar. The warm flush running through her body was terrifying in its pleasure, a driving physical longing astonishing in its intensity. Surely she must leave. This would never do! She *must* leave! But she couldn't.

It was Nikki who decided he would either have to leave now or he'd be recklessly and perhaps disastrously seducing a still-uncertain (bewildered, wavering, but still uncertain) woman. With a tremendous effort of will, Nikki suggested that Alisa should be departing for home since the air was beginning to cool as the sun dropped toward the horizon.

"Yes, of course." Alisa jumped up breathlessly, eagerly grasping the opportunity to escape from an encounter that left her filled with flurries and pulsations, while at the same time, and quite improperly, she chided herself, curiously reluctant to leave. "You're kind to notice. Thank you so much for showing me your catalogues. I haven't had such an interesting conversation in years," she said, and dazzled him with an ingenuous smile.

Nikki rose, and standing quite close to her, was warmed by the unpretentious sincerity of that smile.

"If I might suggest, Alisa," he said, skillfully choosing his words, not wishing to disturb the delicate balance of her desires against the obvious perils she envisioned, "if you'd care to stroll in this direction tomorrow afternoon, I could have one of my servants carry over the Shishkin landscape for you to see, since you feel you cannot take tea at my lodge."

Alisa hesitated only briefly. She eagerly wanted to see the painting, and she also wanted to see Prince Kuzan, and he did say his servant would be present. Nikki's reference to the servant gave Alisa, already susceptible, the needed sop of respectability to arrest her qualms.

"I'd like that immensely. Until tomorrow." Alisa waved gaily and ran off through the delicate birches.

Thank heaven, her husband was in Helsinki on business, Alisa gratefully thought. He normally kept a very careful watch on her activities, but his son, who was supposed to take over the vigil in his father's absence, was rather less concerned than the jealous Mr. Forseus. And Alisa *was* given considerably more freedom *within* the estate. The acres were so extensive and isolated that Valdemar Forseus felt his prize possession relatively safe from strange eyes.

The following morning dawned overcast and drizzly.

Alisa was strangely upset upon awakening to find her maid pulling back the heavy curtains on a gray, cloudy day. She wanted to see Prince Kuzan again, but she didn't know why, and the weather might not permit her to go out. She sat by her window most of the morning, reading to her daughter and trying not to think of his disquieting effect on her.

Nikki, too, woke to strong feelings. "*Merde*," he swore. A seduction in the rain would be troublesome even if she did come out in spite of the wetness. And this was his third and last day to win the wager.

Why was he so eager to make love to Mrs. Forseus? Nikki pondered. He who'd just recently decried the monotony of women. It wasn't the money from the wager; he hardly needed it, and to win or lose the bet didn't signify; on the rare occasions when Nikki lost, he lost as graciously as he won. But he was feeling some strange and remarkable attraction to the chit, an attraction removed from his usual lust. Alisa was virtuous, he reflected; a previously unassailable virtue about to be conquered. That was what was giving him such delicious pleasure.

At noon the sun came out in blazing glory.

Nikki called for his *valet de chambre*, Yukko, and had him fetch the painting. The luncheon basket he had ordered was sent for, and the two men set off toward the rendezvous. Yukko, a friend as well as a servant, having been Nikki's companion since childhood, was better company than nine-tenths of his betters. And the best knife-thrower he'd ever seen. Nikki good-naturedly accepted the teasing directed toward him.

"Don't worry, Yukko. I'll be careful. Just do as I ask. After Mrs. Forseus has had an opportunity to satisfactorily inspect the painting, I'll give you a discreet nod and you take the painting back to the lodge and leave us alone. Urho informed me yesterday when he was saddling my horse that the old merchant is in Helsinki and isn't expected back for two weeks; Urho's sister is a parlor maid at Forseus's. So you see, I anticipate no angry husbands," Nikki said as he grinned into Yukko's widely smiling face.

"In that case, I won't have to stand guard with my pukko to stave off intruders."

"No, Yukko, no need this time. Just go back to the lodge when I nod and try a bottle of my new brandy. Ask Aleksei to find you one; he knows where it is."

Intentionally arriving early once again, Nikki watched as Yukko propped the large canvas against some birch trees, then both men sprawled in the grass, waiting for Mrs. Forseus.

She appeared shortly, slightly breathless, having run the

last quarter verst, fearing she might be too late. In an effort to dissuade herself from meeting Nikolai, she'd postponed her departure until long after Katelina was asleep, and then impetuously decided to go regardless of her fears.

Yukko's presence was reassuring, and the three sat on the grass, admiring the delicate depiction of a birch grove, like the one surrounding them. Shishkin's skill at capturing the atmosphere of early morning, his rendering of lacy ferns, the dawn stillness so powerfully evoked on the canvas, were very impressive. Alisa exclaimed in delight, Nikki was courteously agreeable, and Yukko, after a summary glance at the landscape, ignored the painting and chose instead to observe the protagonists in this elaborate courtship dance.

After a reasonable interval, Yukko discreetly rose and left with the painting. Immediately stepping into the breach with the military precision of a trained field officer (to hesitate is to be lost), Nikki smiled warmly and said, "Could I interest you in some of my chef's concoctions for a *déjeuner sur l'herbe?*" handing Alisa the hamper as he lifted the lid. Any woman would be awed by the sumptuous display arranged in the large basket.

Nikki spread out a damask cloth, crystal, silver, and china while Alisa enthusiastically marveled over the exquisite cold collation; a spiced Cornish hen stuffed with truffles and herbs, pickled artichoke hearts, asparagus vinaigrette, smoked salmon and caviar twirled into delicate pink lily shapes, pâté fluted into a petal-shaped mold, fresh strawberries sprinkled with sugar in a scalloped silver bowl, and pale, golden madeleines artfully arranged in a silver latticework basket. While Alisa set the food before them, Nikki poured champagne into two fine-stemmed goblets.

He handed a glass to Alisa, remarking lightly, "Shall we first drink a toast to the Emperor, since we're drinking his favorite brand of champagne—Clicquot?"[3]

Alisa nodded, wide-eyed.

"To the Emperor," Nikki toasted, and drained his glass.

"To the Emperor," Alisa repeated with a timid smile, and took a sip of her champagne.

Le picque-nicque proceeded gaily, Nikki exerting his considerable charm, with the help of the food, champagne, and improving weather, easily enchanting Alisa, reminding her of all the attractions of the luxurious, entertaining life she'd been removed from for six years.

They chatted cheerfully, laughed at trivialities; he talked to her lightly, fascinating her, hypnotizing her. She listened and responded, heedless of this breach against propriety. She'd been a virtual prisoner of an old and depraved husband for six years, and she was still very young.

And now the joy she'd not allowed herself to hope for came back to her. Alisa delighted in Nikki without reservation, in his burning eyes that held hers, in the caressing compliments he offered her, for the blithe, joyous world he exemplified and that was lost to her forever.

The silly banter stopped abruptly.

A tremulous silence hung between them. Nikki was seated very close to Alisa. He caught her frightened glance and held it.

"No, no," she whispered in fright and began to get up. Ignoring her words, he reached out, caught her shoulders, and pulled her toward him. He knew she would now either freeze in his arms or respond to him. She half opened her mouth and bent her head back; her breath came unevenly, her body trembled under the pressure of his hands. As he kissed her lips tenderly, her arms lifted around his shoulders, her fingertips brushed the soft hair on his neck, lightly, tentatively; she was quivering like a frightened animal.

Almost immediately the enormity of her acquiescence washed over her, and she attempted to break away.

"Loose me," she whispered pleadingly. "Loose me,

please," she cried softly, struggling against his chest, unable to still the wakening desires in her own body.

"No," he murmured thickly, kissing her. His hand slipped under her knees and he lifted her into his arms. Ignoring her timid protests, he carried her under the trees and there on the soft green moss laid her down and began deftly undressing her, all the while murmuring endearments, kissing her lips, stilling her fears with soft caresses, seducing with exquisite gentleness until she closed her eyes and lay still.

Skillful in the intricacies of hooks, buttons, and laces, he opened her dress and, pushing it off her shoulders, untied the straps of her chemise and kissed her shoulders, tasting the rich perfume of her scent. The smell of a woman always roused him; he loved the fresh sweetness. He was wild with desire yet restrained himself, for she was trembling beneath his touch. After removing her voluminous petticoats, pulling off her dainty kid slippers, garters, and silk stockings, he opened the tapes of her lace-trimmed drawers. Slipping them down her slender hips and well-shaped legs, he pulled them free and tossed them aside. A flood of crimson swept over Alisa's face as she lay gleaming white before him while his devouring gaze ranged the length of her splendid, opulent beauty.

Nikki bent and kissed her softly, opening her mouth under the pressure of his lips. Then he gently stroked and caressed her, his fingers sliding over her bare thighs toward the very source of pleasure, and with gentle fingers he gained the opening and toyed delightfully with her until she quivered and shuddered beneath his touch. He could feel her quickening under his titillation. Her flesh was delicious to the touch, smooth and soft and warm. Alisa drew a long breath and opened her eyes. Seeing that she didn't intend to resist him, Nikki kissed her more demandingly. And she turned her face fully toward him and of her own

accord returned his kiss, opened her soft lips to the pressure
of his probing tongue and fierce burning kisses.

She sighed a delicious small sound of surrender and he
smiled against her mouth, gratified.

Quickly stripping off his clothes, he lay beside her, gathering her warm body in his arms. A shiver ran through
Alisa at the contact with his naked skin. Her hands moved
down his shoulders, closed around his back, as though she
would press herself into him forever.

The tender caresses, his long, lean, manipulating fingers,
the lingering kisses, the sweet murmured endearments, had
all served their purpose. Nikki gently lifted her legs, without resistance mounted her, and with a few merciless
thrusts buried himself inside her incredible warmth. Alisa
cried out softly. He was momentarily shocked as he penetrated her, for although obviously aroused, she was tight as
a virgin. She would take some patient, gentle stretching for
the vigorous lovemaking he was used to, he reflected.
Could all the ribald jests and rumors be true? Was her
husband, indeed, too old?

"I'm sorry," Nikki whispered into her tangled hair. "Did
I hurt you?" Her eyelids fluttering, her lips parted in breathless desire, Alisa murmured, "No" as she clung to him, her
arms laced around his powerful body, her legs twined
around his.

Enveloped in her warm, throbbing flesh, he carefully,
gently, explored its luscious interior as she stirred restlessly
beneath him, the pressure of her hands holding him fiercely
tight. With a slow, delicate rhythm he moved in her,
adeptly controlling his passion, slowing his exertions to
savor the tide of pleasure, intent on further rousing Alisa's
senses, deliberately compelling her to need him, compelling her to respond to the exquisite sensual pleasure he was
intensifying with each deep, plunging stroke. He was in no
hurry now, wisely delaying the climax, enjoying each wave

of delight, penetrating and withdrawing with tantalizing slowness.

Soon the last vestiges of Alisa's guilt and fear were swept away before the fury of the untrammeled passion Nikki had adroitly provoked in her newly awakened body, and with a deep, drawn sigh, she lifted her hips to draw him in more deeply.

Nikki continued his slow rhythm, caressing her tenderly, listening to the murmurs wrung from her parted lips by the strange rapture she was experiencing for the first time and which she accepted with a growing passion by arching instinctively to meet each forceful stroke.

"Come, sweet princess, come with me," he murmured softly, touching her neck gently with his warm lips, spoke to her in heated love-words, play-words, words that roused her further.

Nikki had discovered while still a mere youth that whispered phrases, passionate sentiments of affection, a few lustful words, can do more to take a woman over the edge than twenty minutes of the most ardent physical stimulation.

And the flush on Alisa's cheeks was rising, a warm blush of color was spreading down her soft, white heaving breasts.

"Follow me, sweet angel," he murmured tenderly.

She was almost there. And so was he.

Nikki held her crushed to him, his arms wrapped tightly around her slender back, holding her impaled on his rigid, engorged stiffness. His breathing was harsh and rapid, his warm whispers brushed her ear, his masculine scent touched her nostrils, tendrils of damp, dark curls clung to his forehead. He was fully roused, desperate for relief, as if he hadn't had a woman for a long time. As if Tanya no longer existed. Succumbing to his mounting passion, he rode the crest of his desire, no longer restraining his passion, impatient for release. Alisa, too, with guiltless wonder and a long-dormant sensuality abandoned herself to the full glory of her desire. She returned Nikki's kisses wantonly, crushed her mouth feverishly against his, ran her hands over his magnificent body, reveled in the pressure of his firm, muscular frame, hard and demanding against her tender flesh, voluptuously joined him in the selfish, sensual dance of love. She gave herself to him, willingly opened her body for his pleasure, sobbed with a passion too long deferred, keening a quiet, soft cry of rapture as he brought her to an ecstasy she had never known, as he pressed against the mouth of her womb and poured his warmth into her.

She knew in that resplendent moment this was what she'd wanted from the first time she'd seen him and caught that hungry look in those golden eyes; his strength, his wildness, the feel of his powerful body on hers.

Her violet eyes opened slowly and lifted to his, her eyelids heavy with a sweet, languorous memory, and he realized as he gazed down on her beautiful flushed face how men could feel the torturous self-doubts of jealousy. That drowsy, voluptuous, yielding look, the curve of her full red lips, the heightened color, the gentle smile of surfeit—she was a sated woman remembering her lover's caresses. To picture another man plundering the soft riches of her luscious body evoked in him an unfamiliar blaze of jealousy.

Alisa had seen lust in a man's eyes; the fanatic, burning, frankly covetous eyes of her husband when he stripped her or beat her, the surreptitious, carefully concealed lust in the eyes of strangers. At this moment, however, Nikki's golden eyes shone not only with a sensual desire, but also with tenderness as he marveled at the magnificent beauty of the creature before him. He must have her. He would gently teach her the pleasures of her senses, with deliberation rouse her, delicately caress the graceful form and make her his. This beauty *must* be his. . . .

For Alisa, who had only been used, her body torn apart and abused by a selfish, brutal lust, Nikki's glance of passionate tenderness drew her like a beacon of warmth in a cold, black night.

Nikki kissed her lips lightly and murmured as he moved off and lay beside her, propped up on one elbow. "Thank you, love."

He ran a light finger down her belly. "Do you feel content?"

Alisa smiled with a winsome satisfaction, then nodded with a delightful, almost childish openness, putting up her lips to be kissed again.

Her smile brought with it a novel sense of triumph and, bending near, he moved to kiss her. "Sweet nymph, we make a fine pair, Alisa," Nikki whispered as his lips touched hers. She was everything and more than he'd imagined, a nymph, a bacchante, with a natural wantonness that stirred his ardor.

Rising to his knees, he gazed at her lying quietly with her thighs still slightly parted. The seductive lure of Alisa's beauty, her compliant, provocative posture brought his manhood standing proud.

"Look at me, Alisa," Nikki said softly.

She looked at him, embarrassment, shyness, desire all there in confusion, but kept her eyes averted from his obviously aroused masculinity.

"Look at me," Nikki insisted quietly, but she resisted.

After a moment Nikki continued teasingly.

"Look what you do to me." He was laughing and relaxed, while blushing, she avoided looking at him.

"Come now, dearest Alisa. Do as I ask."

She shivered, then reluctantly obeyed. Hesitantly and trembling slightly, her violet gaze rose to his stiff erection.

"Touch me, Alisa," he continued quietly, drawing her unwilling hand to him. "Here, I'll show you how I like you to touch me. Hold me thus." He gripped her hand tightly in his, showing her how to rouse his prick for her satisfaction.

With his free hand he slowly stroked her warm body, rubbing her nipples softly between his fingers till they stood taut and hard, caressing the silky inner flesh of her thighs, probing her soft warmth now wet from his lovemaking. She began stirring under his practiced fingers, breathing irregularly, quivering with the pleasurable sensation mounting within her.

He released her hand and whispered, "Do you want me again?"

Her eyes held his for a moment and she nodded.

"Tell me."

She opened her mouth, then shut it again and shut her eyes, too, in trembling shame.

"Perhaps next time," he whispered with a faint smile and moved over her. He eased himself into her until he could penetrate no further and began to warm her with slow, steady thrusts, exercising all his constraint in order that Alisa would have every opportunity to satisfy her newly roused sexual appetite, so she could fully taste the rapture her senses craved. He continued the steady rocking, turning lightly from side to side, moving inside her with practiced skill, watching her blushing, upturned face and reading from her fluttering eyes how she was feeling, then he set to work in earnest and drew her to new heights of pleasure, finally pleasing himself as he pleased her.

Chapter Three
THE UNBIDDEN SPECTATORS

Alisa was lying quietly now, enclosed within Nikki's strong arms, the trembling of her body having ceased.

Into this wonderland of pleasure, this paradise for the senses, drawled a lazy voice.

"It looks as though you win the bet, Nikki. I should have known better, since your skill in these matters is widely renowned. Must say, I envy you the ride."

Nikki swore and rolled onto his back, his eyes glaring contemptuously at the mocking, derisive smile of Illyich. Cernov was at his side, blandly surveying the delicious display of Alisa's body. He gave the faintest flick of a wink at Nikki.

Alisa lay there, eyes still closed, caressed almost into insensibility. Nikki quickly drew his shirt over her nakedness.

He watched her floating slowly back into awareness from the nirvana of sexuality where she'd so wondrously expired. She opened her torpid eyes, deliciously languorous, still remote, unfocusing.

"You bastards!" Nikki snarled, turning to the two men.

"Now, now, Nikki, don't be vulgar. You know perfectly well I escaped illegitimacy by ten days," Cernov imperturbably retorted.

"Damn voyeurs!" Nikki spat out, a frustrated, blazing anger igniting his mind.

Alisa's lovely eyes opened with a startled look, at last fully conscious of the scene and its spectators.

"Nikki!" she whispered frantically, appalled she was lying almost naked before two strangers.

"I'll give you two seconds to get out of here, or I'll kill you both!" Nikki said in a voice that was solid ice.

Sensible of the reputation Nikki enjoyed as a brawler, the two officers judiciously turned on their heels and left. Cernov, grinning, calmly blew a kiss in Alisa's direction as he wheeled around.

"Who the hell would think Nikki would get angry over some little piece and a frolic in the woods?" Cernov exhaled softly in amazement. "I've never seen him regard a woman as anything more than a serviceable convenience."

"God only knows, but when Nikki's in that murderous a mood, I'm not going to wait around to find out why," Illyich responded with a prudent expediency that had served him well in the past. Together they returned to the lodge to satisfy the desires that Alisa's lush body had stirred within them. Nikki listened to their hasty retreat through the underbrush, then turned to the dismayed woman.

"Forgive me, Alisa, for the crude stupidity of my friends," he apologized softly.

As Nikki watched her silent face, he saw a tear well out of one corner of her eye and trace a course down her rosy cheek.

Damn them, damn them to hell, he thought. Of all the abominable luck!

"I'm sorry," Nikki said aloud, and moved toward Alisa as if to offer what comfort he could.

He'd had vague misgivings and qualifications about this sedu_tion from the beginning, and even more so after their second encounter, but he'd brushed them aside. For Nikki had always lived unhampered by restrictions, ungoverned by rationale, totally unconcerned with consequences. Now he found himself uncomfortably conscious of being the cause of Alisa's pain and humiliation. He felt guilty, and this guilt upset him because it was foreign to his nature.

In addition to the guilt, he was smolderingly furious at his wretched friends. If he'd been honest with himself, he could have understood their puzzled reaction to his rage. For years the men had participated in many "shared" experiences with women. How were Cernov and Illyich to know that in this rare instance they were not supposed to join the fun?

Alisa cringed from Nikki's sympathetic gesture. He hastily stayed his hand in midair.

"Please go," she whispered.

"Alisa, let me explain," Nikki began, forcibly struck by the misery in her tear-filled eyes.

"Please," she remonstrated in a barely audible voice. "Just go, you've had your amusement." Her body involuntarily shuddered. "Just go!" she cried hysterically.

"Very well," Nikki said stiffly. He dressed swiftly, apologizing formally when he withdrew his shirt from her naked form and replaced it with one of her petticoats.

"Please accept my deepest apologies, Madame," he said in a clipped, cool voice as he bowed briefly to her recumbent form, her eyes staring, unseeing, averted from his. Then he walked quickly away, flushed with frustration and anger.

Quite suddenly, all the light went out of Alisa's day. She wept and wept, hugging her petticoat to her as though to keep herself from breaking apart from the great racking sobs of humiliation. She wasn't ashamed of the men seeing her unclothed, she could survive that; she was ashamed for wanting Nikki so, for willingly giving her body to him; he hadn't had to force her, she had wanted him. And she wept for that capitulation, for her loss of will. Strong and resolute enough to withstand an intolerable man and marriage for six years, determined enough to patiently plan and wait for escape from a husband she despised, she'd been brought low by an unfathomable desire for a man with a reputation for treating women casually. Who at this very moment, no doubt, considered her simply another pleasant diversion.

Alisa's life hadn't been happy since the death of her parents; everything she'd loved and cherished had been swept away in a few days when influenza had claimed both her parents within hours of each other. The raging fever that had held them in its tenacious, deadly grip had never broken. Her lovely, gay mother and quiet, scholarly father had eased into a coma from which they'd never wakened. Alisa had often wished in the years following that she, too, could have died, but her young, strong body had defeated the disease.

Then so shortly after, indeed quite improperly so, the incredulous demand of her hand in marriage by old Mr. Forseus, arranged, he'd said, by her father. Unthinkable, but apparently true, since her father's signature was on the document.

If she'd not had Katelina to love after that first year, a child to bring joy to her, she wouldn't have had the strength or courage to continue her existence. Katelina, her darling Katelina, her only solace, had given her reason to live.

Now, the one time she ignored reason, negated logic, passionately made a daring, bold grasp for momentary happiness, she'd been utterly shamed and humiliated. Maybe there truly was no hope for joy or pleasure in her life, Alisa sorrowfully thought. But she *had* been happy, deliriously happy with Nikki for however brief the moments.

And she cried afresh at her wounded heart and pride. She cried for all her sorrows and all her misery these many years and sobbed all the sobs that had been so long suppressed. Then at length, when she'd finally drained all the pent-up tears, she took herself to task with the indomitable spirit that had always sustained her.

Be sensible, you'll survive this mortification, she told herself. She still had Katelina and before long, perhaps they'd be able to leave Forseus and make their way in the world. Arni, her father's old groom, Maria, her old nanny, and Rakeli, Katelina's nanny, were devotedly loyal and always ready to assist her, should that hope become reality.

Alisa washed herself hastily at the river, then dressed carefully and adjusted her clothes into a semblance of order, her face in a spurious repose, and walked home.

Nikki partially assuaged his black rage and frustration by summarily driving Cernov and Illyich out of his lodge, spurring their departure with a string of vivid obscenities. With a considerably more polite choice of words, Nikki convinced his young cousin Aleksei to repair to the town house in Petersburg for a few days until Nikki joined him. The Gypsy girls were promptly ousted as well, piled into a carriage in which they contentedly counted their money all the way back to the city.

Nikki immediately shut himself into the music room

with two bottles of brandy and a brooding anger that turned into a brooding melancholy by the bottom of the second bottle.

He roared for his musicians and commanded they play sorrowful, quiet Finnish love songs, the old familiar songs of Nikki's childhood. His mother's Tzigane ancestors had settled north of Lake Ladoga over a hundred years ago, when a grateful noble had deeded them a large tract of land and citizenship in return for having preserved an only son's life from a runaway horse. Nikki's paternal grandfather had begun construction of Le Repose, northeast of Viipuri, in 1810; the country estate was to become the favorite seat of the Kuzan family. Nikki had been reared there and grew up in an atmosphere of Karelian tradition.

Play "Kalliolle Kukulalle," he would sullenly mutter every second song, and the musicians would lapse again into the sad minor key and play the single melody Nikki wanted to hear.

> *Kalliolle kukulalle*
> *Rakenan minä majani*
> *Sine hajan oman ystävän*
> *Asuman minuu ransani.*

The poignant lyrics spoke of a lover bringing his sweetheart to a secluded forest cabin and plunged Nikki still deeper into an agonizing, gloomy depression. He couldn't dislodge visions of Alisa from his mind. They had shared a sexual response that had struck even the surfeited, world-weary Prince as rare and unique. She was a beauty, unutterably so, artless, dazzling, sensual. He *must* see her again!

At one o'clock in the morning Nikki's glazed, drunken eyes lit with a brilliant flash of an idea. He impatiently waved the musicians away and called for his steward. After sending four riders out with a message for his father's gardener, Nikki, eminently satisfied with his resourcefulness, fell into a drunken sleep, having left adamant orders to be wakened when the messengers returned.

Fifty versts (33 miles) away, in the sunny breakfast room of Le Repose, Prince Mikhail Petrovich Kuzan's principal seat and model estate of 172,000 dessiatins (484,400 acres), Nikki's parents were enjoying the early morning companionship of a breakfast à deux.

"What in the world is Nikki up to?" his mother curiously inquired. She was a petite, dark-haired Tzigane woman, still lovely and slim at fifty.

"Need you ask?" his father replied dryly. "When Nikki strips our greenhouses of ten dozen orchids and twenty baskets of strawberries, I would hazard a guess your dear boy has found some woman who adores orchids and has a passion for strawberries. Let us at least hope this sudden passion for strawberries does not signify yet another *enceinte* mistress. He has populated the world quite adequately already with his bastards."

"Now, dear, don't be too harsh on Nikki," Princess Kuzan remonstrated gently. "He's supporting them all quite satisfactorily, even lavishly, and need I remind you that you quite put him in the shade by your reckless escapades until I tamed you into the joys of domesticity. The rumor mills put his streak of wildness at your door, Misha my dear, for as you well know, the Kuzan bloodlines have long possessed a reputation for vice," she finished sweetly.

Nikki could do no wrong in the eyes of his loving mother. He could be wild and a hellion, but her love was unconditional and she served as a conciliatory influence on the occasions when father and son's obdurate temperaments clashed.

"I could perhaps argue about who tamed whom, and

from whence the taint of wickedness came, but I politely defer to you as a gentleman should," old Prince Kuzan graciously replied, smiling at his wife. Even after thirty-four years, she continued to delight him. The wild Tzigane heritage of the ripe sixteen-year-old Gypsy he'd married had never been submerged. That wildness had been but thinly veiled with the veneer of sophistication necessary to move in Prince Mikhail's aristocratic circles on the rare occasions it suited him to remove himself from the comfortable, elegant seclusion of Le Repose.

"I wish someday Nikki could find a love like ours, Misha," Princess Kaisa-leena Kuzan wistfully murmured.

"We had rare luck, love. It doesn't happen often in this world," the Prince replied with obvious feeling, recalling their first tumultuous meeting thirty-four brief years before.

Chapter Four
THE RECONCILIATION

Early the next morning Alisa was shaken awake by Maria whispering frantically, "Mistress Alisa, Mistress Alisa, you must get up!"

Alisa brought herself up out of a deep dream of Nikki, and reacted immediately when she saw the terrified fear in Maria's eyes.

"What's the matter. Is Katelina ill?" Alisa asked anxiously, sitting up.

"No, my lady," Maria said, wringing her hands.

Alisa visibly relaxed, settling back onto her soft pillow.

"It's much worse," Maria moaned nervously.

Alarm again sparked in Alisa's violet eyes.

"Mr. Forseus has returned." She began looking wildly around the room as if to flee.

"No, my lady."

"What is it, then, for heaven's sake? Speak up, Maria," Alisa insisted.

"A carriage of orchids, my lady," Maria whispered quaveringly.

"A carriage of orchids? What in the world are you talking about?" Alisa asked incredulously as she jumped out of bed and rapidly stripped off her nightgown.

"Well, my lady, you know I always go to the chicken house very early in the morning to gather fresh eggs for your and Katelina's breakfast. As I was slipping out the side door, I saw a strange carriage coming up the driveway and ran out to see who it was. The driver said he was Prince Kuzan's coachman and he had orders to deliver the orchids, and, Mistress Alisa," she continued, aghast, "there are also baskets and baskets of strawberries he has instructions to deliver to Mrs. Forseus as well, and"—she paused to catch her breath—"and also this letter for you. I told him to wait behind the bend in the driveway so he wouldn't be visible from the house, but, my lady, you must hurry, the servants will soon be up."

Alisa had already snatched the heavy envelope embossed with the golden seal of Kuzan from Maria's hand before the old servant was finished with her explanation.

She tore open the envelope and pulled out the single sheet of paper. Swiftly her eyes scanned the heavy, careless scrawl.

"If you don't meet me at the meadow in forty minutes, I shall ride over to see you."

The note was simply signed "N."

Oh, *mon Dieu!* It must have taken the coachman twenty minutes to drive over here on the circuitous roads. This left her a bare twenty minutes to dress, talk to the driver, and cover the distance to the meadow, or else Nikki would be at her door.

"Maria, quickly find a dress for me. After I've gone, if

any servants question you, tell them I went to bring blankets and clothes for Mrs. Niemi's new baby. Put those baby clothes you made in a basket and I'll stop at the Niemis' cottage on my way back. Hurry, quickly now, I don't have much time!"

Within five minutes Alisa was dressed and dashing down the main stairway. The door closed quietly behind her just as the household servants began stirring.

Alisa ran down the driveway to the bend where, thankfully, the carriage and coachman were still waiting. Gasping for breath, she addressed the man severely. "You must return to Prince Kuzan."

"I can't, ma'am. I have my orders. I'm supposed to deliver these to Mrs. Forseus."

Alisa looked in wonder at the glistening open landau, the Kuzan signet initialed on the door, the highly polished green lacquerwork and green velvet upholstery an ideal foil for the stunning display of enormous, resplendent yellow and lavender orchids, orchids in baskets, orchids spilling out of shallow basins, orchids carpeting the floor, interspersed with a prodigious number of wicker baskets containing perfect red hothouse strawberries.

"*I* am Mrs. Forseus, and am on my way to see Prince Kuzan now. If you don't return to his lodge immediately, I promise you he'll be angry."

"I don't know, ma'am. Prince Kuzan was quite explicit about my instructions," the man uncomfortably equivocated.

"I'm sure I'll be able to change his mind. Please, please, go back!" Alisa implored frantically.

You might be able to at that, the coachman reflected admiringly as he looked at the beautiful, breathless young woman before him. He knew Prince Kuzan's susceptibility to beautiful women and had spent many a nocturnal vigil wrapped in fur robes in carriage or troika, waiting for the Prince to reappear from some lady's boudoir.

"Very well, ma'am," he agreed, but added carefully, "if you promise to explain to Prince Kuzan."

"Oh, I will, I will!" Alisa finished in a rush of grateful relief. "Thank you." She waved and disappeared into the forest.

With a quiet cluck of his teeth and a pull on the reins, he turned the landau around and retraced its journey.

Alisa ran through the woods, afraid she'd be too late; would he really come to the house to find her? Horror! Please, please, make him wait, she prayed silently.

Her heart gave a leap of pure happiness. She would see Nikki again!

If you had an ounce of pride, she told herself. Well, she didn't when it came to Nikki. She wanted to see him with all her heart.

Alisa broke from the shelter of the birches into the meadow, the dew lacy and sparkling on the grass, the early morning sun casting long shadows across the glistening meadow. Suddenly she saw the tall figure of Nikki leaning against a tree, restless, impatient, fitfully slapping gloves to thigh as he moodily contemplated the toes of his boots. Alisa stopped abruptly, confused emotions coursing through her.

Looking up at the slight sound, Nikki beheld Alisa hesitantly arrested at the edge of the grove, her gold-red hair tousled, loose tendrils falling around rosy, flushed cheeks, her breasts heaving with the exertion of the headlong rush through the woods, her yellow flower-printed linen dress damply clinging at the hemline from the dew's wetness.

Their glances met.

In his eyes she saw some strange emotion. Was it relief? The transient expression vanished in an instant. Nikki smiled and started forward, opening his arms wide in welcome. Alisa hesitated, then dropped her basket and ran flying into his open arms. Nikki enfolded her in a crushing embrace.

"Thank you for coming," he murmured against her hair in an odd voice. "Forgive me," he quietly added as he clasped her tightly, burying his face in her hair, taking in the smell of her, the scent and feel of clean, silken hair and sweet young flesh, the exquisite sensation of her body against his.

As Alisa clung to him, tears of joy ran freely down her cheeks. She was lost to the world in his arms, oblivious of right or wrong, or duty or conscience, aware only of a thrilling happiness.

For them the world held promise once again.

"I can't stay long," Alisa whispered nervously.

"I know. May I see you this afternoon?" Nikki asked with a husky urgency.

"Yes," she answered, surrendering heedlessly, renouncing with a giddy delirium any thought of propriety.

"At one, then, I'll meet you here. Hours to wait. That will be hell," he groaned softly against her ear.

"I must go!" she fearfully murmured.

"I'll walk you back," he insisted quietly, still not releasing her from his strong arms, not wanting her to leave.

"No! You mustn't. Please! If someone should see you," she pleaded, lifting her lids to gaze into Nikki's warm, golden eyes, already kindling with an insistent passion. "I'll be here at one," she promised.

Rising on tiptoe, Alisa brushed Nikki's mouth softly with trembling lips, turned, pulled free from his grasp, and fled, picking up the basket that had been abandoned at the edge of the meadow. She still had her errand to complete.

Chapter Five
THE BLISSFUL INTERLUDE

Nikki was waiting long before one, thinking only of holding Alisa again, of feeling the warmth of her body against his.

When she came and saw him, her face lit up as he knew it would, no coquetry, no pretensions, just a guileless, naïve happiness, her marvelous violet eyes shining with pleasure, her gaze disconcertingly direct.

Nikki took both her hands in his and, surveying the smiling face, bent his head and tenderly kissed the tip of her nose.

"What do you want to do today?" he asked gaily. "This is our first day together. Come to my lodge. I've sent everyone away but the servants. My home, my servants, my estate, and I are at your disposal." His warm smile caressed her. "Anything you want you shall have, anything you want to do, I will do," he offered with a joyous expansiveness.

Alisa looked up into his handsome face and shamefully blushed.

"Well, if you insist, we shall do that first," he teased.

The music room, Nikki's favorite, immediately caught Alisa's fancy. Alcoves strewn with embroidered pillows fronted each large gothic framed window; the walls and vaulted ceiling were entirely mosaicked in glittering lapis lazuli, gold and ultramarine green tiles, portraying sinuous, entwined vines, flowers, and birds. The effect was breathtaking.

When they walked into Nikki's sitting room, a large portrait gazed down on them—his mother painted by Winterhalter. She was small, dark, beautiful, seated in a gilded chair with Nikki at eight years, sturdily erect, angelic, childishly handsome at her side, his toys scattered on the rug before them. A great tenderness flooded through Alisa when viewing the child that he had once been.

"Your mother is very lovely," Alisa said as she looked at the young woman depicted many years before.

"Yes, she is," Nikki agreed. "You must meet her sometime soon," he continued with a marvelous, open assurance.

"Oh, no! I couldn't," Alisa protested in embarrassment.

"Nonsense. *Maman* is a Tzigane and has a very realistic outlook on life. She'll adore you, just as I do. Come here now," he said impatiently, "enough talking and sight-seeing. Let me hold you." He pulled her through the doorway into his bedroom, transformed since the return of the landau into a bower of orchids.

· · ·

Thus began the first day of a week of afternoons they were able to spend together; a carpe diem existence, two mutually obsessed creatures making love through the warm springtime hours, both avoiding thoughts of the future. Particularly for Alisa, this decision to disregard the future was absolutely essential to her present happiness. Nothing must spoil these few days with Nikki.

For them there was only the wonderful, passionate, extravagant present. Young lovers lost to the world, conscious only of each other's presence. They drew every sensation from every transient hour, from every exquisite touch, look, caress. Their sexual pleasures were of the simplest, old-fashioned, natural, a unique bond of affection enhancing the rapture as they satisfied their lusts in a simple variety.

As an accomplished aficionado of Eros, Nikki had long ago learned the pleasure of afternoon *amours*. One was refreshed from having but recently risen from one's night's sleep and eaten a light lunch. The mind and body were fresh, vital, vigorous, not staled by hours of drinking or gaming, as was the case with a midnight rendezvous. Not that he was adverse to late-night assignations, but he knew that he performed more ardently, more zealously, more resiliently in the gentle hours of afternoon.

The second afternoon Alisa timidly inquired as she lay in Nikki's tender embrace, "Do you think perhaps—that is to say—do you think you should use some precautions?"

Nikki opened his eyes, lifted his head a scant inch off the pillow, and said drowsily, "French letters? Condoms? They spoil the pleasure; I never use them." He reached out to touch her hair. "You wouldn't like them, my love." His eyelids fell and he dozed off, still holding her tightly to his rugged form.

Alisa knew she should force the issue for her own safety

and protection, but she didn't want to spoil their little remaining time together.

Nikki hugged her closer and they both slept.

Instinct told Nikki, when he was alone and away from Alisa's tempestuous excitement, that he was getting in too deep this time, that this wasn't another light flirtation or trivial affair, but regardless of this premonition, he plunged boldly in. He hadn't enjoyed himself so much for months—more—years. It was a time of deepest content.

Alisa, too, lived in the bewitching, sensual present, grasping at the opportunity to postpone the end of these halcyon days. If time could just stand still.

She resolutely refused to consider the future. She wouldn't, she wouldn't, yet she cried inwardly when conscience raised its unwanted head above her repression. She deserved some gaiety, some brief taste of love, she told herself, and for the most part, Alisa was blissfully happy. Since living in *"durance vile"* for six years, who could blame her for ignoring the admonitions of her conscience, the call of duty?—when charming, handsome Nikki was bathing her senses in rapture and extravagantly indulging her caprices.

No such irresolution or discordant meditation preyed on Nikki's mind, for he'd long eschewed regrets as both useless and fatiguing. He had quite simply decided that he would bring Alisa back to Petersburg when he returned and install her in a comfortable house on the Quai des Anglais. If the neighborhood was good enough for the Emperor's mistress, it was good enough for his.[4]

Nikki never pondered over or curbed his selfish wishes. He had never had to. Alisa was delightful, lovely, vivacious, intelligent (the latter quality hitherto avoided in Nikki's amorous adventures). But her overwhelming quality, the major attraction, the most fascinating enticement in this week of tumultuous pleasure, was purely sensual. This woman roused him, teased him, fired his jaded senses to new, exquisite limits. Her spontaneous response as he instructed her in the delights of the flesh, her first tentative, then more assured forays into the game of love, her guilelessly greedy appetite for pleasure, stimulated and whetted Nikki's weary spirit.

Surely he would be a fool to walk away from the pleasures Alisa offered him. She was the fetching, enchanting antidote to the ennui that had threatened to engulf him.

Over the years Nikki had, with caution and skepticism, scrupulously avoided any permanence in his relationships with women, preferring married women of his class, already lawfully tied, or else expensive tarts and actresses easily satisfied with lavish gifts and generous purses of gold. He avoided the obligation to provide an establishment for any one woman for even the transitory duration implied in those arrangements. Nikki's fierce independence had survived all attempts to ensnare, and clinging women had always been anathema to him. He turned quite cold and remote when pressed by the importunities of an ardent female. But now Nikki was quite willing to make the necessary adjustments to his normal, selfish regimen. To have Alisa comfortably settled convenient to his town palace would offer him the most pleasant recreation.

One afternoon, as Alisa lay nestled snugly in Nikki's arms, drifting back from the idyllic depths of pleasure, he quietly said, "Today must be our last day at the lodge. I received a message this morning that necessitates my attendance with the Chevaliers Gardes at the Emperor's review Sunday. You must come with me. Pack what you need tonight; I'll send my carriage round for you in the morning."

Alisa wished she'd misunderstood, but knew she hadn't. Nikki had simply said, "Come with me" as if it were the most natural thing in the world, nothing more, no promises, no assurances; she was to him merely another woman of a certain class.

Happiness that he wanted her was overlaid with shock and dismay. But the thing that shocked her most—the daughter of landed gentry, well-bred and gently reared, was that she wished with all her heart she could disregard her conscience, her parents' ideals, and answer simply—I will come.

If she hadn't a daughter who must have opportunity for a normal life, she might have been even more tempted to say I will.

Sighing unhappily, Alisa reminded herself that she'd known this all must end when Mr. Forseus returned home. This "pleasant interlude" (what a deceptively benign term for these tumultuous stirrings of her heart) had merely ended a few days earlier than expected.

"I can't," Alisa softly replied.

Nikki's complacency was abruptly shattered.

"Why not?" he questioned in faint irritation, unused to negative replies.

"I have a daughter to consider" was her straightforward answer.

Nikki hesitated momentarily. Of course, he should have remembered—what was the child's name? It escaped him. A girl, she had said. After a short pause Nikki replied decisively, "Bring her along."

"No, I can't," Alisa repeated.

Now fully awake, Nikki asked with a sort of baffled impatience, "Why ever not? You shall have as large a house as you wish. I'll hire a niania and a governess—an English one, everyone seems to prefer English ones. There, that's taken care of," he said with satisfaction.

God, why couldn't she just say yes. Nikki was so good to her, and God knows she deserved some happiness after all those miserable years. Why *couldn't* she say yes? Even when Nikki tired of her, Alisa knew his generosity wouldn't allow her to become destitute. With all her heart she wanted him. The precepts of a lifetime held firm, however.

"No, Nikki. It wouldn't do," Alisa retorted with a quiet sadness.

Nikki's irascible temper was rising. Was she like all the rest after all? Holding out for a larger prize, for more remuneration, jewelry perhaps, maybe a more sumptuous house, the right kind of horses and carriage? Had he been deceived by the artless sincerity and air of innocence? He thought not, but apparently he had.

He'd pay her price if it wasn't too high. He wanted her and, hell, he gambled vast fortunes at a single throw. Certainly he could afford whatever her asking price was.

"Tell me what more you want, then," he drawled coolly, determined to outbid her demands.

"I don't want anything from you, Nikki," Alisa's unhappy voice replied. "You've given me one week of blissful happiness, and I knew it would have to end when Mr. Forseus returned from Helsinki. I'm sorry. I must think of my daughter."

"You told me yourself you won't stay much longer with that sadistic lecher." Nikki spoke accusingly, for Alisa had in the course of the last week, to her own immense surprise, confided to Nikki the whole wretched story of her marriage when he had questioned the vestiges of bruises on her tender flesh. (That first afternoon in the meadow, events had moved too rapidly for him to be certain, but the following encounter, the next afternoon, in his bedroom at the lodge, when time and the lack of spectators permitted a leisurely appraisal of Alisa's beautiful body, the faint discolorations were apparent.) Alisa had, at first reluctantly and then more volubly, as the pressure of six years' enforced silence were lifted, described her coerced marriage at fifteen, Forseus's bizarre aberrations and cravings for a nubile young girl-woman to rekindle his flagging desires, his abrupt rejection of her for several years after the birth of their daughter, and his renewed sadistic demands that he had forced on her twice lately.

Alisa's ungainly body during pregnancy had repulsed Forseus, and after Katelina's birth he'd fearfully shunned the baby as an incarnation of the devil's child. Forseus's religious fanaticism (often mutually complementary to sexual deviation) had convinced him that a birthmark on Katelina's leg was the devil's sign. He'd been appalled by the pale pink birthmark in the shape of a half moon and from the day of her birth had refused to have any contact with the child.

Nikki was enraged at her story. That old man was the man who possessed Alisa, owned her, slept with her, touched her, caressed her, abused her. God, how could she, he thought angrily. And, damn him, Forseus was a savage monster even by the none-too-exacting standards of humanity afforded contemporary husbands.

"I know I said I would leave him someday, but I must first find some employment," Alisa explained patiently.

"Damnation!" Nikki was furious now. He wasn't having his way. "Work?" he incredulously inquired, his face blank for a moment with disbelief. Immediately denying the staggering heresy, he demanded, "Why work when I'll take care of you?"

He really didn't understand, Alisa thought with a feeling of despair. For Nikki, a woman's dignity, her pride, were at best nebulous, and more aptly much overrated. In his experience women almost universally opted for security rather than independence. Rich or poor, highborn or low, they were all the same to him. But Alisa was not cut from the same mold. She, too, had a stubborn inclination and an inordinately determined will of her own. How else had she survived Forseus?

"You wouldn't understand, Nikki. There's such a thing as a woman's dignity and pride. I'm not a whore to be acquired for the price of a house and a governess and a nanny."

"Damn right I don't understand!" he said through clenched teeth, trying to control his rage while groping vaguely for some reason for Alisa's violent affront, the entire issue of a woman's dignity and pride beyond his comprehension. Woman's pride? Sweet Jesus! Their pride was between their legs!

"You won't come, then?" he continued hotly, furious at having his wishes thwarted, irritated at Alisa's monumental naïveté that presumed there was a whore in the world he would have offered the luxurious, privileged existence he'd offered her. By God, he'd even consented to allow her damn brat to tag along.

"No," she replied stiffly.

"Very well," his voice was steely, "allow me to thank you for a pleasant week." Nikki rolled over and pulled open a drawer on the bedside table. Taking out a purse of roubles, he tossed them on Alisa's naked belly.

"It's been amusing," he said coldly, one sardonic eyebrow raised.

Alisa lifted the purse from her stomach, gently set it on the floor, rose from the bed, and dressed as rapidly as her numerous petticoats permitted.

Nikki watched sullenly, not uttering a word. He let her go and then laughed scornfully at himself for allowing passion, once again after all these years, to overcome his usual cool reserve. Stupid fool! he chastised himself.

Seconds after the door closed behind Alisa, Nikki reached for the bellpull and when the servant arrived, requested in a dangerous voice, "Three bottles of brandy, *immediately*."

As the afternoon shadows turned to evening dusk, even the three bottles of brandy failed to dislodge or dull the cold fury of his thoughts.

Damn inconsiderate slut! He'd offered her a pampered, luxurious life, the considerable influence of his protection, and a damn sight less sadistic treatment than that peasant she was married to gave her. I am not a whore, she had said. Insufferable arrogance— Why, oh, why would none of them ever admit to being what they were?

Chapter Six
THE DÉNOUEMENT

"Where the devil is she? I told you to keep watch over her!" Valdemar Forseus shouted wrathfully at his large, lumbering son.

"She couldn't have gone far without a horse or carriage," the middle-aged son calmly replied to his father, who was livid with rage, having already harangued his son for several minutes. Forseus's sparse gray hair was standing wildly about his bald pate, his small, sunken eyes flashed with anger, his carefully manicured, blunt peasant hands clenched and unclenched on his riding quirt.

"We weren't expecting you for six more days," the son continued with the puzzled simplicity of a dull intellect.

"That's obvious!" Forseus thundered. "Is that devil's brat with her?" Forseus asked suspiciously.

"No, I saw Katelina out in the orchard with Rakeli."

"Very well, get out of my sight!" Forseus spat out irritably. "I should have known better than to expect any competence from you. You take after your mother, you lout!"

Far from being disconcerted by this tirade, the simple, ponderous son merely turned on his heel and walked slowly back to the stables, where he was most happy and content, brushing, feeding and talking to the horses. After years of listening to his father's fulminations, they scarcely made an impression on him.

Forseus stalked into the house, threw his coat, hat, and quirt on the hall table, and bellowed for his butler.

"Bring me some kvass into the study," he instructed grimly. "Leave the door open," he ordered as the butler set the pitcher of kvass before his master and retreated from the room.

For forty-five minutes Forseus sat, sunk deeply in his leather chair, drinking steadily, his scowling beady eyes trained on the hallway.

The object of this vigil finally opened the front door and walked into the hall. Alisa's eyes widened with alarm immediately as she spied the coat and hat on the table in the center of the foyer. A startled catch of breath froze in her throat as an ominously calm voice spoke from the study.

"Out for a stroll in the spring air, Mrs. Forseus?" her husband inquired smoothly as his eyes flicked shrewdly over Alisa's figure, observantly taking in every detail of her ensemble. He hadn't amassed a fortune as a merchant because of a lack of perspicuity, and at once noticed the rumpled skirt of the dress and the damp hem and slippers. "Down by the river, my dear?" he questioned suspiciously. "Rather a long way from the house, isn't it?"

Alisa stood frozen in her tracks. The unexpected arrival was quite out of character for the punctilious, meticulous Mr. Forseus. Her mind rushed through a hundred excuses, none suitable, that might allay the sinister direction of her husband's inquiries.

"Yes," she flushed helplessly, unable to present a calm façade with the rising terror in her soul.

"Yes?" he repeated softly, his anger flaring higher as fanatic jealousy displaced reason. Forseus had wanted Alisa as a collector might want a fine painting, in order to possess it. She was a showpiece, another possession to be flaunted and displayed as further indication of his wealth, but not valued more highly than any other representation of his fortune, no more than his blooded stallion or his antique carpets or his gun collection.

He had also wanted her to demonstrate to the world that by virtue of his fortune, he was now august enough to marry into the gentry. He had also coveted the young girl because his flagging sex drive at sixty-one had required more and more stimulation, and young virgins were an obsession with him. After the novelty of the first few months of marriage had worn off, however, even Alisa's young, tender body was no longer enough to rouse his ardor.

Mr. Forseus had left her alone at that point, finding stimulation in the brothels catering to deviates who sought young girls. But even those had failed to satisfy him of late. Quite by accident, in a drunken rage, three weeks earlier, he had struck out in anger at Alisa and was astonished to discover that beating her had stimulated him sexually. Not sufficiently to consummate the act, but it became satisfaction in itself.

"Perhaps, Mrs. Forseus," her husband suggested smoothly, raising his obese bulk from the deep chair with some difficulty, "you would accompany me on a stroll, since you seem to enjoy the out-of-doors so much."

He walked up to Alisa, still frozen in her tracks, gripped her arm below the elbow in an iron grasp, and steered his frightened wife out into the waning afternoon sunlight.

He forced her in the direction of the barnyard, relentlessly keeping up a trivial chatter that grated on Alisa's raw nerves and tremulous fears. Opening the door of a shed with a key he kept on a chain at his waist, Forseus pushed her inside the empty granary and shut the heavy door.

"Now, then, Mrs. Forseus," he breathed with a fanatic gleam in his eyes as he stripped off his coat and rolled up his sleeves, "we might discuss where you were this afternoon."

Reaching out to a hook on the wall, he took down a length of rope, tied a knot slowly and carefully on one end, let the knot drop to the floor, and wrapped the excess length around his hand.

"Now, my dear, we begin. Where were you?" He swung the rope sharply and caught Alisa on her shoulder. She shuddered from the pain, but spoke not a word, nor would she look at him.

"Come, dear, lost your tongue?" he sneered coldly, lashing out again and striking Alisa viciously across her breasts. The strength of the blow dropped Alisa to her knees. God help me, she prayed silently, for she didn't dare tell him the truth. He would certainly kill her then. If she could just tolerate the torture, steel herself to keep from screaming in agony, perhaps, merciful God, perhaps, after a time, she would be lucky enough to faint.

Ten minutes later Forseus was breathing hard and just about to cease, when Alisa lost consciousness and sank gratefully to the floor and the beckoning solace of a black oblivion.

After rolling down his sleeves, wiping his perspiring face with a silk handkerchief and carefully adjusting his suit coat on his shoulders, Forseus quietly walked out of the shed and locked the door behind him.

.   .   .

Much later that evening, after explaining to a suspicious and distrustful Maria that Alisa had gone to Viipuri shortly before sunset, he ordered a tray of food and a glass of wine brought to him in his study.

When the house had quieted sufficiently and it appeared all occupants were sleeping, Valdemar Forseus carefully maneuvered his way through the moonlit shadows of the barnyard, unlocked the shed door, and deposited the tray on the floor beside his still-unconscious wife.

Before departing, he drew a small vial from his waistcoat pocket and poured half the contents into the glass of wine.

Chapter Seven
THE NECESSARY OPTION

Alisa woke in the early hours of morning and lay for a moment with her eyes still closed, flooded with a hopeless, bottomless despair so overwhelming, she could almost taste it. Her eyelids blinked open; she saw the knotted rope hanging back again on its hook on the wall and instantly renewed terror gripped her mind, tightened her stomach. Her one brief chance for happiness was gone, sent away by her own words. Any future offered only terror and abject misery. Her life ahead was completely empty of hope.

She felt extremely weak, and when she moved to a sitting position, a sharp pain began to throb in her temple. Seeing the tray before her, Alisa reached out to soothe her parched, dry throat with the contents of the wineglass, but the food remained untouched.

Almost immediately a vast drowsiness overcame her, but

Alisa thought this the natural result of her battered and fatigued body requiring needed rest. Her violet eyes dropped shut and her breathing slowed into the labored cadence of a heavily drugged repose.

Maria hadn't believed Forseus's lies for one minute and had solicited Arni's assistance in trying to find Alisa. Rakeli wouldn't be able to long allay the growing fears of Katelina.

Early next morning, returning surreptitiously up the servants' back stairway, Arni informed Maria of his findings. He'd seen Forseus as he emerged from the house at dawn and watched him go directly to the shed, enter the building and remain inside briefly. On reemerging, Forseus had carefully relocked the door, bidden a stable boy to saddle his horse, and left for Viipuri. Arni had discovered the destination upon questioning the lad.

Peering through one of the cracks in the log structure of the shed, Arni distinguished the body of Alisa lying on the floor, apparently asleep. When Maria was informed, her alarm mounted.

"What are we to do? He's beaten her again, you can be sure." Nothing went unseen or undetected by a personal maid who was also a loyal friend.

"We must get her out. Mistress Alisa has been wanting to leave. We can't wait any longer. Dare we steal some of Forseus's horses and make our escape while he is in Viipuri?"

"I don't know," Arni replied cautiously, "Forseus's arm is long and his money can buy much. I think we should appeal to Prince Kuzan. He's much more powerful than Forseus. He could protect Alisa where our poor credit could not."

Maria, Arni, and Rakeli, Alisa's old servants from her

parents' home, had protected and aided Alisa as best they could in the years since she'd been forced to marry Forseus. Carefully concealing their loyalties for fear of Forseus dismissing them, they had been able to smooth some of the sorrow of her existence.

They were all very aware of her relationship with Prince Kuzan since Maria had insisted Arni follow Alisa that morning when the carriage had come from Prince Kuzan, to insure their mistress was in no danger. After viewing the tender reconciliation in the meadow, Arni assured Maria that the Prince was not a dangerous villain intent on harming Alisa. On the contrary, he had brought an obvious ecstatic happiness to their young mistress, and her faithful servants were silently pleased to see Alisa singing again after years of quiet, hopeless despair.

If the question of morals were to be raised, the inhuman marriage forced on the young fifteen-year-old girl they loved was the most immoral of acts in their minds. That union was a travesty of the bonds of marriage, obscene and repulsive.

"You're right, Arni!" Maria exclaimed with renewed hope. "Go quickly and tell Prince Kuzan. He won't let our Alisa be hurt!"

Racing down the back stairs and out to the stables, Arni saddled one of Forseus's swiftest horses and was galloping down the long driveway in less than five minutes.

That same morning, Prince Kuzan was being dressed for his return to the city. He was still in a black fury, kicking furniture about, cursing loud and long in three languages with a fluency that amazed even Yukko, abusing his steward and any other servant who was unfortunate enough to come within his line of vision.

Nikki's troopers who had accompanied him out to his

hunting lodge were mounted in the courtyard, nervously eyeing each other and hoping Prince Kuzan's rage didn't descend on their heads.

For the last twenty minutes, as their horses restively sidled and fidgeted beneath them, a steady stream of explosive invective had been issuing from the open windows of the lodge. Initially, the cursing had resounded from the second floor, and presently the main floor rang with violent verbal denunciations as Nikki descended to spread his wrath democratically on breakfast, butler, cook, and steward. The coffee was too hot, the eggs were too cold, the butler didn't pour the brandy rapidly enough—the arrangement of luggage in the front hall grossly offended him, so the poor steward was frantically having footmen dispatching the offending luggage out of sight of their master. It was quickly loaded into the waiting wagon and sent out of view around the corner of the building.

Ten minutes more and three healthy bumpers of brandy later, Nikki emerged from the front entrance and critically surveyed his troop now drawn up in parade-ground precision. Even the careful scrutiny found nothing to criticize. The Prince threw himself into the saddle and swept one more glance around his familiar environs. Each vista only served to further remind him of Alisa. We walked there. We sat down there. Alisa admired those flower beds. I showered her in rose petals from that climbing rambler. The sun was warm on their bodies that day. Damn her voluptuous memory! And that's what it was, he irritably reminded himself, nothing more than a memory!

The black bulk of his favorite horse, Koli, was comfortingly familiar beneath the saddle. Nikki made a soft clicking noise with his tongue, and Koli swung his ears back, anticipating his master's command. Nikki's grip relaxed on the reins and he moved his horse forward at a slow walk. There was no shouted command. A slight sigh was heard, a

passing zephyr as the troopers inhaled a breath of relief.
They were on their way at last! Saddles groaned as men
gripped harder with their knees.

Nikki could hear the harnesses of his men's mounts jin-
gle behind him and the pad of hooves on the soft dirt of
the road. The troop traveled slowly in the warm air of the
spring morning, following the road that curved languidly
over pine- and birch-clad hills and valleys, traversing the
vast Kuzan estate.

Nikki's thoughts were on Alisa. After three bottles of
brandy, after a restless, tormented night of little sleep, after
relentlessly reminding himself that he was a fool—after all
that he wanted her still, and that insistent feeling couldn't
be dismissed.

Within twenty minutes the southern border of his hunting reserve was crossed. He must force thoughts of Alisa
from his mind. Too much mental recrimination was debili-
tating. The past was gone. Their brief affair was over. Nikki
gently spurred his horse to a trot. With the trot, the ring of
metal harness intensified and softly resounded in the quiet
morning air. As Nikki nudged Koli gently with his knees,
they increased to a canter. Seconds later, feeling only the
lightest of pressure from Nikki's legs, the black stallion
snorted, changed his pace with that faint encouragement
from his rider, and the troop was in full gallop. Nikki surveyed the road ahead. He began to visibly relax as the
comfortable rhythm of a familiar horse, the warm spring
air, and the exhilaration a full-out gallop always evoked
soothed his churlish temper. In seven hours of hard riding
they'd be in Petersburg.

Arni had ridden cross-country to the hunting lodge only
to discover that the Prince had left for Petersburg thirty
minutes before. Lashing his horse, Arni continued in frantic pursuit of the Prince. He couldn't hope to overtake
Prince Kuzan with that great a head start unless he cut over

the fields and through the forests. Arni dug his spurs into Forseus's bay mare. The horse leapt the first fence and charged across the plowed field.

As Nikki's troop was riding in correct formation, following the Prince's blooded stallion, a rider became visible, galloping diagonally across their line of vision from east to west. They all granted he must be a fine rider to be forcing his mount that recklessly across that uneven field. Soon he could be heard shouting something, wildly waving his arms, but the message was lost in the morning breeze. As the man galloped hell-for-leather directly toward them, Nikki drew to a halt. A few moments later Arni thundered up, sawed his horse to a rearing stop before Nikki, who was firmly keeping his skittish animal in check before the flailing hoofs of the rearing horse, and gasped out his message, "Alisa's in danger! Forseus has beaten her and locked her in the shed! She appears unconscious and—"

Arni's sentence was left hanging in the air as Nikki savagely swung his horse around and charged back past the halted ranks of his troopers. He waved his sergeant to give orders to follow.

There was no time for speculation, little enough time for thought. Alisa was in danger. No doubt because of him.

Within seconds the troop was once again in full gallop. Nikki forced the huge black hard, pressing him furiously.

Damn sadistic misogynist! He'd break Forseus's neck with his bare hands! Beaten her again, had he? It would be the last beating that old reprobate would ever administer! He'd see him burn in hell!

Arni had kept pace with Nikki. Nikki kneed Koli alongside the groom and shouted, "How long ago did you leave her?"

"About forty minutes ago!" Arni yelled in reply.

Nikki prayed he wasn't too late. All his frustrated fury of the morning had a new outlet—Valdemar Forseus!

Koli was flagging by the time Forseus's driveway was in sight, his mouth foaming, his flanks running with sweat. Nikki kept him at a gallop up the long driveway. Nearing the main house, Nikki snatched the pistol from his saddle holster and twenty troopers followed suit. He spun Koli sideways, reining hard to ease around the east wall of the house, and rode headlong into the stable yard, glanced briefly around the outbuildings, spied the shed, and hauled his stallion to a stop in front of the building.

Jumping down, he tossed his pistol aside, flung his huge frame against the locked door, and both hinges shattered at the violent impact. Two of his men who had dashed to his assistance lifted the door away.

In the dim light of the empty room Nikki saw Alisa's figure lying motionless, her tattered clothing scarcely covering her bruised and torn flesh. Rapidly divesting himself of his braided tunic, he wrapped Alisa gently in the garment and gathered her from the dirty floor into his arms.

She was so still! My God! Had Forseus killed her this time? He carefully scanned her pale face, so close to his, and was relieved to see faint color on her cheeks. Walking outside, he carefully laid her on the ground on a blanket hastily retrieved from a haversack, covered her lightly with another blanket, and began snapping orders.

"Find Forseus for me! I want that foul monster dragged out from wherever he is. Fetch some brandy for the lady! I want some lint and warm water! Immediately!"

Everyone scattered to obey his commands.

Arni was kneeling at his mistress's side, tears of rage in his eyes. Then he peered at her more closely. "I believe she's been drugged, Prince," he cried.

Nikki leaned over the slight, almost still form and felt for a pulse. Slowly he pulled her eyelids back to reveal vacant red eyes. Carefully closing the lids once more, he nodded agreement. "You're right. We must have her away from that fiend. You were right to come for me."

"What can we do?" Arni asked, terrified.

"Find her daughter and her maidservants." Nikki was aware of Alisa's affection for her old servants. And certainly Arni's loyalty must be rewarded with safety from Forseus's wrath. "Do you wish to accompany your mistress?"

"I go where Miss Alisa goes," Arni said gravely. "I promised her father."

"Very well, assemble those servants who wish to come with us, her daughter, and a change of clothing for Alisa. Take nothing more from this barbarous pig Forseus. After I've dealt with him, we'll leave."

Maria came to Alisa within minutes with warm water to bathe her face, but the drugged woman didn't respond and could accept no brandy.

The troopers' careful searching turned up no master of the house. Frightened servants explained that he and the son had ridden into Viipuri early that morning.

"As well," Nikki muttered grimly. His father wouldn't have appreciated Nikki murdering a neighbor.

Alisa was placed in Nikki's arms once he mounted, and the cavalcade slowly retraced the route of its headlong chase. Arni held Katelina while Maria and Rakeli rode behind two sergeants. Returning within the hour to the Petersburg road, the troop continued to the first post stop, where Nikki's luggage wagon and carriage had been left instructions to wait. The servants, Katelina, and Alisa were placed into Nikki's beautifully sprung landau and continued the journey south.

Aleksei greeted the strange group of guests late that afternoon when they and Nikki entered the town palace of pink Finnish and Siberian marble, situated just east of the Hermitage on Millionnaya, the most genteel street of old Petersburg. The serene classical palace facing the Neva was built between 1768 and 1785 as a present from the Empress Catherine II to her favorite Platon Kuzan.

A doctor was immediately called to Alisa's bedside and pronounced her out of danger. The dose of laudanum had been powerful but not fatal. For two days and nights Nikki kept servants around the clock at Alisa's bedside to monitor her needs as she drifted between sleeping and waking. On the morning of the third day, when he checked in to see what her condition was, Alisa was reclining comfortably against numerous lace-trimmed pillows, totally awake.

"You're looking much better this morning." Nikki smiled warmly in greeting. "For the past few days it's been like having the Sleeping Beauty in our midst."

"I must thank you for rescuing me in such a fairy-tale fashion." Alisa smiled gravely in return. "Maria told me everything. I'd despaired of surviving Mr. Forseus's last tantrum." Tears came to her eyes. Kneeling by her bedside, Nikki gently brushed them away.

And later to Nikki's insistent questioning Alisa related the proceedings after she'd arrived home to find Mr. Forseus there. Nikki paced the room as she told him of her beating, of finally becoming unconscious. Murderous thoughts sprang to his mind.

"He'll never again dare touch you, by God," Nikki said grimly as Alisa finished her story. Then once more he went to her and took her hand. "You're safe here with me."

"Oh, but I can't accept your hospitality for long. Surely, your parents won't like strangers in their home."

Not wishing to enter into that argument again, Nikki temporized placatingly, "You're not quite yourself yet, so please accept my hospitality, at least temporarily, and as for my mother and father, they haven't entered this threshold in over three years, much preferring the air of the country. So rest assured, you'll not be disturbed.

"Now, please, ask for anything you require, and I hope your health soon returns, although you're looking remarkably fit this morning," he added with a languid smile. "Perhaps you could join me for dinner this evening. Now I must be off briefly for regimental duties. Au revoir."

"Au revoir, and thank you again. I hope I'll be able to repay you someday."

You shall, dear, you shall, Nikki reflected as he strode down the hall resplendent in full regimentals, the silver braid brilliant against the white superfine tunic, his dark hair still damp from his bath and curling at the nape of his neck over the stiff, silver-embellished collar. With an uncharacteristic flash of romantic sympathy he'd not only refrained from touching the beautiful, warm sleeping woman so inviting in her helpless vulnerability, but had, more remarkably, eschewed other women in the past three days. No Gypsies on the Islands, no Countess, no ballet dancers. With a curious whimsy the Prince rather fancied waiting for the sleeping lady. He hadn't realized he had such high-minded instincts, but it wasn't all earnest moral principles, for he'd spent a lot of time in taking cold baths and chastising himself for acting in such a ridiculous manner.

Nikki was in charity with the world and in such superb spirits that morning that even an insistent note from his mistress, Countess Amalienborg, greeting him at breakfast didn't deter his fine humor. Sophie had apparently heard of his house guest (gossip travels fast below stairs) and had requested his company at a small card party that evening. He scrawled a short acceptance across the bottom of her perfumed stationery and dispatched the message by footman.

Just as well, he reflected. Countess Amalienborg had been an enduring mistress over almost two years now, notwithstanding Nikki's occasional short flings with an actress or Gypsy. However, he'd become faintly tired of Sophie's proprietary airs in public lately. Tonight would be an ideal opportunity to courteously break off their longstanding friendship. A skilled lover, Sophie had served well in the past as a palliative to his boredom when he craved extraordinary acrobatics in bed. She was always successful in bringing his blood up, although he thought her the lowest kind of bitch, for she'd do anything to oblige him. But then there were other times when he didn't care if he lived or died, and on those occasions he surpassed even Sophie's audacity in bed.

But lately even her practiced accomplishments were palling. A bank draft or jewels? Which would she prefer as a parting token? Out of innate laziness and indifference he decided on the money, called Ivan in, and was assured the bank draft would be on his dressing table before dinner that evening.

"Thank you, Ivan, you're ever efficient."

Deferentially, Ivan inquired of his well-disposed employer so obviously in buoyant spirits this morning, "Did you enjoy the art catalogues you requested?"

"Immensely, Ivan, immensely! You don't know what pleasure they brought me." Nikki chuckled.

Puzzled, but cheered at his master's new interest in art, Ivan bowed himself out of the breakfast room.

Could one wonder at the cause of Prince Kuzan's enormous good humor? He'd had his way after all. The object of his amorous interest, but recently outside his grasp, was now ensconced in a splendid gilt bed mere feet from his suite next door, and in addition, supremely grateful for his efforts on her behalf. So very convenient.

Nikki positively glided through the onerous, petty details of regimental paperwork necessary to his position that fine early spring morning. Within the hour he'd dispatched these trivia and had returned home only to find that Alisa was dozing once more. Not an impatient man, under the circumstances (he had all the time in the world) Nikki let Alisa sleep quite peacefully most of the day.

Sending a note in the late afternoon, he inquired if she had any preferences for dinner and informed her he would await her company in the drawing room at seven.

Nikki, elegantly attired in black evening dress and white satin waistcoat, relaxed before the open window on a large tapestry settee, one foot in its patent evening pump resting on the windowsill, and slowly sipped a fine Madeira. Seeing him sitting there, all well-bred grace, one lost sight of the brute power beneath the silken raiment unless one paused to note the width of the shoulder or the thickness of wrist, unless one marked the thigh muscles flexing on the leg so casually at ease on the sill.

He turned his head at the sound of the door and automatically came to his feet, advanced across the enormous parquet floor with his customary poise, and gave Alisa an elegant bow.

"My lady," he said very formally while smiling down at her in a most distracting fashion from under those heavy brows, "please join me in a Madeira before we dine. The weather is quite exceptional and I've been enjoying the prospect of the Neva across the quay."

Alisa was dressed in her only ensemble.

"I'm afraid I'm not adequately dressed for dinner," she stammered slightly, overawed by the magnificent rococo room resplendent with gilt, putti, stuccoed reliefs, and real Bouchers and Fragonards. Awed as well by Nikki's casual grace and the distinct overt difference between the unsophisticated, natural man she'd known in the country and this supremely dégagé courtier so at ease in this enormous palace, wearing his luxurious attire carelessly, as though being point-de-vice was as comfortable as old slippers. She felt like the proverbial country mouse.

"You're ever the epitome of beauty, my dear," Nikki amiably replied in a smooth drawl. He could sense she was embarrassed at her lack of elegant dress, was himself so used to dressing for dinner, he hadn't considered the awkwardness it might cause Alisa. He observed to himself that he would put her wardrobe to rights immediately, and then attempted to placate her embarrassment by apologizing. "Forgive me for dressing so conspicuously, but I've an engagement after dinner I must attend, hence this attire." Alisa was surprised to feel a strange and uncomfortable jealousy at his remark.

"Come sit by me and we'll enjoy the saffron sunset. You look the picture of health once again."

Maria had bathed Alisa and washed her magnificent hair; the vibrant recuperative powers of youth had quickly restored her peaches-and-cream complexion, and she did indeed look refreshingly glowing.

"Thank you, I feel very well."

Nikki chatted casually, never referring to anything personal, putting Alisa completely at ease, teasing and entertaining her with the trivial, innocuous gossip about town. Zacouska preceded the dinner and Nikki directed Alisa to a small anteroom, where a table was spread with caviar, cheese, rusks, sardines, oysters, olives, liqueurs, and vodka.

"I understand zacouska is becoming quite comme il faut in France this year. We Russians have known for centuries that several glasses of liquor much improve that *mauvais quart d'heure* that generally precedes European dinners. Do try one small glass of chilled vodka, my dear." Without waiting for an answer he proceeded to pour them both one.

"To your regained health." Nikki raised his glass in salute.

The dinner was superb; Nikki's French chef surpassed

himself for his young master who so rarely dined in. Perhaps the new house guest would change the Prince's normal pattern, the chef reflected with a Gallic lift of his eyebrows. He would be able to serve his delectable coq au vin, his exquisite crème bachique, his savory potage à la crevette. Ah! *Vive la femme!* He could display his skills again. Bah! He had become tired of only serving breakfasts at two in the afternoon.

Nikki came home quite late from Countess Amalienborg's card party, his brows drawn together in a lowering scowl. An evening's entertainment of charades and a bellowing Italian soprano had preceded the cards. By God! Sophie's amusements were banal. Needless to say, it had been quite late before he was able to affect a private conversation with Sophie. The amiable parting Nikki had envisioned had not been all that amiable. When he'd politely offered his adieus and his handsome bank draft, the Countess had bitterly and impertinently bearded him about his new mistress.

"Installed in the room next to yours, Nikki, I hear, and drugged when she was brought in," the Countess had said maliciously. "Losing your touch, dear? Surely between your smooth tongue and big cock, you don't have to resort to force?"

"Don't be coarse, *chérie,*" Nikki said flatly. Damn gossiping doctor, Nikki thought irritably, the news must be all over town by now. Normally immune to gossip concerning himself, he preferred not having Alisa's name bandied about.

"When I lose my touch, Sophie dear, I'll let you know," Nikki murmured coldly. "Perhaps your husband and I will then be able to share a mutual interest in cards. Whist is all he's good for at present. I still endeavor to amuse myself in more active ways."

"With your 'active' ways," she sneered, "next thing you know, your little mistress will be handing you another brat."

"Perhaps," he replied.

"Perhaps? Is that all you can say? You, who are near to setting some kind of record for bastards?"

"These things are rather inevitable," Nikki continued, exasperated with Sophie's spite. "Not every woman is in such an enviable position as you, dear, who can bed without restraint and never experience a qualm, thanks to your barren womb."

"No doubt your newest trollop is not so disposed and will soon present you with the unwelcome news of impending fatherhood yet again!" Sophie taunted.

"Whether that comes to pass or no, I fail to see how my affairs are any concern of yours," Nikki drawled, trying to keep his anger in check.

Seeing she had pushed the quick-tempered Prince too far, and averse to losing such an accomplished bed partner, the worldly-wise Sophie sensibly changed her tack.

"Stay the night, Nikki," she breathed softly, "I haven't seen you in weeks."

Glancing at his gold and champlevé enamel wristwatch, he absently toyed with the unusual alarm mechanism that upon release reminded its wearer of the hour by tapping the wrist.

"Not tonight, Sophie," he said politely.

"I don't suppose you'd say no if your newest bed warmer asked you," Sophie snapped, her brief attempt at cajolery vanishing.

The Prince raised his eyes from his timepiece and there was a glint in his eye. "That, my dear, is quite another matter."

"Rude, odious wretch!" the Countess spat out.

He only laughed. "As you very well know from past experience, Sophie, my pet." Bowing infinitesimally from the waist, he left the scented boudoir.

The irritating Countess had taken some of the edge from his good spirits. Arriving home, Nikki waved off the solicitous butler, let himself into his study, and relaxed over several brandies, allowing the annoyance of Sophie's impertinence to wash away. An hour later Nikki was comfortably soothed. The presence of Alisa in his own home was a powerful distraction. There might be problems with his malicious ex-mistress, he thought. But to hell with the problems; all he could think of was the woman upstairs; the problems could wait.

He rose from the chair near the window and slowly walked up the wide marble staircase. A small gaslamp was burning low near Alisa's bed. Nikki stood a long time and watched her peacefully sleeping; she was so fragile, her breasts rising and falling gently beneath her silk negligee, her long lashes resting on her soft white cheeks, one arm thrown above her head, her red-gold hair like liquid copper in the mellow light, in casual disarray on the satin pillowcase. Unbuttoning the silver buttons of his evening jacket, Nikki dropped it on the floor at his feet. He removed his clothes slowly, devouring her with his gaze. When he deliberately dropped his black patent shoe on the floor, her eyes opened instantly.

She saw him in the soft glow cast by the lamp, and for a second glimpsed the brief bewilderment of his emotions. The look was gone in a flash and the bed dipped as his weight came down on it. His head lowered and his parted lips moved over hers gently, forcing her mouth open, slowly, languorously, teasing her senses as his hands ran over her body and lifted her gown.

He could feel her beginning to respond to him. Slowly

he undid the ribbons of her silk gown and pulled it from
her shoulders. He touched the hem and raised it past her
softest place. Finally, her arms pulled him to her and he
knew the long days of his enforced celibacy were over.

He took her time after time that night, wanting her to
need him, wanting her to cry out for him, reassuring himself that she really was his, that he had her in his bed, in his
house, at his demand. Perplexing emotions raced through
his subconscious but he felt most the need for reaffirmation
of his dominant role in their relationship, a role most gratifying when she was pleading for him to grant her release in
exquisite pleasure. Alisa loved him that night hopelessly,
incoherently, as again and again he wakened her body to
bewitching sensation. Each touch made her feel her body
for the first time, as if in a rebirth. And finally sated, they
fell asleep coiled around each other, arms and legs entwined, the warmth of her breath on his chest, the powerful beat of his heart beneath her ear.

Chapter Eight
THE RECALCITRANT MISTRESS

Early the next morning the bedroom door burst open and one small curly-mopped, red-gold head popped into sight, babbling excitedly in Finnish.

"Momma, Momma, Look what Uncle Nikki bought—" She stopped abruptly, broke off, and immediately switched effortlessly into French.

"Uncle Nikki!" She let out a squeal of delight when she spied him lying in bed next to her mother.

Katelina tightly clutched a large china doll with long flowing blond hair in her chubby arms and flew across the marble floor, her splendid new velvet robe and dimity nightgown streaming out behind in her impetuous dash toward the huge, gilded four-poster bed majestically installed on a dais over which four flying cupids suspended a gold and mother-of-pearl half shell. Katelina was an engaging and lively child, a beautiful little girl with all of her mother's good looks and devastating charm.

Scrambling into bed like a frisky, rambunctious puppy, she promptly discarded her doll and threw her plump arms around Nikki's neck, excitedly entreating, "Will you take Rakeli and me to the toy shop again today? Please, please!" she implored, her dark eyes wide with hope and expectation.

The Prince smiled amiably at the small girl clutching him and said, "You may speak Finnish to me, my pet, I, too, have a Finnish mother." (He had unwittingly spoken French to Katelina the past few days and she had responded in kind.)

In the days Alisa had been ill and recuperating, Nikki had spent a great deal of time with Katelina. The first time he'd stood in Alisa's room and seen the young child crying pitifully, it took several seconds for the tableau to register as reality. A young child crying sorrowfully in his house was so alien that his reaction was delayed. Nikki hadn't talked to a small child or been within touching distance of one in years. Having heard the wailing for over an hour since his return that first afternoon, and surmising that the nanny and maid were unable to stop the distress, Nikki decided to lend a hand in an attempt to mitigate her unhappiness.

Nikki was by nature kind and cheerful, as any of his friends would agree, and altogether capable of tenderness and gentleness as well, as any of his lovers would concur. Nikki's phenomenal success with women was not due solely to his remarkable handsomeness and princely fortune, although, in the glittering society in which he moved, those were often attributes enough. His conquests were due as much, if not more, to his charm, his ability to give a woman pleasure in the drawing room as well as in bed. He could be jesting, tender, gentle, interested, and concerned as the mood moved him, and this charm was marshalled in an effort to soothe Katelina's fear while at the same time making his beautiful mistress better able to recover from her overdose of laudanum.

During the days of Alisa's recovery, Nikki had offered adventures to the young child that soon took her mind off her fears. Katelina almost immediately adopted Nikki as a kind of vice-uncle and behaved toward him with an uninhibited and sometimes embarrassing affection.

Turning quickly to her mother as if it were the most natural sight in the world to see her with Uncle Nikki in bed and hardly pausing for a breath, Katelina rattled on, reverting back to Finnish. "Oh, Momma, the toy shop is just beautiful. Everything is most—" She stopped. "Rakeli said I shouldn't be so greedy, didn't you, Rakeli?" She turned her wide eyes toward her nanny, who had tarried doubtfully by the door upon seeing Prince Kuzan. Katelina's brief regard for humble courtesies over, she rushed on breathlessly. "But Uncle Nikki said that I was a little princess and I could have anything I wanted. Didn't you, Uncle Nikki?" Katelina beamed widely into Nikki's amused countenance as she perched on his broad chest.

"That's right, moppet," said her benevolent "uncle."

"Oh, Uncle Nikki, could we *please* go again today, *please?*" she begged delightfully, and gazed with pleading brown eyes into Nikki's face.

"Of course, dear, you shall have another doll if you like."

"Oh, Nikki, I would *much* rather have a train!"

Nikki's eyes twinkled gaily as he shot a sidelong look at Alisa, grinned faintly, and said, "Already an independent young lady not content to play with dolls. Very well, minx, the train it shall be," he finished indulgently.

"Oh, Momma, isn't Uncle Nikki *just* wonderful?" Katelina pronounced with all the uninhibited candor of her five years.

Nikki turned to glance wickedly at Alisa and smirkingly asked, "Yes, Momma, aren't I *just* wonderful?"

"Say yes, Momma! Say yes!" Katelina insisted, bouncing with excitement and delight.

Before Alisa had to answer that awkward question, Katelina blithely continued her chatter.

"Momma, I'm so *very* glad you're feeling better. Nikki said I must be *so* very quiet for *so* long. I'm glad I don't have to be quiet *anymore!*" she finished emphatically.

Unable to hold her youthful enthusiasm in check, she continued bouncing up and down as she inquired relentlessly, "When can we *go*, Uncle Nikki, when can we *go?*"

"After you eat breakfast and Rakeli dresses you," he answered patiently, "then we'll leave. Now, go and get ready."

The volatile little body that gave every indication of a perpetual motion machine grabbed the doll, immediately slid off the bed, and bounded across the large room. At the door she paused, one hand in Rakeli's, one plump fist clutching the enormous doll by her blond hair.

"May I have strawberries and cake again for breakfast? May I, may I, Nikki?" she entreated her new and generous uncle.

"Of course, dear, whatever you like."

"*When* can we leave?" she repeated again with the impatience of her five years.

"In about an hour," Nikki replied, then, looking down at Alisa, warm, tousled, and languid in bed beside him, he reconsidered. "Make it an hour and a half, Rakeli," he said matter-of-factly. The door shut behind the small whirlwind, and Alisa remarked gratefully in a low, quiet voice, "Thank you for being so kind to Katelina while I was ill." Nikki took Alisa's hand in his and very simply replied, "You're welcome." He went on teasingly with an affectionate grin, "I've had to entertain that little brat for three days while you have been lazing in bed. Rakeli was at her wit's end, with Katelina insisting on crying at your bedside and you still in a half-drugged state, unable to respond to her. Maria couldn't check the tears either, so the task fell to Aleksei and me to devise some schemes to distract Katelina and keep her from disturbing you.

"We slid down the grand staircase on silver trays, dressed her as Empress in lace tablecloths (I was a reluctant Emperor, I might add, and Katelina manifested the true imperiousness of born royalty by ordering Aleksei and me about shamelessly), we sailed paper boats in the monteith bowls, I had the grooms bring the new kittens from the stables, and Maria fetched her some new clothes from some children's modiste Ivan knew of."

Nikki was massaging Alisa's wrist absently with his thumb.

"Thank God you began to feel yourself once again yesterday afternoon, because I'd taxed my ingenuity to its limits and had quite exhausted my meager repertoire of amusements for children. I'm afraid I'm woefully out of practice. My memories of childhood pleasures are extremely dim, overborne, no doubt, by the myriad and vastly more pleasurable adult pastimes. I'm happy to see," Nikki said with a flame of passion kindling in his golden eyes as he turned to her, "that you have been restored to vibrant, blooming health once again. I've sorely missed your warmth these last few days.

"You're my delectable, enticing bed warmer," Nikki said with a natural proprietary air as he ran his finger up her bare arm. "You suit me admirably," his husky voice added.

Alisa felt panic rise within her at his words. Uncertain, confused, aware of the dangers in succumbing to Nikki's seductive charm, she wondered how deeply her untutored emotions had entangled her. Each touch, each caress, seemed yet another strand woven in the net that was

slowly but inexorably enveloping her. Faint with helpless-
ness at her situation, she was still heavy with love, heedless
to all but desire.

Nikki was caressing her now with both hands, slowly
running his fingers down her soft curves. He bent his head
and touched her warm, inviting lips. And then Alisa had
no further time to reflect as her passions rose to meet his
demands.

Sometime later, Nikki rose from the rumpled bed.

"We must hurry and dress if we hope to meet Katelina's
schedule." Saying this, he turned and walked stark naked
with a most unaffected composure to the door of the adjoining dressing room. Pausing in the open doorway, he
reached one long arm out for the bellpull, remarking, "I'll
ring for the servants to draw your bathwater. I hope rois-
terous Rubenesque nymphs and black onyx Turkish sunken
tubs don't offend you, but our ancestor Platon was not
distinguished for his refinement and leaned rather toward
an erotic purism." Neither expecting nor waiting for an
answer, Nikki shouted for his valet and strode out of the
room.

Fifteen minutes later Nikki sauntered back in, the valet
bustling after, easing a crisp white shirt onto the muscular
shoulders.

Alisa swiftly pulled up the sheet and covered her shoulders.

"Aren't you out of bed yet? Tut, tut, dear, Katelina will
be fidgeting."

"I know. I'll get up directly. But the bed felt so comfortable."

"You'll like the toy shop. They have the best selection in
the city." As the valet hovered about, buttoning the gold
shirt studs, adjusting the turquoise cuff links, straightening
the soft collar to the right degree of perfection, Nikki carried on an easy conversation explaining the direction of

the establishment where Katelina's train was to be found, noting the beautiful day, discoursing convivially on Katelina's impetuous charm, until he suddenly realized Alisa's responses to these mundane observations were rather stilted. Glancing over to the bed, he saw an obviously distressed and embarrassed figure clutching the bed linen to her chin.

"That will be all, Georgi." He crisply dismissed the valet.

"Yes, my Prince," said the diminutive man, and quickly left the room.

Walking over to the bed, Nikki leaned over and kissed Alisa's cheek. "Forgive me. I didn't realize Georgi disturbed you."

"It's silly, I'm sure, but, well . . . I'm not used to having a manservant in my bedroom."

"Of course, dear. I should have considered. I'll dress myself from now on."

"Oh, no! I don't want to cause trouble for your valet . . . and . . . how will you manage?" Alisa stammered apologetically.

"Nonsense! Georgi will find his extra leisure no hardship, I assure you, and I'm perfectly capable of dressing myself. Men don't have all those frippery buttons and laces women do. Now, come, my sweet, into your bath, or Katelina will complain vehemently at the delay. I'll go and explain to Georgi."

In an incredibly short time Nikki returned through the dressing room doorway extremely well-turned out in a fastidiously tailored coffee-brown frock coat of exquisite fit across his broad shoulders, a finely tucked open-neck lawn shirt, brown brocade waistcoat, and pale biscuit trousers resting the required bare half inch from the ground over his brown kid half boots.

Alisa was being dressed by Maria while Katelina sat upon a tufted hassock, watching with a very unusual and quiet patience. Alisa was turned out in her only dress, which had been miraculously washed and pressed overnight, a navy and green striped silk serge skirt and a green silk blouse clasped high under her neck with a cameo brooch. Nikki had instructed Maria to find a wrap in his mother's wardrobe, and Maria was now arranging the soft folds of a navy blue pelisse edged in silk braid over the voluminous skirt.

Alisa's golden coppery hair had been arranged simply, pulled back and up on top of her head, long curls falling down her back, soft tendrils framing her delicate face. Studying Alisa critically from head to foot, Nikki said, "We must see to some clothes for you, Alisa. I'm afraid the gowns left in Mother's room are sadly out of date. However, that pelisse will do. And you, moppet, look quite elegant." He grinned as Katelina jumped from her seat upon hearing Nikki speak and rushed toward him. Maria had found on her shopping expedition a dress of white organza with pale green ribbons that fit Katelina admirably as well as a short green coat and an enormous pale yellow straw sailor hat decorated with long green taffeta streamers.

"Shall we, ladies?" Nikki inquired with an elaborate flourish, and Katelina tumbled out of the room a full five yards in advance of Rakeli, who ran after her impetuous young charge.

The landau, with its top down, stood ready outside the main entrance, its coachwork freshly beeswaxed, its four horses so well groomed, their gleaming chestnut coats seemed to have been brushed with oil. After everyone was comfortably seated, the coachman, in his best livery of green velvet, set the animals into a fashionable high-stepping trot.

It was impossible for Katelina to sit tamely on the velvet upholstery. She hopped about, asking questions, excitedly pointing out items that interested her and demanding and getting most of Nikki's attention. Alisa was pleased to see that adjusting to a new environment was evidently not going to be a problem for her daughter. With Katelina's natural curiosity, vitality, and open, affectionate nature, each new experience was avidly enjoyed. As Katelina's father had studiously avoided her since her birth five years before, no emotional pangs of separation had developed since leaving Viipuri.

Katelina had wrung a promise from Nikki to ride to the Summer Gardens first, and as they approached the Gardens, the other occupants of fashionable carriages out to enjoy the balmy temperatures were astounded to see the city's most sought after bachelor riding with a beautiful young woman, a nanny, and a child!

Two smartly uniformed Chevalier Gardes astride magnificent blacks rode up to the carriage as Rakeli and Katelina were disembarking to take in a short expedition to feed the swans. The coachman finished tying the horses to a hitching post and retired to the shade of a nearby tree.

Both officers bowed deeply from their saddles and the fair-haired young lieutenant remarked politely to Nikki, "Good morning, Nikki, I don't believe we've met your charming companion before."

"No, that's right, you haven't," Nikki replied rudely. "Now, get about your business," he added discourteously, and sketched them a brief salute. With no rebuke possible to that direct cut, they wheeled their horses and left, puzzled at his response.

"It looks like our Colonel has discovered a new bit of fluff he's jealously guarding," the young blond subaltern remarked to his companion with a chuckle as they continued their leisurely canter down the Admiralteski.

"Nikki in public with a child is enough to shock the most redoubtable aplomb. Do you think it's his?"

"Can't say. With that red hair, the little girl looks like her mother, not like Countess Souvanieff's last child that bore the stamp of Nikki Kuzan so blatantly, it fair took your breath away."

As these speculations were being bandied about farther down the avenue, Nikki and Alisa were interrupted once again by a passing horseman. Major Cernov, riding up to the open carriage, doffed his hat in greeting. Nikki's face set into a scowl.

"So nice to see you *once again*, Mrs. Forseus," Cernov said pointedly with a lopsided grin, and his Oriental eyes narrowed speculatively.

Alisa flushed hotly at the insinuating tone of the greeting and at the eyes that stripped her.

"Good morning," she returned coolly, angered at the bold scrutiny he was directing at her.

"Haven't seen you at the Yacht or Nobles' Clubs lately, Nikki. LaSalle Square and the islands seem quite dull without you, but now I can see good reason for your absence."

"I didn't know my absences were noted with such assiduity," Nikki observed dryly.

"Come now, don't be so modest, Nikki; as you well know, your activities have been substantial material for on-dits and observation since you were a mere stripling."

"Surely people have better things to occupy their time than listen to absurd gossip. In point of fact, don't you have some more pressing business, Gregor? We wouldn't want to detain you," Nikki said, brushing off yet another attempt at conversation.

"As you wish, Nikki. Your servant, Madame," Cernov said soothingly as he took the rather direct suggestion amiably. Taking a silk wipe from his sleeve, Cernov flicked an imaginary speck of dust from his spotless cavalry boots, pushed the kerchief back into his sleeve so a few inches trailed elegantly below his silver-braided cuff, wheeled his horse to leave, and winked at Nikki.

"If Tanya's pattern should reoccur, please inform me. I'd be interested in the merchandise."

"Don't get greedy, Cernov," Nikki quietly retorted. Cernov's long, flowing mustache only twitched as his thin lips smiled faintly. "I'm a patient man, *mon ami,* no hurry." He gently spurred his horse to a trot and disappeared into the stream of carriages and riders.

"What did that insolent cur mean by merchandise?" Alisa asked, knowing full well what he'd meant. "And who is Tanya?"

"Don't get your temper up, dear. Tanya was an old friend and Cernov knows very well that you're under my protection, so he won't bother you, I'm sure."

"Under your protection?" Alisa sputtered, flushing vividly as the obvious and unmistakable clarity of his explanation struck her. Of course, she should have realized. How very stupid of her. The full implication of what the public reaction to her situation would be left her momentarily stunned, devoured with shame. She was exceedingly thankful, for the first time since her parents' death, that they *weren't* alive to see the terrible depths to which she had fallen, the sordid fate outlined for her.

All those years with that beast Forseus she'd patiently waited until Katelina was older and had planned on leaving, having saved some money as she could, with the expectation of that flight. Now, through nothing more than her own sensuous weakness in succumbing to the devastatingly charming advances of Prince Kuzan, she was deprived of even the comfortless life of Forseus's estate.

Irritated at the masterful certainty of Nikki's assumption, and resentful to be treated once more like a piece of property, she coldly said, "I don't recall placing myself under your protection."

"Come now, love," Nikki said reasonably, "if you recall, when I found you in that shed, your alternatives were surely limited; more severe beatings and possibly death if Forseus had continued drugging you. Hardly a choice of options, I should think. And consider it now," Nikki urged amiably, "plenty of advantages, especially if one has already shown a *decided* partiality for the man one has as protector. I'm not considered ungenerous, and if you contrive to please me in the future as well as you have to this date, we shall deal together quite easily."

Taking umbrage at his arrogant presumption that her role was to please *him*, Alisa indignantly said, "I haven't any *decided* partiality for you, you arrogant lecher, and furthermore—"

"Give me three minutes alone with you, my dear," Nikki interjected suavely, "and I feel sure I can restore my credit on that account."

Her eyes dropped shamefully before his candid regard, but she was angry enough to thrust aside the brief feeling of embarrassment, continuing belligerently. "Maria has some money of mine she brought with us. I'm not in *need* of protection."

"Not enough to buy you one decent gown, let alone support yourself, a child, and three servants," Nikki disagreed bluntly with his typical disregard for tact.

"Well, then," Alisa insisted heatedly, "I'm relatively well educated, young, and strong. I can obtain a position as governess."

"I agree in principle with your idea, but unfortunately, the pressures of existence in this world of travail serve to daunt the most optimistic hopes." His words were uttered in a lazy, mocking drawl. "For you, the role of governess"— the sarcasm in his voice was all too apparent—"is quite a pleasant conceit, my dear. You *will* forgive my speaking frankly, but I fear you are lacking in a sense of the realities of things.

"*If*—I say, *if*—any wife in her right mind would allow a

provokingly beautiful young woman like yourself to enter her household, I'd wager a small fortune, the master of that house would be sharing your bed within the week. Consider the folly of the notion, love. At least with me there'd be no indignant wife to throw you and your retinue out into the street when her husband's preferences became obvious. And since I have a rather intimate knowledge of many of these wives, I think my opinion is to be relied upon. And as your protector," he continued equably, "I, of course, feel an obligation to maintain your daughter and servants in luxurious comfort."

"I am not a plaything to be bought!" Alisa said feelingly.

"Ah, my dear, but you are. Confess, it is a woman's role, primarily a pretty plaything for a man's pleasure and then inexorably as night follows day—a mother. Those are the two roles a woman plays. It's preordained. Don't fight it," he said practically.

Alisa would have done anything, she felt at that moment, to wipe that detestable look of smugness from Nikki's face.

"Perhaps I'll take Cernov up on his offer after all," she said with the obvious intent to provoke. "Is he richer than you? I must weigh the advantages if I'm to make my way profitably in the demimonde," she went on calculatingly. "Since I'm merely a plaything, it behooves me to turn a practical frame of mind to the role of demirep and sell myself for the highest price in money and rank obtainable. I have a certain refinement of background without the stench of the ghetto, which is surely worth a few roubles more, and I play the piano, though, I must confess, with more skill than talent; of course, I embroider a fine stitch, hardly of interest in the boudoir, I fear. I dance rather gracefully, if you *will* pardon the immodesty of boasting; sketch and paint, am fluent in Latin, French, German, again, alas, of little consequence once the lights are out."

With an uncharitable pleasure Alisa noticed her words had the effect of erasing the objectionable look of smugness from Nikki's face, to be abruptly replaced by a glowering frown.

"Desist in the cataloguing if you please," he broke in rudely, and in a dangerously cold voice murmured, "Let us not cavil over trifles. You're staying with me." Alisa involuntarily quailed before the stark, open challenge in his eyes, and her heart sank in a most unpleasant way.

"So my life is a trifle?" she whispered, trembling with a quiet inner violence.

"You misunderstand, my dear," the even voice explained with just a touch of impatience. "It's simply that I don't intend to enter into any senseless wrangles or debates over your attributes and the direction in which your favors are to be bestowed. Madame, you're to remain my mistress." His lips smiled faintly but his tawny gaze was chill.

Alisa closed her eyes momentarily as she reached the final point of renunciation of all the ideals of her youth. Then, lifting her chin resolutely, she said sarcastically, "In that case, I suppose I must thank you for your generous hospitality."

"Not at all," Nikki coolly replied. "I expect my generosity to be amply repaid."

Rakeli and Katelina returned at that moment to cut short the sharp retort Alisa was about to utter. They gaily jabbered on about the swans and flowers and statues as Nikki turned to speak to Alisa.

"We'll stop at Madame Vevay's next. She isn't Worth, but since your wardrobe must be replenished immediately, we'll settle for a local modiste," Nikki said, giving the coachman a signal to leave.

The first of her commands, Alisa resentfully thought, in her role as mistress.

"Does that require an answer, Lord Prince," she inso-

lently inquired. "You must help me acquire the proper conduct for one of my class."

"I look forward to the tuition," he quietly replied, his
voice not carrying beyond her ears. "Somehow I feel you
have a natural talent for at least a portion of the require-
ments," he finished, amusement rife in his tone.

Alisa coldly sat next to Nikki, her ankles crossed neatly,
her hands folded together in her lap, and lapsed into an
outraged, vengeful silence, answering only in curt monosyl-
lables when he addressed her directly. After several rebuffs
to his conversational sallies, Nikki leaned over and whispered teasingly into her ear, "Maybe Forseus wasn't crazy
after all when he beat you. You're singularly provoking and
impertinent for a woman."

She shot him a look of black fury and hissed, "You have
yet to see my full impertinence, sir."

"In that case, I look forward to the future with pleasant
anticipation," Nikki retorted, and a level gaze of challenge
issued from under half-lowered lids.

Rakeli and Katelina were so engrossed in their sight-
seeing that they were oblivious of the sotto-voce *contre-dit*
going on across from them.

Within minutes they were alighting before the fashionable façade of Madame Vevay. Nikki, in an agreeable
mood, as he always was when he had his own way, was all
courtesy and easy manners as he escorted them into the
gilded establishment of the haute couturière of Petersburg,
the interior in flattering emulation of Worth's in Paris, all
green silk, gold, and mahogany.

Seeing the elegant equipage depositing its passengers,
Madame Vevay came sweeping toward the door with a
finely controlled hauteur and was momentarily arrested in
mid-glide when Prince Nikolai Kuzan stepped through her
delicately grilled plate-glass doors, escorting a ravishing
beauty, but most startling, and the object of Madame

Vevay's rapt amazement, pulling a young child in tow. The sight was enough to stagger the most rigid demeanor, but Madame Vevay, ever resourceful, rapidly regained her composure and, holding out both hands, warmly greeted the Prince and his party.

"Prince Kuzan!" she gushed with an extremely deferential familiarity. "So lovely to see you!"

"A pleasant morning to you, Madame Vevay. May I present my"—he paused delicately, and smiled faintly—"my—ah—cousin, unfortunately recently widowed, and her charming daughter." A suitably grieved expression accompanied his malapert lie concerning Alisa's "dead" husband.

Alisa flushed brightly pink to her ears and Katelina bobbed a correct little bow as Nikki grinned broadly. He was paying Alisa back for her challenge to his authority and for her rudeness on the ride to the dress shop. Nikki was making certain her possibilities for finding work as a governess were abruptly dashed. Everyone would know within hours of their leaving Madame Vevay's that Alisa was Nikki's newest mistress. That delicate pause had peremptorily put her in her place. Alisa realized this too. He is daring me, she thought, to contradict the implication, and what's more, he's quite prepared to be even more explicit if I dare. Her courage melted away at such public disgrace.

Madame Vevay was delighted at the prospect of dressing such a vivid beauty, a beauty enhanced by the fresh innocence Alisa wore without pretense. Maybe it was her tender youthfulness that appealed to Prince Kuzan's jaded palate. This mistress was scarcely more than a child herself. Her slender voluptuousness would set off Madame Vevay's most recherché creations, and this "cousin's" status didn't confine her to prim, demure fashions. Madame Vevay could already envision a use for that Byzantine tussah in her warehouse.

"I have a magnificent fabric that requires just such a striking beauty to do it justice," she cooed, and just such a munificent benefactor to absorb the staggering cost of the rare fabric she reflected silently. What a delightful combination in these two splendid young creatures.

Katelina was tugging insistently at Nikki's hand, totally unconcerned with matters of fashion.

"Nikki, Nikki, *when* can I get my train? You promised!" she wailed, jumping up and down. Prince Kuzan, in a totally uncharacteristic move calculated to raise eyebrows and drop open the mouth of anyone privy to the scene, bent over kindly to the tugging and pleading little girl and in a soothing Finnish dialect quieted her tantrum.

Searching in his pocket, Nikki handed Katelina several silver roubles, stood upright, and deposited a packet of roubles in Rakeli's hand.

"Now are you happy?" he asked the beaming young child. Then he gave instructions to Rakeli and explained. "If you're finished at the toy store early, just have Feodor wait outside until we complete our purchases. Now have a good time. Feodor knows exactly where to go. Give your mother a kiss good-bye, little brown eyes," he ordered softly.

The bouncing child threw her arms around her mother's waist and lifted her face for a kiss. Alisa smiled at her happy young daughter and bent to kiss her.

"Say thank you to Prince Kuzan," she admonished gently.

"*Thank you*, Uncle Nikki!" Katelina cried as she dashed toward the door, Rakeli in hot pursuit.

Uncle Nikki? That designation raised even Madame Vevay's unflappable eyebrows. Prince Kuzan had never publicly recognized any of his natural children. He was generous and thoughtful concerning their support, but didn't acknowledge them, except monetarily, in any fashion whatsoever. His life-style, to this point, hadn't embraced the world of children. He simply moved in circles in which children were never seen or discussed.

His wasn't a malicious disregard but rather a selfish indifference. Everyone in town was aware of the trust he had funded for Countess Souvanieff's last child. Bank clerks and servants were notorious gossips, and no bit of scandal passed unnoticed below stairs.

So, to see the cold reserve, the unrufflable hauteur of Prince Kuzan yielding to a dynamo of enthusiasm was unprecedented. And he spoke Finnish to the little tyke in public; he had never even deigned to speak Russian outside the barracks before, French being the exclusive language of society. Surely this fresh, young, dazzling matron at his side must have some powerful attraction. Madame Vevay was consumed with curiosity.

"If Madame will follow me, please," Madame Vevay said graciously to Alisa, this obviously clever woman who had managed to induce Nikolai Kuzan to abandon the habits of a lifetime and actually appear solicitous in public to nothing less than a pert child. Madame Vevay gestured toward an open doorway into a private fitting salon.

But the imperturbable Prince showed no indication of politely accepting a dismissal from anyone. Instead, he followed the two women at a leisurely pace into the salon, seated himself comfortably in a gilded brocade fauteuil which creaked indignantly under the impact of his weight, stretched his long legs out before him, impeccably clad in the biscuit-colored trousers, and leaned back at ease. He looked thoroughly at home in this elegant green and gold showroom, as if he were frequently a visitor to the inner sanctums of fashionable modistes, when, in fact, Nikki normally waited with impatient indifference outside in the anteroom while his mistresses selected their dresses, showing not the slightest inclination to concern himself with their purchases.

Madame Vevay, disconcerted at Prince Kuzan's presence in the room, stammered in confusion, but quickly recovered and inquired inquisitively, "Monsieur is interested in selecting the fabric and designs?"

"But of course," Nikki replied blandly, as though this, too, were a perfectly normal practice of his. In a pleasant tone he explained, "My cousin and I don't believe unduly in the old-fashioned tradition of mourning, so I don't want any somber black or gray crepes. Some vivid, bright colors, I think," he said consideringly, flicking a leisurely glance up and down Alisa's body as she stood flushing angrily before him. With a bold crudeness he added quietly, "While the thought occurs to me, we'll order two dozen silk negligees, an assortment of colors, and the usual lace and ribbon froufrous."

"Very good, Monsieur, two dozen it will be. If you will excuse me one moment, I'll gather my designs and perhaps one or two dresses for Madame to try on for size."

Alisa, furiously embarrassed at Nikki's presence, after Madame Vevay left the room, snarled, "I hope this charade is amusing you, Prince Kuzan!"

"You always amuse me, darling, in countless and delightful ways," he replied, looking at her insolently from under half-lowered lids, his superb self-confidence evident in every word.

Madame Vevay bustled back into the room, her arms full of sketches, fabrics, and dresses, and set about her business.

Nikki watched appreciatively as Alisa's blouse and skirt were removed; soon she stood blushing in corset, chemise, and petticoats, the delectably lovely swell of her breasts rising above the tightly laced stays.

Madame Vevay was astonished to see multiple bruises

lightly visible on the ivory purity of Alisa's flesh, and considered silently. Does Prince Kuzan beat her? He had a reputation for profligacies as well as a taste for the bizarre, but she'd never heard rumors of perversions. Nevertheless, this woman had been badly beaten and not too long ago. A new quirk of his? she pondered, her curiosity about this relationship further roused.

Slipping a white beaded silk creation over Alisa's head, Madame Vevay made a few tucks and adjustments after buttoning up the back securely. The gown was of white silk, the skirt entirely covered with white bugles. The tunic was, like the skirt, of white silk and was edged with a rich trimming of colored silk embroidery worked by hand on the fabric itself. The sash at the back was embroidered to match, and the whole length of sash was surrounded by a deep white fringe of bugles. Vivid violet velvet ribbon outlined the flounces and ruffles terminating in bouffant bows at shoulders, décolletage, and hip.

"Come closer, dear," Nikki demanded. "You look very lovely in white."

Alisa reluctantly drew closer but remained outside his reach.

"Come *here*, love," Nikki firmly said, holding his hand out to touch her as she unwillingly stepped a few paces nearer.

Was the young woman that afraid of him? Madame Vevay conjectured, although she realized it was safer to stop speculating about the private lives of reckless patricians like Nikolai Kuzan. He was much too rich and well connected to antagonize.

Nikki clasped Alisa's hand, straightened his posture somewhat, and pulled her between his legs.

"Turn around now so I can see the dress from all sides," he murmured softly, and twirled her slowly. The silken skirts brushed against his legs. Under his careful scrutiny

Alisa turned, her slender form exquisitely shown off in the revealing gown, cut daringly low in the bodice.

"I like it," the Prince declared emphatically. "We'll take this one, Madame Vevay."

"It's much too extravagant!" Alisa whispered, Nikki's presence unnerving her. "Where can I possibly ever wear something like this?"

"Why not at dinner tonight with me?" he softly said. "You'll quite improve my appreciation of dining en famille and I might decide to stay home this evening. Even the entertainment of the Yacht Club's gambling rooms can't hope to match your allure."

Shame overcame her at his unequivocal description of her role. And then anger at his casual appropriation as though she existed only for his amusement.

"You can't force me to dine with you and serve as your 'entertainment!'" Alisa retorted, looking mutinous. "I'm not going to!"

"Aren't you, by God?" Nikki responded, and, to Alisa's distinct chagrin, a smile of the most unalloyed amusement appeared on his face. "We shall no doubt see. Now, try on that other dress," he said authoritatively, and pushed Alisa gently out into the center of the salon. In a louder voice, intended for the modiste's ears, he said, "The second dress, Madame Vevay."

Nikki's eager gaze surveyed the slender body slipping into a dark green silk-twill morning dress trimmed in green velvet, and he smiled lazily at her as she bent to straighten the skirt and spilled provocatively out of her corset. It was one of his favorite aesthetic diversions, watching women dress. With a succulent, luxurious beauty like that she should wear sables, the natural ones with the golden vaguely foxy tint to complement her hair, he mused. He would wrap her in sables this winter.

Madame Vevay was clucking and fussing, keeping up a steady inane chatter.

Meeting Nikki's gaze, Alisa quickly dropped her seductively lashed violet eyes before that unmistakable long, burning glance.

Damn her, the lure was overpowering, he thought as he shifted uncomfortably in his chair. He could just *look* at her and forget everything else.

Nikki had a disturbing impulse that perhaps this *amour* was not going to be like all the rest, an uneasy sensation of being drawn in beyond the usual barriers he studiously maintained against emotional involvement. But he'd never turned aside because of a premonition before. Temperamentally he denied withdrawal, or retreat, or too much introspection; he lived life rashly, like a bold and bruising hell-for-leather rider, and if that was the quickest way to a broken neck—the consequences be damned!

As a connoisseur of fine female flesh and style, Nikki was aware that Alisa was more beautiful than most, while instinctively, and temperamentally, one of the best women to give pleasure in bed. His feelings weren't necessarily any more involved; he thought she was just a rarer jewel, a more precious bauble, and he'd be a fool not to react to these unique and delightful attributes. He began to understand Forseus's reluctance to let Alisa out in the world.

Raising a languid hand, he beckoned Alisa toward him. She approached slowly, wearing her most *jeunesse dorée* look, young, petulant, sullenly beautiful.

"Smile, love," Nikki drawled. "You're supposed to bring me pleasure."

A fixed tight smile appeared.

"Now," he said equably, unperturbed by the grimace, "if you could contrive to behave as charmingly as you look, one could hardly ask for more."

"That's impossible, under the circumstances!" whispered

Alisa, casting a glance of contempt upon Nikki's smiling face.

"One can but hope," Nikki murmured as he pulled her down on his lap. He liked to touch her, as if it gave him some kind of ownership.

"Madame Vevay, bring your sketches. My cousin and I will select some of your designs to have made up, hopefully, very quickly."

"Oh, *certainement*, Prince. There will be *no* delay, I assure you."

"Please, Monsieur," Alisa whispered faintly, giving Nikki a sidelong pleading glance, her position as his mistress so flagrantly exposed when he held her on his lap—for all the world to see.

"No," he said simply, in command of his world and hers, no explanation beyond that required for a man of his unconditional power. And he held her tightly while he peremptorily ordered a wardrobe that brought the light of avarice to Madame Vevay's greedy eyes. Nikki noted Alisa's distress as the procedure went on for a protracted time and he almost felt sorry for her. But not quite.

He would have to buy her an extravagant *bijou*, he thought. She gave him so much pleasure, he must try to erase the distress. Perhaps he could assuage the bitterness she felt at being a kept woman. That emerald necklace he had seen last month at Fabergé's. Such lavish gifts had always been highly successful in the past. All women were irresistibly warmed by the brilliant sparkle of emeralds and rubies.

"That will be all, Madame Vevay. My cousin will wear this becoming morning dress and we can expect a minimum number of dresses to be delivered within two days, the rest to follow?"

"Yes, most assuredly!" the modiste promised him. She

would bring in extra seamstresses to fill this order immediately, she thought.

"Thank you, then, Madame, we'll see ourselves out."

She accepted her dismissal graciously and amid effusive thanks left the green and gold salon.

"I have no doubt overwhelmed you," Nikki said teasingly, "by my generosity and superb expertise in female fashion. I trust you approve my taste and"—he paused briefly—"please accept my apologies." He grinned suddenly. "This shameful conduct is quite common to me."

"Why, Nikki?" she asked quietly. "Why all this? Why me?" Alisa questioned, looking at him with resentful liquid eyes, perhaps questioning herself as well for not hating him more. For not hating the man at all—but only his careless authority over her life.

Because I have need for your body that drugs my mind, he thought. Because you and your charming daughter warm my spirits, he thought. "Because," he said instead.

Alisa, still seated on Nikki's lap, attempted to coldly stare him entirely out of countenance, but his amiable smile continued to play on his handsome face. "I should hate you," she softly said.

"But you don't," he said as softly.

"Still, for all that," she quietly declared, "I won't be your mistress." Her statement stopped him for a moment, so opposite were their opinions—but he wished her to be happy, so he perjured himself without a qualm. "Can we be friends, then?"

With the unpredictability of her sex, she did a complete volte-face and suddenly she smiled. "I'd very much like to be friends."

"And Nikki, you're much too generous both to me and Katelina."

Tears abruptly welled into her beautiful large eyes. "How

can I ever repay you?" A poignant smile of gratitude flickered across her mouth.

"Nonsense. It gives me pleasure. Now, don't cry, darling," Nikki said in an oddly constrained voice. "You and Katelina both bring me enormous joy." He kissed Alisa tenderly. "Come, now, no more tears, let's go and see the child's new train."

The next week flew by. Nikki did contrive to stay home every evening, and Alisa tried not to think at all; she only felt. Nikki was sorely missed at the Yacht and Nobles' Clubs gaming tables, but when his name came up, the raised eyebrows and leering glances explained his sudden propensity for the comforts of home.

"If I had that beauty warming my bed, no one should see me about town until I was too old to care or dead from trying," one coarse but expressive young officer remarked.

"Nikki deigns to show up for morning reviews," another man noted, "and immediately leaves at noon when they're over, and rumor has it he's cast off Sophie."

Alisa and Katelina in Nikki's morning absences had been squired around by Aleksei, who felt honored to be seen in the company of such an intriguing beauty. Alisa, on her part, enjoyed the pleasant companionship of Nikki's youthful cousin, who generously gave up his time to escort them sight-seeing. Nikki found that sort of thing a bore, and Alisa would never see the beauties of Petersburg if she waited for him to accompany her. In the course of the next few days she and Katelina saw everything of interest. They saw the Winter Palace just down the street from Prince Kuzan's pink marble palace. The Winter Palace, not yet completely restored since the fire in 1863, was now colored brickred by Stussov and Brullov instead of its original pale green. Aleksei conducted them not only through the Hermitage galleries with its magnificent École Russe, but through suites of rooms not accessible to the ordinary visitor. They strolled through the Summer Garden with its shady walks and innumerable marble statues which Peter the Great had collected from Italy, visited the very first palace occupied by Peter the Great, the Summer Palace, built on a modest and intimate scale by Trezzini in a section of the Summer Garden. They viewed the forbidding Fortress of Peter and Paul, magnificent rather than beautiful, built across the Neva. They whiled away one whole morning at the Kunstkamera, the first library and museum in Russia with its collection of curiosities ranging from Chinese manuscripts to stuffed birds but particularly noted for its stupendous collection of Scythian jewelry.

Another morning of sight-seeing disclosed the wonders of Tsarskoe Selo with its dazzling interiors, the Amber Room,[5] its walls completely paneled in amber, pale as honey, the glass-beaded room, the Malachite Room, Cameron's Lyons Room, the walls and furniture covered in pale yellow Lyons silk woven with a pattern of branches and little birds, Catherine's own "snuffbox," which is what she called her private boudoir, paneled with opaline white glass and gilt appliqué ornament. The doors were framed in columns of ultramarine-colored glass.

Another morning took them by steamer down the tideless, saltless Gulf of Finland to view Peterhof, Rastrelli's fabulous yellow and white country residence built originally by Peter the Great to rival Versailles. On the grounds were two Imperial palaces and many little summerhouses adorned and fitted with every beauty that wealth and taste could achieve. The gardens eclipsed the finest in Europe, crowned by the magnificent cascade and gilded fountains shooting glittering spray that flowed into the sea.

Color abounded in the city architecture and pale, delicate hues delighted the eye at every turn: The lemon-yellow and white of the Admiralty and Pushkin Theatre, the rich blue of the Smol'nyi Cathedral, the coral of Menshikov's Palace. All the rococo façades stuccoed in beautiful pastels, lilac, salmon, pistachio-green served as a foil for the starkly Neo-Classic Russian Empire architecture of Alexander I and Nicholas I. Beautiful sparkling canals intersected the three main arteries that spread from Admiralty Square. Alisa was truly affected by the beauty of this Venice of the North.

Unknown to the small party of sight-seers, each day two other attendants accompanied the group. Scrupulously remaining in the background, not a difficult task in the polyglot babble of the diverse nationalities and costumes jostling each other in the capital of the Empire. The streets contained quantities of barbaric costumes. There were Cossacks from the Don, Georgians from the Caucasus, Tatars, Persians, natives from Central Asia, Chinese, Laplanders, as well as the motley crew of Russian peasants, priests, monks, nuns.

In this floating stream of humanity Forseus's trackers silently stalked their quarry, persistent as a conscience. Alisa had not once ventured alone outside the marble palace, but they patiently waited, the six men changing shifts every eight hours, so one pair of men, four earnest eyes, knew Alisa's whereabouts twenty-four hours a day, and only waited for an opportunity in which she was alone to carry her back to her husband. Forseus wasn't so foolhardy as to come to grips publicly with such an illustrious, powerful figure as Prince Kuzan. Those persons privileged to have the Emperor recognize their family in friendship were above the law, and Forseus knew it.

The days of sight-seeing occasionally concluded with a drive out to the Point, where the fashionable world went to see the sun set across the Gulf of Finland. It was a beautiful sight, the sky glowing crimson and gold, the bay as smooth as glass, reflecting the beds of rushes that rose here and there, one or two boats serenely gliding over the glistening water. Alisa would sometimes stay until the crimson faded into evening's twilight. These beauties of nature, however, were wasted on the unseen eyes, steadfastly fixed on their prey.

One morning several days later, Nikki was in his dressing room, struggling into his uniform; he was already a half hour late for formation and becoming frustrated. Finally, fully attired in white tunic with red facings and dark trousers with red stripes, he sat on a low chair, thrusting his foot into an immaculately polished riding boot, cursing softly.

"Where the hell is that damn valet when I need him," he muttered distractedly. Alisa, garbed in a pale aquamarine flower-embroidered silk wrapper, had been watching him from the doorway.

"If you recall," Alisa chided him gently, "you distinctly warned your poor valet more than ten days ago that you didn't want to be disturbed by him in the morning until further notice."

"I did?" Nikki asked, raising his head and lifting one eyebrow quizzically at Alisa. Breaking into a broad grin as she flushed under his gaze, he said, "So I did, didn't I?" He chuckled. "And now I pay for my pleasures by having to contend with dressing myself," he teased.

"Could I help?" Alisa offered as she moved toward his seated figure.

"No, dear, don't bother," he amiably replied, sliding on his second boot. "I'm fussing for no good reason. I'm quite able to dress myself. I'm just in a damnable hurry. My late arrivals are beginning to raise comment."

"Nikki?" Alisa began hesitantly. "Do you have one minute to spare?"

"Of course, love," Nikki remarked placidly as he stood before a large cheval glass and began adjusting the silver epaulets on the tunic of his undress uniform. He was buckling on his belt, and when Alisa didn't continue, he prompted her quietly, "What is it, my dove?"

"Well—" she faltered, unable to find suitable words to continue.

"Well?" Nikki rejoined, looking at Alisa intently as he noted the obvious timidity in her demeanor.

"I'm . . . that is . . . I'm quite sure I'm pregnant," Alisa blurted out, and nervously dropped her eyes from the piercing glance that quickly ranged the length of her body.

"How sure?" Nikki asked conversationally, his composure unruffled by the disclosure.

"About three weeks sure," she answered, astonished at Nikki's calm reaction. Alisa hadn't known what to expect, and her nerves had been on edge the last few days, trying to bring herself to break the news. It wasn't unheard of to be promptly sent packing upon presenting tidings like that. And she had nowhere to go.

"Please, sweetheart, relax, you look quite anxious. I flatter myself I am as hardened a reprobate as most men, and I indulge in numerous vices," Nikki stated with a faint smile, "but rest assured, casting pregnant females into the streets is not one of them." He looked at Alisa closely. "One must expect such things, after all," he continued tranquilly. "Surely you didn't hope to escape that condition for long when one considers the diligence with which we pursue our —ah—friendship," he drawled.

"You're not angry?" Alisa asked, incredulous.

"Angry? Whatever for? Come now, dear, give me a kiss good-bye. I really must be off, for Cernov's jests are becoming cruder every day, and I'm damned late."

Since she'd realized she was pregnant, Alisa had been uneasy. Anxiety was uppermost in her mind. She hadn't hoped for another child from her marriage with Forseus and had given up such thoughts. But she also hadn't wished to become pregnant by Prince Kuzan, especially since their relationship was so undefined. This child nurtured within her body, a living, breathing extension of herself, couldn't be forgotten, set aside, or rejected. It had overwhelmed her thoughts the past few days, and now she was relieved to have shared her secret.

Nikki, for his part, accepted the fact calmly as part of the order of things, a circumstance bound to happen. For Nikki, a pregnant mistress was a reasonable consequence of their irresponsible self-indulgence. He really must buy her some extravagant toy, some bauble to cheer her up, was his immediate reaction. He perceived his obligation in this as in all other responsibilities of his rank. He had affectionate feelings for Alisa, the habits of a lifetime refusing to acknowledge any more powerful emotions.

Alisa in the time-honored tradition of keeper of the womb was compelled to accept what goodwill Nikki offered; she had no money, no home, no relatives to turn to. But she had other reasons, less prosaic reasons; she passionately loved this quixotic, reckless, enigmatic, oddly gentle man.

"When I return this afternoon, we must keep your appointment at Madame Vevay's," Nikki casually said, picking up his gloves. "She sent me a note yesterday, informing me that several more of your dresses are ready for the final fitting." Walking over, he clasped Alisa gently in his arms and kissed her a tender au revoir. "Until this afternoon," he murmured.

He blew her another kiss as he stood in the doorway. "Oh, one request, my sweet." Apprehension gripped her. Vulnerable in her current position, she waited for that first

move of detachment. "Please, for the sake of the child,"
Nikki said, "would you mind not smoking cigarettes? I
know it's terribly fashionable, but I have vague apprehensions of our child being born with soot on his face. Do you
mind?"

"That's all?" Artless, her astonishment showed.

A brief puzzlement passed over his face. "That's all I can
think of," he replied. "Would you, then?"

"Of course," she murmured, still slightly stunned by his
unruffled response to her disclosure.

"Thank you, my dear. I stand relieved. Why don't you go
back to bed and rest until I return. Aren't *enceinte* women
supposed to be constantly fatigued?" He grinned.

And that was the end of that.

Fortunately the sight-seeing trips had been curtailed,
since Aleksei's presence was now also required at his regiment, for of late, Alisa's mornings were punctuated with
spells of nausea. Perhaps she *would* climb back into bed;
Katelina could have her lessons in the bedroom this morning.

After a light luncheon, Nikki and Alisa arrived at
Madame Vevay's. Nikki seated himself in his usual comfortable sprawl, blue frock coat open, hands clasped across
the middle of his embroidered linen waistcoat, legs clad in
light gray trousers outstretched before him. He watched
Madame Vevay slip dress after dress over Alisa's head,
make a variety of adjustments with pins and basting, clucking and chattering all the while.

"Madame Forseus!" she wailed after ripping out the bast-
ings on the sixth dress in a row. "I will never be able to
finish these gowns. Every fitting requires further adjustments. Madame is putting on weight!" she chided.

"Perhaps it's my chef's incomparable menus, Madame

Vevay," Nikki softly said. "I fear he's been outdoing himself since my cousin has been in residence."

Madame Vevay stood back, arms akimbo, and closely surveyed the blushing Alisa. With eyes narrowed, she replied coyly, "Monsieur and Madame, if the chef *continues* to outdo himself, perhaps I should put additional darts in the waistline which could be taken out as needed."

"Excellent idea, Madame Vevay," Nikki heartily responded. "Please do that on all the remaining gowns and we'll cause no further delay in their construction. Is that all right with you, my dear?" he asked Alisa politely.

"Yes, that will be fine," Alisa answered faintly, wishing she could disappear into the floor rather than continue being the object of Madame Vevay's comprehending speculative gaze.

As they were driving back home in the carriage, Alisa fretted over the humiliation of Madame Vevay's shrewd scrutiny. "She knows. Did you see how she looked at me?"

Nikki took her hand in his. "How can it matter if she knows or not?" he said with a negligent shrug, squeezing her fingers lightly, soothing her dismay. "Don't give her a second thought, love. I'll protect you from any more knowing looks if they bother you. Motherhood is eminently natural, and one should never be ashamed of such a state. However, if you're disturbed, I shall determinedly stare down or set to anyone in the future who attempts to disconcert you. I confess"—his eyes gleamed wickedly—"I've quite a notorious reputation in that regard. Should we advance dinner by two hours today and allow Katelina to join us? Would you like that?" he asked with unwonted cajolery, hoping to distract Alisa from her wounded pride and rueful musings.

"Am I being foolish?" she said with a small sigh.

He exhaled a sigh too, wondering how much or how little to say. "Honestly?" he inquired.

"Of course, honestly," she replied.

He was struck afresh by her naïveté; the world he knew was so different.

"Well, honestly, then, darling, you can't give a damn what people say."

"I must learn that, then."

"If you live with me," he said with a grin, "it would be wise."

She took a moment to consider, and then her smile appeared. "You must remind me at times."

"Good. Now, do we eat early or not?" Uncomfortable with emotional issues, he preferred activity. "And can we bring Katelina down from the nursery?"

"Oh, Nikki, that would be lovely!" Alisa beamed.

"Let's talk to Pierre when we return. He could concoct some suitable dish with which to surprise Katelina."

"That's a marvelous idea. She is inordinately fond of rice pudding and—"

"Strawberries and cake," Nikki interposed obligingly.

"And also petits fours . . ."

The rest of the journey passed with the lovers holding hands and comparing notes on the dishes most enjoyed by themselves as children.

It pleased him to please her.

The following morning Alisa and Katelina were in the study, working on Katelina's lessons, which had been neglected during their round of sight-seeing, when a tall, erect, gray-haired man abruptly walked into the sunlit room and treated them to a lowering scowl.

His glance altered approvingly upon noting the fashionable elegance of Alisa's jonquil-yellow morning dress which set off her trim form and red coiffure to perfection, and determined with a practiced eye that it was not surprising that Nikki was behaving so uncharacteristically. After seeing the dazzlingly lovely, well-bred young woman, Prince Mikhail understood why Nikki had committed the indiscretion of ensconcing his mistress in his own palace. Thank God she's a lady, he observed, and quickly took in the young child at the woman's side.

"You must be Alisa," the old Prince said bluntly.

Alisa rose in confusion, immediately recognizing the unmistakable resemblance to Nikki, the same imperious air of one born to command. She colored becomingly and bowed deeply, her eyes demurely downcast. Katelina, with a glance from her mother, quickly rose and bobbed a curtsey.

"Yes, Monsieur, I am, and this is my daughter, Katelina."

"Nikki's newest paramour, eh? Quite unlike him, you know, to settle for one woman. Had to come myself and see what she was like," Nikki's father uttered with perfect equanimity.

Alisa's emotions were thrown into complete confusion, tumultuously rushing and tumbling one over the other. Her first panic-stricken thought was to send Katelina from the room.

In great agitation she whispered to her daughter, "Run along, dear, and find Rakeli. She'll take you out in the garden."

As Katelina skipped out of the room after a curious look at the formidable old man, Alisa drew herself as erect as her slight frame would allow and, looking the old Prince directly in the eye, said with asperity, "Have you had an edifying look, sir, for if you have, perhaps you'll excuse me."

"Now, now, my child, don't take issue at my bluntness. I'm just not one to stand on ceremony," Prince Mikhail said kindly, the heavy brows relaxing somewhat from their normal severe expression. "Undeniably exquisite, Nikki's choice, if I do say so myself," he continued with a faint smile. "Come now, I shan't eat you. Do sit down. I'll ring for tea and sherry and we can become acquainted."

Within minutes a flustered servant brought in tea and sherry and set them on a low malachite table between the two settees where Alisa and Prince Mikhail faced each other. The Prince chatted with Alisa in his wonderfully open, relaxed way and entranced her quite as easily as his son had. Nikki's unfailing charm was most decidedly inherited, Alisa observed.

The prince, in turn, studied Alisa, which was his reason for visiting the palace. After hearing the first smatterings of rumor concerning Nikki's newest paramour, the old Prince had immediately sent his barristers a message requesting a thorough investigation of this new "cousin."

The malicious letter sent by Countess Amalienborg had been unnecessary, as Prince Mikhail was never far removed from the pulse of gossip, but appreciated by its recipient for reasons not intended by its sender. Nikki had obviously renounced that slut after all these years. This fact was a great relief to Mikhail Kuzan, who had been fearful that perhaps in a rash moment some drunken night, Nikki might offer her more than an affair, and while the old Prince would indulgently allow his only child to commit almost every indiscretion, that one he would not have allowed. Prince Mikhail had never intended to have Sophie Amalienborg for a daughter-in-law.

Then the startling news that Alisa was Valdemar Forseus's wife had required further inquiries in the Viipuri area. After three weeks the old Prince was fully informed and in control of an entire dossier on Alisa, her parents, the marriage to Forseus (which in itself raised a few questions), and her new "friendship" with his son, Nikki. He kept this information to himself as he drew the young lady gently into conversation, wanting to discover for himself just what sort of woman his son was enamored of. And enamored Nikki certainly was, to have her openly living in his palace, plus, the old Prince understood with astonishment, deserting the gaming tables and keeping himself home every night.

"Tell me about your daughter," he said pleasantly when they'd explored the subject of Petersburg's museums and architecture. And Alisa went on in the doting way of mothers, describing her precocious daughter with obvious pleasure.

After beholding this striking beauty before him, in the course of their conversation, Nikki's extremely curious behavior was no longer baffling, Mikhail Kuzan reflected wryly. You had to give the boy credit for good sense. If Nikki was becoming serious about a woman after all these years of casual *amours*, he couldn't have selected a more delightful creature. Alisa's marital state was of little importance to Mikhail Kuzan. His thorough investigation had revealed the magnitude and frequency of Forseus's debauchery and his abuse of his young wife. Although Prince Mikhail was not unfamiliar with brutality in human behavior, Forseus had turned out to be a master of the craft and he felt no compunction to restore this young girl to that beast. A discreet word from the Emperor and the problem of divorce would be resolved.

The Prince sipped steadily on the sherry, emptying half the bottle in the course of their conversation. Soon they were getting along famously and Alisa had lost some of her awe and shyness. Alisa drank her sherry slowly, and after having her glass filled the second time began feeling nauseated. Her color waned and a thin film of perspiration broke out on her forehead and upper lip. After gallantly attempting to control the waves of sickness for several minutes, Alisa, desperate that she would embarrass herself in front of

Nikki's father, asked in a faint voice if she could be excused and rose carefully from her seat opposite the Prince.

After observing his wife through five pregnancies, the prince was well aware of the obvious symptoms of an unsettled stomach in the morning.

"Of course, my dear, you're excused. By the bye, when are you in the way of making my son a father?" he calmly inquired.

The shock of his knowledge eclipsed the nausea by sheer horror, and Alisa sat down heavily.

"How did you know, sir?" she whispered, fearful Madame Vevay's tongue had run wild so rapidly.

"I've held my wife's hand through five pregnancies, my dear, so I am well acquainted with that greenish look around the gills. The marked pallor of your complexion so early in the morning, coupled with your proximity to my son these few weeks past, prompted me to make a calculated guess as to the inevitable consequences," he said dryly. "Prince Nikolai's amatory exploits are rarely attended by any prudence. It was to be expected," he said gently.

"Now, my dear, do you want him?" the old Prince asked flatly in his oddly abrupt conversational manner.

She seemed to ponder her reply. "It's very complicated, sir. There are several reasons—"

"You want him," he broke in quietly.

"You are very astute, Monsieur."

"I have that reputation," he concurred.

"Yes, I'm afraid I do," Alisa sighed softly, then quickly rushing on in explanation. "But never, sir, if he does not want me." She continued in a subdued voice. "Having lived through one disastrous marriage, I would never wish that on anyone. It's much too terrible."

"Spoken very forthrightly. I like that. Very well, my young lady, you shall have him," Mikhail Kuzan declared with decisive, unruffled composure, with the usual Kuzan insensitivity to the delicate shades of human relationships. If Nikki couldn't find this charming, delightful, unutterably beautiful young woman compatible, he obviously had no sense, and it was up to his father to mend his stupidity. The old gentleman surveyed her with distinct admiration.

"Please put your feet up on the settee and I'll ring for a cool compress. My wife will be delighted to hear the news. She had quite despaired of Nikki ever finding anyone suitable. You'll meet her later. She's traveling more slowly, having insisted on bringing several servants and eighty pieces of luggage. Perhaps you would be more comfortable in bed?" he soothingly suggested as he noticed the unnerved appearance of the young woman.

"Yes, I should, I'm sure."

"Allow me, my dear." Prince Mikhail gallantly offered his arm and escorted Alisa up the stairway to her bedchamber.

Returning down the marble staircase, the Prince crisply informed the butler that he wished to see his son *immediately* when he set foot in the palace.

"I'll be in the library. Bring me a light lunch and a bottle of brandy."

"Very good, my Prince. May I say in behalf of myself and the staff, it's a pleasure to see you once again in residence." The old butler beamed happily, having served the old Prince since before his marriage.

"You'll be seeing a great deal of us in the near future. It seems I must take a hand in my son's affairs." Prince Mikhail grinned familiarly at Sergei.

"We do what we can—eh, Monsieur?" Sergei responded, and winked.

·   ·   ·

Upon arriving home at his usual hour, Nikki was astonished to receive the sharp message from his father. Questioning Sergei accomplished little except to warn Nikki that his father had met Alisa. Nikki entered the library slightly annoyed at the peremptory order.

His father was seated behind the polished expanse of an André-Charles Boulle desk veneered in marquetry of tortoiseshell, natural colored woods, engraved pewter, brass, and ivory.

Father's eyes met son's. Both were cool and aloof, except the father's held a touch of disdain as well.

With a resigned sigh and a casual gesture of his hand, Prince Mikhail offered a chair to Nikki.

Nikki ignored the courtesy and obstinately remained standing, leaning negligently against the Palladian window jamb, looking rebellious, angered at the curt summons from his father, resentful at being made to feel like a young cub about to be upbraided for some defiance of parental authority. However, because of the deep respect in which he held his father, Nikki was attempting to suppress his normally ungovernable temper. He set his teeth.

Silently, with maddening deliberation, Prince Mikhail regarded the tall, broad-shouldered, impeccably dressed figure of his only child. Under this scrutiny Nikki's eyes lifted, met his father's, and held for an instant before a lazy flicker turned his expression suddenly remote, but not before his father noted the sullen stubbornness and the barely concealed anger.

"To what do I owe this unexpected visit? It's been three years since you were last in the city."

Nikki didn't really expect an answer to this flippancy, and he wasn't disappointed. With the exception of one ironically raised eyebrow, Prince Mikhail ignored the remark, his attention more significantly engaged in adjusting the ruffle on his shirt cuff. The ruffle suitably disposed, he once more lifted his eyes.

Prince Mikhail Kuzan enunciated evenly, the words clear and precise in the hushed stillness of the vast library.

"I have indulged you in every way, have I not, Nikki?"

"Yes, Father," Nikki responded shortly, watching his father warily.

"Have I ever said you nay, or gainsaid you in any of your desires?"

"No, Father." The words rapped out, sharp and decisive.

"I have overlooked all your numerous peccadilloes and reckless escapades these many years past, never interfered except to intercede when extenuating circumstances of your—ah—affairs have occasioned the need of a mollifying or palliating presence."

Nikki stiffened at the reproach.

"I believe I have rather adequately conducted my own affairs, if you please," he replied curtly. "I don't recollect having had any need for your assistance."

"You will allow me to point out your error, my boy. An example. Perhaps you recall the dark-haired child born to Countess Souvanieff last fall. Since she and her husband are both exceedingly fair and their other three children towheaded and blue-eyed, the conspicuous coloring of the last boy child did not go unremarked. Furthermore, if you remember, your pursuit of that fair lady was not in any way discreet. With your usual bland blindness to reason and prudence, your coach and lackeys were left waiting outside her door until dawn, time without number. That Adelaide blue brougham ornamented with silver, which you bought from the Duke of Devonshire after his state visit here, is one of a kind and elicits considerable attention, while your red and blue sledge is equally conspicuous with the golden bells and gilded, tasseled harness you affect.

"Even though I'm rarely in town, my sources of gossip

are speedy and reliable. I expected, daily, to hear of yet another duel, and you know how those last few contests of honor (although how the term *honor* comes into a fight over some woman's favors, I fail to discern) terrified your mother. I *do not* like to see your mother disturbed and unhappy," Prince Mikhail intoned ominously.

After a deliberate pause, he continued softly. "Since Count Souvanieff was out of the country so often, it's conceivable that he was ignorant of his wife's affair, or perhaps your notorious reputation as a duelist may have dictated his caution. In any event, Count Souvanieff is not altogether a fool and was outraged at being cuckolded. Since you have a string of women constantly in your wake, he thought it ungenerous of you to turn your eye appreciatively on *his* wife. In this instance you incurred the indignant displeasure of a minister not without influence and power. You were remarkably close to being summarily cashiered out of the Chevaliers Gardes for that unheeding disregard for appearances."

The old Prince heaved a small sigh.

"Fortunately my wealth and position bear some little consequence as well, and even while infrequently in town, my substantial connections prevail undiminished. In deference to our old and close friendship, the Emperor was persuaded there was no conclusive proof the child was yours."

"It appears your—er—connections are to be commended. I owe you my belated thanks," Nikki's equable voice drawled as he gave a stiff bow in his father's direction.

Prince Mikhail met his insolent glance squarely.

"Quite so. Now, enough of this sparring. What do you intend to do with Alisa?"

"Do? What am I expected to do?" Nikki inquired sardonically. "I'm well satisfied with the relationship. I find Alisa delightful and charming in spite of being overeducated for a woman. As you know, I have never been overly fond of clever women."

"*That* fact has always been fairly obvious," his father replied dryly. "I am informed that Alisa is carrying your child."

"My compliments, sir, on the efficacy of your sources. I was informed but yesterday myself of the impending blessed event. May I make so bold as to inquire whether you've discovered if it's to be a boy or a girl?"

"Very amusing, I'm sure," said the old Prince with a slight lift of the brows. Prince Mikhail went on gelidly, his gray eyes snapping with contained fury at Nikki's impudent disrespect. "*Is* the child yours?"

"Apparently."

"How can you be sure?"

"I've no reason to doubt her word. Rest assured, she shall be well taken care of," Nikki continued, icily polite. "I'll buy her a house and set up a suitable establishment in which to rear a child of mine. Alisa and her two children will have every comfort. As her protector, I can offer her a safe, secure, and luxurious refuge."

"Is a protector enough?" his father gently inquired, frustration smoldering beneath the quiet rebuke.

"Surely I'm not to consider a mesalliance?" Nikki protested righteously.

"Remember, my boy, your mother is a Tzigane," the low voice dangerously reminded him.[6]

"Forgive me, sir," Nikki hastily apologized, an embarrassed flush coloring his neck. "Of course, I didn't mean Mother. You know she's very dear to me."

"If you will recall, my pompous young cub, before your haughty airs carry you too far, our princely title is due to our ancestor Platon's prowess in Catherine the Great's bedchamber. When our noble family dispatched their fine young scion, then a mere count, to court in hope of advancing the family interests, don't think for a minute they weren't reasonably certain his strapping good looks would attract the insatiable eye of the Empress. The Kuzan family acquired numerous properties and additional titles thanks to the good offices and vigorous stamina of young Platon. And no doubt, if we were to search far enough back in our 'illustrious' family tree, we would discover the first 'noble' Kuzan was probably nothing more than a highly successful brigand on the caravan route east.

"Scrutinize any old prominent family in Russia and you will find, at base, a mercenary, a powerful warlord, a chieftain more shrewd or ruthless than his fellows. On such a base as that, the rank and fortunes of the first families rest, so do not speak to me of mesalliance.

"The honorable course of action would be to marry Alisa," his father admonished sternly.

"Honorable?" Nikki laughed derisively. "I'm to mend the nonexistent honor of some petty merchant's wife at the altar?" he sneered arrogantly. "Since when have either you or I been unduly concerned with a fine sense of proprieties? I find it ironic in the extreme that you should be trading little homilies with me about propriety and honor. You know yourself, most of our recent, illustrious progenitors were loose-living, self-indulgent wastrels whose chief diversion was irregular relations with a variety of women of every class and nationality. And with the scapegrace way you racketed around society for so many years, as rumor asserts, you'll forgive me if I find your present posture singularly out of character. In any case, it's out of the question, since Alisa is already married," Nikki finished with an easy, smug smile.

"That insignificant detail can be readily remedied," his father said curtly. "Money and influence buy most anything, as you have no doubt noted," he continued with unmistakable cynicism, "since you have had a stable of tarts both highborn and low for your convenience these many years. And damn! I like the chit!"

"Then it's a pity you're already married"—Nikki smiled genially as he once again relaxed comfortably against the window jamb and crossed his arms lazily across his chest—"for *you* could do the honorable thing by Alisa since you seem to revere her so highly. *I* am not the marrying kind, and if and when I do reach the stage when I'm inclined to settle down and set up my nursery, rest assured, I will select some suitably docile young girl just out of the schoolroom who will be biddable and content to spend her time in the country, raising my heirs. I certainly will not choose to ally myself with someone who has shown on more than one occasion a most unsettling stubbornness of character. I would be guilty of the greatest inane rashness, it seems to me, to burden myself with a self-willed woman. Nevertheless, I do feel a certain obligation to Alisa, since I figured rather largely in the loss of her former life."

"This 'obligation' does not extend to marriage, however," his father jibed.

"Hardly. If I were *obliged* to marry every female who bore my children, I would have been married long ago to that lovely moujik girl you so considerately put in my way when I was fourteen," Nikki serenely remarked.

"Enough!" Prince Mikhail rose swiftly, hitting the desk with his fist as he thundered his command. He stood regally upright, his tall, spare frame still vigorous at sixty-eight, the strong aquiline features haughty, his cold gaze piercingly set on his recalcitrant, insolent heir.

"I have reached a decision!" the old Prince stated with a majestic unequivocality, flagrantly disregarding all Nikki's protestations. "You *will* marry Alisa! She's not one of your brazen sluts to be used and cast aside. I've waited long enough for a legitimate grandson to carry on the name. You are thirty-three years old and so far have demonstrated a

marked reluctance to allow yourself to be persuaded to select a wife, although every tabby in town has been on the
scramble for you for her daughter.

"With the spirit of folly in which you conduct your affairs, the odds for you living a long life are exceedingly
slim, and I want a grandson to inherit. You have, by some
fortuitous miracle, finally coupled yourself with a fine,
young, well-bred woman instead of the usual loose women
you are wont to favor, and I have a fancy to have Alisa as
the mother of my grandson. Heaven knows what she sees
in you, but if she wants you, she shall have you!"

"Just like that?" Nikki was no longer casually lazing
against the window but standing rigidly upright, his face
pale with dismay. "You command me to marry Alisa?" he
asked, incredulous. Nikki's eyes narrowed as he tried to
hold his growing anger in check. "What if I refuse?" he
inquired softly through clenched teeth.

"Let us simply say you shall be extremely unhappy in
exile on my estate in Siberia with my Finnish lukashee
guarding you and no women available for your comfort.
You've never felt the full force of my displeasure. Be
warned. I can and will coerce you to see things my way. In
this instance I will not be opposed." Each word of the last
sentence was enunciated precisely, in a carefully modulated
murmur as frigid as the Arctic permafrost.

In his entire life Nikki had never experienced the unconditional fury of his father's temper. For him, the wrath
had always been allayed, repressed, controlled. Fate had
chosen to relentlessly deprive Prince Mikhail and Princess
Kaisa-leena of their other four children, each in the early
stages of infancy. Nikki was, in fact, the only one to reach
the age of twelve months. The small graves neatly lined
one side of the east wall of the mausoleum at Le Repose,
the dates pitiful evidence of the frailty of infants when
pitted against the dread childhood diseases. The firstborn,

robust, sturdy Nikki had then become the sum total of all his parents' love, hopes, and expectations. His utterly devastating charm, even as a child, endeared him to his parents even had he not been the sole survivor and only heir to the immense and centuries-old Kuzan fortune.

"You will escort Alisa to the Golchoffs' birthday dance this evening," his father stated flatly.

"Is that a command?" Nikki asked bitterly, a black scowl darkening his brow.

"Yes, it is. That will be all." Satisfied that he'd settled the matter, Prince Mikhail curtly dismissed his son.

The interview was over.

Nikki left the library dazed by the unfamiliar anger of his father, but equally overwhelmed by a frustration and resentment far more dangerous. To have an indulgent parent manifest a violent volte-face was devastatingly humiliating to a grown man addicted to having things his own way.

It was not to be tolerated! Nikki seethed inwardly. To be ordered about like a minion! And now the two strong, determined temperaments of father and son presaged a clash of indomitable wills. Nikki had the disadvantage of years and a reckless brashness not yet tempered by prudence, but he had an optimistic conceit that a way would be found to circumvent the autocratic dictates of his father.

The far more experienced old Prince had a knowledge culled from an acute and cynical perception of the world and human foibles during sixty-eight years of keenly observing the machinations of society. He knew that he would have his way and *that was that*.

Nikki left the house in a high pitch of anger and spent the rest of the day at the Yacht Club rather moodily gambling.

Earlier that afternoon Prince Mikhail's wife had arrived

and, after seeing to her unpacking, had waited in the east drawing room for Alisa to present herself. Prince Mikhail had alerted his wife that this was not Nikki's usual choice of paramour, and thus she was prepared to like and accept Alisa before even meeting her.

The ladies spent a delightful hour together—talking of their homelands, exclaiming over Alisa's forthcoming child. When Alisa begged to be excused to rest for dinner, Princess Kaisa-leena went in search of her husband to tell him she, too, approved of Nikki's choice.

That evening Prince Mikhail entertained both his wife and Alisa at dinner and explained to them that Nikki would join them for the Golchoffs' party. Prince Mikhail received a note just as they were finishing the meal.

I have been unavoidably detained. Please accept my apologies. I shall join you at the Golchoffs'. N.

The note was a direct challenge. Nikki's father smiled faintly. The boy had spirit—that he had known for years and was not naïve enough to anticipate a compliant, dutiful son. Nevertheless, he could afford to play a waiting game for the moment. One must not press one's authority with foolhardy zeal. No doubt Nikki's regard for his parents, or at least his consideration for Alisa, would overcome this initial resistance. Prince Mikhail felt sure Nikki would appear later in the evening.

"Nikki is detained and will join us later," he noncommittally explained. "Ladies, allow me the pleasure of escorting two such charming beauties. We have time for a hand of cards before we leave."

At ten-thirty the trio walked out of the drawing room into the hall and through the double doors swept instantly open by two footmen in Kuzan liveries. The tall, stately Prince in black evening dress, its severity relieved solely by the prestigious Order of St. Andrew suspended from its pale blue ribbon, was flanked on either side by a slender woman, each beautifully garbed in rustling silk, their dainty stature further enhanced by the majestic size of their escort.

The small "intimate" birthday celebration consisted of a crush of three hundred guests. Alisa, presented as a relative of the Prince, was accepted graciously by their host and hostess, ever ready to accommodate any of the whims of Prince Mikhail.

Gossip had, of course, preceded Alisa's introduction into the restricted exclusivity of the crème of Russian society, and some disapproving glances were cast at the exquisite red-haired beauty, but no one dared cross swords with Prince Kuzan or his equally arrogant son. Their credit guaranteed every door would open to their protégé, and she was now surrounded by a veritable, if spurious, fog of respectability.

"A formidable assemblage of support, I'd say," one guest sniffed. "Prince Mikhail hasn't breathed the city air these three years past."

As Alisa was being introduced to one rather erect, forbidding matron arrayed brilliantly, if not garishly, in purple silk and plumes, she had a taste of the old Prince's commanding power. When the intimidating purple-clad female cast a baleful eye on this "cousin" and offered a frigid greeting, Prince Mikhail said very suavely, "I do not in the least understand, Anna Feodorovna, how you can afford to stand there, risking my displeasure with your censorious expression when you know as well as I do that not so much as one arshin of the seventy-thousand tons of steel rails just ordered from the Creuzot works will be laid in the area of your husband's wheat fields without the approval of the Minister of the Interior, who is a very old and dear friend of mine. Now, curtsey prettily and bid a pleasant evening to our cousin." He smiled thinly.

The grande dame acceded to his wishes. Alisa received a rather strained good evening.

"You are excused, Anna," Prince Mikhail murmured. As the woman's stiff back receded, the old Prince observed. "Damn hen-witted female. She was never a woman of intuition—eh, Kaisa-leena?" He peered down at his petite, dark-haired wife and grinned widely.

"I think you have enlightened her somewhat, Misha." She smiled back at him.

"Come now, Alisa, who else haven't you met?" And then abruptly changing his mind he grumbled, "Bah! I'm not going to introduce you to any more old hags. Let's see who we have here otherwise," he murmured, surveying the room.

Many of the women watched this new beauty with undisguised, malicious envy, noting each detail of Alisa's appearance, but they prudently held their tongues, while the men took full advantage of Alisa's first essay into public free of Nikki's jealous presence. Everyone did agree, though, this newest mistress was in Nikki's usual style: beautiful, provocative, sensual. Alisa was immediately surrounded by a phalanx of charming, solicitous men, each attempting to flatter, praise, and please her. She danced endlessly, thoroughly relishing the party and the attention of admirers, although she quietly and regularly searched the crowd for a sign of Nikki. He'd not given her any explanation of his absence that afternoon.

Alisa was seated facing the door, looking delicately beautiful in a ball gown of two shades of lilac silk, patiently waiting for the six gallants who had rushed off to satisfy her request for a glass of champagne, when she saw the tall, unmistakable figure of Nikki. Unhurriedly he strolled across the vast expanse of the room, quite as if he were not four hours late to act as her escort. Alisa was unable to check a rising resentment at his bold impudence.

He seemed oblivious of the hundreds of eyes swiveling to regard the encounter between Nikolai Kuzan and the new "cousin" with whom he was consorting, who now, with the imperious audacity only old Prince Kuzan was capable of, had been taken under the wing of the family. To have Nikki appear at a ball would have been a rarity enough to occasion their stares, but this gesture for the obvious sake of his newest inamorata was not to be missed, for Nikki Kuzan never did anything to oblige anyone.

No one believed for a minute that Alisa was a cousin, but in society one soon learned the necessity of never "noticing" in public. The Kuzans, as one of the oldest and most powerful families in Russia, predating the Romanovs by several centuries, were above the normal conventions; hadn't the old Prince married a young Gypsy girl eighteen years his junior with total aplomb during the reign of Nicholas I, and forced society to accept her? And even if one would have liked to demur, one did not dare aggravate Prince Mikhail's obstreperous temper which had been famous throughout Russia for fifty years.

Nikki's languid stride slowly brought him face-to-face with Alisa, seated on a brocaded Louis XV settee. The brittle glitter of considerable drink shone from his golden eyes.

"You have deigned to make an appearance," Alisa mockingly stated.

"As you see, Madame"—he bowed elaborately with his usual self-composed air that made her want to strike him— "I have a distinct feeling that not only my father, but these hundreds of curious, gaping people, will be supremely dismayed if I do not take a turn with you, so please," he continued in a lazy drawl, "do me the honor."

He reached out for her hand in a graceful gesture.

Alisa burned with annoyance and declined the obviously acid invitation. "I'm sorry . . . Major Khreptovich and Count Soltikoff and several others have gone off to bring me champagne and . . . will be back directly." To her vexation, she felt herself blushing under the intense scrutiny of his glittering, inebriated eyes.

Nikki in one swift movement grasped her hand in an iron grip and spat through tight lips, "They can wait my convenience."

Pulled unceremoniously to her feet, she felt a muscular arm around her waist and her right hand clasped in a strong hold that offered no opportunity for further resistance. She was swept forcibly off onto the floor and, gliding into a waltz, found herself dancing with quite the most adept partner she had ever had. He danced superbly, as he did all things, but with his usual bored elegance.

After avoiding his eyes with deliberate coolness and concentrating instead on the third button of his collar, her silence was interrupted by Nikki remarking rather grimly, "Well? Mrs. Forseus? What are your plans?"

Alisa's eyes rose in response to the icy tone and met his cool stare. She lifted her chin belligerently as the uncivil inquiry raised her fighting spirit. "What are *my* plans? What a monumentally censorious tone, Monsieur, as if the responsibility is exclusively mine. Without your damnable wager I should never have had the misfortune to make your acquaintance, and had you not so assiduously 'wooed' me once again in Petersburg, I would not now find myself in the unenviable position of carrying your child!"

"As I perceive, Madame, you would hardly be classified as an innocent after having lived with that perverted lecher Forseus, and don't forget, my dear, that my attentions were rarely repulsive to you. Why, as recently as last night, your response was, shall we say—er—selfishly demanding?" he finished with silky malice, one eyebrow raised sardonically while a parody of a smile creased his lean cheek.

Alisa's indignation rose at the ignominious truth of his statement, for she was mortified at the ready response

Nikki's bold and passionate advances invariably drew from her. She always succumbed to his consummate skill and experience, her senses betrayed by the exquisite torture of his touch.

The creamy skin of her cheeks glowed rose at the direct cut, and she endeavored to pull away from his grasp and leave the floor. Dropping her hand from Nikki's shoulder, she twisted her fingers from his grip. Undeterred, Nikki only tightened his hold on her slender waist and quickly regained her right hand, this time in a viselike grip so ruthless that tears of pain sprang into her eyes. He pressed her closely against his tall frame and calmly continued twirling expertly down the long ballroom, scarcely having missed a step in the smoothly flowing rhythm of the waltz.

"That's better," Nikki said approvingly. "Really, my love, aren't we offering enough of a spectacle already without resorting to childish tantrums? For me to be on a ballroom floor should keep the matrons' tongues wagging for quite some time. It must be some four or five years since I have graced a polite social function. Consider yourself quite the belle of the ball to have captured my attention in such an unusual public display of my regard."

By this time the musicians were staring rather fixedly at the combatants with disastrous results to the tempo of the dance; half the waltzers were also quite obviously staring, while the other half were politely pretending they hadn't observed Alisa's flushed face, Nikki's grim expression, and the tempestuous dialogue passing between Prince Kuzan and his newest paramour.

"Rest assured, Prince Kuzan," Alisa said formally, "I do not solicit your public displays, or your private displays either."

If Nikki chose to eschew his responsibility in a typically masculine fashion, she refused to plead or grovel for aid.

"Once it is discovered I have a husband living, my reputation will be ruined, and an illegitimate child can hardly further damage a reputation already sunk below reproach. You can cease directing your tender and public attentions toward me, and I will with great pleasure rudely repulse you, in which case you will be absolved from any further tiresome dangling after me."

"Nothing would suit me better, Madame," he brutally said, "but curiosity impelled me to ascertain if perhaps your intentions were in the opposite direction. After a rather candid conversation with my father this afternoon, I wasn't altogether certain of your earnest desires," he added with suspicious emphasis.

Nikki's irritation was further provoked as he uncomfortably recalled the confrontation with his father and the express command issued him.

Alisa gazed at the Prince, almost speechless with indignation. But she collected herself in a moment more determined to make her position clear.

"Do I understand, Monsieur," she said in glacial tones, "that you envisioned me clinging to you? What monumental arrogance! I fear I must disappoint your expectations. Unfortunately, you see"—her soft whisper held a world of fury—"that is a dramatic tableau I find myself incapable of enacting even to save the child from some unknown fate. Recourse to you as some permanent but unwilling protector I find wholly repulsive!" She fixed her basilisk eyes on his.

Unexpectedly, this snappish diatribe resulted in a bright, boyish grin, a most engaging smile that was immediately followed by a deep, relaxed chuckle. Nikki's formidable, glowering countenance was overcome by a benign amusement.

"What a lovely spitfire you can be, most engaging," he murmured softly as he gazed into the seductive beauty of Alisa's flushed face, her violet eyes glowing with anger, her breathing irregular from the violence of her emotions.

Feeling relieved, he said, "I should have known you weren't behind the damnable fiat delivered by my father."

Alisa's eyes opened wide in astonishment as she stared incredulously into Nikki's now-placid gaze.

"What fiat?" she demanded hastily.

"An unequivocal command to marry you." He smiled lazily at her surprised face, her lips parted in wonder. "Now I can inform Father that his coercion is unnecessary since you're as antagonistic to the union as I am," he explained amiably.

"What an utterly preposterous notion in any event, since I am already married. His idea surely cannot signify." Yet her heart was beating rapidly at the thought.

"On the contrary, my dear, Father is not one to be contradicted or nonplussed in any of his idiosyncrasies, as I discovered for the first time today," he said tranquilly, his self-assurance restored.

"Well, in this instance he must. The idea is absurd."

"Agreed!" Nikki unchivalrously replied.

The music stopped and the dance ended.

Nikki stood looking down at Alisa, lightly holding her voluptuous warmth in his arms.

"Monsieur, you may now be excused from my unwelcome presence. Please feel free to grace the dance floor with some other fortunate object of your attentions," Alisa said sarcastically.

"Very well, dear, as you wish." Nikki released his hold, honored her with a weak inclination of a bow, and, to Alisa's chagrin, very ungraciously accepted her petulant suggestion as he moved away with the easy stride of a cavalry officer and spent the rest of the night dancing with Countess Amalienborg. The Countess preened with unmitigated pleasure at receiving Nikki's attention. Now everyone could surely see that Nikki was still enamored of her and that little bitch she gleefully noted, didn't mean anything to him.

Alisa felt her spirits sinking with a sudden odd pang as she watched them. Only the twin fiends of stubbornness and pride kept her from succumbing to the unhappy feelings generated by the spectacle of Nikki and his old mistress dancing across the room. They were a picture of handsomeness, for the Countess was a tall, dark-haired beauty with a classic profile, a noble body of Venus most admirably displayed in black lace with a daringly cut décolletage, and Nikki's attractive dark looks and magnificent size suited her to perfection.

I hope her dress is ripped to shreds by those spurs, Alisa hatefully thought.

Prince Mikhail was furious with Nikki's behavior, and after seeing Alisa's distress, he insisted they leave. That ungrateful whelp would pay for this discourteous display, he reprovingly vowed. Could he have that slut of a Countess sent to Siberia? It was a thought.

In the early hours of the morning Nikki reluctantly accepted the Countess's invitation to accompany her home and with a perfunctory preoccupation fondled and caressed her in the carriage when she slipped his hand under her skirt.

Now he lay on his back on her bed, the Countess's head resting in his groin. He watched the reflections of her activities in the mirror above his head with a certain detachment—as if he weren't involved in the scene. Her head shifted and her mouth began to move once again with a soft, sucking sound. She had one of the most magnificent bodies, he observed, and one of the most degraded imaginations he had ever known. He rated her on a par with Cora Pearl,[7] an encomium of the first order, but by and large he was a man of normal proclivities, a sensualist fastidiously indifferent to the practices of the deviates. Within seconds these casual musings ceased as his entire nervous system was forced to concentrate on Sophie's delicate manipulations. A little later the flickering mirrored vignettes of Countess Amalienborg's movements had stilled, she had swallowed, and Nikki closed his eyes and breathed deeply. He relaxed in the silence, not wishing to see or talk to her.

The black-haired Venus slowly eased across his body, running her hands up and down his torso, cupping her fingers gently around his testicles. He shook off her hand.

"Not now, Sophie."

"I want you to dominate me, Nikki!" she moaned. Those damnable long fingers of hers were perversely effective. Her skill was remarkable. He was rigid already.

"Hurt me, Nikki!" she pleaded, pulling at him to enter her.

Christ, tonight he didn't like her in this mood, and she was irritating the hell out of him, Damn her! He took her then like a dog and forced her to do his bidding. But Nikki's black mood served only to further excite her. Minutes later he rose from the bed, disgusted.

Why did he always get involved with women like Tanya and Sophie, who wanted tyranny in the bedroom?

"Nikki, where are you going?" she cried, attempting to cling to him. "Stay with me!"

Three times was too much. He was feeling tired and hadn't wished to see Sophie again in the first place. If it weren't for wanting to spite his father and Alisa, he wouldn't have even addressed a civil hello to the Countess at the Golchoffs.

"I'm fatigued and long for my own bed," he replied curtly as he dressed rapidly.

"You just long for that harlot sleeping in your bed!" the Countess screamed in anger. "What about my pleasure?"

Nikki was pulling on his boots and closed his eyes in revulsion and weariness. He eased himself slowly from the chair, turned to the door, and as he walked out of the room, said coldly, "I'll send your wolfhound in for your pleasure. I understand he's one of your special perversions. Adieu, Sophie."

On the ride home he rested his head gratefully against the velvet squabs and attempted to rid himself of the loathing Sophie engendered in him. He reminded himself that Sophie's perversities hadn't always disgusted him—in fact, her extraordinary expertise had been a major element in her attractiveness. What was happening to him? All he could think of was Alisa. Day and night, her beauty, her artlessness, even her stubborn temper. He chuckled. God, he missed her. After tonight Sophie was definitely off his list.

Arriving home, he slowly walked up the stairway and down the long marble hallway into his rooms. Without pausing, he continued through the adjoining doorway into Alisa's bedchamber, wanting to look at her peaceful beauty and rid himself of Sophie's taint. He'd expected Alisa to be sleeping at this late hour, but she lay wide awake, propped up against a bolster of pillows, the faint light of a single lamp dancing her shadow across the wall. Before he had time to speak she acidly remarked, "You positively reek of a woman's perfume!"

"Countess Amalienborg's," he replied candidly, unused to the necessity of explanation. He walked closer to her bed.

"How dare you!" Alisa retorted in affront, drawing away from him.

"How dare I?" Nikki's eyebrows rose in genuine perplexity. The idea of explaining his actions to a mistress was unthinkable.

"It's unspeakable! Coming here warm from another

woman's body! You're despicable, detestable!" she cried, her eyes blazing with indignation.

"Is that a fact, Madame," he responded almost gently, goaded by her challenging posture. His eyes held a distinct menace. "Mistresses should not harangue. It isn't wise," he quietly reminded her.

"I didn't choose to become your mistress, and I don't choose to conduct myself wisely at this late date!" Alisa snapped back, unabashed by those dangerous eyes, for frustration and resentment were making her reckless. It had been a long, sleepless night with images of Nikki and the Countess prevalent in her thoughts.

"It seems, then, that you need some schooling in the duties and behavior of mistresses," Nikki remarked with narrowed eyes glaring.

"I need no instruction from the sordid likes of you, *if* you don't mind!" the haughty, undutiful mistress replied.

"*If* I don't mind? But I *do* mind, Madame," Nikki returned silkily. "You see, I dislike acrimonious contre-dits when I'm in the humor for an amenable mistress to comfort a black mood."

"Get your 'comfort,' you whoremonger, from that whore Sophie! As you may have noticed, I'm not in an amenable mood!" she spat out angrily.

"Please, Mrs. Forseus, don't be vulgar. Vulgar women I can find by the score." Nikki's lips curled into an unfriendly smile while he thought resentfully: Two bitchy women in one night. By God, it's too much! First the lingering bad taste over Sophie's tantrum and now totally unnecessary goading from this indignant woman.

"You just do as you please, don't you?" Alisa continued, angrily clutching the bedclothes to her heaving bosom.

"As I please!" Nikki snarled, the black rage and irritation of the long day, his interview with his father, the long afternoon and evening drinking at the club, his required appearance at the Golchoffs' party, the unwanted ministra- tions of Sophie, and now this screaming, shrewish virago all finally burst into an uncontrollable fury. Needless to say, twelve hours of drinking brandy did little to curb or tran- quilize his foul disposition.

"Perhaps I can persuade you to alter your 'mood,' " Nikki enunciated evenly as he walked slowly toward the bed, beginning to unbutton his tunic jacket. "Move over," he said unpleasantly through gritted teeth, continuing to strip off his clothes. Lifting first one foot and then the other onto the silk counterpane, he unbuckled his spurs and dropped them on the floor.

"Damnable boots!" he cursed, sitting heavily on the bed; it was impossible to remove them without help. He turned to Alisa and pulled the bedclothes from her.

"Put your back to these boots, Madame, or I'll ride you shod. At least Sophie knows enough to help me off with them."

"I suppose that whore serves you gladly!" Tears sprang to her eyes.

"Yes, and now *this* whore will serve me, gladly or no. Bend to the task, my dear."

He lay on the bed and flung one foot into her lap.

"Pull, dammit, I'm in a hurry!"

As Alisa struggled with first one tall, slim patent leather boot and then the second, Nikki stripped the leather breeches from his hips and dropped them onto the floor. Lying back on his elbows at the foot of the bed, he surveyed his seething mistress with a cold, predatory gaze.

"Don't you dare touch me!" she cried.

"Dare? I dare? Mrs. Forseus, you bait the wrong man tonight." His tone was dangerous. "Now, my sweet, take off that negligee, or it will be in shreds in seconds."

Alisa lunged for Nikki's face with bared nails as he came at her, clawing instinctively for his eyes. He snapped his head back and the vicious nails raked one cheek, leaving deep furrows that immediately sprang red. A new shock of anger surged through him.

His hands closed on her shoulders with a grip so painful, she winced.

"Don't scratch my face." His voice was soft with an unnatural calm. "I abhor having to give explanations." There was a strange light in his flashing eyes and a cruel twist to his mouth as he said, "Now take off that gown or I will."

"No." Her eyes blazed.

"You're being foolish." His voice was no more than a whisper.

"Will you beat me?" she sarcastically inquired.

His smile was unpleasant. "Why don't I leave that for your husband?"

"Now, my dear, acquiesce like a good girl and service me in the way of mistresses," he demanded as his hard, mocking eyes roved over her quivering form. "It seems my misfortune to be plagued tonight with unpaid whores who suddenly have principles. Really, my dear, isn't it a bit late for these theatrics of affronted honor?"

Alisa uttered an infuriated cry and flung herself at him. Releasing her shoulders, with lightning speed Nikki caught her hands in his grip, deceptively casual but cruelly tight, wrenched them behind her, and bent her back on the bed beneath him.

Violently her knee came up and he arched back just in time, loosening his grip on her wrists. For a brief second Alisa twisted free and swung both legs over the side of the bed. Plunging his fingers into the heavy waves of her hair, Nikki savagely pulled her back, rolled over her, pinning her arms at her sides. As he forced a knee between her legs, they found themselves in close contact, and they glared at each other, both panting, incensed, blood running down Nikki's swarthy cheek.

Tears of frustration rose in Alisa's eyes as she lay exhausted, pinioned helplessly despite her struggles. With a sardonic quirk Nikki lowered his blood-stained face and sought her trembling mouth, kissing her thoroughly, insolently. Alisa's efforts at resistance were futile against such strength and brutal determination. With a stubborn perversity Nikki held her immobile and caressed her, forcing her to kiss him, filling her mouth with his thrusting tongue, slowly, lingeringly, destroying thought or opposition. A familiar heat insinuated itself deep within her, a slow, steady throbbing desire, and soon she no longer wished to struggle, she ached for him, longed to embrace him. But the animosities of the long night alone while he was with another woman still rankled, and she refused to grant him the satisfaction of responding. She lay inert beneath his touch, knowing this servile passivity annoyed and frustrated him.

"Am I discharging my duties properly?" she softly taunted him. "Is this befitting subservience, my Prince? A tame enough mistress, my lord?"

With a superhuman effort he kept from slapping her for her audacity and, cursing softly, swore to himself that he'd hear her beseech and plead for him soon. His skilled hands roved her body while his lips followed and caressed each tender fount of pleasure. He cupped her full breasts and lowered his mouth to tease and warm each soft nipple until they peaked proud and rigid, then he moved down her satin-smooth belly into the down beneath, and farther still until his hands and tongue had probed and titillated the soft regions of pleasure and she moaned softly and moved fitfully and arched in search of his pleasing tongue. Raising himself up and over her body, he glided slowly into her wet, lubricated warmth, then moved gently backward and forward, slowly forcing himself deeper with each gentle stroke. Her legs gripped him, and she rose to meet each sensual thrust; her violet eyes fell back voluptuously. The fire of passion threatened to consume them both, but Nikki deliberately restrained himself. Alisa wrapped her arms tightly around Nikki's muscular back and pulled him to her. Suddenly Nikki withdrew.

Alisa cried out in dismay, as suddenly she was empty and alone.

Lifting himself up and leaning both hands on the bed, Nikki looked into her startled, confounded eyes and said softly, "Ask me."

"You do this to humiliate me," she whimpered, trying to pull a sheet over her naked, throbbing thighs.

"Ask me," he repeated inexorably.

"Please," she sobbed quietly.

"Please what?" he questioned mercilessly.

"Please," she caught her breath, faltered, then whispered, "make love to me."

"Say, fuck me."

She didn't answer.

"Say, fuck me, or I'll leave."

A pause, then she whispered, "Fuck me." Her lips burned at the word.

"Does it matter that I have come from another woman now?" he persisted. He began again to tease her damp, soft crevice, moving his fingers slowly, gently.

She hesitated. "No, Nikki," she said at last. She moved her legs to make herself wide for him.

"Are you ready for me?" he cruelly continued, stroking her harder. Almost hurting her.

"Yes," she murmured, her eyes closed, too ashamed to look at him. Nikki exhaled a deep breath of satisfaction, his desire for vengeance gratified.

Dropping down, he took her then, no longer in fury but in hunger. She drew him deeper and deeper into herself, shuddering in ecstasy with each plunging stroke, holding him fiercely against each withdrawal. She was wild, begging him with her body to stay inside her. He brought her to a tumultuous climax and lay quiet in her as the waves of pleasure died away, then brought her up to the peak again before he allowed himself to reach fulfillment.

"My compliments to a bewitching, dutiful mistress," he whispered, kissing her tenderly. He fell asleep cradling Alisa in his arms. But she found sleep elusive, mortified by her body's traitorous desires.

Chapter Nine
THE BEGUILING BELLE

Rising early the next morning without disturbing Nikki, Alisa dressed and went downstairs to breakfast. A melancholy pervaded her thoughts as she regretted the passions that put her so mercilessly under Nikki's domination, while a slow anger remained over Nikki's gross perfidy in coming straight from Sophie's bed to hers. She toyed with her breakfast in an abstracted silence, responding only mechanically to the friendly conversation of Nikki's parents as they attempted to restore her normally cheerful spirits. Kaisa-leena sympathized with her son's lovesick mistress and sought ways to comfort her; she was not too old to remember the torment of loving with the despairing gloom of youth. The old Prince fulminated blackly, personally disposed to thrash his son if it would do the least bit of good. Sighing resignedly as he viewed the folly of that useless endeavor, he decided instead on a course of action that might be more successful. He wanted Nikki to marry this fascinating young woman who was bearing his grandchild but balked at the use of naked power to achieve his ends. He could, of course, quite literally compel Nikki to wed the girl, but preferred less harsh measures. But he would not be gainsaid; he would bring his recalcitrant son to heel one way or another, by force if necessary, but first— a more subtle attempt.

"Alisa, my pet, after that disgraceful spectacle created by Nikki and Sophie last evening at the Golchoffs' ball, might I hope to persuade you to move your quarters to our wing, at least temporarily. I think that scapegrace son of mine deserves a setabout. Would you be receptive to the idea? Kaisa-leena and I would be delighted to have you in our apartments." (And in a palace boasting ninety-two bedrooms, the distance factor was considerable from the parents' east wing to the son's west wing.)

Alisa's eyes lit up in relief. The perfect solution to her dilemma. She couldn't control herself when Nikki was pressing his suit, and it would serve him right for his arrogant, dominating attitude. She would simply remove herself from the temptation of Nikki's soft lips and practiced hands. Memories of last night's tempestuous act of union outraged her whenever she recalled the humiliation he'd forced on her. She lifted her chin determinedly and smiled.

"An excellent idea, Monsieur, for I fear your son has very little use for me after all." Would this retaliation even suit? Indeed, would Nikki even care? She knew with a desperate hopelessness that she cared very much if he missed her. A pang of great loneliness, even amid the devotion and friendship of Nikki's parents' concern, enveloped her. She was as alone as she had been for the past six years. One could ultimately rely on no one but oneself in this world, and sometimes the emptiness of that solitude was overwhelming.

"We shall see about that, my dear child. I think the young fool will find your absence provoking."

Later in the day, after Nikki had gone out, the change was effected. That evening at dinner, when apprised of the alteration, Nikki didn't rage or threaten. In fact, Alisa noted with consternation, he scarcely evinced any noticeable sign of acknowledgment. The drumming pulse in his temple would have been visible to only the most astute observer as Nikki casually drawled, "I see, Father, you're up to some scheme. Pray don't be disappointed if I fail to rise to the lure."

He consumed his meal with his usual careless indifference, perhaps imbibing one or two more glasses of wine than normal, politely asked to be excused when the third course was served, declaring he had recalled an urgent matter requiring his attention, rose unhurriedly to his feet, drew himself up to his full commanding height, courteously bid his adieus, and strolled in immaculate evening dress out of the dining room.

Prince Mikhail accompanied Alisa and Princess Kaisaleena to a dancing party that evening, and when Alisa caught sight of Nikki walking in with a very young lady dressed demurely in pale pink organza, the shock was like a dagger in her heart. Her despair wasn't improved when, later in the evening, Countess Amalienborg with her customary disregard, sat down next to Alisa and, leaning confidentially close, began inquiring in an apparently polite fashion of her relationship with the Kuzans. Alisa was too disconsolate to parry the swift ripostes.

"Come, come, my dear, the green-eyed monster is too apparent. Your heart is in your eyes, *chérie*." Without pity, the worldly, smiling woman continued. "It is only natural he should have wanted you; you are quite a diverting little beauty and he is, after all, a healthy young animal, but, my dear, please don't pine so openly. He's an incorrigible rogue and has affairs without number, all of which are short-lived. Nikki is the most notorious rake in town, has a horrid temper, and every scrap of scandalous rumor you hear of him is true. But because of his outrageous charm, wealth, and breeding he's still the most eligible *parti* in Petersburg and received in even the most reserved drawing rooms; in point of fact, I've just learned that he paid a morning call today on sweet little Emilie Belkenkoff, on whom he is dancing attendance tonight. This remarkable visit quite effectively threw Emilie's mother into delighted speculation. Nikki simply never calls on sweet young chits in the daytime."

The significance of the timing of that visit was very clear. He'd not even known she was moving from her room that morning. The transfer hadn't taken place till late afternoon. She was evidently only another of his short-lived affairs. Alisa's temper blazed, the melancholy burned away in a fire of resentment. Her violet eyes under her heavy lashes turned royal purple to match her royal rage.

"This morning?" she inquired coldly.

"This morning," Sophie cooed.

Had Nikki taken the notion in his head to court the pink-frosting confection? He'd always declared his intention to settle on a biddable schoolroom miss, and if he chose to pay addresses, no young miss could remain entirely indifferent to his practiced charm and handsome good looks. Someone like young Emilie, who couldn't be over seventeen, must be in love at first sight. Alisa glanced up to see Nikki across the room, bending solicitously over a seated Emilie, talking quietly with an admiring attention upon that sweet, upturned face.

Soothingly patting Alisa on the knee as she rose to leave, Sophie's malevolent intentions fully realized, she said with an air of benevolent condescension, "I am sure, *chérie*, that you'll find a very suitable husband from among these young blades panting after you. Someone eminently more suitable to your station in life. Nikki can, after all, as a Prince of one of the finest families, look much higher than a poor, obscure young widow with a child, and young Emilie's antecedents are impeccable."

"No doubt it will be refreshing. After Nikki's usual dalliance with, as you say, obscure widows and"—Alisa pointedly continued—"jaded sluts, a bonbon of such obvious naïveté as Emilie will be a welcome change."

The thrust hit home, for the Countess turned swiftly on her heel and left in a huff without replying.

Alisa watched Nikki dance with the dainty young girl, a sugar-plum kind of female, all pink and white and softly rounded, dressed in multitudinous pink ruffles adorned with crème roses. Her pale corn-silk hair had been fashionably arranged, pulled up high and bouffantly in front, while glossy golden curls cascaded down the back of her neck and onto her smooth white shoulders. Indeed, it would have been hard to find fault with her appearance. Nikki was carrying on his customary charmingly insouciant conversation, to which the innocent young girl could only blush or giggle in reply.

For the twentieth time that night, Nikki made one of those bland social remarks necessary to occasions such as this. "You waltz quite enchantingly, my dear." He waited patiently for the inevitable. It came after half a heartbeat—the trilled little flight of nervous laughter. Nikki gritted his teeth and glided into a wide turn. He felt sorry for the nervous, sweet thing. She was out of her league, unpracticed in elegant badinage, but sympathy didn't necessarily behoove obligation, he abruptly decided. Smothering a yawn, his attention wandering to contemplate a ripe brunette with shiny ringlets and a practiced eye who was scrutinizing him. Through force of habit he gave the blooming brunette a wicked wink over the cornflower-blond head.

Thankfully, the waltz ended and he returned young Emilie to her beaming mama, who was probably already measuring him for the marriage bed, then sauntered slowly across the floor toward Alisa. As he approached the swarm of young swains milling around Alisa, the crowd parted and quickly drifted away under the steely gaze Nikki bestowed on each of them. After curtly nodding dismissal to one of Alisa's lingering admirers more foolhardy than the rest, Nikki drawled, "Must you, Madame, constantly surround yourself with such lovesick pups? I should think you'd find the conversation tedious."

"You should talk, Prince Kuzan. Aren't sweet, witless young misses equally tedious? I swear, that little blonde appeared to do nothing but blush or titter," Alisa answered him acerbically.

"Alas, Madame, quite true, and while she's not entirely witless, she's as near to it as makes no difference"—Nikki sighed and shrugged eloquently—"so I think my duty dances for the evening will now suffice. I fear my background of vice and dissipation has little acquainted me with the pleasures of virtuous young women."

The direct cut was blunt and deliberate.

Alisa's eyes sparked in anger as she purred spitefully, "Perhaps what you need, Prince Kuzan, is an introduction to more virtuous pursuits. Who knows, you may not be totally sunk beyond redemption. A few evenings or afternoons in the company of that pink and white miss might be rewarding."

"Egad, woman, are you mad? Two dances was enough to give me a headache. I'm off to take the perfect remedy now

—a bottle of brandy. Would you care to join me, my sweet?"

"Thank you no, I shall continue to converse with these young gallants in hope of raising myself somewhat from the depths of depravity, as you so frankly put it. These young blades have a refreshing youthful charm."

Nikki had no idée fixe on women's morality, but his views on his mistress's morality were decided.

"As you wish, just so long as you offer no more than conversation. I prefer your charms to remain exclusively mine," he finished, his eyes amused as he noted Alisa's angry response.

"We are not all indiscriminate whores like Countess Amalienborg, Monsieur."

"How *very* reassuring, my love." Nikki raised her hand to his lips and brushed Alisa's fingertips with his warm breath while he gently massaged her palm. "Adieu, my love, until later," he murmured imperturbably as Alisa flushed pink at his touch and tried to snatch her hand away. Deliberately holding her hand a few moments more before relinquishing it, he grinned faintly, gave a swift bow, turned on his heel, and began strolling toward the card room.

Alisa willed herself to control the rising pulsations Nikki's touch had evoked. Damn him! His merest touch set off sensuous ripples through her veins. She shook away the disturbing tremors with grim determination and looked up, smiling lightly at Lieutenant Polovtsev who was the first to reappear at her side.

Chapter Ten
THE ANGRY LOVER

For the better part of a fortnight now, Alisa had been squired around a frantic whirl of parties, dances, and dinners by Prince Mikhail and Princess Kaisa-leena; the Prince determined to see that Alisa was enjoying herself regardless of Nikki. Removing Alisa from Nikki's embrace wasn't without a shrewd intent on the part of his father, who knew his son's need of women. For Alisa it was pure anger and revenge; she'd show Nikolai Mikhailovich Kuzan she was quite capable of having a marvelous time without him.

In spite of Alisa's vengeful intent, she woke up one morning after a particularly grueling evening and decided she could no longer continue. She must get away. She was exhausted, sick, and nauseated again. The ball last night had lasted until four. After returning home she'd slept poorly. All the feverish activity was taking its toll; she found polite enthusiasm more and more arduous to summon. One must always appear cheerful, vivacious, and interested, when the only person she was interested in scarce recognized her in a crowd. This wasn't working; no matter how kind Nikki's parents were, she resolved to leave, out of a combination of fatigue, despondency, and grief.

Alisa sent a footman with a message to Aleksei, requesting him to escort her shopping in an hour. Hastily dressing in a sedate walking costume of brown silk, a coarse straw hat lined with velvet perched on her curls, she gulped a cup of tea in an attempt to ease the nausea. Then she went to her jewel box and, with only a moment's hesitation, plunged the splendid emerald necklace Nikki had given her into her reticule and rushed downstairs to find Aleksei already in the front hall, waiting.

"Thank you, Aleksei. You're always to be depended on."

"You know I'd do anything for you, Alisa." In his nineteen-year-old puppy infatuation, he sincerely meant it. She explained in the coach what she intended to do, and they set off for 28 Morskaija, the street where the finest shops were situated. Aleksei promised to help; he could find an apartment for her; of course he'd be delighted to assist her.

The jeweler who'd sold the necklace to Nikki was more than obliging about buying the emeralds back.

"*Certainement*, Madame, we'd be more than willing."

The price offered astounded Alisa; she could live three years on the proceeds if she were frugal. Profuse thanks were exchanged, and the business was concluded.

Alisa returned to the palace in prodigious fine spirits, sustained by thoughts of thwarting Nikki. She would leave and fie to him! Aleksei said she had but to ask and his time was hers.

"In a few days, Aleksei, we'll go apartment hunting. You can help me find my new home."

The idea of living alone didn't hold as much pleasure as the day progressed. Alisa lay on her bed that afternoon, moodily contemplating life without Nikki. Could she do it after all, now that her pique of anger had passed and she wasn't as irritable and tired as this morning.

Her musings were interrupted as a sharp rap sounded on her door, and in his usual way Nikki walked in without waiting for a reply. Still dressed in buckskins and tweeds from an afternoon ride, he strode, ill-humoredly glowering, over to the bed and tossed the emerald necklace at Alisa's feet.

"Mrs. Forseus," he said in a glacial murmur, a wintry smile on his face, "I wish you wouldn't be so ready to dispose of my gifts. It smacks of the mercenary, designing professional. If your need of pin money has reached these proportions, I'm sure you could have easily approached my father or myself."

"How . . . how did you find out?" Alisa stammered, since no more than four hours had elapsed since her visit to the jeweler.

"Mr. Fabergé and I are acquaintances of long standing, so he informed me immediately when the necklace I purchased so recently had been resold. With all due sincerity he felt I should know that my inamorata was quite desperate for funds. Have you gaming debts, my dear?"

"No!" she snapped. "I'm leaving and I need money."

"If it's Cernov, I'll—" His scowl deepened and he glared at her.

"Don't be ridiculous," Alisa tartly replied, giving him back look for look. "I'm simply getting my own apartment."

Nikki's brow lifted as a flicker of relief shone in his eyes.

"If that's all you want, why didn't you say something?" The tense crease between his brows relaxed.

"You've not been exactly available these many days past, Monsieur."

"Rest assured, my love, the oversight will be remedied. I'll have Ivan find you something suitable tomorrow. This damn living in my parents' apartments has been hellishly inconvenient."

A smile broke across his handsome face. "It'll be pleasant to have you for myself again without my parents' affronted breath constantly on my neck."

"I think you misunderstand, Prince," Alisa flung back at him defiantly. "I wish to live alone. *Alone!*" she distinctly enunciated.

His smile disappeared in an instant.

"In that case, Madame, you will stay here. I'll not have you available for all the lecherous acquaintances of mine to patronize. Keep the money, but if you attempt to leave, I'll have you locked in . . . and to hell with Father," he growled.

"Remember now, I mean what I say," he said ominously. "If you try to flee, I'll run you to ground within the day, and if I'm put to that irksome exertion, you'll find my temper disagreeable. Dammit, Madame," he exploded, "you *will* do as I say!" And so commanding he turned and left the room.

Like a bird in a gilded cage, she dismally reflected. Why was she so unhappy, so desolate. If he would just say he cared, she sadly thought. Why couldn't he say he cared?

The party-going resumed, both Alisa and Nikki perhaps even more deliberately provoking to each other. Out of spite, for the effort was excruciatingly boring, Nikki occasionally paid homage to young Emilie, preferably at a ball or a party where he didn't have to endure long stretches of her undiluted company, but by and large Nikki had returned to spending his evenings at the club. His gambling and drinking were deep and heavy, his remarks often bordering on the insulting. A defiant recklessness spurred his actions and even his closest friends judiciously chose to tread warily, not eager to provoke his sarcasm or find themselves at the other end of his dueling pistol.

Precisely at two each night Yukko would appear at his side, the cards would be discarded regardless of the hand, irrespective of his gains or losses; Nikki would rise slowly, offer polite excuses to his partners, and stroll out of the club, followed by Yukko.

Each night, in turn, curious, watchful eyebrows were raised as Prince Kuzan's late appearance was duly noted at the parties, routs, or festivities graced by his beautiful "cousin."

Invariably, he would sullenly lean against one of the walls, drink in hand, nursing his anger, and follow with glowering eyes the slender figure of Alisa as she whirled past in a waltz or flirted brightly with the young officers.

One evening an old tabby approached Nikki and remarked injudiciously with a jolly little titter, "It appears your cousin is quite surrounded by admirers, and just when it had been rumored that you had developed a tendre for the poor creature." (The "poor creature" in this instance was laughing gaily at some sally from young Count Berzlov. She was arrayed in a sumptuous creation of green gauze and diamond brilliants decorated with sprays of silk apple blossoms tied in place with green velvet bows, her ripe, luscious bosom a foil for the magnificent emeralds.) Nikki watched her and seethed.

"It seems you are most alarmingly hindered by rivals. For one must admit your cousin is beautiful as sin."

"Countess," Nikki replied as calmly as his inebriated mind was capable, "my 'cousin' "—he purred the word maliciously—"occasionally lacks discrimination in her friendships. But let me suggest, Madame, that in the future perhaps I shall remedy her shortcoming," he finished acerbically, bowed insolently, and walked away.

Since being locked out from Alisa's bedroom, Nikki's temper hadn't been improved by his unaccustomed celibacy. Emilie was untouchable, had he even felt the inclination, which he didn't. There was little challenge in such a simpering child, and little pleasure, too, he imagined. The four incidents with dancers hardly counted; merely a perfunctory performance briefly engaged and as rapidly forgotten. Other women simply didn't look interesting anymore. Damn Alisa's alluring ways! He couldn't shake from his thoughts the beauty and sensuality of this unique, infuriating minx.

It had been a long, frustrating, exceptionally irritating two weeks. With a palpable but losing effort he was attempting to maintain some semblance of control over his growing irritation.

They met quite by accident one evening, two nights later.

Alisa, having been left by her partners, who went solicitously to fetch her an ice, heard a familiar chuckle and whirled around. Nikki was standing almost directly behind her, lounging against a pillar.

For over a fortnight he'd treated her with coolness when they met at a social affair or in the rooms of the Kuzan palace. The golden eyes that stared into hers were both insolent and admiring.

"*Merde*, you look demure. A creditable feat for a whore clothed in that gown. Are you displaying your wares for the highest bidder? The gauze of your bodice almost reveals more than it covers." The sarcasm coiled around her, silky smooth and faintly menacing as he approached.

"At least, should I choose to accept one of the bidders, I can offer him warmth in bed, which is more than you'll get from that pale confection of a mechanical doll you have been squiring around. How is she in bed, by the way?" Alisa retorted angrily.

"Not much good," he lied. "But one can always find someone else to warm my flesh, my dear, should I tire of the giggling," he coldly declared as his eyes lingered on her pretty breasts which were almost completely exposed. "May I compliment you on the effectiveness of your ensemble. Never have I seen wantonness so beautifully unclothed. One's imagination quite runs apace. You fairly invite ravishment dressed in such a fashion," he bluntly went on as his bold glance swept Alisa's form in the blue silk ball gown draped with a tunic of tulle trimmed with cut-outs of lace appliqué. "We're all waiting breathlessly to see if your gown will contain those luscious breasts so precariously balanced above these wisps of tulle," his sneering voice intoned as his long, lean index finger insolently flicked the offending blue tulle ruffles.

"Don't touch me," Alisa whispered hoarsely.

"They're probably taking bets in the card room right now as to whether you stay in or out of your dress tonight. May I offer my services in helping you out of it?" Nikki leered. "Although, no doubt, every man in this room will be equally eager to offer you the same assistance."

A red flush rose up Alisa's slender neck and flamed on her cheeks.

"Blushing, my love? Outfitted in this gown that leaves so little to the imagination? I would have conjectured you were beyond maidenly blushes and soon into a new bed."

"And thanks to your excellent tutoring, Prince Kuzan, my new bed partners won't be disappointed in my accomplishments," she spitefully cooed.

"Did I remember to teach you everything?" Nikki paused in mocking thoughtfulness. "In any event, I'm sure your resourcefulness will prevail, but just a word of warning.

Although your lovers, no doubt, won't be disappointed, you might be." He grinned.

It was too much. Alisa turned and walked away in a furious rage, damning his insufferable arrogance.

The next several of Alisa's partners were nervously disconcerted to find their waltzing even more carefully followed by the coldly watchful eyes of Prince Kuzan, who was now holding up another pillar and refreshing himself rather regularly as the footmen went by with champagne. One might almost think he was trying to get drunk as he tossed down a glass, reached for another and repeated the action.

Lt. Bobrinski in the deep throes of infatuation made the mistake of waltzing Alisa through the large arcade into the conservatory. Nikki with apparent calm drained his champagne glass and followed. Alisa and the lieutenant were seated on a delicate iron bench under the brilliant display of a blossoming gardenia tree. Lieutenant Bobrinski was ardently pouring out his love to an embarrassed Alisa, offering her his hand, his heart, his rather considerable wealth.

With a baleful eye and a temper goaded beyond civility, Nikki surveyed this tender scene and then walked boldly up to the couple, interrupting Alisa in the midst of her confused acknowledgment of the deep honor she felt in having Pavlov regard her with so much affection.

Nikki's imperturbable voice finished Alisa's flustered statement by drawling, "Tempting as your offer is, Pavlov, my friend, I'm afraid Mrs. Forseus rather counts on having me for a husband."

The Lieutenant began protesting.

Quite pleasantly Nikki told him to be quiet, then continued. "If you will excuse us, Pavlov," Nikki said coolly, fixing him with a look of such cold malevolence that the young Lieutenant stammered his adieus and hastily retreated.

"Must you always interfere?" Alisa flashed angrily.

"You wouldn't really consider marrying the pup, would you, my dear?" Nikki drawled.

"A lot more than I would ever consider marrying you," she retorted rudely.

"Ah, may I disagree with you, my love? But then, as the saying goes, since nobody asked you," he murmured dampingly, "I fear we shall never know. And then, darling, think what a shock Pavlov would have if you were to give birth to a child before you had time to marry or shortly after the ceremony. Now, if the child were Pavlov's, there would be no problem, even if it was born six months prematurely. As he well knows, being a direct descendant of Catherine the Great and Orloff, there is no stigma attached to illegitimacy if one's rank in society is lofty enough. But his family might frown on unanticipated progeny."

"Pavlov knows me as a widow just recently bereaved. A posthumous child is not without precedent," she spat out irritably at Nikki's smug countenance.

"Not, however, when the child is born bearing my stamp," he quellingly retorted. "These black, wolfish features have an embarrassing inclination to reproduce," he softly murmured. "So you see, a posthumous child in my image might require a bit of explaining. Am I not right?"

Refusing to answer his insolence, she said instead, wishing to wound as deeply as possible, "Maybe I should just not bring this pregnancy to term and put a stop to all these senseless arguments."

"Do not," he said in an awful voice, "even consider it." His tawny eyes smoldered. "It's too damned dangerous. Illyich's little actress bled to death last year because of a botched abortion. Let me assure you, it wasn't a pretty sight."

His words had the desired effect as Alisa paled visibly.

"At least these men treat me with respect and courtesy,"

Alisa retorted, annoyed at Nikki's checking her riposte, allowing the obvious comparison to hang in the air.

"Everyone has their own approach to the citadel, my love," Nikki returned brutally. "Don't delude yourself, *chérie*, they all have their tongues hanging out for the same thing, but some cloak their desires in a soothingly deceitful address."

"May I disagree with your coarse intimations of my suitors' intentions. I've received several proposals of marriage. This isn't the first. Is that a fine enough indication of my beaus' regard for the proprieties?" Alisa smiled smugly.

Nikki's eyes were cold as he met her mocking gaze.

"Other marriage proposals? You have? Married? Married?" he repeated. "If you were to be so foolish, I would make you a widow soon enough, by God!" He swore softly and long. "Married? By Christ, we'll see about that!"

She was his, by God; he'd wakened her to womanhood, had drawn the female from her shell of naïveté. She wasn't fair game for every drooling, callow youth, every lustful eye, every practiced man-about-town. Wasn't his mark on her, wasn't she carrying his child? How dare they address marriage proposals to her, he thought with the unmitigated audacity of a Kuzan born and raised. He would tolerate this charade no longer! Locked out of her bed, her person guarded by his parents like an unblemished virgin, an untouchable holy relic. He *would* have her again, he decided, his anger dangerously roused.

"I've watched you flirt and entice and coyly cast out lures for the last two weeks. My acquiescent temperament has reached its limit. You will flirt no more!" he quietly growled.

"Acquiescent!" she snorted. "Sooner try to convince me that the world is flat or that the sun rises in the west, you arrogant bastard!"

"Acquiescent," he whispered through clenched teeth,

and meant it, for what else had curtailed his rising fury these past weeks if not that sterling trait. He wasn't unfeeling and could understand the angry motives that prompted Alisa's light amorous bantering these several days, but when marriage proposals resulted, he drew the line. Nikki's altruism never stretched so far as to sharing his mistress.

To hell with them all! He'd take Alisa away tonight to Mon Plaisir, his estate north of Lake Ladoga. Remote, sequestered, irrevocably off the beaten path, the thought of a summer with Alisa in that distant fastness of forest and kallio brought his blood up.

"You've permitted every whoremaster here tonight to ogle your bounteous charms. I think it's my turn," Nikki said, his face contorted in fury, his breathing deep and heavy.

"Come now, dear, we go. Your flirtatious days in society are over. I've put up with all the interference from Father I'll tolerate. My independence from his control began years ago."

"He'll stop you!" Alisa warned, a rising note of hysteria in her voice as Nikki took her arm and began forcing her toward the door.

"I wish him luck in that endeavor," he coldly replied, and then unexpectedly broke into a warm chuckle. An exhilaration raced through him. The inaction and restraint, the stifling protocol of society he'd labored under for weeks, were cast aside. He was his own man again! His old mad recklessness invigorated him. One could be prudent only so long and then must break away.

Taking Alisa's hand in a vicious grip, Nikki pulled her protesting through the conservatory, thankfully empty of people at the moment. He slammed through double French doors, dashing them aside with a powerful sweep of his arm, causing them to shudder indignantly on their metal frames. Oblivious of the shocked stares of partygoers on the terrace, he tossed up the kicking, screaming Alisa and flung her over his shoulder. In this embarrassing position her pummeling fists uselessly bombarded Nikki's strong back while he held her feet firmly in his left hand, concerned with protecting his manhood from her kicking toes.

"Put me down, you monster, you brute!" Alisa screamed, beating ineffectually against the broad back, cursing him furiously.

Blandly ignoring her screams of outrage, he didn't even break stride as his long legs carried him and his rambunctious burden across the sweeping lawn toward his waiting carriage.

Walking purposefully down the long row of carriages, Nikki found his equipage, opened the door, and unceremoniously dumped Alisa onto the floor. Climbing in behind her, he curtly directed Feodor to drive back to the palace and slammed the door shut with a crack.

Immediately he was set upon by a scratching, clawing, screaming wildcat. For days now, he'd been forced to contain his fury, his resentment, his frustration. There was a limit. *Diable*, there was a limit! his mind thundered.

The horses had hardly begun to move, when Nikki seized Alisa in one sweeping motion and shook her viciously by the shoulders, leaving bruises on her flesh.

"I will not tolerate having you trifled with by other men!" he roared, the suppressed vexation of watching Alisa flirt and laugh and dance and posture before other men's frankly lustful gaze finally released.

"You're mine!" he thundered. "No man will trespass on my property! Do you understand?" He gripped her tighter and, struggling to regain his composure, spoke in a low, hard voice. "Do you understand?"

Alisa's eyes narrowed, her nostrils distended in anger. He shook her again.

"Answer!" he roared, the brief moment of control snapped.

Alisa spat on him and laughed at his discomfiture.

"Christ's blood," he growled, wiping his face with his sleeve. "I'll have the taming of you yet."

Grabbing a handful of her copper curls, he pulled her head back until her eyes were wide with fear. Then he stuffed his silk handkerchief into her mouth, muffling her whimpering to a whisper, and tied his neckcloth around her head as a gag. Her wild eyes watched him rip the blue ruffles from the hem of her gown and truss her hands and feet together.

When the carriage reached the pink marble palace, he grimly alighted from the carriage, closed the door, and issued orders rapidly to Feodor.

"Mrs. Forseus fell asleep, please don't disturb her. Make ready a second carriage, bring along another coachman and four grooms; two outriders on mounts are also needed. Have everything ready in fifteen minutes."

Being neither deaf nor blind, Feodor didn't believe for a minute that Mrs. Forseus was sleeping, but, inured to the idiocies of his young master, he only presented an impassive face and an affirmative response to his orders.

Nikki sprang up the stairs to the front door, eager to be packed and off before his parents discovered Alisa's absence from the party. The startled butler was the recipient of numerous and curtly barked orders. Footmen were to carry down the luggage to the waiting carriages outside, maids were to be sent upstairs to help with the packing. Get Ivan his secretary immediately, he needed money and a letter sent to his regimental commander, requesting leave. Have the chef pack some food, vodka, and brandy, everything to be accomplished in no more than fifteen minutes. Understood? Sergei quailed before the dangerous look in Prince Nikolai's eyes.

Nikki bounded up the stairs to waken Katelina and whisper to her that they were going to the country. She was, always to him, a vivid recollection of the bright freedom and wonder of youth. Katelina, ever amiable to her favorite Nikki, had already tumbled out of bed and was collecting her toys.

"Uncle Nikki, will you teach me to ride a horse as you promised and take me hunting like you said?"

"I certainly will, *lapsikulta*," he pronounced solemnly, for he treated her with the courtesy of an equal, never condescending to patronize her childish delights. "I'll let you ride a horse, take you hunting with me, and even teach you to drive your own pony cart."

"*Uncle* Nikki! What fun! I'll dress very quickly," she promised.

Nikki gave her a kiss and a quick hug, imparted instructions to Rakeli and Maria to have Alisa's and Katelina's clothes packed in ten minutes, and walked to his room to settle affairs with Ivan and select some of his favorite old clothes for hunting.

Within an incredible twenty minutes, the small caravan was on its way, Katelina, Rakeli, and Maria settled comfortably in the second carriage, Arni riding guard outside, Nikki and Alisa traveling in the first carriage with two outriders in the vanguard.

As the carriages left the outskirts of the city behind, Nikki silently untied Alisa and removed her gag, neither gentle nor repentant.

Alisa closed her eyes as the gag was taken from her mouth. Slowly she breathed deeply, trying to gain some semblance of composure for what she was about to say, as they eyed each other coolly.

Finally she spoke, pronouncing each word slowly and distinctly, having, in the angry solitude of her wait, discarded numerous and varied epithets and invectives.

"I am not your baggage to be trussed and ordered about," she said with a cold fury.

"You are now," he said grimly and unequivocally, not a flicker of tenderness in his tawny eyes. "At Mon Plaisir *I* am lord and master. *Everyone* obeys my bidding," he continued icily, emphasizing the pronouns. "And now we'll have our first lesson in obedience, my lovely baggage."

He felt himself harden with lust.

"You will not flirt with Lieutenant Bobrinski or any other man again, will you?" He reached for Alisa and pulled her resisting body to his.

"I will if I choose," she spat out, still defiant.

"You will not." In swift movements he threw her facedown across his lap, tossed her skirts back, and pulled down her lacy drawers. Her lovely bottom was exposed. Hand poised above the soft pink flesh, he mildly asked, "Will you now?"

Alisa shook her head, stubbornly refusing to give in to his demands.

His hand came down and spanked her, leaving pale red marks on the smooth circles of flesh.

"Speak up, darling. I can't hear you." His hand descended again on her tender skin.

She could feel him stiff and rigid against her belly.

"We'll return to this question later, my love," he sighed softly, his passion rising fast, a throbbing stiffness hard against his trousers. "It's time for your second lesson in obedience. The very motion of a carriage is enough to rouse my passions, and you're so conveniently close."

"Off with your clothes now. Let me gaze upon my property. I feel a need for your services."

Nikki turned her over and began pushing his and her clothes aside, too much in a hurry to undress. His large hands held her face while his lips fiercely found hers, his open mouth demanding, insulting, his face dark with passion.

"You—you're just like the worst of all men!" Alisa rasped breathlessly as he released her lips.

"*Just* like?" inquired Nikki sardonically as he settled her with a casual effortlessness beneath him, adjusting her position precisely as he wanted her, his strong arms holding hers against the hard carriage seat.

"Worse!" she panted, unable to move against his powerful strength. His excitement was so intense now, he shuddered at the second's delay. But have her he would, for nothing else mattered.

"Or better, mayhap, my dear?" He smiled arrogantly and faintly as he mounted her and without preliminaries he rammed himself in clean up to the hilt.

Alisa gasped. Despite an effort to steel herself, a cry was torn from her lips as a particularly fierce thrust penetrated deeply. He finished in seconds, withdrew, wiped himself off on her petticoats, and adjusted his clothes. Then he resumed his position on the seat opposite and stretched out comfortably, leaving Alisa feeling used and furious.

"A dog could do better!" she said in disgust.

He turned his head with a slow, deliberate motion, his eyes cold and blank. A brief second elapsed, and then the familiar derisive expression played across his face.

"My dear," Nikki replied softly in mock dismay, "I do hope you don't consider taking up Sophie's perversions. So very vulgar, you understand." So saying, he shut his eyes and with an infuriating, calm indifference, proceeded to fall asleep.

Alisa pulled her clothes around her naked body, turned over on her stomach, and wept.

·   ·   ·

They traveled steadily for the next five days with only brief stops to rest the horses and break their fast. Nikki didn't touch her again, he barely acknowledged her existence, further exasperating Alisa, who longed to stir up some reaction when she railed at him in anger. For most of the journey Nikki slouched low in the seat, his long legs propped up on the seat opposite occupied by Alisa, a bottle of brandy his constant companion.

On the evening of the fourth day, after having traveled with Katelina in the second carriage, entertaining her with tales of fairies and elves most of the day, Nikki climbed back into Alisa's carriage and lay back against the seat.

Alisa immediately began hurling denunciations at his head, trying to ease some of her resentment at being so arrogantly and tyrannically abducted. Further adding to her anger was the fact that Katelina looked upon the whole journey as another delightful adventure being supplied by her darling uncle Nikki, and even Alisa's old and loyal servants were quietly pleased to be going back to the country; they much preferred their familiar pine forests to the bustle and dirt of the city. Even Rakeli and Maria seemed to be on Nikki's side, and they would look uncomfortably away in embarrassment when Alisa would deliver some malicious remark to Nikki in their presence.

After patiently and quietly listening to the string of invectives for several minutes, Nikki held up his hand wearily in an attempt to stay the tirade directed at him.

"Please, my dear, no more." He heaved a small sigh. "Your violent sentiments do not stimulate my interest. I am by nature a very mild man."

Like Genghis Khan was benevolent! Alisa snorted derisively.

Nikki continued unperturbed. "And actually, I prefer considerably more passivity in a woman. So do try and be more silent. In fact this constant heckling may be dangerous, don't you see? My restraint is not unlimited, and it's been four days now." His heavy lids rose slowly, revealing a gaze suspiciously sardonic. "I'm surprised you have such a gift for inciting abuse. It must be your long apprenticeship under Mr. Forseus's tutelage." He paused. "I view as odious my brutal attentions directed at you that first evening in the carriage. Most unprecedented; perhaps I could be excused as having been under unique pressures and then, of course, you are decidedly provoking with your tempestuous tantrums. Forgive me. It won't happen again."

"I suppose that's something I have to be thankful for," Alisa snapped.

Ignoring the sarcastic retort, Nikki continued in his calm, equable tone that explained but neither petitioned nor beseeched its listener.

"I must warn you, however, as soon as we arrive at Mon Plaisir, if you continue to remain recalcitrant to my ah— demands, some methods of persuasion will be necessary, although, rest assured, they'll be more pleasant and subtle than those I so hastily and imprudently resorted to five days ago."

"You're all kindness, to be sure, Monsieur," Alisa retorted angrily, "but I shan't be long at Mon Plaisir. You can't make me stay."

With a husky laugh that indicated that he thought otherwise, Nikki replied quietly, an ironic smile in evidence, "I disagree, but do, by all means, put it to the test. In my present humor," he went on grimly, "after having listened to your insults for four days and five nights, I feel inclined to let my chivalrous nature lapse momentarily. Even my benign patience is not interminable."

The cold, steely look in his eyes restrained the angry retort Alisa was about to make, and she lapsed into silence. The rest of the journey passed in a frigid hostility. They reached the estate late that afternoon.

In 1796 Nikki's grandfather decided to build a wooden country villa on his forest tract far north of Lake Ladoga, a retreat from the frenzied pace of court life. Using hundreds of serf-artisans, this large structure was built completely of wood, with the ax alone (saws, chisels, and drills were used only for decorative details), and had not a single iron nail or other metal part. It was built "by the eye" and became a remarkable demonstration of the spontaneous expression of the folk genius.

The central eighty-foot-long, three-story block was flanked by two wings extending the overall length of the façade facing the lake to one hundred and sixty feet. Elaborate open-work eaves projected over the log walls cut flat on both exterior and interior. Intricately carved moldings framed each window and doorway, vast carved panels were inset in walls, delicate spindle-railed balconies projected from the second floor bedchambers, while a huge baroque pediment flanked by carved whole tree-trunk pilasters distinguished the main entrance doors.

By the spring of 1798 the villa was completed, the interior as beautifully crafted as the exterior. Chandeliers, mirrors, door frames, the parquet, were all made of wood, some gilded, all of superb execution. The scrollwork on furniture, frames, and candelabra: incredibly carved garlands, roses, cornflowers, figures, animals, all were made of wood by men unable to write their own names.

The rooms all bespoke the quiet charm of the hand craftsman; softly waxed floors, fur and woven rugs, tapestries, handwoven linens, crocheted lace, embroidery in the traditional tomato-red stitchery (in Russian, the words "red" and "beautiful," both *krasnyi,* are identical), while fresh flowers were arranged in huge vases throughout the house.

All these splendors were only briefly glimpsed by Alisa as Nikki immediately carried her up to his chambers in the

East Wing, laid her on the bed, turned without a word, walked out of the room, and locked the door.

Returning back downstairs, Nikki directed the servants and Katelina into the West Wing, where they were to be housed. Seeing that the little girl was settled comfortably, he explained to her as well as to Rakeli and Maria that Alisa wasn't feeling well because of the arduous trip and she would remain in her room for a few days until she felt stronger. He promised Katelina to take her riding the next day and told her to come and see her mother in the morning and wake him up. The servants didn't resist Nikki's suggestions that Alisa be afforded seclusion for a few days, because he'd charmed them as well as Katelina and they didn't view him as anything but kind and generous. He was courteous to them and politeness itself to Alisa and Katelina in their presence. He'd even accepted Alisa's spiteful remarks during the long journey with a benevolent, restrained calm.

In fact, Rakeli annoyed Alisa by her constant praises of Prince Kuzan. He is so much nicer than old Mr. Forseus, she would say with a completely unassailable simplicity.

Nikki returned to the bedroom in the East Wing after having ordered some supper sent up. He found Alisa pacing agitatedly back and forth between the huge bed and the bay windows that overlooked the acres of lawn sloping down to the lake shore.

"Don't wear a path in my Carabagh rug, love. You might as well relax. You're here for the duration."

"How long will that be, pray tell?"

"As long as I desire your services. If you contrive to amuse me, I may let you out sooner."

Her mouth dropped open in astonishment.

"You're going to keep me locked up?"

"Precisely."

"You can't! I'll scream, I'll tell Rakeli and Maria what a

monster you are; I'll make your life hell!" she cried in high dudgeon.

"Upon further contemplation, my dear, I think you won't. Now," he said briskly, "let's be practical. You're three hundred versts from the nearest town. I'm the master of this estate and its employees. If you attempt to inform Rakeli or Maria or Katelina or anyone else of your, shall we say, retirement for health reasons, I'll lock you up in an isolated cabin that is two miles deeper in the forest and inaccessible to anyone but me. I'll inform Katelina and your retainers that you've returned to Petersburg for a short stay and venture to entertain Katelina myself, which shouldn't be too difficult. You may have noticed, we're great friends. After she goes to sleep in the evening, I shall slip away to your forest cottage and have you entertain me for the night."

Alisa's heart sank in dismay as she listened to Nikki's voice explaining her alternatives.

"Now, if you should, instead, choose," he continued amiably, "to remain here in this room and obey me, I'll allow Katelina to visit you every morning as you are both in the habit of doing and I'll also allow you to sit on the balcony outside the bay windows and watch me tutor Katelina in riding and driving a pony cart. She's delightfully pleased with both prospects. If you undertake to be biddable and obedient, I'll permit you to see Katelina and your servants. If you disobey me, you'll be locked in my cabin. I'm sure you'll agree to my terms when you consider the great advantages to seeing things my way."

Alisa sat on the bed, her mind racing to find some alternative, some way out of the trap she was caught in.

"Really, dear, I don't like to press you, but do come to a decision soon, for if you choose to be obstinate, I must spirit you away to the cabin tonight. You understand, with morning," he said deprecatingly, "the difficulties would be endless."

She had no choice, Alisa reflected bitterly. She couldn't think of a single pathway out of this tangled web. If she stayed at the villa, at least her opportunities for escape would be greater and Katelina would be close.

"Very well," she said sullenly. "I'll stay here."

"Marvelous. I thought you'd accede; after all, you're a clever woman. Now, unless you plan on sleeping in your dress, I suggest you wash off the dust of the road and get into something more comfortable."

As if on cue, a timid knock was heard; Nikki unlocked the door and a procession of servants entered. Two footmen carried an enormous ceramic bathtub which several more servants then filled with steaming hot water. Stacks of linen towels were left on the dresser and the cavalcade withdrew as silently as it had entered.

"Madame, please be my guest," Nikki gestured grandly.

Alisa would have liked to curtly refuse the offer, but after five days in a dusty, rocking carriage, the temptation of a warm, soothing bath was too much to resist. One searching glance around the room indicated neither dressing room nor screen. A mental shrug dismissed the issue. Surely it was a little late to be unduly concerned with modesty. Alisa kicked off her high-heeled yellow kid slippers and reached behind her neck to undo the countless buttons marching down the back of her lemon-yellow traveling costume.

"May I offer my assistance as lady's maid?" Nikki drawled softly as he leaned back against one of the enormous carved posts of the bed.

"Thank you no!" Alisa snapped. "I'll manage."

Several minutes later, despite her best efforts, she was unable to reach all of the succession of minute covered buttons. Nikki watched her contortions, a slight smile playing about his mouth. Alisa looked up once and shot him a murderous glance, whereupon he quickly composed his features into a sham solemnity.

Several seconds later: "Please, dear, accept my services or your bathwater will be disagreeably cool. Since we must out of—er—necessity dispense with personal servants, I beg you forget our differences and permit me to valet you these following days. I hardly relish the idea of seeing you in that same dress day and night."

If looks could kill, he chuckled to himself as he viewed the fuming, piqued woman opposite him.

Alisa didn't deign to reply but merely turned around, offering her back to his ministrations. Several minutes of cursing later, which uncharitably cheered Alisa, the tiny buttons were all released.

"My God, Madame, those hellish loops are surely not meant for masculine fingers. A greater deterrent to lust I've never encountered."

"If I know you, sir," Alisa said with sweet malice, "you wouldn't let such trivial defenses arrest your passions."

"It presents a certain dilemma, I will admit, and leaves one with only two choices. To make love to a clothed woman or to send a lady back home with her dress ripped in two. Now, the former course, unless excessively drunk, I abhor on principle—so very crude—and the latter I abjure out of prudence, for husbands and servants are apt to notice small matters such as tattered dresses when ladies return from afternoon visits or rout parties."

"Surely, sir," Alisa couldn't prevent herself from saying, "you'll understand if I find it singularly difficult to see you as either refined or prudent."

Not particularly goaded by Alisa's acrid remarks, since he had her exactly where he wanted her, quite literally under his fingertips, he yet had an irresistible compulsion to nettle her as retribution for the five days of vituperation he'd suffered on their journey north.

"Crude like this, *chérie?*" he impudently murmured, ripping the ties from her petticoats, which fell to the floor on top of the folds of lemon-yellow silk.

She stiffened.

"Or imprudent like this, Madame?" he softly whispered, slowly turning her around to face him. One hand drifted from her arm over the swell of her breast, his slender fingers slipping between her full breasts, then, firmly grasping the material of both chemise and stays, he gave a firm wrenching tug, and silk and lace ripped from top to bottom. They, too, joined the garments on the floor.

"Any more provocative remarks, my dear?" he said with a lazy smile as Alisa stood crimson with shock before him, clad only in delicate gossamer drawers. Then he laughed softly, saying, "I see, my dove, your temper is at its usual fine pitch. Have a pleasant bath." He flicked aside a red curl that had fallen across her breast, bent over slowly, and sought a soft pink nipple between his fingers. He pinched gently, then harder. A wild tremor drove through Alisa, and Nikki smiled triumphantly, pleased with his power over her. "Reluctant as I am to leave you just now, the dust of the road offends me, so I'm off to bathe in the lake. In deference to your—ah—delicate condition, I knew the forty-five-degree water temperature would not appeal to you."

With a blown kiss he was gone, the quiet click of the lock echoing in the silent room. Alisa burned with shame at her treacherous body and Nikki's recognition of her response.

Within the hour both Alisa and Nikki were refreshed from their baths and together once again in the large room, mauve and golden rays of the sun striking through the thick atmosphere of silence. Nikki was sunk deep in a down-cushioned chair, calmly reading, while Alisa moved restlessly about, her thoughts in a confused turmoil, her emotions warring within her mind, all conflicting considerations ultimately overridden by anger at Nikki's arrogant mastery over her. Damn him! There must be some way out!

But the servants knocked on the door soon after and dinner was carried in. Two footmen set it out on a table near the tile fireplace.

"We will serve ourselves, thank you, Anastasia," Nikki said courteously to the beaming peasant woman who was directing the placement of the dishes.

"Is there anything more your lordship will require tonight?" she asked.

"No, nothing. I'll ring for you in the morning and Mrs. Forseus will select a menu for the day."

The servants cast surreptitious glances at the sullen beauty who was standing near the window, tapping her foot in exasperation, scowling till her brows drew together over dark, heavily lashed eyes. The door closed behind the retreating backs of the cook and footmen. Nikki walked over to the door, locked it, and replaced the key in his waistcoat pocket.

"Don't be so foolish as to contemplate stealing the key while I sleep. I warn you, you'd find the cabin extremely lonely when I caught you and brought you there. And catch you I would; my Finnish trackers are nonpareil in their trade and have taught me since childhood a certain degree of proficiency as well."

Moving over to the table, Nikki lifted the covers on the silver dishes tastefully arranged on a hand-woven beige linen cloth; the crystal and china sparkled in the candlelight of four tall tapers.

"A magnificent meal. Come, dear, sit down. Look, I ordered all your favorite foods, although I apologize for not offering sterlet.[8] We left in such a rush, you'll forgive the oversight." A flicker of a grin appeared.

And indeed he had bespoken her food preferences, Alisa noticed as she sat down and glanced over the sumptuous array before her: mushroom soup Madeira, duck au bigarade, brook trout in white wine sauce, cucumbers in sour cream, buttered baby carrots, wild strawberry tarts, large crusty rolls of dark rye, and almond dragées to complete the repast.

Nikki lounged comfortably in a large bergère that had been pulled up to the table.

"I would like a glass of champagne," he quietly ordered, adjusting the cuffs on his well-fitting chamois jacket.

"I'm not your servant," Alisa snappishly replied.

"You are now, my love, for you see, if you don't do as you're told, you don't eat. It's very simple, très simple," he breathed softly. (Having watched Alisa's healthy appetite increase due to her pregnancy, he'd thought himself diabolically inspired to have devised such an affable form of persuasion.)

"You wouldn't!" she gasped in horror.

"Try me," he said flatly.

Her eyes blazed in anger.

"I would like a glass of champagne," he repeated.

Alisa stubbornly sat where she was, seething with indignation, telling herself she'd starve before she did what he commanded.

"Dear, dear, I can see you're going to be difficult. I was so looking forward to a pleasant evening." Putting the covers back on the heated dishes, Nikki helped himself to champagne and drank several glasses as he relaxed in his chair, watching the firelight, refilling his glass, occasionally offering an idle bit of gossip as conversation, which was pointedly ignored by the tight-lipped, seething beauty opposite him. In this same tranquil, easy manner he drank a bottle of Clicquot and was opening the second when he apologetically remarked, "I can't wait for you any longer. Please excuse my discourtesy; I believe I'll eat." He helped himself lavishly to each of the foods, pulled his chair slightly closer to the table, and began eating slowly, resting between mouthfuls to drink his champagne. Nikki maintained a steady, quiet dialogue, praising the flavor of the duck, remarking on the delicate hint of fennel in the trout sauce, activating the salivary glands in Alisa's mouth so she had to swallow often. He pretended not to notice.

Alisa hadn't eaten much that day, in fact, the entire five days had been pick-up meals and cold collations as they journeyed into this wilderness. She was inordinately hungry, bombarded now with the sight and delicious aromas of all her favorite dishes, and as Nikki had surmised, even more ravenously hungry due to her pregnancy. Damn his black soul, she was starving and he sat there chewing his food so slowly and carefully, you'd think he was a taster for some foreign potentate. She swallowed hard once again.

After some minutes of leisurely dining, Nikki softly reiterated, "I'd like some champagne," and he held out his goblet.

Alisa hesitated a long moment—then, forcing aside her pride, she rose and poured the stemmed glass full of the bubbling liquid.

"*Now* may I eat?" she inquired sarcastically.

"Soon, dear. I'd like you to feed me first. It will teach you obedience. My comforts come first."

Gritting her teeth on the reply that sprang to her tongue, Alisa stood beside Nikki and dutifully fed him. He smiled up at her encouragingly between bites, blandly disregarding the glares she returned. Much later, when he deemed himself finally satisfied, she returned to her chair, sat down, and reached for the food.

Nikki rapped her knuckles lightly with the hilt of a silver knife, arresting her hand in midair. Alisa gasped.

"Forgive the delay, but I'm afraid there's one more lesson yet, my sweet. I never quite received the proper replies to my questions that first night in the carriage. Perhaps you've reconsidered your answers. I stated that I'll not tolerate you being trifled with by other men. Do you recall?"

Alisa sulkily shook her head and peevishly replied, "That hardly remains a problem out in this desolate part of the world. I'm three hundred versts from the nearest dance or party."

"You may not be here forever. I want an answer," he said shortly, fixing her with a steady look. "Are you going to flirt with other men in the future?" he patiently inquired.

She looked at him woodenly, refusing to answer.

"Are you?" he questioned, a scowl darkening his brow.

"I may," she replied, yawning, her devil of a will incorrigible.

"What?" he hotly whispered, swearing roundly. Reaching across the small table, he took her face between his powerful hands and, glaring at her, whispered, "What did you say?"

She tried to glare back belligerently, but her eyes fell before the fury in his.

"No," she gasped softly.

His hands slowly relaxed their cruel grip and he released her face and leaned back in his chair while a faint smile lifted his lips.

"You're learning to be sensible, my dear. Come here and sit on my lap; I'll feed you now."

"I can perfectly well feed myself," she spat out, her violet eyes filled with resentment.

"Come," he commanded quietly, and she went.

Nikki fed her slowly as he held her on his lap. She ate and ate, the flavors delicious, the variety magnificent.

"I'm full. I would like to return to my own chair."

"A little more," Nikki insisted patiently.

"No." Alisa clamped her mouth shut obstinately like a small child.

"Come, love, a few more bites. I want my baby to be fat and healthy, and I delight in your curves filling out," Nikki murmured as he slipped his hand into the bodice of her negligee. "Such full, soft breasts," he whispered. "They fairly cry to have someone suck them. Take off your gown, chérie, so I can caress your divine breasts."

"No, Nikki," she protested, drawing back from him, "they're so tender lately."

"If I promise to be gentle?" he murmured huskily as he lowered his head. Her protestations were immediately quieted as pleasure surged through her senses when his lips touched her nipples.

"Ah, love," he softly sighed, lifting his head briefly as he ran his hands over her swelling hips and looked into her languorous eyes, already sinking into sensuality. With an indrawn breath she felt the world drifting away and experienced a shivering thrill as his fingers glided between her legs.

"You've changed your mind. I know you better than you know yourself," he whispered. "You've learned well but still won't admit you were made for love. It's no sin to acknowledge your desires." His long, lean fingers were probing, caressing, making her wet with passion and desire. "Your body needs me as much as I need you." He lifted her in his arms and carried her to the beautifully sculptured pine bed lavishly decorated with carved flowers and leaves.

"Tell me you need me," he whispered as he lowered her onto the bed.

"I need you, Nikki. . . ." Her dark eyes entreated, her soft voice implored, her hands reached up to draw him near.

Chapter Eleven
THE STALEMATE

There was little sleep that night, for the Prince after almost three weeks of missing Alisa in his bed had an immoderate hunger for her. She always offered her initial resistance, but he wooed her and inevitably prevailed. Her senses passionately responded each time, and she hated herself after for that betrayal. By dawn Alisa was sore and tender and swollen.

"No, Nikki, please, no, I can't bear any more," she whimpered. He caressed more softly but he wouldn't stop. He slid between her legs, spread her thighs, and within minutes he had once again brought them both to a frenzied ecstasy. Kissing her gently as he withdrew from her warm body, Nikki whispered apologetically, "Forgive me; you bring on a fever in me that won't be quenched."

Later that morning, in an atmosphere once again heavy
with hostility, for in the cooler moments, removed from
Nikki's passionate embrace, Alisa still raged at her bondage, he silently began opening Alisa's trunks and portman-
teaus, pawing through clothing with a fine disregard for
wrinkles.

"Leave them, Monsieur," Alisa said icily from the huge
bed. "I'll unpack them myself."

Ignoring her, Nikki continued in his search until he
found the articles he wanted. All twenty-four of the as-
sorted negligees and peignoirs ordered from Madame Vevay
were located. Taking out only the peignoirs, Nikki hung
each one in the armoire, shut the trunks, unlocked the
door, and in one swift motion shoved the luggage out into
the hall.

Walking back into the room, he scooped up the yellow
dress and petticoats still in a heap on the floor, threw them
over his arm, and proceeded to move toward the door.

"What in the world are you doing? You can't leave me
without any clothes!" Alisa protested, aghast, rising from
the bed, a silken sheet clutched to her full breasts.

"*Au contraire*, my dear. I can and I do."

"I need my clothes!" she cried in frustration.

"Let me assure you, my love"—a wicked leer lit up his
wolfish yellow eyes—"your activities will require no clothing. I leave the peignoirs merely in deference to modesty
should you care to take some air on the balcony."

"You—you're despicable, loathsome; I hate you!" Alisa
sputtered, sinking back onto her pillows in chaffing frustration.

"My, my, how soon we forget," Nikki murmured in mock
dismay. "Why, no more than two hours ago I recall you
crying rather plaintively for my presence."

Laughing at Alisa's discomfiture as she flushed pink to her hairline, Nikki turned and left the room. She hated him then, hated him for making her melt in his arms, making her forget all his iniquities forced upon her with only his expert touch.

The situation remained thus for almost a week. Alisa was confined to the room. Battle lines were drawn, heated words exchanged—a stalemate between two tempestuous, willful temperaments. The only reverses were those suffered by Alisa when Nikki skillfully, patiently roused her senses to a passionate need for him. As soon as the sexual skirmish was over, the advance was beaten back. He gained ground only to lose it once again when her sensibilities calmed, when her tremblings ceased.

One afternoon Nikki was seated, reading, in one corner of the large bedroom, while Alisa sadly stared out the window at the beautiful lawn and garden, the sparkling surface of the lake in the distance dancing in the light breeze, a landscape still refused to her. She'd been locked up in this room for six days now, forced to accede to Nikki's wishes, and her nerves were taut.

Nikki glanced up from the page and quietly watched the stubborn set of Alisa's back as she stood immobile before the windows, barefoot, her shapely form wrapped in a sea-green lace dressing gown, silhouetted against the brilliant afternoon sunlight.

Within seconds his erection was rigid. My God, he only had to look at her and he wanted her. She went to his head like a drug. He was going to push himself into insensibility in a few more days at this rate, although, he reflected lecherously, it was a pleasant way to go.

"Chattel," Nikki said provokingly, "come here."

Alisa spun around.

"Go to hell!" she said, glaring at the lounging figure in the cushioned chair.

Why did he taunt this woman? Nikki wondered. It was unprecedented for him to want to totally possess any female. In all his former liaisons Nikki had remained deliberately aloof, never wishing to satisfy more than a casual lust. This independent, strong-willed creature was a challenge to him, a piquant change from the accommodating women in his past. And that fierce determination was like a tossed gauntlet. It raised his blood. He *would* possess her totally; she *would* bend to his will. An irrational impulse drove him.

"Come here," he repeated softly, and crooked a finger. She didn't move, favoring him only with a silent, poisonous look.

"The cabin deep in the forest waits you," Nikki reminded her in a mellifluous murmur, his sweet tone belied by the dangerous glitter in his eyes.

She came then, eyes downcast, walking slowly across the room and stopping several feet distant from the sprawled legs.

"Reconcile yourself, Alisa," he said gently, "for I mean to keep you near me."

She opened her mouth as if to speak, and he stayed her with a raised finger. Shaking his head slowly in baffled self-disgust, his voice dropped to almost a whisper.

"Don't ask me why again; I don't know. I can't tell you. All I know is you're in my blood; I need the taste and feel and scent of you. I want the warmth of your skin next to mine in the morning when I wake; I want to know you're here to welcome me when I return." He glared almost in bitterness at Alisa. "I want to fuck you day and night." She shuddered before the crudeness of the remark and the piercing savageness of his fierce eyes.

"And"—he laughed a short, bitter rasp at the painful, unfamiliar sense of possessive jealousy she raised in him—"I feel an unaccountable need to keep you for myself. No other man shall touch you. Stay willingly or unwillingly. It scarce matters to me, but rest assured, my little dove, you *will* stay. Now, take off your clothes. I have need of you." Her hand reached up and began unbuttoning the front of her dressing gown.

He had won another round.

Nikki drew Alisa to him and caught her in a powerful embrace; his fingers grasped the curls at the back of her neck, tightening, forcing her head back as he pressed ruthless, demanding kisses on her lips, her throat, her trembling breasts, branding her as his in a savage assuagement of the uncomfortable, compromising sensations she engendered in him.

A sweeping movement slid her robe aside, off her shoulders, and it drifted to the floor. Scooping her high against his hard, muscular chest, he carried her to the bed, settled her beneath him, and penetrated the soft, warm flesh that held him in thrall with silken bonds of mindless desire. He fiercely resented his passionate bondage and savagely invaded her, each powerful stroke an exorcising of his frustration. Alisa's soft, whimpering cries finally pierced the confusion of his black anger, and he was aware of hurting her. Taking her face gently between his hands, he tenderly kissed her tears away, murmuring apologies, whispering quiet entreaties, gently rocking in a slow rhythm that caressed and stroked and roused.

She wanted his love but he gave her passion. In the dark recesses of her soul she wanted to be his wife; he wanted only a sensuous mistress.

Soon they both forgot all else but their need for each other as the driving ecstasy reached consummation and they met once again on the only common ground that offered them both surcease.

· · · ·

In the mornings Alisa watched from the balcony as
Nikki patiently taught Katelina to ride her pony and han-
dle the reins of the small red pony cart. A warmth of feeling would rush over her then; he was so good to Katelina. If
only he didn't insist on owning *her* in such a feudal display
of authority, leaving no dignity or pride. Damn him, damn
him for making her want him, for after six days of continu-
ous lovemaking, morning, afternoon, and night, Alisa's
passions were roused by Nikki's merest touch, her body
addicted to the titillation of its senses—a brushing hand, a
soft caress enough to instantly activate the sensuous nerves
that cried for, yearned for the exquisite torment and pleasure of satiation. Her need grew more intense with indul-
gence.

And that night was no different from the rest; a war of
words and thoughts, Alisa persisted in her verbal assault.

"Why do you insist on humiliating me? Women aren't
simply things, playmates in bed. We have feelings too.
We're equal."

"Equal?" he retorted in astonishment. "Nonsense! Why
would a woman want to be equal? Isn't it enough to be
normal and happy? You're beautiful," he murmured, reaching for her. "Come here." The audacious thought summarily left his mind as Alisa's seductive image provoked his
desires.

She resisted his advances as she always did since they
had adopted their lines of battle. Within seconds Nikki
pushed her aside in disgust.

"*Sacrebleu!*" he exploded. "You're insufferable. Why do
you always fight me? Why do I always have to force you?
Can't you admit your desire? Do you think I don't know
when a woman wants me? You wanted me from the first day
I met you."

I know, she sadly thought.

"There's nothing more gratifying or flattering to a man

than to have an irresistible woman want to be his lover.[9] You, it seems, are incapable of confessing to these natural feelings."

He glared at her lying beside him. Then he took a deep breath and exhaled. "You win. I'm leaving tomorrow. You can stay or go, I don't care. I'll not bother you again. Take your damnable pride and dignity and I hope you find them good company! Ivan will set up a trust in your name at the bank in Petersburg for our child. It will be adequate to offer you and the child financial security. And I trust you'll find some accommodating man to bolster your insufferable ego."

Nikki turned his back to her and immediately fell asleep.

Alisa lay frozen beside him. How could he? How could he be so unfeeling? He was leaving her in the morning and he could sleep as though all the world were in peaceful accord.

Alisa tossed fitfully as her awful pride waged a battle against her love for Nikki. How could she love a man who only used women, who ridiculed and railed against clever women, who spoke of setting up a nursery someday with some compliant young chit. How could she love him? Had she lost all reason? She meant no more to him than any of the women who had been dogging his heels since he entered manhood. And when he left her, she'd be desolate, life would hold no joy, no meaning, her future would stretch bleak and empty. Is hellish pride worth that desolation and unhappiness? she wondered. Was her body so inviolable and precious that she couldn't give it freely to the man she loved? But he didn't love her, she piteously cried. She needed him to love her.

He'd given her so much, though, his time, affectionate attention to Katelina, gifts beyond belief, tenderness in making love. Wasn't that enough? Must she chain his independence as well? Was she asking for more than he could give? Maybe it was enough that he wanted her passion.

Then her voice of reason would whisper devilishly. Had she no sense? Had she no pride? To which she confessed, sadly—no. With Nikki she had no pride.

And what good was pride if she lost Nikki? she asked herself with a brutal honesty. She loved him.

She realized as the early glow of morning touched the room that she wanted Nikki unconditionally, on any terms he chose. A restless sleep finally overcame her tortured thoughts and she dreamed of demons tearing her away from Nikki's arms, of dark wastes and lonely vistas in which she sat desolately alone. Full daylight brought relief from the nightmares, if not the anxiety, prompting them.

Alisa rose just as the sun crept around the linen draperies, determined to keep Nikki there if she could. Standing before the wash stand, she deliberately banged and clanked the china pitcher and basin in the spurious act of washing.

When Nikki's easy breathing changed from sleep to wakefulness, she wiped her hands, slowly raised her gown, and seductively stripped it from her body, lifting her arms high above her head and stretching languorously like a cat waking in the sun. The early morning rays shining through the coarse linen draperies bathed her body in a soft, golden, iridescent glow.

Nikki, watching, thought her, in that pose, as beautiful as Rosso's nymphs in the Gallery at Fontainebleau. Lithe, sensual, the sun gilded her soft curves of breast and hip and thigh, warmed the pure white flesh, accentuated the bloom of womanhood. By God, she was deliberately seducing him, he realized, and he willed himself to resist the provocation.

"It won't work," he said evenly, the simple statement dropping ominously in the quiet room. "I'm leaving this morning." He paused briefly, running his eyes boldly over her luxuriant curves. "And I don't like you performing like a whore," he finished coldly.

Hands on her hips, lips petulantly pursed, Alisa murmured softly as her violet eyes held his, "You're always telling me I must learn to accept my passions, my sexuality. I'm simply taking your advice," she said softly, advancing toward the bed, slowly melting over his supine form and kissing him lingeringly, searingly, on his lips, brushing her hand against his stiffening prick, caressing his powerful muscular chest with light fingertips.

"Take me one last time before you go. I'll leave you something to remember me by," she breathed, the soft words tantalizing.

Nikki strangled a curse, inveighing his faltering willpower but losing his fight against Alisa's passionate lips. She bent her head low, gentle lips touched the engorged red head, a moist tongue drew him into her, and all resistance ended.

He groaned and gathered her up into his arms. "Come here. My leave-taking can wait," he whispered hoarsely. And Alisa clasped Nikki to her with a frenzy of hope and desire, withheld nothing, giving her love with a wild, reckless abandon, wanting him to stay with her, wanting to make him need her as much as she needed him. For the first time, their mating was a complete union of two hearts, two spirits, two passions, their yearning for each other totally fulfilled.

She drew him deeper and deeper into her as if she could hold him to her forever, chaining him to her with bonds of warm flesh. He brought her to climax after climax, marveling at the ardor she contained; the final relinquishing of her heart as well as her body reflected in the intensity of her passion. During her convulsions, he lay rigidly still inside her, affording her the maximum of pleasure, letting her feel the full impact as each trembling wave washed over her. Finally he could no longer hold himself back and poured himself, shuddering, into her, his heart pulsing violently. In that final moment he experienced a feeling of contentment and blazing sensation beyond his wildest memories of pleasure.

He kissed Alisa tenderly, pushed her tousled red-gold curls back from her forehead, gently cradled her in his arms. The scent of mating hung heavy in the room.

Quiet tears filled her eyes and lashes.

"Don't cry, Alisa *lemmikki*, I won't leave you," he promised softly.

She smiled faintly and brushed his lips, so close to hers, with her fingertips. "Thank you," she murmured as her tears overflowed, and she cried for herself, for her enslavement to this man. She would do anything to lie with him, to have him near her, and she cried for the loss of her will.

Nikki was all gentle kindness. She was his now, completely, wholeheartedly. He was joyfully triumphant. He sent for breakfast and her trunks of clothes. Her imprisonment was over.

After they dressed and breakfasted, Nikki had a swing hung under the rose arbor near the house so Alisa could sit in the warm sun and watch Katelina go through her paces with the pony on the large lawn.

Katelina jogged along happily on the small pony as Nikki spoke encouragingly to her, prompting her to hold her hands lightly, to remember her seat, to keep her elbows in. The tousle-haired youngster successfully followed all his instructions letter-perfectly.

Nikki adored Katelina in a casual way. He'd provided money for Katelina's lifetime with his usual careless liberality, an act that served also as a sop to silence his conscience which chided him to provide some measure of permanence in Katelina's life. Insistent, nagging remonstrances that urged him to commit himself legally to his lovely mistress, the expectant mother of his child.

Mother and "Uncle" applauded loudly as Katelina's mischievous face lit into a beaming smile of joyous glee when she completed the circuit of the lawn in fine form.

"Mother dear," Nikki murmured as he sat next to Alisa on the wide swing, "Katelina is charming," he said with pride. "If your second child is as delightful, you will have doubled my pleasure."

Alisa's heart melted at his whispered affection. He cared for her and Katelina and for his yet-unborn child. He made no promises, never even in the height of his lovemaking did he tell her he loved her, offered her no future, only a passionate present. But he did care and she clung to this small compensation for her surrender.

"And I intend to keep you pregnant, at my side, populating this glorious wilderness," Nikki whispered playfully. As he realized what he'd just said, a new unfathomable sense of the future with Alisa struck his consciousness. He immediately rose and paced beside the swing so she couldn't see his face, so false hopes wouldn't be raised within her heart. Resolutely he sought to shake off the unfamiliar feeling. He struggled for control. *Mon Dieu*, it would never do, this giving way to emotion.

How *did* he care for her (he dared not use the word "love")? Love was anathema to him. He reveled in his independence, fiercely clung to his singular existence. It suited him to bow to no one, man or god, and certainly never to humble oneself for a woman, never again. He wouldn't allow himself to dwell on these unfamiliar sensations Alisa stirred in him. He'd not permit a woman to breach his inner private citadel again, although the storming was exquisitely accomplished with soft words, soft lips, and soft thighs.

She pleased him, that was all, so he would keep her, but only until such a time as she no longer pleased him.

"You think of me only as a brood mare," Alisa pouted prettily. Now that their war was over, she enjoyed being openly flirtatious, seductively suggestive. "You're imperious and peremptory to even suggest such a thing as keeping me pregnant."

"But not excessively repugnant, for all that." His eyes twinkled a little as he stopped pacing and joined her at the swing.

"No, not completely, my lord," she posed demurely.

Nikki smiled lightly at the soft mouth fixed in a pretty moue, delighted with her attempt to gratify his wishes, to appeal to his stated preference for a soft passivity in a woman.

"Not only as a brood mare, love; you enchant me in a variety of ways, but, I'll admit, the thought of you nurturing my child within your body warms me with a pleasant conceit." He bent low over her to place the palm of his hand against her rounded, swelling form. *His child.*

Katelina was squealing for Nikki's attention, and he rose to stroll over to the insistent little girl on her pony. He spoke a few words to her and walked back to Alisa while Katelina kicked her chubby legs into the pony's ribs in an effort to make the animal move. At the moment, the pony was more interested in cropping the daylilies and Siberian wallflowers on the edge of the flower beds.

Nikki glanced in Katelina's direction as he stood near Alisa. "I promised Katelina I'd take her squirrel hunting this afternoon, and she's holding me to the promise. Will you be all right alone for a few hours? I reluctantly leave you, but must honor my word to that persistent little brat." He grinned. "And I won't ask you along, for I don't want you riding. You must be very careful of our child. Shall I call Rakeli or Maria for companionship while we're absent?"

"No, I'll be perfectly fine alone. Perhaps I'll stroll down to the lake. The only glimpse I've had of it until today has been through the bedroom windows." She smiled mischievously through half-lowered lashes.

"Sorry for my damnable temper, love. I'll endeavor to bridle it in the future. The entire estate is at your disposal" —he indicated with a sweeping wave of his arm—"but don't wander too far into the forest. You might become lost."

"I won't, Nikki."

"Now, you're sure you'll be all right alone?" he asked anxiously as he bent to kiss her.

"Of course, dear, and don't shoot too many poor squirrels."

"No, we won't be gone that long. Au revoir." He blew her a kiss as he strode away, extricated the pony and rider from the flower bed, and disappeared around the corner of the West Wing, heading toward the stable block.

Alisa sat on the swing for a short time after the hunting party left. It consisted of Nikki, Katelina, Arni, Yukko, and three trackers. The sun was comfortably warm, and Alisa daydreamed blissfully. She walked around the flower gardens, beautifully cared for by an army of gardeners, then moved in the direction of the lake. On reaching the sandy shore, she strolled along the soft white sand of the bay that swung away in an easterly direction from Mon Plaisir. Within minutes the house disappeared from sight behind the tall, dark pine trees lining the shore. Alisa stooped occasionally to select a small, flat piece of shale and skipped the rocks across the luminous sparkling water. She walked for some ten minutes, careless of her distance from the house because there was no chance of becoming lost out in the open of the lake shore.

Finding a large, flat boulder, Alisa sat on its broad expanse and gazed out on the lake, knees drawn up under her
chin, arms clasping her legs, letting the lassitude of the
warm sun and light lake breeze bathe her; contentment
filled her soul.

Hearing an unexpected sound behind her, she whirled
around.

Valdemar Forseus was standing five feet away, his small,
deep-set eyes peering with a dangerous mockery at the terrified face of his young wife. She froze in horror at the sight
of those fanatically piercing eyes.

"So, Mrs. Forseus, you have led me a merry chase," he
breathed softly. "We were beginning to despair of ever seeing you outside the house. That whoremonger of a Prince
guards you well. But, alas," he sighed, a sinister smile playing across his grotesque face, "not well enough. And, of
course, I'm a patient man."

A rapid flash of his arm and two gigantic men appeared
out of the trees and strode swiftly to his side. "My trackers,"
he conversationally remarked, "my sweet young wife. Men,
the object of this long and diligent quest," he politely introduced them, his wrath barely concealed beneath his rigidly controlled demeanor.

Alisa was dumb with alarm as wave after wave of silent
terror flooded her consciousness. Why had she wandered so
far from the house? Why had she so stupidly assumed Forseus would accept her flight from him? God, where was
Nikki? She began to tremble in the sure knowledge that
Forseus would kill her, certainly if not now, later, after he'd
used her to suit his devilish will. He was insane, sadistically
taking delight in causing pain. God, Nikki, help me, she
sent up a silent plea, her nerves stretched taut in panic.
Flashing, blinding spots of light suddenly danced before her
eyes and oblivion took pity.

She crumpled in a swoon at the feet of the three men.

"Pick her up," Forseus ordered sharply. "We must make haste."

One tracker effortlessly lifted her body and the three men walked back to their horses tethered in the pines. The men mounted, Alisa was settled across one man's chest, and the party spurred their horses. Once back on the road, neither quirt nor rowel was spared as the riders furiously pressed their horses south.

Mercifully, Alisa remained in a faint for several hours, the agonizing terror of Forseus's proximity locked outside of her conscious mind.

She regained consciousness in the late afternoon when they were forced to stop to change horses. They mounted her on a small bay, her hands tied to the saddle pommel. Forseus spoke scarcely more than three words to her, carefully restraining his anger in front of the two trackers. To bring back a runaway wife was legal enough; he could expect their help, but even these primitive men wouldn't accept the punishment he was going to inflict on his contrary wife once he had returned her home.

"You will rot in hell, Jezebel, and your carnal urges will be punished as you deserve," he whispered evilly that evening as they stopped briefly to water their horses at a stream. "I hope you last long enough. I wouldn't want my pleasure curtailed." As if to prove his point, he cruelly tightened the cinch on his horse's saddle and heaved his great bulk back onto his mount.

Alisa trembled involuntarily, prayed for courage and strength to sustain her. The full horror of her capture was beginning to overwhelm her. And although she told herself sharply to remain calm, her panic was reaching nightmare proportions.

• • •

The squirrel hunt lasted longer than anticipated, since Katelina was enjoying the excursion. Shadows of twilight were slowly creeping in from the forest as the small group rode back into the stable yard, a tired but satisfied little five-year-old nestled in Nikki's arms.

Walking into the large hallway carrying the fatigued child, Nikki hallooed for Alisa, cheerfully anticipating a welcoming kiss from his lovely mistress. He handed Katelina over to Rakeli and strode up the broad wooden stairway to the bedroom, so eager to see and hold her, he didn't even stop to shake the dust from his boots and clothes. This morning had been magnificent. God, *she* was magnificent; beautiful, sensual, intelligent, and she loved him. His world was near perfection.

"Alisa!" he called out. "Alisa, we're back!" Nikki cried as he opened the door into the bedroom, lit now with the last rays of sunset glow. "Katelina is becoming a very excellent rider for—" He paused on the threshold as his eyes swept the room, searching for the familiar form, the auburn hair.

The room was quiet and empty. The muscles in his jaw tightened. Turning sharply, he retraced his steps down the main staircase, shouting for Alisa. The housekeeper came running from the back hall and explained quickly, "I haven't seen Madame for hours. She was walking in the garden last I saw her."

"You mean you haven't seen Mrs. Forseus all afternoon?"

"No, sir, I haven't," she answered fearfully, for the Prince was scowling mightily.

Nikki thanked her gruffly and proceeded out the front door, racing down the entrance steps in three long strides, the tiniest twinge of apprehension beginning to mar his perfect mood. Within seconds he'd turned the corner of the West Wing and peered across the broad flower beds, all gaily blooming, a few bees still busily humming from flower to flower.

No Alisa.

A larger fragment of doubt replaced the vague apprehension as he walked purposefully back to the entrance, thundering loudly for the housekeeper. He ran up the stairs. Having heard the roar of Prince Kuzan's voice in the kitchen, she was at the door to greet him.

"What is it, my lord?"

"Assemble all the servants—immediately! I can't find Mrs. Forseus." Within the minute a glowering Nikki was addressing a long line of maids, gardeners, and footmen.

"Has anyone seen Mrs. Forseus since I left for my ride?"

The answers came in a confused babble, but when all were sifted and deciphered, apparently no one had seen Mrs. Forseus since early afternoon, when she was strolling in the yard.

A fierce rage began to smolder in the quick-tempered Prince. So all the theatrics this morning, the tears and sighs, the loving words, had been just that—theatrics. She had probably coolly plotted the drama and he, driven as usual by his genitals, had fallen for her scheme. How else would she have been released from the prison of the bedroom? Very clever of her; the oldest female ploy, when all else fails, use your body.

He swore to himself and then aloud as the servants huddled in a group, glancing nervously at their distraught master. There was no more to learn from them, so he curtly dismissed them, charging them to keep out of his way.

"Yukko, bring me two bottles of brandy," he demanded, incensed. Nikki stalked off into his study, infuriated at having been deceived by the feigned sincerity of Alisa's loving scene that morning.

Damn her, damn her lying heart. He'd drag her back by the hair! He'd beat her! He'd show her not to trifle with

him! But even as he stormed and raged, the more pragmatic side of his nature challenged—why bother? Why
bring her back? He'd been ready to leave her this morning
anyway; the decision had simply been taken out of his
hands. Maybe that was what piqued him most. Was his
pride pricked because Alisa had chosen to leave him, had
taken away his perogative. And he was made to look the
fool?

When Yukko appeared with the brandy, he attempted to
raise a question about Alisa, but Nikki was only able to
conceive her disappearance in terms of deceit. He con-
demned her duplicity, censuring, damning her provocative
sensuousness, castigating himself for the thousandth time
for his childish credulity. Cunt did that to him. He forgot
all else.

"Nikki, what of Katelina? Alisa would never leave—"
Yukko braved his master's wrath.

"Silence!" Nikki bellowed, and put the bottle to his lips,
draining a third of its contents in one huge swallow. He
looked up with a deadly glare and said, "Are you cham-
pioning that bitch?" He lapsed into Finnish. "I don't want
to hear that trollop's name again! Do you hear? Do you
hear?" Nikki snarled. "Now go. Leave me in peace. Bah!
Women. Who needs them!"

Yukko lifted his eyebrows in resigned disbelief at the last
statement. If there was ever a man who *couldn't* do without
women, it was his master.

"Very well, Nikki," he sighed as he watched his master
grasp the bottle again and pour down another long draft.
Leaving the study, Yukko resolved to look for Alisa himself.
She wouldn't run off now, when she was carrying Nikki's
child. Everyone below stairs knew that. But when Nikki's
temper was up, he didn't listen to reason.

It took Yukko no more than twenty minutes to find why
Alisa had disappeared. Racing back to the house, he found

Nikki slumped in his chair, his face an unreadable mask. Having finished the first bottle of brandy, Nikki was approaching the mood when all the world was of no consequence.

Yukko jerked the second bottle of brandy from Nikki's sullen grasp and said, "Alisa's been abducted. Three men on horseback took her from the east shore of the lake about three quarters of a mile down the beach."

Approximately three seconds elapsed before the news penetrated Nikki's senses. Then he shot to his feet, clapped a strong hand on Yukko's shoulder, and tersely questioned, "Abducted? You're sure?" he asked sharply. "She didn't run away? You're sure?" His eyes were eager.

"I'm sure, Nikki," Yukko answered positively.

"Thank you." Nikki's eyes lit with a hungry hope.

Yukko turned away in embarrassment from his proud young master. The Finnish brotherhood of trackers and woodsmen were by nature and training taciturn, proud, laconic of speech, and disinclined to show emotion. Nikki for a brief moment had exposed his vulnerability and Yukko, with a delicate courtesy, chose to avoid the sight.

When Yukko looked next, Nikki was out the door, dashing down the outside steps, already halfway down the path to the lakeshore. Yukko and Arni hurried to catch up with him. The three men ran down the soft sand, darkening now in the swiftly growing twilight, following Alisa's small footprints.

An awful obscenity exploded from Nikki when they reached the additional tracks around the large lakeside boulder where Alisa's footprints abruptly terminated.

"Are you positive there's three, Yukko?" Nikki asked curtly.

"Yes, three," Yukko replied decisively as he knelt to scrutinize the prints more carefully. "Two big men, one average size."

Rising, Yukko followed the trail into the woods to the place the horses had been tethered.

"They're carrying Mrs. Forseus," Yukko said, glancing compassionately at Nikki striding beside him. Yukko had been with Nikki ever since he was a small boy given as a serf-companion to the young master. He knew all his moods, his pleasures, his idiosyncrasies, so he'd watched with almost unbelieving amazement as Nikki had altered his life for this young woman. Extending a sympathetic hand, he touched Nikki's shoulder.

"We'll catch up with them, Nikki," he solemnly promised. "They can't have more than a four-hour start on us and won't be able to travel as rapidly with Mrs. Forseus. She can't sustain a headlong pace."

Nikki cast a swift glance around the small clearing that had sheltered the horses, shutting his eyes briefly in despair. There was no doubt who'd abducted Alisa, and the knowledge of Forseus's cruel sadism shook his composure. Resolutely dismissing the awful visions, he started back to the house, running full out, his long legs outdistancing both Arni and Yukko. Dashing into the stables, he ordered the grooms to saddle six horses, then he swiftly returned to the house and explained to a fearful Maria what had transpired. He warned her not to alarm Katelina.

"We should be back in two days. Tell Katelina anything, anything at all to pacify her until we return."

He strode into his study, lifted down an ivory-stocked Winchester model 1866, lever-action carbine, the best in the world, purchased in Paris, as well as a serviceable Belgian Colt Navy Model Revolver, crammed his hunting jacket pockets full of shells, and shouted for the cook as he ran back outside to the stables.

The horses were almost ready; the cook breathlessly appeared and Nikki ordered food to be packed for three days' travel.

"You've five minutes to prepare it before we leave," he snapped. The cook scurried back to the house, crying for the kitchen maids.

"Empty the stables," Nikki commanded sharply. "I want every horse with us. Two grooms will be needed to return the fatigued animals. *Vite! Vite!*" He snapped his fingers.

Arni and Yukko were checking their harness, the mounts dancing and sidling in the nervous activity of the stable yard. Horse after horse was led out and strung together with long braided leads.

Nikki slammed the rifle and revolver into his saddle holsters, took one look around to determine everyone's readiness, and flung himself up into the saddle. Koli pawed in sensitive anticipation, eager to be off. The cook and her helpers came flying out from the kitchen, carrying rucksacks that were hastily fastened to the saddles.

Within seconds the party thundered out of the stable yard, Nikki setting a dangerous pace in the twilight shadows.

Chapter Twelve
THE CHASE

The horror of some injury befalling Alisa kept running through Nikki's distraught mind as he leaned into the wind. If Forseus had harmed Alisa or his child in any way, he would see him burn in hell before another day passed, Nikki vowed as fear for Alisa's safety rode with him. He knew Forseus's mind wasn't normal. He derived pleasure from subjecting Alisa to indecent aberrations, from hurting her. God, what if he killed her, what if she were dead already? His pulse rate soared while his heart plummeted. A suffocating despair gripped him. Nikki dug in his spurs, furiously pushing the horses, forcing them unmercifully until they were unable to go on, their mouths foaming, their coats glistening with sweat. Without pausing for more than three minutes, the beaten horses were unsaddled and left with a groom, the tack transferred to fresh animals, and

Nikki, remounted, was three hundred yards ahead, whipping his new mount to pick up the pace.

The damn fool will kill all his horses, Yukko muttered as he threw himself onto his vigorous new mount and put spur to horseflesh. Thousands of roubles of prime bloodstock were being driven into the ground.

The largest horses were needed to support Nikki's weight and they, in their brute strength, had a stamina and endurance beyond an average horse's powers. Nikki was well ahead, picking up and following a glaringly obvious trail. Forseus was traveling in headlong flight; no care was taken to cover his escape. He was either confident no one could overtake them or too frightened to take the time to be cautious. It didn't matter. Either way, he'd die, and soon, Nikki promised himself.

They watched for signs of change or separation.

One horse had faltered—a light track—the horse carrying Alisa. She must have been remounted, for a different animal was now supporting her slight weight. They were gaining on the fugitives. At the wicked, reckless speed Nikki was urging, it was just a matter of time. Nikki's party were all mounted on Stryelet horses now, which had been left for last, having the stamina to cover long distances without flagging. They counted on the fact that Forseus would have to stop for food and rest, however briefly, and Nikki would gain valuable time, for no one in pursuit remotely considered rest. Nikki wouldn't stop until Alisa was safely with him once more, or—God, no, he didn't dare think.

He dug the bloody rowels into the horse's ribs.

By four o'clock in the morning, waves of exhaustion were sweeping over Nikki. He hung on to wakefulness with stubborn determination. He mustn't close his eyes. Darkness pulsed around him, the rhythm of the horse was soothing. Had he dozed momentarily? With effort he levered his eyelids open. It wouldn't be long now. He had to remain awake. They flew southward in the velvety night, the blackness of the forest pines flashing by.

As the sky lightened, Nikki knew that Forseus couldn't be far ahead. The fugitives didn't have the advantage of fresh horses, and their mounts had to be exhausted, maintaining no more than a slow trot.

Nikki and his trackers came up on the encampment in the gray mists of early dawn. Frantically his eyes searched the glen for Alisa, for some sign of her. Finally his glance caught a glimpse of her dress lying beneath a rock outcropping, and his heart almost stopped beating. Was he too late? Had Forseus beaten her beyond endurance? Horrible visions of her lying in a pool of blood, losing her baby from the terror and brutality of her abduction, flashed through his mind as he leapt from his horse and bent to retrieve her torn gown. He barely heard the voices of Arni and Yukko threatening Forseus and his men into submission as he prowled from place to place, looking for Alisa.

"Alisa," he called, beset with alarm, "Alisa . . ." panic tightened his stomach; there was no sign of her anywhere. He heard a rustling in the underbrush and turned, thinking to tell Yukko to help him in his terrible search. And then he saw her.

She was bound and gagged, her eyes wide with terror, her chemise her only covering.

"Alisa," he cried, relief flooding his brain. Racing to her, he quickly untied her and pulled her, sobbing, into his arms.

"Are you all right?" he asked anxiously.

She nodded speechlessly against his chest.

"Did he . . . the babe . . . are you . . ." He couldn't say the words, but he had to know.

"There wasn't time," she gasped. "Thank God, there wasn't time."

"Your dress is torn as if . . . I found part of it."

"He ordered me to undress in front of him. When I refused, he tore my clothes from me and then he tied and gagged me." The words rushed from her as if to exorcise the horrible memory. "He sat drinking, watching me, as if planning his next assault. Then I think the journey and drink together proved too much for him and he fell asleep." She closed her eyes against the horror of her memories.

Nikki kissed her. "It's over," he murmured. "I'm here. You're safe. . . ." And swiftly shrugging out of his leather jacket, he covered her trembling shoulders. "Wait here," he whispered, "I'll be with you soon." He didn't want her to witness his vengeance on Forseus. She'd have nightmares enough.

Following the voices of his faithful servants, he came to a camp clearing where three men stood under the guns of Arni and Yukko. Nikki immediately recognized the evil countenance of Forseus.

He could think of nothing now but killing the man who had stolen his mistress. In a low, savage voice Nikki said, "Prepare to meet your maker, Forseus."

Forseus stared at Nikki with a bestial ferocity, his eyes flecked with insanity, and when he spoke his words were uttered with the finality of the deranged. "The Jezebel deserves to die for her sins," he intoned, the fire of a zealot burning in his eyes.

Snatching his pukku from its sheath, Nikki leapt at Forseus, driving him helplessly down on his back, forcing his advantage of size and strength ruthlessly. Wild with loathing, Nikki's eyes raged with venom. The point of his hunting knife flashed in the air.

Instantly springing into action, Yukko stayed Nikki's knife hand, talking rapidly while he held back the shuddering strength. But his master was too strong. Nikki shook him off and lunged for Forseus, who had risen to his feet.

As he was about to strike a murderous blow, Alisa ran forward, Nikki's jacket clutched tightly to her, her eyes alarmed.

"No! stop!" she cried, "please, I don't want that man's blood on my conscience. Please, Nikki!"

It was the only voice that could have stayed Nikki's hand, and even then he hesitated before pulling back from Forseus's chest. He gazed up at Alisa, indecision in his glance, and then he rose abruptly, releasing the man he'd held helpless beneath him. Pointing his knife at the man's loins, he said, "I'll not kill you, but if I should see your face again, you'll not survive."

With the fanaticism of insanity, sustained by an aberration he called religion, Forseus screamed, "God will punish you for your sins!"

"Will he indeed?" said Nikki icily. He picked up Alisa and mounted his horse. Then, wheeling his mount, he rode out of the clearing, followed by Arni and Yukko.

They traveled home slowly, Nikki holding Alisa closely to him, both filled with an enormous sense of gratitude and relief, their essential spirits at peace. The miles passed in a silence of contented exhaustion. Much later, Nikki looked down on the red-gold curls, the delicate face dozing lightly on his chest, and said softly, "I love you," very simply and without emphasis, the raw terror of almost having lost Alisa still brutally fresh in his mind.

Through the mists of a light half-sleep Alisa responded faintly to that staggering statement with a small, satisfied smile.

Nikki placed a gentle kiss on her tousled curls.

They were going home.

Chapter Thirteen
THE HALCYON DAYS

The first evening back at Mon Plaisir, Nikki and Alisa retired contentedly to their bedchamber after putting the lovable Katelina to bed. Nikki had ordered a sumptuous dinner to be served to them to celebrate Alisa's homecoming. Numerous sterling candlesticks illumined the small table à deux, lending a lyrical poetic brilliance to the scene.

Arranged before them in precise rows on Lanerschy decorated china plates were unbelievable quantities of succulent, lightly scraped asparagus. Instructions as to their preparation had been stipulated: no more than seven minutes of the plunged stems in boiling water or heads will roll, Nikki had teasingly commanded of his beaming cook.

Finger bowls were laid out, and a large sauceboat of melted butter rested between the two services. Nikki silently reached across the small table with his long arms, rolled up the sleeves of Alisa's dressing gown, did the same to his linen shirt-sleeves, and admonished her in a thoroughly relaxed drawl as he reached for his first spear, to please forget etiquette and enjoy the pleasure of the delicious vegetable.

Alisa hesitated momentarily as she contemplated launching into the plate full of asparagus as Nikki was doing. As she paused, one hand daintily raised above the plate, Nikki muttered, typically heedless of decorum, "Yes, I know asparagus is a great stumbling block in a refined ladies repertoire," he said, smiling, "but, à propos shoddy table manners, I must confess, they would never cause me to reject such a charming companion." Gazing up at the most audacious man in the Empire, Alisa ironically murmured, "How reassuring. I need not pack then, should I dribble butter down my chin."

"Dribble it anywhere you like, darling." Nikki's voice held a velvety undertone.

"I do adore the libertine in you," Alisa acknowledged with a lazy smile, reaching for a spear.

"I noticed . . . once or twice that you did." Nikki's grin was wolfish.

Alisa, already consuming her first tender spear, smiled and said full-mouthed and muffled, "Eat now, darling. You'll need your strength."

This harmonious, genial companionship continued through the entire four courses of superbly prepared food, and Nikki, in a gentlemanly fashion, forwent the lonely port and cigars and directed his attention to the lady's entertainment.

And later that evening, as they sat by the fire, he pulled her to him, looked deep into her eyes, and said again, "I love you."

Alisa gazed up at him in tearful disbelief. "I thought it

was a dream. But you did say those words before, when we were coming home."

"I almost lost you," he quietly said.

"I've loved you from the first," Alisa whispered.

"It's a word I've avoided—til now."

"But—I'm so lovable," she teased.

He smiled down at her, feeling strangely blessed, an uncommon sensation for a man of his repute. "Yes," he said, and then his voice turned husky. "I'm a lucky man."

In the following days, these lovers, so similar in their volatile temperaments and yet so dissimilar in the outward appearances of their past lives, settled into an intimate companionship. They slept and ate and laughed and talked and *agreed*. They entertained Katelina and read together and walked the estate hand in hand. The rhythm of their days was serene and languorous; the rhythm of their nights passionate and intense. They lived in a cocoon of love, preoccupied with their own concerns, oblivious of the outside world.

The summer nights were very short now, and many evenings after a sauna they'd sit on the porch of the bathhouse, perched over the shore of the lake, and watch the pale iridescent colors of the setting sun far into the evening hours. Even the land of the midnight sun seemed to be presenting an extravagant, sumptuous backdrop to these glorious, halcyon days. Often on these evenings, when it was warm and still and heavy with the scent of grasses and clover, they would sing together, all the old Finnish folksongs. Nikki's bass and Alisa's soft soprano in concert with Katelina's lilting, high-pitched voice blended in pleasant harmony.

Their relationship, at one time so turbulent and violent, was in these days without flaw. Late one evening, after putting Katelina to bed, Nikki and Alisa were sitting in the library; Nikki was drinking his way to sleep as was his

custom, but slowly now and with none of the reckless in-
temperance of the past. The Prince was happy, not the
usual frenzied exhilaration that had often passed for enjoy-
ment or the satisfied lust that offered a certain consolation,
but truly a deep, contented happiness. He watched Alisa
from under lowered lashes as she sat across the Turkish
carpet on a small settee, engrossed in Winckelmann's *Exca-
vations at Pompeii*. Her peaceful beauty reached out and
struck him afresh. She was his, proud now to be his, and
she was to have his child. A strange sense of fulfillment
soothed his mind. He actually looked forward to the event.
He wasn't just happy because she was happy, but happy
within himself.

Could he have stopped the passage of time, he would
have then. He was content. In the past, he'd always lived
for the uncertain future, hoping to find tomorrow an assuagement of his restless ennui. But now he wished for
neither past nor future. He was experiencing a happiness
that had eluded him for twenty years and he wanted to halt
the progress of time.

Unknown to the participants of the sunny, contented
household at Mon Plaisir, Nikki's father had been informed
by his servants of the dangerous abduction attempt by Valdemar Forseus.

Prince Mikhail was in a fine choler, storming and cursing
as he paced around his study in Petersburg one warm summer morning. Damn, insolent pup! He'd wait no longer for
Nikki to come to his senses. Alisa could have been killed
by that insane lunatic Forseus.

I've waited long enough, biding my time while he thinks
only of his amusements, the old prince muttered impatiently. I even *explained* to him my firm desire for a legiti-

mate grandson, he fumed. I don't have to request. He will obey, he furiously raged.

Prince Mikhail stalked from his study, bawling for his barrister, his secretary, his Finnish trackers; he raved and fumed.

"I want an audience with Alexander II as soon as possible," he commanded his secretary curtly. "Alisa shall have a divorce before the next sun sets. Send for my barrister. He must inform Valdemar Forseus of the divorce and offer him a settlement to sugar the action," he snapped briefly.

"Johanos"—he turned to the leader of his trackers—"I want Nikki back here as soon as possible. Go up to Mon Plaisir and bring him back. I don't care how you do it. I'll write a note informing him of my wishes while you're saddling your mounts."

Prince Mikhail turned and disappeared into the study, while Johanos raced out the door, crying for his cohorts. Within a few moments a group of trackers were in the saddle and hurtling out of the courtyard while Prince Mikhail stormed about the hall, raging still.

Princess Kaisa-leena came running down the stairway, roused by the noise and commotion. "What's going on, Misha?" she inquired breathlessly as she reached his side, searching his tempestuous face for some answer.

"That damnable son of yours, that's what's the matter!" he roared. "He's coming home. He'll be less impudent soon, by God!" He gave her a terse outline of his plans, then stalked away, cursing still.

Kaisa-leena sighed resignedly. She could envision the embroiled household already. Father and son, both with indomitable tempers, at each other's throats. She must do her best to sooth the ruffled feathers, but she wondered this time whether she had any chance of success.

Chapter Fourteen
THE RELUCTANT BRIDEGROOM

Three days later, Nikki stood in the library at Mon Plaisir, holding his father's note in his hand.

He had read with mounting horror the short, crisp missive.

Alisa's divorce is being "accelerated"[10] *by the Emperor while your marriage plans proceed. Please be so kind as to return immediately. My trackers will expedite your removal.*

I'll bet they'll "expedite" my removal, Nikki reflected with a ghost of a laugh. The barest civility was accorded when his father used the word "please," but the implication of coercion was eminently plain as Nikki glanced out the window and noted the fifteen men dismounting and stretching their limbs after their three days of hard riding.

He'd never truly believed that his father would have the audacity or ruthlessness to dragoon him and had felt quite safe and content at this remote northern retreat. But here it was—simple, direct, and certain. He was to be married.

He sighed and slumped into a soft leather chair, kneading his brow with his left hand and getting into a fine sweat at the thought of his father's plans. Nikki had been successfully avoiding this tender trap for half his lifetime, had considered himself quite proficient at the art. Now he could see that his efforts had prospered only because of his father's sufferance.

Lord, he had no inclination or partiality to spend the rest of his life playing checkers with the Governor of Archangel. He knew his father's warning about a future at his estate in Siberia was no idle threat now.

So here he was on the brink of marriage; you can see what can come of an apparently harmless diversion. He'd like to wring Illyich's neck. But he did love Alisa, he supposed, in a way that was not entirely carnal and he felt quite sure she was in love with him.

There was no point in wasting his wits and digestion ruminating over his folly, Illyich's evil wager, or his father's astonishing new sense of priorities. *Mon Dieu*, if his father wanted a grandson, he would happily round up any number of those, but not, unfortunately, legitimate ones, and that seemed to be the kernel of the immediate problem. Why suddenly had his father developed such a fine taste for propriety?

He was snared, not a damn thing to do about it but grin and bear it; either that or molder in Siberia for forty-odd years. A wife need be no great encumbrance if one has money, and they do have their conveniences, he thought; but all the same, it was a distressing, abominable piece of madness. He kept swearing to himself as he rose from the chair and walked upstairs to inform his mistress of her imminent change in status.

Alisa was seated at the mirror, brushing her hair, and smiled at Nikki as he walked into the bedroom.

"My father has obtained your divorce and I have been commanded to marry you, and, it appears, Madame, that we are to be married post haste," Nikki stated, a note of grimness apparent beneath the lazy drawl.

The smile died on Alisa's lips, and she turned to face him. Her lips trembled in anger. "Please inform your father that no one has to marry me," she said, resentful of Nikki's obvious reluctance. "Having endured one unsatisfactory marriage, I don't care to venture into a second that has all the prognostications of being a disaster, with you as unwilling husband. As you well know, I don't wish a forced marriage," Alisa indignantly finished.

"I'm of a like mind," Nikki declared with unfeeling candor. "And our new relationship is so agreeable lately that I scarce believe it possible," the carefully modulated voice remarked with its old derisiveness. "But, alas, neither of us has any choice in this matter. If I refuse," he went on in a soft restrained voice, "my future entails a dreary life on Father's estate in Siberia, which I'm in no mind eager to pursue. He will, no doubt, treat you more tenderly for the sake of this grandchild he's bent on having. *Certainement*, he will remove you to his dacha on the Crimea so the little tyke will have the creature comforts of sun and beach." He paused thoughtfully. "Although, if one must be shackled to someone, I daresay you'll suit." Nikki flicked a bold glance over the beautiful face and form of the affronted woman standing opposite him in dishabille, a filmy morning robe but imperfectly covering her. The future child was just beginning to make his presence known; Alisa's belly rose slightly beneath voluptuous, trembling breasts as she haughtily regarded the arrogant, lean figure confronting her.

"I'm afraid I cannot return the sentiment, for you do *not*

in the *least* suit me!" she snapped, furious at his nonchalance, the underlying trace of contempt, that almost flippant incivility.

Nikki shifted his weight and advanced menacingly. Alisa involuntarily shrank back to the dressing table as the cool golden gaze stared caustically into her own mutinous eyes. Forcing her against the edge of the table, Nikki leaned forward slightly to within three inches of the flashing eyes and murmured, "I beg to differ with you, Madame, for in one area, at least, we suit to perfection, or else you are capable of the most artful pretense since Delilah gulled Samson out of his hair."

"I won't marry you!" she cried.

"It's customary to wait to be asked, Madame," he snarled, at which point he ground his teeth in exasperation and hurled the dressing table mirror through the bedroom window.

Alisa burst into hysterical tears at Nikki's violent display of anger, their peace and contentment shattered as abruptly as the mirror. Running to the bed, she collapsed facedown, sobbing into the pillows because she wanted him, and then didn't want him because he no longer wanted her.

Nikki stood in the center of the room, rankled and incensed, clenching and unclenching his fists as he gazed at Alisa, tumbled on the bed. Her robe had been pushed up as she fell, her beautiful white body exposed to the waist.

What a luscious roses-and-cream exterior and passionate nature underneath, he mused as his kindling sensual desire gradually inundated his temper. Walking slowly to the bed, he pulled the robe from Alisa's shoulders. She shuddered beneath his touch. He lay down and kissed her cheek. She turned away. Nikki unbuttoned his pants and turned her toward him; she lay quivering against him for a moment, then lifted her face for a kiss. His lips came down on her parted lips, and he climbed on top of her, boots and all.

Several moments later, Alisa lifted a provocative glance and whispered seductively, "Do you find me a nuisance to have around?" and moved her bottom deliciously beneath him.

"A nuisance I'm persuaded to retain," he groaned softly, the feel of her heavenly, his erection swelling again, and at that moment he decided marriage to Alisa had its advantages. Long moments later they were both lying exhausted and content in each other's arms.

Lord, this passionate creature would soon be his wife. And an alarming thought crossed his mind. If she had lain so easily with him, had there been others before—or since?

A fierce jealousy possessed him. Would he be justified, he wondered, in keeping her locked in her apartments in Petersburg? Even though the civilized niceties were often paper-thin in Petersburg, such medieval techniques would cause a damnable scandal, he decided. On the other hand, would it matter to the noble Kuzan family if one more scandal were added to their long list? Perhaps the concept was antiquated in the bustling, modern capital city of the Empire. Wives weren't locked up anymore; sent away to remote convents, perhaps, but that recourse, he very selfishly decided, would deprive him of Alisa's companionship and warmth in bed.

Lifting himself on one elbow, he slid out from her heated warmth and fixed Alisa with a piercing scowl of censure. Her face was softly flushed, her eyes dreamily abstract.

"Listen to me," he said evenly, and shook her gently back from the depths of her passion.

"If I ever catch you seriously flirting, I'll shoot your gallant. And if you compromise my name, I'll shoot you." He had no intention of playing the cuckold; he'd have to keep an eye on her; she had tumbled easily enough for him. "Am I perfectly plain?" he inquired sharply.

"Perfectly," she murmured complacently, and sighed,

blissfully sated. Moments later, however, when reality was more real, not entirely happy with the style of his capitulation, she said, pouting, "But you don't love me anymore."

"I love you, dear. There, I've said it again."

But his tone was dismissive, as one would say, "Thank you for coming, the butler will show you out." "You only desire my body," Alisa insisted pettishly. "You command me to obedience and yet you promise nothing of yourself."

"I won't deny I desire your flesh, I'm a man, after all, and you a lush flower of love, and if I promise you nothing, I can't change. I'll give you shelter and food and the luxuries of life; I will see our child wants for nothing. He or she shall have everything money can buy. I can't promise more. I can't promise you I'll love you forever when I don't know. Don't cry," he soothed as tears fell from Alisa's eyes. "We have, right now, more happiness than I've ever dreamed possible. But don't ask me to give up my independence. I cannot."

And remember for both of us, he thought to himself as he tenderly kissed her tears away, remember these blissful, unutterably happy days, these golden summer weeks; remember for both of us because I can't promise for myself.

Nikki was able to momentarily forget the daunting prospect of marriage while involved in the throes and immediate aftermath of making love, but that evening Nikki resorted to several bottles of brandy to escape the impending demise of his bachelorhood. Such finality, it was appalling. Alisa nervously sat beside him, reading, as he gloomily drank himself into oblivion.

The next morning he felt shaky as he hauled himself into the saddle and in a state of philosophic resignation began the journey back to town; two carriages carrying Alisa, her daughter, and servants, the grooms and outriders, fifteen trackers, and a reluctant bridegroom rode forth with two of the trackers flanking him the whole way. They even followed when he stopped to relieve a call of nature.

"Really," Nikki protested. "This 'protection' is quite unnecessary."

"Sorry, Lord Prince," the taller one solemnly intoned. "Orders from Prince Mikhail."

It appeared the old boy was dead serious and Nikki finally resigned himself to the constant company of the two enormous men. They even slept on either side of him with a light leather braid knotted around his waist and their wrists.

Arriving back in town five days later, Alisa was immediately whisked away by Kaisa-leena for dress fittings and other womanly pursuits necessary to organize a gigantic wedding.

Prince Mikhail summoned Nikki to his study within minutes of their return and flatly informed Nikki that he would be married in two days time. The invitations had been delivered and even on such short notice the responses were all in the affirmative. No one ever declined an invitation from Prince Kuzan, and furthermore, this wedding had all the indications of a delicious scandal. It would have been humanly impossible to keep the curious away. Prince Nikolai Kuzan actually marrying; all the servants' gossip hinted at an exceedingly recalcitrant bridegroom and an *enceinte* bride only one week divorced. How delightfully titillating. Whom would the child look like? Most assuredly Nikki, for one could not contemplate for a second his marital capitulation to a woman carrying another man's child. And yet—speculation ran on.

For two days Nikki's bodyguards followed him everywhere; discreetly, of course, in order to arouse as little gossip as possible. On the eve of his wedding, Nikki descended the marble staircase splendidly attired in white linen mufti, for the summer heat had settled on the jewel of the Baltic. His faithful companions at his heels, Nikki stopped on the last step, turned, and glared at the two guards who had stopped respectfully three steps higher, their pleasant faces tranquilly composed in spite of Nikki's obvious displeasure.

"Good God!" Nikki complained irritably. "Enough's enough. I'm just going to my stag tonight and promise on my mother's soul that I'll be back in time for my wedding tomorrow."

Johanos just shrugged his shoulders and spread his hands in apology.

"Sorry, Lord Prince, your father's orders." He stared impassively into space.

"Damnation!" Nikki exploded. "If you say 'father's orders' one more time, Johanos, I swear, I'll do you bodily harm." He strode, cursing, out the door into the summer night, vowing to drink them under the table. Then he'd be free of their unwelcome company.

He should have known better than to attempt to drink a Finnish woodsman under the table. The brandy and champagne flowed freely. All Nikki's fellow officers and friends were bent on teasing him remorselessly as Nikki, whom everyone considered the least likely to succumb to wedded bliss, was about to leave the ranks of bachelorhood.

With a drunken earnestness and a maudlin sentimentality over losing one of his drinking cohorts to Parson's mousetrap, Illyich cornered Nikki late in the evening and whispered conspiratorily, "I never thought you'd do it, Nikki. Why in hell's name do you consider marrying your mistress? I thought your greatest fear was the marriage block."

"That, my dear Astrakan," Nikki replied smoothly, "is

my second greatest fear. The first is that of freezing my vitals off on my father's estate in Siberia."

Illyich's eyebrows rose.

"So you perceive, perhaps, my friend, how things go on at the Kuzans. Although when one considers that half the genius and energy of Russia has been interred in Siberia for two centuries, it's entirely possible that its domestic society has improved, but I prefer not to be put to the necessity of discovering whether this is true," Nikki finished, and the unwelcome thought induced him to refill his glass once again.

"So that's it. My sympathies, *Mon Colonel.*" In his usual kind humor, Illyich attempted to cheer his friend. "But she's very lovely, eh? And warm in bed, I warrant. Things could be worse, Nikki. Think of the advantages."

"Somehow, at the moment, I can see only the disadvantages," Nikki muttered. "A pox on the female sex, Astrakan," he stated sourly. "Here, you need a drink."

Both glasses were refilled and tossed down.

Several hours later one of the youthful officers in Nikki's regiment who was not fully apprised of the true feelings of his colonel made the gaffe of offering his felicitations on the coming nuptials.

"Go to hell!" snarled the Prince.

The following afternoon, a pale and silent Nikki faced his father across the library desk.

"You returned home after dawn. I trust you enjoyed yourself at your bachelor party," Prince Mikhail said in a polite, distant voice.

Nikki lifted his shoulders in an eloquent shrug and remained silent.

"I won't keep you long, so you may retire to gather your strength for the ceremony and festivities this evening.

However, I have a few simple remarks I wish to leave with you.

"You are to see to Alisa and to that other life. I trust I can with confidence leave them in your hands. I hope it is unnecessary to tell you that I expect a tighter bridle on your excesses. I don't care to hear rumors like those already circulating about Vladimir. The Emperor is quite irritated."[11]

Nikki didn't deign to respond.

"I advise you, Nikolai," his father continued, unperturbed, "that I would be pleased if you did not amuse yourself with Sophie again. Although I'm certainly worldly enough to understand that faithfulness is not a necessity in every marriage, indeed in few, apparently, may I remind you that Sophie is brazen enough to possibly cause public embarrassment to Alisa."

"Sophie's not one to be easily put off, Father."

"I wish you to make the effort. She is a decadent slut at all accounts; *une femme facile*, in contrast to Sophie, takes on the aura of saintliness."

"You speak from experience, no doubt?" Nikki's eyebrows rose as he flashed his father a questioning glance.

"Naturally." The Prince didn't lower his gaze.

In spite of himself, Nikki grinned. "I'll be damned! You must admit, sire, she is nonpareil in her bawdy role. A damned fine cunt."

"I am relieved to learn," the old Prince said mildly, "that your heart is not involved."

Nikki laughed harshly, raised a lazy eyebrow, and commented rather caustically, "Hearts are not in Sophie's style, *mon père*, only stiff cocks."

Blandly ignoring this vulgarity, Prince Mikhail tranquilly resumed his lecture. "Your mother and I will retire to the country immediately after the festivities. Take care for the mother of my grandchild." His voice was all the more deadly for not bearing the slightest trace of emotion.

"While I'm all for family, Father, I fear I don't have the dynastic instinct as strongly as you," Nikki replied with a quiet contempt.

"I don't need your impertinence," Prince Mikhail said in that same chilling murmur. "Simply do as you're told and reflect on the consequences of my wrath if you don't."

He waited patiently for ten seconds, and upon receiving no answer, rose from his chair, saying, "Please be on time at the chapel; we are curtailing the service in order to alleviate any unnecessary standing for Alisa." He walked from the room, leaving Nikki slumped in his chair.

Nikki sat there for almost half an hour, his mind blank of any thoughts or emotions, his body fatigued from the long night of drinking. Hauling himself to his feet, he retraced his steps to his room and fell into a deep, exhausted sleep. The next thing he knew, he was being shaken awake. His bath had been prepared and all his silk finery spread out ready for dressing.

Within the hour Nikki was traversing the numerous hallways and passageways that led to the family chapel. His cousin Aleksei and Aleksei's brother were standing as witness for him and followed closely on his heels as he strode rapidly and mindlessly to his wedding. The chapel was small, holding no more than two hundred persons. When Nikki entered the gilded and stuccoed room flooded with the flickering light of thousands of candles and perfumed with the scent of tens of thousands of flowers, a sigh broke from the assembled guests. He was fifteen minutes late.

Nikki strolled across the front of the chapel and took his place under a large canopy of trelliswork interwoven with orchids. That moment Alisa reached the main door and began to walk down the aisle. A beautiful chant began. She was breathtakingly flawless in a crème-colored silk overlaid with deep flounces of magnificent lace, her pregnancy perfectly concealed beneath the current fashionable tunic which draped yards of material gracefully across the skirt front and pulled it all in successive folds to the back of the waistline. The increasing waistline, which had been the despair of Madame Vevay, was hardly evident to anyone who had not known Alisa's original lithe slenderness. A small tiara of diamonds set with cameos (a gift from Prince Mikhail) crowned her red-gold coiffure and held in place the yards-long hand-made lace veil, valued at one thousand roubles an arshin. The veil was of the most exquisite texture, the design of roses and lilies so truthfully wrought that the flowers seemed raised from the surface. Full twenty feet trailed gracefully behind. A pendant necklace of emeralds from Nikki was around her neck, and Aleksei's gift of diamond earrings hung from her ears.

Nikki caught his breath and paused to absorb her beauty, then stepped forward boldly and took her hand in his, drawing a quiet, subdued bride to his side. They both stood on a strip of satin and were given a lighted candle to hold, which they retained throughout the service. The priests wore dark blue velvet, much embroidered in silver, and began reading the ceremony.

Nikki and Alisa both put rings on their right hands, a glass of wine was given them, out of which they both drank in turns three times, the priest holding it. Then elaborate golden crowns were brought in, which the officiating priests waved before them and which were then held over their heads by the best man, who became very tired and had to change arms. The priest began to deliver a long and beautiful recitative portion of the service in a magnificent bass voice, but abruptly cut the anthem short after a meaningful curt nod from Prince Mikhail. Nikki's father had been keenly observing Alisa, and noted a slight pallor beginning to appear.

The ceremony was blessedly abbreviated, and after intoning the benediction, the deep voice of the Russian Orthodox priest pronounced them married before the eyes of God.

Alisa clung to Nikki's arm as they passed from the chapel, feeling faint from the closeness of the small room filled with people and heavy with the sweet odor of flowers and incense. Nikki hadn't exchanged more than a dozen words with Alisa in the past two days, for despite his attempt to graciously accept the imperious commands of his father, a nagging anger consumed his thoughts.

Rationally, Nikki realized that Alisa was just as much a victim of this farce as he, perhaps more, because she was burdened with an unborn child. But judiciousness wasn't holding sway in his emotions lately, and he quite unjustifiably and irrationally blamed Alisa for his predicament.

"Chin up, my dear," Nikki whispered sarcastically as he pulled Alisa's trembling body up with a tight grasp under her arm. "You wouldn't want to faint before all these pantingly inquisitive guests."

"I wouldn't feel like fainting now if you could learn to keep your pants buttoned up," she hissed petulantly as Nikki single-handedly held her upright and guided her out into the hall.

"Remember the old proverb, my love. A dog doesn't worry an unwilling bitch," he retorted ignobly, and Alisa blanched visibly at the bitterly insulting remark.

Now she did look ready to faint. Quickly, Nikki slipped his arm under her knees, picked her up, walked rapidly to a curving staircase, and ran up a flight of stairs. Once out of sight of the hundreds of guests, he continued more slowly to Alisa's room, the long train and veil billowing behind them. She rested gratefully against Nikki's black silk lapels.

Discordant emotions raced through both their minds. Nikki wanted her and didn't want her, afraid of permanence, while Alisa wanted him at all cost and deplored her submission and bondage. But she was mostly aware of a desperate fatigue; she was tired of parrying Nikki's acid remarks or frigid indifference, and she was too weary to fence off any more verbal ripostes. Her sensibilities were bludgeoned, her nerves frayed. Nothing mattered anymore. She was beyond hostility, beyond apology, beyond caring for pride. She was in his arms, comforted by his strong embrace. It was the only place she longed to be.

Walking into her room, Nikki laid her on the bed, strode into his chamber next door, and returned within seconds with a bottle of brandy and two glasses. Quickly pouring Alisa a glass, he plumped up the pillows behind her, arranged her unprotesting form in a half-reclining position, and handed over the glass.

Pulling up a chair near the bed, Nikki sat down with the bottle and the other glass, poured himself a full bumper, put his long legs up on the satin counterpane, and said mockingly in his casual drawl, "Shall we both sheath our talons and attempt to amiably muddle through this charade. It seems you are mine now for the rest of our lives, and one must survive, after all. To our future, dear. Do you think we have one?" he jibed in a soft murmur, noting the still-pallid color of Alisa's complexion.

"Am I supposed to beg for your favors?" Her voice was scarcely audible. "I won't, Nikki—so the future is in your hands."

His golden eyes held hers, for a long moment and then instead of answering, he casually said, "You'd better drink your brandy quickly, or you won't last many minutes more, my dear. You look quite pale." Lifting his glass in salute, Nikki drained it in one swallow. Over the rim of the glass he held her eyes for another long, speculative moment, his glance cool, measured, unreadable. Alisa found she could not look away, transfixed by the depths of those golden eyes. Was it possible she'd discerned an unease registered briefly? The expression closed abruptly, his eyelids fell, his hand reaching out to refill his empty glass. The moment was over.

"Come now," he insisted half kindly in his natural lazy tone, "you must summon the necessary energy to withstand the lengthy receiving line of our well-wishers."

Obediently Alisa drank slowly; the liquor burned down her throat and coursed through her bloodstream, soon reviving her failing senses.

With an amiable courtesy Nikki entertained Alisa quite cheerfully for the next twenty minutes, single-handedly emptying two-thirds of the bottle while Alisa's color returned. Alisa glanced at Nikki, comfortably sprawled in his chair, and smiled faintly. "You're appearing less irate about this marriage."

"Alisa, my sweet, I'm becoming more reconciled to the prospect by the moment." The brandy and Alisa's serenity had improved his humor.

They were interrupted just as Nikki was about to kick off his shoes, thinking, to hell with the guests. Alisa looked so radiantly lovely, perhaps they should start the honeymoon immediately. His irritations could seldom withstand the dual pressures of plentiful liquor and a languorous female within reach in bed.

Princess Kaisa-leena opened the door, and stepping halfway over the threshold, inquired solicitously, "Do you feel well enough to come down? The guests are impatient to toast the bride and groom."

Nikki smothered a curse in deference to his mother and dropped his patent-leather-clad feet to the floor. He extended his hand to Alisa. "Shall we, my dear?" he inquired pleasantly.

Alisa and Nikki stood in the receiving line next to Prince Mikhail and Princess Kaisa-leena for over an hour, greeting the guests to the accompaniment of the mechanical phrases necessary to the occasion—*"Enchantée,"* "So nice to meet you," "Thank you so much."

Several grand dukes of both generations attended, and after watching Alisa sink into a deep curtsey for a second grand duke, Nikki satirically murmured, "You won't be able to curtsey that low much longer, my blooming young wife; your belly will get in the way."

Alisa cast him a wrathful look of indignation, and Nikki smothered a chuckle as he turned to greet yet another distinguished guest. Several moments later Major Cernov paused before them and, taking Alisa's hand in his, raised it to his lips. He held it for a moment longer than necessary while he murmured suggestively, "You're more lovely each time I see you, Madame."

"You honor me with the compliment, Monsieur," Alisa replied flirtatiously, paying Nikki back for his mockery, while Nikki stood at her side, wondering what would happen if he smashed Cernov square in the mouth. He restrained the urge, for that would be a ripe piece of gossip indeed, the bridegroom fighting a rival at his wedding.

Abruptly Nikki turned to his parents and said, "We are done with these civilities. If anyone else wants to congratulate us, they can put it in writing. Come, my dear, you look fatigued." Gripping Alisa's elbow, he drew her to him, reestablishing possession, and whisked her away to a quiet alcove, where he snapped his fingers for a footman carrying a tray of champagne glasses.

"Put the tray down," Nikki said, and motioned at the table beside the sofa. Quite oblivious of his responsibilities to his guests, Nikolai Kuzan proceeded to empty the contents of the glasses while he grimly clasped Alisa's hand as she sat next to him on the green satin upholstery. He burned with jealousy at Cernov's remark and swore aloud several times between draining glasses while he dwelt on the gall of his old friend. Damn his impudence! Alisa enjoyed this indication of jealousy after having endured Nikki's bland indifference for so many days.

With his usual disregard for the courtesies of society, just as the dinner guests were filing into the supper room for the magnificent array of dishes produced by the Kuzan chef, Nikki pulled Alisa to her feet and pushed her ahead of him through the throng of well-wishers and up the stairs to the nuptial bed.

Quite foxed by this time, Nikki couldn't decide which bed to use for this momentous occasion—the termination of his bachelorhood and the beginning of his husbandly duties. Should he use the bed in his room or the one in Alisa's? Solving the dilemma by deciding to take turns in both, he hastily disrobed himself, pulled off Alisa's voluminous gown, and eased off her petticoats as she giggled from the several glasses of champagne he'd pressed on her.

Picking Alisa up, they collapsed on the bed, kissing and laughing. Then he kissed her long and carefully, fondling her ripe body until she trembled beneath him, threw her arms around his neck, and eased herself beneath his throbbing stiffness, entering into the spirited loveplay with abandon. They were always in amorous accord regardless of their other differences and it was no sense of husbandly duty or adherence to his father's admonitions that kept Nikki near his wife all night.

The following morning, Prince Mikhail and Princess Kaisa-leena took their leave for Le Repose amid kisses and hugs, exclamations of fondness and kind good wishes, with the exception of Nikki and his father, who stiffly and formally bade good-bye to each other, the strain in their relationship painfully clear.

As his carriage passed through the dusty streets of the city, Prince Mikhail relaxed his stern, forbidding expression, reached over, clasped the small hand of his wife sitting beside him, and said wearily, "I hope I've done right by that young woman. Have I been too harsh to insist on their marriage?"

"No, Misha, our son resists the fact that he loves her; he'll come to accept it someday, and Alisa loves Nikki, of that I'm sure. It's important for the coming child to have both a mother and a father. Don't despair, all will be well," she said quietly, and patted his large, strong hand. Silently she whispered a Tzigane charm for the happiness of the union, for she knew how unyielding, independent, and demanding Nikki could be. Like his father.

"I won't interfere again," the Prince sighed unhappily. "Perhaps if left alone, they'll build a life together for our future grandchild." Secretly he was not very hopeful, but at least the child would have a name, and the vast assets and resources of the Kuzan family as its patrimony. Money couldn't buy happiness, but at least it offered luxury in one's despair, the old prince reflected cynically.

Before many weeks had passed in the pink marble palace on the Millionnaya, Nikki began to fall into his old habits. At first he had grudgingly but dutifully run the rounds of parties, drums, balls, and picnics with Alisa, but always bored, indifferent, and obviously discontent as he either stood on the sidelines, drinking and watching Alisa, or else disappeared into the card room for hours. In less than a month he no longer made an attempt to hide the fact that he found these functions intolerable.

Aleksei had more and more taken his place as escort, and lately almost exclusively squired Alisa to the festivities she chose to attend. Aleksei adored Alisa with the dogged infatuation of youth and was ever ready and eager to indulge her whims. Alisa appreciated Aleksei's youthful spirits and candor and thanked him with heartfelt sincerity for being a companion to her. His was a friendship she valued all the more as Nikki's interests drifted away to other pursuits.

Aleksei raged inwardly at the callous indifference and discourteous treatment Nikki gave his wife, but kept his indignant thoughts to himself. A verbal brawl with Nikki would accomplish nothing for Alisa's happiness, and in the cool tenor of Nikki's current mood, he didn't want to risk being forbidden the freedom of the house and Alisa's company. The young man fretted but held his tongue.

Soon Nikki began staying away from home nights, comfortably easing back into the habits of twenty years. Alisa sobbed in sorrow and rage the first time it happened. The pain Nikki saw in her face forced him to hurl back at her with a suppressed ferocity, "Damn you, stop whining! You knew what I was like when you married me! Did you not?" And then his voice dropped to a chilling murmur. "My whoring and drinking were well known to you, Madame, before you chose to become my mistress and then my wife. Surely it's not a shock to your delicate sensibilities. Do not, at this late date, become full of nonsense about honorable and virtuous conduct. You were hardly a model of propriety yourself."

"You need not insult me," Alisa whispered unhappily.

"By God, a *femme facile* can be insulted now," he said, wishing to hurt. "What next? Rockets to the moon, no doubt."

"But"—his eyes narrowed dangerously—"do not consider flirtations, Madame, or that you have a freedom of— hmm—shall we say—outside friendships. I've warned you in that respect. No man touches my wife. Whatever children are born of this marriage will be Kuzan by parentage as well as by name. And I would appreciate, Madame, in the future, if you would have the goodness to refrain from concerning yourself in my affairs."

Alisa cried in private at Nikki's casual freedom, but if

she sometimes renewed that line of conversation, he simply walked away, so as the weeks progressed, she accepted his behavior because she had no other choice. But she wanted to scream, Go away! Go away! If you don't care for me, go away! Why should she be forced to suffer his reluctant forbearance as life companion. But the growing child, now kicking in her womb, the need for some security in a thoroughly male-dominated world, required that she accept the grudgingly offered hand.

How can he be the same man? she thought with despair. Previously he was capable of great kindness, so gentle yet so passionate when she was his mistress. Now he was cool, indifferent, an unresponsive man who happened to live in the same residence. She was paying a high price for her child's name. Once the seed is planted, a man can ignore, or circumvent, or disavow; paternity is an elusive state, but the receiver of his "gift" has no such option.

Alisa decided to make the best of this imperfect world. She would not retire from life, but chose instead to devote herself to Katelina and, in the future, to the new child as well. Her second child would have a name too. Her husband, though it wrenched her heart to conceive of it, could resume his former life—apparently he already had. But she wouldn't humiliate herself and beg for crumbs of affection.

And yet, she often broke into an uncontrollable torrent of unhappy tears. Her mind couldn't control her wounded heart.

Nikki never visited her bed anymore. She knew his need for women, and her heart was consumed with pain at the thought.

Nikki spent his evenings gambling at the clubs, silent, taciturn, grim, quick to anger, while his friends remarked that marriage must not be agreeing with Nikolai Kuzan. He'd even missed the annual war games at Tsarskoe late that summer, pleading an extended leave for reasons of health. The easy masculine camaraderie of the officers would have been intolerable in his present humor.

He was drinking deep, and whispers warned to stay clear of Prince Kuzan; he was primed for trouble. When tired of brandy and gambling, Nikki could invariably be found in one of several Kirgiz night cafés on the islands, drinking black coffee with lemon essence and opium, sweetened with sherbet, or smoking hashish. Both drugs soothed his frustrations, mellowed his irritations, and assuaged his melancholy.

He would, with studied punctuality, arrive home before Katelina wakened and wait for her in the morning room, where she would run down to chatter with Nikki while eating her breakfast. Dressed in his evening clothes, he would wait by the dying fire, feeling no sense of urgency or anything beyond a detached, dreamy interest in seeing his favorite moppet.

Nikki was considerate of Katelina in every way, bringing her lavish quantities of toys and giving every attention to her dialogue. When it was time for Katelina's lessons in the morning, Nikki would retire to his bedchamber and sleep the day away, rising in time to join Alisa and Katelina for dinner in the enormous formal dining room. Dressed once more for an evening out, he would gossip cheerfully with Katelina while talking with a polite civility to Alisa. Once Katelina was tucked in bed, he disappeared for the night without a word of explanation.

One evening at the dinner table, Alisa gathered her courage to ask Nikki if he would be available for a dancing party she was giving at the end of the week. He hesitated briefly, asked again what day it was to be held, and then said with his customary cool voice, "I'll contrive to attend, Madame. Please remind my valet the morning of the occasion to wake me in time to dress."

· · ·

Alisa was dressed and waiting in the drawing room the night of the party when Nikki sauntered into the room at ten o'clock, carrying a glass of brandy, already his fourth since putting Katelina to bed. He was attired with his usual negligent elegance in a superbly fitted brown velvet suit that showed his magnificent body off to advantage. An enormous turquoise and diamond pin fastened his carelessly tied cravat and sparkled in the brilliantly lit room. Alisa couldn't help herself as a press of confusing emotions smothered her. Nikki's presence still took her breath away, and she was conscious of an unavoidable stirring of admiration.

Casting one desultory glance at the splendid exotic floral arrangements that graced the room, he walked across the polished parquet, stopped halfway into the room, and in a slow drawl remarked, "May I compliment you on your toilette, Madame? You are shown off to excellent advantage this evening."

A warm glow blazed through Alisa at these first complimentary words she had heard from Nikki in weeks. Was he really proud of her good looks? In the fifth month of her pregnancy, Alisa was wearing a slightly Empire gown of emerald-green satin with ruching and ruffles of green velvet and embroidered Byzantine brocade decorating the flounces of green satin and outlining the décolletage. Her beautiful breasts now further enlarged by pregnancy were swelling magnificently above the green satin bodice. Nikki's emeralds rested on the soft mounds of flesh while the enormous pendant hung suspended in her deep cleavage. A wreath of white violets and green velvet ribbon was woven into her fashionable upswept curls.

Alisa's warm glow was short-lived as Nikki tartly said, "However, may I caution you not to bend over too far, or you may fall out of your gown." A slow anger rose in him at the sight of so much of Alisa's flesh exposed to the public eye, but he restrained his waxing jealousy and tossed off his brandy instead. Walking over to a side table, he refilled his glass, then perched on the edge of the table, idly swinging one velvet-clad leg.

"Décolletage is fashionable, as you well know," Alisa coolly replied.

"Indiscretions are fashionable too, Madame, but that doesn't mean you're allowed one," Nikki insolently retorted.

Receiving no answer save a narrowed glance from hot violet eyes, Nikki continued. "May I offer you a brandy, Princess. Personally, I find a need to fortify myself against the coming ordeal."

"If you please, Lord Prince," Alisa retorted formally. "I, too, feel the need of a drink."

They sat for twenty minutes, drinking their liquor in a strained silence before the first guests arrived, walking up the grand marble stairway flanked by twenty-four footmen wearing the Kuzan livery, and were announced by two chasseurs at the doors to the ballroom.

Alisa, frustrated by Nikki's contemptuous stares, drank rather more than usual and was soon flirting outrageously with several of the young gentlemen who paid her court. She was constantly being complimented as the most beautiful woman in Petersburg, and tonight she was in a dangerous mood to accept the flattery as she danced with the young officers and drank champagne with the ardent gentlemen surrounding her.

She even greeted Major Cernov cordially as he came over to pay his compliments and gaze down her low neckline. Alisa smiled at him sweetly, thinking how easily men could be diverted by a pink expanse of bosom.

Nikki stood apart with some of his friends from the

Yacht Club, pouring brandy down with great regularity and only occasionally listening to the conversation concerning the merits of the two new *danseuses* in the *corps dramatique*. His eyes followed Alisa around the room, and his temper rose as the evening progressed. He watched Alisa darting flirtatious glances at young gallants, thinking she was his wife, dammit, and he put away some more brandy as he considered the infamy of her actions.

When Cernov began bending rather too closely to Alisa's dainty ear while leering down her cleavage, Nikki took a drunken resolve.

Vile little slut, teasing Cernov with your heaving bosom. He excused himself from his friends with a studied politeness and slowly sauntered across the room toward Alisa and Cernov, followed by several curious eyes in the group he had just quit.

"Good evening, Gregor," Nikki said quietly, breathing brandy everywhere.

"We will not detain you, Cernov," he said in a cold murmur. "I'm sure you're eager to join your friends." With a short nod he dismissed him. With the immeasurable arrogance instilled in a thousand years of Kuzan nobility, Nikki turned his head the merest fraction and a footman came scurrying out of the noisy crowd.

"Princess Kuzan is feeling indisposed and desires to retire to her apartments. Please escort her."

Alisa had no choice. If she refused, Nikki was entirely capable of provoking a scene in front of her three hundred guests. She went, her anger blazing high.

Experienced host that he was, Nikki signaled the musicians to begin again, abruptly breaking the still hush of expectancy that hung in the enormous ballroom. Nikki left immediately after, taking himself to the Kirgiz café, while the guests continued to dance without either host or hostess, and only a delicious scandal to occupy them.

Early the next morning, as the horizon lightened to a shimmering pink, feeling mildly apologetic for his drunken peremptory conduct the evening before, Nikki woke up a furrier on his way home and purchased some gifts for Alisa and Katelina. He'd promised himself last spring he'd dress Alisa in sables, and the weather was coming on winter. Snow could be expected in a few weeks.

When Katelina and Alisa arrived in the morning room for breakfast, Nikki occupied his usual comfortable chair by the fire, still dressed in brown velvet. Katelina scrambled onto his lap and began exclaiming over all the flowers still decorating the palace and Chef's promise to serve party food for breakfast.

"Come, Uncle Nikki." She paused. "I mean—Isa," she remembered quickly. Nikki had insisted on adopting her. Strong-arm methods, in addition to a small fortune, had persuaded Forseus to sign the consent papers. He'd explained to Katelina in the Finnish language Katelina preferred to speak that she was to call him "Father" now that he had married her mother. Katelina had gaily clapped her hands in delight and remembered on most occasions to make the change from uncle to father.

"Come, Daddy," she implored him, "and eat some party food with me."

"Look first at the presents I have for you and your mother," Nikki insisted.

"You should eat some breakfast, Nikki," Alisa suggested as she sat across the room, noting his appearance. He looked pale, more fatigued than usual.

"Very wifely, I'm sure," he commented ironically, but ignored her suggestion. "Bring those to your mother." He handed two enormous boxes to Katelina. She brought first one and then the other to Alisa, who was seated at the table, watching Nikki and Katelina. Why can't Nikki share some of that kindness and love with me? she thought sadly.

He blames me for the marriage, but if I had known how miserable he was going to be, I would have refused. We were so happy those few weeks in the country. Now she was like some alien presence in his town palace, an albatross of duty around his neck.

Katelina was tearing off the silver wrapping and pulling out a gorgeous ermine cape with matching hat and muff trimmed with white velvet ribbons. Nikki helped her put on the new ermine finery, and she whirled around the room, jumping on a chair to gaze at her image in a mirror, then ran out of the room, looking for Rakeli to show off her new outfit.

Alisa slowly unwrapped the largest box and exclaimed in wonder at the splendid sable cape ensconced in silk tissue. Nikki lounged in his chair, watching her.

"Try it on," he ordered quietly, and Alisa's momentary happiness was shattered by his tone of command, however softly spoken. "I want my wife to be adequately dressed," he added.

That's all he cares about, she thought hotly, remembering her unhappy departure last evening from her *own* party.

She tossed the cape around her shoulders and sullenly turned around, the superbly soft fur whispering as it twirled.

Nikki smiled faintly. He preferred her petulance to the moroseness she'd affected lately. "Open the other one," he prompted her.

Alisa ripped the wrapping violently aside and lifted out a short, snug-fitting, waist-length jacket of ermine trimmed with seed pearls.

"I can't wear it," she said with malicious delight at being able to refuse his gift. "It's too tight. It won't fit while I'm pregnant."

"Forgive me, a man's unpracticed eye, I'm afraid. Such a pity. Perhaps you can save it for Katelina when she grows older, for it won't fit you next winter either."

"It certainly will," Alisa replied waspishly. "I haven't gained that much weight. My figure will be quite returned by next winter."

"So sorry to disappoint you, Madame, but my father is so set on legitimate heirs, I intend to punctiliously demonstrate my filial piety and keep you pregnant. If he wants heirs, he shall have heirs."

"You aren't going to use me for a brood mare!" Alisa exploded angrily.

"I'll allow you a two-month rest after the birth of this child, but," he warned, "I shall plant my seed in you once again."

"The only part for which you are providentially qualified, no doubt," Alisa said scathingly.

"No doubt," Nikki agreed equably, "and a gratifying part, I might add, with your soft, luscious body as participant. Ah," he sighed lightly, a smile playing across his handsome face, "I quite look forward to my duties as stud for the Kuzan family and intend to pursue my function with great assiduity. If you do your part, Madame, little Kuzans should arrive with punctual regularity."

And so in this acrimonious, malevolent atmosphere of wedded bliss, the young Prince and his wife continued. As the weeks flew by, Alisa became ungainly and awkward as the child grew. She relinquished most of her social activities and remained home with Katelina and occasionally Aleksei for company. Nikki persisted in his carefree bachelor life, solicitous to Katelina, but indifferent to his wife, now great with child.

Prince Mikhail, with his usual host of reliable informants, was kept apprised of the movements of his son and family. He was told that Nikki was living like there was no tomorrow, drunk or sleeping most of the hours of the day and night, while he and his wife had no more than a nodding acquaintance. Prince Mikhail wondered how long it had been since Nikki was sober. The old Prince viewed the situation with deepening, grievous concern. Not sure of his son's reception, he had Kaisa-leena write to inquire whether they would be welcome for Christmas and received from Nikki a polite but clear "no," explaining Alisa's delicate health made entertaining impossible as she approached the end of her term.

Prince Mikhail, now greatly distressed, decided to wait until after the birth of the child, and if the marriage didn't improve and Alisa was genuinely unhappy, he would offer to help her in obtaining a divorce. The procedure was eminently simplified by his friendship with the Emperor. He simply couldn't have Alisa's wretched misery on his conscience. He'd foolishly hoped for a reconciliation between his son and Alisa, but Nikki stubbornly refused to give up his licentious living. He would leave the choice to Alisa. Whatever she wanted, he would support her decision.

Nikki, Alisa, and Katelina spent a quiet Christmas. Nikki indulged Alisa's request to celebrate the holiday in the Lutheran fashion, since Katelina was familiar with those activities, so the festivities lasted many days, beginning with Christmas Eve on December 24 and continuing through the Russian Christmas on January 6. Katelina was deluged with enough gifts to fill a room and accepted the largesse with equanimity.

Nikki presented Alisa with a three-strand necklace of extremely rare black pearls. The black pearl, the jeweler had explained, was now the summit of every *elegante*'s ambition, and due to its rarity was the most expensive jewel to adorn a lady's jewel case.

A second gift of a large photo portrait of Katelina had been contrived after many whispered conferences between father and daughter. Nikki had taken Katelina for two sittings at the fashionable "artistic photographer" at No. 4 Morskaija, until they were both satisfied with the portrait. A mischievous face framed in ermine peered seraphically from behind a frothy muff, and Katelina had signed the photo with her unsteady five-year-old hand.

An unpleasant stab of guilt struck Nikki as he accepted Alisa's gift to him; a watercolor sketch she had done at Mon Plaisir the past summer. A wash of warm memories enveloped Nikki, and a reminiscent smile softened his harsh-featured face for a brief moment.

Nikki actually stayed home several nights in a row to spend the holiday with his winsome daughter. He read her Christmas stories and joined in the songs, surprising everyone by singing them from memory. He remembered his own early Christmases with a child's memory and tried to give some of that delight to Katelina. With a rueful pang he had to admit that these evenings *en famille* offered a contentment and satisfaction that no liquor or opium could promote. How long had it been since he'd sung Christmas songs?

Alisa was pleased to have Nikki sitting with her before the fire, and her emotions leapt in happiness to have him near. She resolutely steeled herself to expect his disappearance soon, but she would bask unreservedly in the luxury of his kindness and company while she could.

Nikki watched Alisa as she read to Katelina or played the piano while they sang, and marveled anew at the beauty and charm of this woman who was his wife. He would find himself occasionally lapsing into recollections of their weeks at Mon Plaisir or in vague musings about the child she was carrying. Alisa was charming in cashmere dresses of a loose, flowing style suitable for ladies "awaiting a blessed event," as Madame Vevay so delicately put it.

For the first time in his life he thought about becoming a father. He even felt a kindly concern for Alisa's travail, soon to begin. She was small and fragile and the child was already extremely large. He must ask about her doctor, he considered absently, and then was coaxed into joining them in play and forgot the subject.

However, with Christmas over, Nikki embarked once again on his chronic, restless rounds of gambling and drinking, descending a little further into his own private hell. His melancholy deepened, his drinking increased, his boredom he could have cut with a knife.

Chapter Fifteen
THE VOLTE-FACE

Returning home at his usual early hour one morning, Nikki found the palace already a bustle of activity. Maids were running up the stairs, footmen were scurrying on errands, even Sergei momentarily forgot to divest his master of his sable topcoat, gloves, and walking stick, instead, blurting out forthwith, "I'm so glad to see you, Lord Prince, we were not able to locate you last night."

Nikki gripped Sergei's shoulder in alarm when he heard the nervous protestation.

"What's the matter, Sergei?"

"The Mistress, sir, she went into labor last evening and is having difficulty."

"Where's the damn doctor?" Nikki roared as he dug his fingers into Sergei and shook him. "The doctor is here,

Lord Prince, but says he can do nothing. The baby is too large. It will not come."

Nikki released his hold on Sergei, tossed his gloves and stick aside, and raced up the steps, bursting furiously into Alisa's bedroom. The drapes were drawn, the room was stifling, gaslights burned low in all the fixtures. Rushing to the bedside, Nikki looked fearfully at Alisa's still form. Her skin was translucently pale, her fists clung weakly to sheets tied to the bedposts above her head, small beads of sweat lined her upper lip, and damp hair curled around her pallid face.

"Where's the damned doctor?" Nikki spat out to Maria, hovering near. Alisa's eyelids didn't even flutter at the sound of his voice. Holy Mother, was she dead already? He quickly bent to feel her pulse. It was extremely weak but not irregular.

"Where's the doctor?" he repeated in a louder whisper as he shrugged out of his fur coat, suffocating in this hot, close room. He twirled around and searched the darkened room.

"Here, Lord Prince." A little man moved forward. Nikki eyed him belligerently.

"What in hell's going on?" he growled in a repressed roar.

The poor doctor wrung his hands in panic. Prince Kuzan's temper was notorious. This Prince could send him to Siberia within the hour if he so chose. Dare he tell him the truth? Dare he tell him the child was too large and wouldn't be born? He could cut the woman open and probably save the child, but not all women survived that surgery, and she was very weak already. Without the surgery, both mother and child would die.

"Well, Doctor?" Nikki asked impatiently as he glared down at the hesitant, uncertain figure.

The little man decided on the truth. If worse came to

worst, he could appeal to Prince Mikhail, who had a reputation for justice.

"Have you no tongue?" Nikki demanded furiously.

The doctor gravely told him the truth; at best, he might be able to save the child. He could do no more.

Nikki, in a blinding rage, picked up the little man bodily and flung him out the door, then he roared for Ivan and all the servants. Within seconds a crowd was assembled around him.

"I want every midwife in the city here within ten minutes!" he bellowed. "Ivan, check with that incompetent who calls himself a doctor and get names and addresses. Send out the troikas to pick them up. Immediately!" he stormed, and swung back into the bedroom.

The stable boys set a new record that morning harnessing up the troikas, and as the last buckle was wrenched into place, the drivers lashed the horses and sped off, the sleighs flying over the crisp white snow.

Within ten minutes the first midwife appeared, and within twenty minutes a score of women were standing in the hallway outside Alisa's room.

Nikki, who had been watching Alisa in an agony of despair and fear, returned to the hallway and scrutinized the assembled women. Several he dismissed on the spot as being too dirty and pushed the others into the room to Alisa.

After examining her, most of the women shook their heads and refused to touch her. They believed she was going to die anyway, and if they assisted, they would be blamed when she died. None of them cared to incur the wrath of Prince Kuzan.

One woman said very simply, "There's not much hope, Lord Prince, she's very weak, the baby is much too large, but I'll try."

His world reeled madly. No hope? Alisa would die? All

his wealth and power were helpless. Despair opened like a black chasm. He resolutely shook it off. Nikki released his breath which he'd been unconsciously holding, dismissed the other women with a wave of his hand, and in a voice deep with emotion said, "If you cannot save them both, sacrifice the child; take it out any way you have to; I don't care, but I will not lose my wife. Do you hear?" he whispered fiercely. "I will not lose my wife!"

The woman shuddered at the piercing eyes staring at her and couldn't answer such a statement. Was he mad?

Alisa lay in a deep, unconscious state from which she would frequently drift up and hear the muted words and quiet sobs of the servants, the whispers and the questioning voices. Time became disjointed, erratic; fragmented vignettes fluctuated madly, images of her and Nikki at Mon Plaisir, mindless longing for peaceful oblivion from the pain, visions of the pine forests and clover fields of her childhood. Take me away, take me back. There must be something more than this wrenching, brutal, unnatural pain—this unbearable agony of labor.

Why, she moaned, had she ever lain with Nikki in that spring meadow and wanted him to make love to her? She had forgotten how painful, how devastatingly wicked, how agonizing the contractions of labor were. The pain crept over her slowly and then sank in like fangs of a crazed animal, ripping and tearing her apart until she screamed in frenzy. She would cling to the sheets, pulling until her arms ached with the effort, twisting, turning, trying to elude the monstrous, ruthless, unceasing beast.

Now nothing hurt anymore. She floated powerless in a sequence of dreams and blackness and whispered sobs. She's dying. The baby won't come. Dear God, was she dying? Was it she they were whispering about? She wanted to see Nikki and Katelina. I have to explain to Katelina. She's so young. She won't understand. She wanted to see

Nikki. Nikki! she screamed, Nikki! In her floating world and to those around the bed a pitiful faint whisper spoke— Nikki.

"I'm here, my love," he answered brokenly, and she opened her eyes slowly, and in a golden haze of light his swarthy face, those tawny eyes, looked lovingly into hers. Her hand fluttered up to touch him, but she hadn't the strength to lift it.

"I love you," he whispered. She smiled faintly at those words she'd not heard for many months. She tried to say I love you too, but the sound wouldn't come.

What were they doing to her body? Don't touch me, she wanted to say, leave me alone. The blackness enveloped her golden haze and she thought how remarkable that a dead woman can still hurt so.

The midwife was instructing Nikki quietly. "Press down on her stomach, she has no more strength for contractions. I'll work my fingers in and try to force the baby's cranial plates together. If we can just inch the head through, we can pull the baby free."

She ruthlessly cut the opening wider. Her sensitive fingers edged into Alisa, probing and pressing, feeling for the bony plates that would compress and ease the size of the skull. For three minutes she worked, sweat dripping from her brow. Nikki did what he was told, exerting pressure on Alisa's swollen abdomen when commanded, repeating to himself in a hopeless inaudible monotone, Help her. Help her, God. Sweet Jesus and all the Saints, help her.

At last the fullness of the baby's head slid through, and a great sigh was heard around the room. Nikki's bitter despair lifted, and he dared to hope. Very slowly the midwife guided out first one small shoulder, then the second, the long torso emerged, and finally the chubby legs. The baby was a boy; fat, healthy, and now vigorously bawling in a nurse's arms.

Nikki scarcely glanced at the child whose birth might have come at too high a price. Alisa's hands had released their limp grip on the sheets. He looked up at the midwife.

"Will she live now?" he asked with a look of anguish, desperately afraid of the answer.

"She's young, Lord Prince, and if no hemorrhaging begins, she has a chance."

"Thank you," he said quietly. "For your work today, you shall live in comfort the rest of your life. And if my wife lives, all the generations of your family will never want. I can't lose her." Nikki moaned and his great dark head bowed over the bed as he wept unashamedly.

He kept a vigil through the night, not daring to sleep for fear the faint breathing would stop; offering a thousand penances to God if he would let her live; invoking every charm and superstition and childhood prayer to succor the frail, battered body of his wife.

In the awful hell of guilt and shame tearing at his brain, one thought reeled over and over, I love her and she cannot die. And now he knew he had loved her from the first, even while he suppressed and denied the human passion within himself. He'd never intended to love her, had sworn never to love any woman again, didn't intend for her to fall in love with him. It began as sport, a game to idle the time away, and now he couldn't help himself. Was it too late now, too late to try to make her happy, to give her the love she deserved?

He dropped his head into his hands and whispered, "Please God, let her live. . . ."

Hours later, in the lightening dawn, Alisa's eyelids fluttered open and Nikki jumped from his chair. Her eyes moved to the figure bending over her and she saw Nikki through a golden haze.

"Is the baby born?" she whispered weakly.

"Yes, love, a boy." He reached for her limp hand.

Her eyes sparkled in triumph. "You have your heir." She smiled faintly.

At too high a price, Nikki agonized, but smiled in return and simply said softly, "Thank you, love, for a fine son. Is there anything at all you want? Anything in the whole world?"

Alisa smiled again and whispered faintly, "Will you stay home some nights now?"

"Every night," he promised, and thought, just live so I can stay home with you every night. Just live!

"It was worth it, then . . ." Her words trailed off as she gave a contented smile and sank back into a deep, untroubled sleep.

Nikki stayed by her bedside night and day for three days. Her pulse was weak but never failed. He talked briefly to Katelina each morning and then immediately returned to his vigil. He was unkempt and haggard, gaunt, exhausted, but now, on the third day, hopeful. Alisa hadn't hemorrhaged and he'd been able to feed her some light broth the previous day. He could almost dare be optimistic.

Nikki had sent for his parents immediately after the birth of his son, and his mother had competently taken charge in the nursery. At first seeing his father, Nikki had begun to apologize, but Prince Mikhail brushed aside his attempts indulgently. "Apologies aren't necessary, my son. I, too, was young and fiercely independent once. I only hope you can find as much happiness with Alisa as I've found with your mother. All the hashish in the world can't replace the comfort of a woman who loves you," said the old Prince with a wink. "I think you will not be frequenting the Kirgiz night cafés so often, now, eh, my boy?"

"No, Father, most assuredly not." Nikki laughed softly.

.   .   .

Several days later Alisa, feeling quite strong again, was sitting up in the gilded bed, holding her large, healthy son and cooing into the pale blue eyes already full of golden highlights. Nikki came into the room and marveled at the beauty of the scene—Alisa, her rosy complexion restored, playing with his fine, robust son. His child; immortality in his image; his mark left on the world.

Motioning for the maid to take the baby away, Nikki walked over to Alisa and seated himself on the bed. "Don't you want to hold your son?" Alisa asked.

"My dear, I've done all the holding of babies I intend to this day. Katelina insisted we take Sasha on our silver platter rides down the stairs, so early this morning we spent most of an hour exhibiting this delightful occupation to the youngest member of our family. I held Sasha in one arm, Katelina sat between my legs and we sailed down the marble stairs amid squeals of excitement from that hellion of a daughter we have."

"Good Lord!" Alisa's eyes opened in alarm. "Sasha's too young!"

"Indeed, Madame, I must agree," Nikki rejoined, eyes twinkling, "for after the third ride, he promptly fell asleep in my arms and missed the next four trips." His eyes softened. "You look very lovely this morning."

"Thank you, and thank you for staying at my bedside for so many days. Rakeli informed me that you were very solicitous," Alisa said teasingly, feeling giddy, tremulously joyful.

"Well, I hope, Madame, I know my duty," Nikki replied in mock dismay. And then he said seriously, "I'd like to talk to you."

Alisa's heart sank. Now that she was out of danger, perhaps he would no longer feel any concern for her. She lay back against her pillows, prepared for the worst. "Yes, Nikki," she said fearfully.

"As soon as you are recovered sufficiently, I'll have you taken out into the country. I have a great desire for my children to be reared away from the dirt and bustle of the city."

So that's how he's going to manage, Alisa thought bitterly. She remembered his promise to stay home every night with her. He wouldn't have to break his promise this way. She'd be out of the way and he could come and go as he pleased.

"I shan't do it! I won't stay in the country!" Alisa replied defiantly. Already her mind was racing to find alternatives. Prince Mikhail and Kaisa-leena would understand. Perhaps divorce, freedom for both of them, was the only answer. But now she felt too tired to care. Her defiance slowly died.

"Perhaps you could be persuaded to stay if I were to accompany you. You see, quite unaccountably, I have developed an overwhelming penchant for country air."

Alisa's tired glance lifted swiftly, glimpsing Nikki's merry eyes and smile, and suddenly she felt blissfully happy.

Nikki clasped both her hands in his and, holding them in his sure, strong grip, said gently, as he looked into her dark violet eyes, "And in addition, I'm unfashionably besotted with the woman I married." Alisa put up her arms in an open, childlike gesture of need. Nikki enfolded her in his arms.

"We will be happy, you and I. I'll see to that."

"Yes," Alisa murmured softly as Nikki bent to kiss her tempting lips, "you've always been able to see to that."

As Nikki lifted his mouth from hers, Alisa softly queried, "Nikki, could I ask something of you?"

"Of course, love," he whispered huskily, nibbling at her ear.

"Would you consider giving up such mistresses as Sophie, who are constantly in company with us? I never know what to say to them and feel so foolish and awkward." It was half statement, half question.

He paused for a moment, contemplating a lie, but he couldn't dissemble after all, and having lived a life renowned for the uniqueness of his depravities, he didn't want to be forced into a posture he could in no way carry off.

"I will forswear one day at a time, I promise you that."

With a mischievous glance Alisa murmured, "And I, my Prince, can go my own road too, then? It's the sophisticated fashion. We will both discreetly look away on occasion."

Nikki threw back his head and laughed.

"You damned impertinent minx. You still don't know your place. Will you never learn submission and duty? Remember, I know how to guard my own. My God, woman." He grinned. "I suppose we shall bicker and scrap incessantly and be at each other's throats from morning to night."

"I suppose so, my Prince," Alisa replied, flashing a teasing look up through heavy lashes, "but it *does* keep your mélancholy at bay, and I *do so* enjoy the making up."

Epilogue

An elegant chapel was constructed at Mon Plaisir, and when Alisa questioned the enterprise, Nikki sheepishly explained that he had promised to erect the church if God spared her life during Sasha's birth.

"Good Lord, who will use it except the servants?" she asked, incredulous, but a tiny glow of pleasure was lit somewhere within her heart at the sentiment.

True. It wouldn't be used often except by the servants. But occasionally, he knew, he would enter the holy sanctuary alone, and alone give thanks that the woman he adored was still with him—in marriage and in love.

The Prince did indeed fill his nursery, not by force, as he had once threatened, but rather with the full acquiescence of his affectionate wife, who assured him that all births were not as difficult as Sasha's. A nursery wing was added by necessity after their third child was born, and Prince Kuzan was often known to remark that he quite heartily approved of the concept of filial piety, and was doing his damnedest to satisfy his father's desire for heirs.

Nikki also admired the old Persian saying: Three things are most pleasing in the eyes of God: to conceive a child, to plant a tree, and to write a book. Someday, he said, he would consider moving on to subjects two and three.

Nikki appeared in town infrequently, and on those sporadic occasions he was usually accompanied by his family. During these visits he proudly displayed his beautiful and growing children, and the pink marble palace resounded with their noise and activities. His clubs would see him rarely, and to other women he was to all practical purposes lost forever. They would repine and cast soft sighs after the tall, handsome Prince, but he very happily ignored them and found his satisfaction and contentment in the company of his beautiful wife and enchanting children.

As their firstborn son Sasha grew to manhood, the boy showed a marked affinity to embrace the same dissipated life once enjoyed by his father.

"Sometimes I think you positively encourage Sasha's debauchery, condoning any hellish scheme he concocts, overlooking the most blatant escapades," Alisa would occasionally remark testily to the Prince.

"Now, dear, let the boy have his head."

"Yes, that was always your maxim, you lecher, and look what happens. You know," she said darkly, "when I discovered the younger children's governess in bed with Sasha, he was scarce fourteen."

"I know, dear," Nikki soothed placatingly, "but that didn't happen again. Sasha, no doubt, took your motherly advice to heart."

After that indiscretion, Nikki had taken his reckless son aside and warned him about too blatantly offending his mama. "I'll spare you my advice which I conceive you will in no part accept at this youthful stage, and only recommend, for the sake of my domestic tranquility, my boy, that perhaps the summerhouse on the point by the lake would be more discreet."

And so the boy went on, but that's another story.

Notes

1. The remark concerning the Elector of Saxony was, needless to say, not meant literally, for Prince N. Kuzan had some way to go on that score. Augustus the Strong, Elector of Saxony, was aptly named, since he had the distinction of siring 354 illegitimate children. (page 15)

2. The art of tracking wild animals by their footprints was brought to perfection in Russia by a certain tracker known by the name of Lukash—Big Luke—whose methods were quickly adopted by others, so that presently all professional trackers came to be known as Lukash, plural Lukashee. The original Lukash was in the employment of Polovtseff. (page 37)

3. Owing to the frequent severe attacks of asthma to which Alexander II was subject, he rather dreaded going to bed at all, and when he was suffering from this chronic complaint, he would remain at work at his desk all night, keeping himself stimulated, although this is denied by the people in his immediate entourage, by occasional sips of champagne; Clicquot being his favorite brand. A shower-bath in the morning would suffice to freshen him up. (page 44)

4. Alexander II became enamored of Princess Catherine Dolgorouky and made her leave the Smolny Institute (a fashionable finishing school for patrician young ladies) at the age of sixteen, before she had completed her studies. She went to live with her eldest brother, Prince Michael Dolgorouky, to whom Alexander II presented a very beautiful house on the Quai des Anglais. The ground floor was occupied by Princess Catherine, who had her own domestics and carriages. (page 68)

5. The Amber Room is encrusted with exceptionally fine amber. Originally the room was arranged by the architect Schlueter for the Prussian King Frederick I. Peter the Great admired the room on one of his journeys and Frederick agreed to exchange it for fifty Russian soldiers over 6'7" for a special guard troop. (page 122)

6. Prince Mikhail Kuzan fell in love with the young Gypsy. The traditions of the tribe are strict. If a girl has a love affair, even if it be with a Prince, she must set up an establishment. The ceremony of marriage is not complicated. There is no need of priest or registrar. Any man who takes a Tzigane must obtain the consent of the chief of the tribe and declare that he intends to live with her maritally; further, he must pay a ransom to the chorus, for he deprives it of an artist bringing in a good profit. Prince Mikhail, after a

whirlwind courtship of five days, submitted to all the demands of the Tzigane regulations and paid the high ransom, for every rate is doubled for Princes, especially love ransoms. (page 138)

7. Cora Pearl, the daughter of a humble London music master, in spite of her coarse features and vulgar tongue, and due to her lovely body, rose to the rarefied heights of the highest paid courtesans in the Empire of Napoleon III. (Sums such as 5,000 francs, which was equivalent to 200 English pounds or about 1,000 American dollars, were not unheard of for twelve hours of her company.) Prince Gortchakoff described Cora Pearl as "the acme of sensual delights." A journalist of the day wrote of her "almost superhuman knowledge of the art of love" while M. Kracauer, in his biography of Offenbach, says, "she was able to keep in the front rank, because of her inordinate talent for voluptuous eccentricities." (page 151)

8. Sterlet was the famous luxury brought to Petersburg from the Volga, and the Black and Caspian Seas. Even in winter they were transported alive and shown swimming to the guests as they passed through the hall at a dinner party; and when they are ready for the fish (the third course in Russia) they are cooked. In winter they cost from ten to fifteen dollars apiece (c. 1850), which makes a dinner an expensive affair, as every guest has a fish. (page 192)

9. This is not an original thought, as you can see, but I find this charming sentiment appealing for its universality, both encompassing and traversing the ages. The original quote from Harriette Wilson's Memoirs follows: (Harriette Wilson, by the way, was one of the high-class courtesans of early Regency England)—Lord Ebrington to H. Wilson c. 1810:

Nothing can be so gratifying and delightful to my feelings, as the idea of having inspired a fine woman with a strong irresistible desire to make me her lover, whenever the desire is not a general one. I remember having once made the acquaintance of a woman who was greatly to my taste, and who, as I almost fancied, was disposed to favour me in return. After much difficulty I obtained her consent to indulge me with a private meeting and she agreed to come into my chariot, in which I took her up at the end of a retired lane at the back of her father's house. She was a young widow. We were scarcely seated, when her very natural frank and flattering exclamation of "Oh how very happy I am, to find myself at last here alone with you," produced such a pleasant effect on me that I have never forgotten it. (page 202)

10. Although it was not difficult to obtain a divorce in Russia, witnesses were needed to attest on oath and in the presence of the priest that either husband or wife was unfaithful. This was very easy as far as gentlemen were concerned for all of them were unfaithful, but it was different in regard to ladies.

An example of the Emperor's favors:

Prince Bariatinsky did not succeed in obtaining his divorce because his wife, Lydia, had been prudent enough to remain faithful. But for highly placed nobles, in moments of insuperable difficulty, there was always recourse to the Emperor.

On the cover of the file case presented to him, the Emperor, without examining or caring what the documents contained, wrote as a favor to the Prince, the words "Please accelerate."

Two days later a gentleman asked Lydia Bariatinsky

whether she had noticed her husband with his wife at the theater.

"What wife?" the Princess asked.

"The wife your ex-husband Prince Bariatinsky has married," he answered.

"How can that be since I won't give him a divorce?" The next morning Lydia Bariatinsky learned that her husband had obtained his divorce in 48 hours, thanks to the Emperor's words, Please accelerate, and that the Prince was already married again. (page 227)

11. When Alexander II sent for his son Vladimir and informed him that a Princess of Mecklenburg-Schwerin had fallen in love with him and that he, the Emperor, wished his son to marry and settle down, the handsomest of Alexander II's sons is reported to have remarked, "Poor girl!" Upon which the Emperor indignantly inquired what he meant by that exclamation and received this reply, "What sort of a husband shall I make, Sire? I am drunk every night, and cure the headache of the next morning by getting drunk again." (page 236)

About the Author

Susan Johnson, award-winning author of ten previous novels, lives in the country near North Branch, Minnesota. A former art historian, she considers the life of a writer the best of all possible worlds.

Researching her novels takes her to past and distant places, and bringing characters to life allows her imagination full rein, while the creative process offers occasional fascinating glimpses into complicated machinery of the mind.

But perhaps most important . . . writing stories is fun.

Indulge yourself with
PURE SIN
a new novel of sizzling seduction and
dangerous pleasures
from Susan Johnson,
the mistress of erotic historical romance.
Coming soon from Bantam Books

Here's a peek at this dazzling novel. . . .

Virginia City, Montana, April 1867

She met Adam Serre on the night his wife left him.

He walked into Judge Parkman's foyer as she was handing her wrap to a servant, and they nodded and smiled at each other.

"Pleasant weather for April," he said as they approached the bunting-draped entrance to the ballroom together. He smiled again, a casual, transient smile.

"Is the temperature unusual?" Flora glanced up only briefly, intent on adjusting the length of her white kid glove on her upper arm.

Adam shrugged, his broad shoulders barely moving beneath his elegantly cut evening coat. His gaze was on the crowded ballroom visible through the decorated portal, which was patriotically swathed in red, white, and blue in honor of their host's new appointment to the federal bench. "It's been an early spring," he said, searching for his host in the glittering assemblage. "But then the Chinook winds are unpredictable."

Both were curiously unaware of each other. Adam, for whom the previous few hours had been volatile, was still distracted. Flora Bonham, only recently arrived in Virginia City after a long journey from London, was looking forward to seeing her father.

They were both late for the judge's celebration party.

But the sudden hush that descended on the ballroom as they appeared in the doorway had nothing to do with their tardy arrival.

"He actually came!"

"Good God, he's with a woman!"

"*Who's* the woman?"

An impassioned buzz of astonishment and conjecture exploded after the first shocked silence, and Lady Flora Bonham, only child of the noted archaeologist Viscount Haldane, wondered for a moment if she'd left her dress undone and some immodest portion of her anatomy was exposed before the expectant throng.

But after a moment of panic, she noticed all the guests' gazes were focused not on herself but rather on her companion, and she looked up to discern the cause of such avid fascination.

The man was incredibly handsome, she instantly noticed, with a splendid, classic bone structure and dark, sensual eyes that held a tempting touch of wildness. But before any further appraisal flashed through her mind, he bowed to her, a graceful, fleeting movement, said, "Excuse me," and walked away.

Almost immediately she caught sight of her father advancing toward her, a warm smile on his face, his arms out in welcome. Her mouth curved into an answering smile and she moved into her father's embrace.

Two minutes had passed.

Perhaps less.

It was the first time she ever saw Adam.

"You look wonderful," George Bonham said as he held his daughter at arm's length, the brilliant blue of his eyes taking in Flora's radiant beauty. "Apparently the rough ride from Fort Benson caused you no harm."

"Really, Papa," she admonished. "After all the outback country we've lived in, Montana Territory is very civilized. We had to walk only a dozen times to lighten the stage through the deepest mud, the river crossings were uneventful, and the driver was moderately sober. After a hot bath at the hotel, I feel perfectly rested."

He grinned at her. "It's good to have you back. Let me introduce you; I've met most everyone in the last months. Our host, the judge, is over there," he went on, gesturing. "Come now, let me show you off."

But Flora noticed as they joined a group nearby and greetings were exchanged that the man who'd entered the ballroom with her continued to elicit extraordinary interest. Every guest seemed alert to his movements as he crossed the polished expanse of Italian parquet flooring.

No one had expected Adam to appear tonight.

And as he strode toward his host, greeting those he passed with a casual word, a smile, a sketchy bow for old Mrs. Alworth, whose mouth was half-open in astonishment, a flurry of excited comment swirled through the room.

"His wife left him today."

"Probably with good reason."

"Rumor has it she ran off with Baron Lacretelle."

"A mutual parting then. Adam has dozens of lovers."

"He's a cool one to show up tonight as though nothing untoward had happened in his life," an older man near Flora remarked.

"It's his Indian blood," a young lady standing beside Flora whispered, her gaze traveling down Adam's lean, muscled form, her voice touched with a piquant excitement. "They never show their feelings."

He looked as though he were showing his feelings now, Flora reflected, watching the animated conversation between their host and the man who was attracting so much attention. The bronze-skinned man smiled often as he conversed and then he suddenly laughed. She felt an odd, immediate reaction to his pleasure, as though his cheer were beguiling even from a distance.

"Who is he?" Flora asked, struck by his presence.

The woman at her side answered without taking her eyes from the handsome, long-haired man. "Adam Serre, comte de Chastellux. A half-breed," she softly added, his exotic bloodlines clearly of interest to her. "He's even *more* available," the petite blonde murmured, "now that his wife has left him."

"Available?" Did she mean marriage? Never sure of female insinuation since her own conversation tended to be direct, she made a polite inquiry.

"You *know* . . ." the pretty blonde declared, turning to wink at Flora. "Just look at him." And her sigh was one of many—surreptitious and overt—that followed in the wake of Adam's progress that evening.

Flora was introduced to him much later, after dinner, after a string quartet had begun playing for those who wished to dance. When Judge Parkman said, "Adam, I'd like you to meet George Bonham's daughter. Flora Bonham, Adam Serre," she found herself uncharacteristically discomposed by the stark immediacy of his presence. And her voice when she spoke was briefly touched with a small tremor.

"How do you do, Mr. Serre." Her gaze rose to meet his and her breath caught in her throat for a moment. His beauty at close range struck her powerfully, as if she were imperiled by such flagrant handsomeness.

"I'm doing well, thank you," he said, his smile open and natural, the buzz of gossip that evening concerning his marriage apparently not affecting him. "Is this your first visit to Montana?"

"Yes," she replied, her composure restored. He seemed unaware of his good looks. "Montana's very much like the grasslands of Manchuria. Beautiful, filled with sky, rimmed with distant mountains."

The viscount's daughter was quite spectacular, Adam thought with a connoisseur's eye, her mass of auburn hair so lush and rich and heavy, it almost seemed alive, her face dominated by enormous dark eyes, her skin golden, sun-kissed from so much time out-of-doors. He knew of her travels with her father; George Bonham had visited several of the Absarokee camps in the past months. "And good horse country too," he replied, "like the steppes of Asia. Did you see Lake Baikal?"

"Have you been there?" Animation instantly infused her voice.

"Many years ago."

"When?"

He thought for a moment. "I'd just finished university, so it must have been 1859."

"No!"

"When were you there?" He found the excitement in her eyes intriguing.

"June."

"We set up camp on the west shore near Krestovka. Don't tell me you were in the village and we missed you."

"We were a few miles away, at Listvyanka."

They both smiled like long-lost friends. "Would you care for some champagne?" Adam asked. "And then tell me what you liked most about Listvyanka. The church, the Countess Armechev, or the ponies?"

They agreed the church was a veritable jewel of provincial architecture. It was natural the artistic countess would have appealed more to a young man susceptible to female beauty than to a seventeen-year-old girl obsessed with horses. And the native ponies elicited a lengthy discussion on Asian bloodstock. They found in the course of the evening that they'd both been to Istanbul, the Holy Land, newly opened Japan, the upper reaches of the Sahara, Petersburg in the season. But always at different times.

"A shame we didn't ever meet," Adam said with a seductive smile, his responses automatic with beautiful women. "Good conversation is rare."

She didn't suppose most women were interested exclusively in his conversation, Flora thought, as she took in the full splendor of his dark beauty and power. Even lounging in a chair, his legs casually crossed at the ankles, he presented an irresistible image of brute strength. And she'd heard enough rumor in the course of the evening to understand he enjoyed women—nonconversationally. "As rare as marital fidelity, no doubt."

His brows rose fractionally. "No one's had the nerve to so bluntly allude to my marriage. Are you speaking of Isolde's or my infidelities?" His grin was boyish.

"Papa says you're French."

"Does that give me motive or excuse? And I'm only half-French, as you no doubt know, so I may have less excuse than Isolde. She apparently prefers Baron Lacretelle's properties in Paris and Nice to my dwelling here."

"No heartbroken melancholy?"

He laughed. "Obviously you haven't met Isolde."

"Why did you marry, then?"

He gazed at her for a moment over the rim of the goblet he'd raised to his lips. "You can't be that naive," he softly said, then quickly drained the glass.

"Forgive me. I'm sure it's none of my business."

"I'm sure it's not." The warmth had gone from his voice and his eyes. Remembering the reason he'd married Isolde always brought a sense of chaffing anger.

"I haven't felt so gauche in years," Flora said, her voice almost a whisper.

His black eyes held hers, their vital energy almost mesmerizing, then his look went shuttered and his grin reappeared. "How could you know, darling? About the idiosyncracies of my marriage. Tell me now about your first sight of Hagia Sophia."

"It was early in the morning," she began, relieved he'd so graciously overlooked her faux pas. "The sun had just begun to appear over the crest of the—"

"Come dance with me," Adam abruptly said, leaning forward in his chair. "This waltz is a favorite of mine," he went on, as though they hadn't been discussing something completely different. Reaching over, he took her hands in his. "And I've been wanting to"—his hesitation was minute as he discarded the inappropriate verb—"hold you." He grinned. "You see how blandly circumspect my choice of words is." Rising, he gently pulled her to her feet. "Considering the newest scandal in my life, I'm on my best behavior tonight."

"But then scandals don't bother me." She was standing very close to him, her hands still twined in his.

His fine mouth, only inches away, was graced with a genial smile—and touched with a small, heated playfulness. "I thought they might not."

"When one travels as I do, one becomes inured to other people's notions of nicety." Her bare shoulder lifted briefly, ruffling the limpid lace on her décolletage. He noticed both: the pale satin of her skin and how the swell of her bosom slipped tantalizingly beneath the delicate lace. "If I worried about scandal," she murmured with a small smile, "I'd never set foot outside England."

"And you do."

"Oh yes," she whispered. And for a moment both were speaking of something quite different.

"You're not helping," he said very low. "I've sworn off women for the moment."

"To let your wounds heal?"

"Nothing so poetical." His quirked grin reminded her of a teasing young boy. "I'm reassessing my priorities."

"Did I arrive in Virginia City too late then?"

"Too late?" One dark brow arched infinitesimally.

"To take advantage of your former priorities."

He took a deep breath because he was already perversely aware of the closeness of her heated body, of the heady fragrance of her skin. "You're a bold young lady, Miss Bonham."

"I'm twenty-five years old, Mr. Serre, and independent."

"I'm not sure after marriage to Isolde that I'm interested in any more willful aristocratic ladies."

"Perhaps I could change your mind."

He thoughtfully gazed down at her, and then the faintest smile lifted the graceful curve of his mouth. "Perhaps you could."

"How kind of you," Flora softly replied in teasing rejoinder.

"Believe me, kindness is the last thing on my mind at the moment, but people are beginning to stare. It wouldn't do to besmirch your reputation on your first night in Virginia City. And I like this waltz, so allow me the honor of your first dance in Montana." He was avoiding temptation as he swung her out onto the floor, cutting short a conversation that had turned too provocative.

But he found dancing with the alluring Miss Bonham only heightened his sensational response to her, and everyone in the room noticed as well. A palpable heat emanated from the beautiful couple twirling across the floor, and people turned to watch as they passed.

She wore violet tulle elaborately ornamented with moss green ribbon and ivory lace, a dazzling counterpoint to her pale skin and auburn tresses, to the severe black of Adam's evening clothes. The diaphanous froth of her gown and her lush femininity were a counterpoint as well to Adam's harsh masculinity. And later as they danced, when a silky tendril of Flora's hair fell loose from the diamond pins holding her coiffure in place, Adam bent his head and lightly blew it aside. At his intimate, audacious gesture, simultaneous indrawn breaths from scores of wide-eyed guests seemed to vibrate through the room.

And a molten heat flared through Flora's senses.

Even as she shut her eyes against the exquisite sensation of his warm breath on her neck, she felt his arm tighten around her waist, as if he too were susceptible to urgent desire. And she understood suddenly why women pursued him. Beyond his obvious beauty he offered a wild, reckless excitement; oblivious to exacting decorum and every watchful eye, he did as he pleased. Heedless, rash, direct. And she felt him hard against her stomach.

She was far too beautiful, too impetuously unconstrained, and even as he moved against her in the dance, his arousal pressed into her yielding body, he struggled to retain a pragmatic grip on reality. Only short hours ago he'd vowed to give wide berth to pampered patrician women. But she's not precisely pampered, his libido pointed out, allowing him the rationalization he craved. She's lived in tents in far corners of the world most of her life. There. It's all right, his heated voice of unreason said. And as his erection swelled, he found himself surveying possible discreet exits from the room. "Can you leave?" he bluntly asked, deliberately omitting the familiar seductive words. He didn't wish to be so aroused by her. His irrational, heated desire disturbed him; he would prefer that she refuse.

"For a short time," she said, as bluntly as he.

And for a moment his surprise showed.

"If it would ease your discomfort," Flora softy said, her dark eyes touched with violet squarely meeting his, "I could seduce you."

"Do you do this often then?" His voice was cool, but his grip tightened at her waist.

"Never." The brush of her thighs against his as they turned in graceful slow loops around the floor seemed patent contradiction.

"Should I be honored?" A certain insolence colored his words.

"If you wish," she tranquilly said. "I prefer the concept of mutual pleasure."

His reaction to her last two words was immediate. She could feel it. "Could I interest you in a view of Judge Parkman's new garden?" Adam brusquely queried, turning them toward the terrace doorway.

"It depends on the view."

His head snapped around from a swift survey of an exit route and he found her smiling up at him.

"I'm serious," she said, but a teasing impudence gleamed from her eyes.

"I'll see what I can do," he gruffly declared. "Do you need a wrap?" A half-remembered politesse.

"How chivalrous," she said with a smile, "but I think we're both comfortably warm. It must be the dancing."

"Or *uncomfortably* warm," he muttered, gazing down at her with heated black eyes. "And dancing has nothing to do with it." They'd reached the border of the dance floor, and with an edginess Flora found equally tantalizing and disturbing, he wordlessly guided them around two potted palms to the terrace door, pushed it open, and pulled her outside.

He stood on the flagstone, his hand firmly gripping hers, scrutinizing the garden that was almost bare of flowers this early in the spring, the foliage of hedge and bower only half-formed leaves. A decision apparently made, Adam turned toward the back of the stone mansion, moving less swiftly so Flora could keep up. Then, leaving the terrace, he walked across the carefully raked gravel of the back drive into the dusky entrance to the carriage house. With the large double doors open, the spring moonlight illuminated the front third of the interior, which Adam carefully noted before moving further back into the shadows.

He seemed to know where he was going, for he strode surefooted to a landau set against the wall, abruptly swept her into his arms, and deposited her in a tumble of violet tulle on the wide, satin-upholstered seat.

"Should we put the top up?" Flora murmured, stripping off one long kidskin glove as Adam unlatched the lacquered door and stepped into the open carriage.

He shook his head. He'd selected the landau for its

roominess and open top; he'd made love in enough closed carriages to know the merits of space. "Will your father look for you?" he asked as he seated himself beside her and slid into a comfortable sprawl.

"Not since I turned eighteen and came into my own fortune." Her smile was pale in the dim light.

"You're very unusual," he softly said, grazing at her.

"You are too. You must know that." She was unbuttoning her second glove at the wrist.

"One's constantly reminded," he drily said, stretching his arms above his head, then relaxing again. "Acting Governor Meagher and his drunken volunteers are currently dividing their time between Con Owen's saloon and their inebriated pursuit of Indians." He shifted his posture slightly. Restless, he was questioning the wisdom of his libido-driven actions. "My clan is trying to stay out of their way."

"You sound resigned."

"Armed and alert actually. It's safer."

"Are you in Virginia City often?"

He shook his head again. "I prefer my ranch, but Judge Parkman's a friend." He sighed. "And of course Isolde was added reason."

"Has she truly gone off with the baron?" Flora's voice was hesitant as she slid the second glove free.

He didn't answer for several moments, and Flora thought she'd overstepped politeness again. Then he laughed, a warm intimate sound in the darkness. "I certainly hope so." He turned to her and, raising his hand, touched her cheek lightly with the back of his fingers. "This is a mistake. You shouldn't be here. I shouldn't be here. Our garden promenade wasn't a sensible idea. We should go back inside."

"We should." Her voice was hushed, her mouth only

inches away as she let her gloves slip through her fingers to the carriage floor.

He drew in a deep breath of restraint. "Lord, you're tempting. . . ." Her skin glowed in the shrouded moonlight. Her shoulders, unsheathed arms, the swell of her breasts above the low neckline of her gown seduced the eye; the opulent jasmine scent of her perfume enticed his senses.

"Kiss me," she whispered, because she couldn't help herself any more than he.

"No." But he didn't move.

"Then I'll kiss you."

The Very Best in Historical Women's Fiction

Rosanne Bittner

_____	28599-8	EMBERS OF THE HEART .. $5.99/$6.99 in Canada
_____	28319-7	MONTANA WOMAN $4.99/5.99
_____	29033-9	IN THE SHADOW OF THE MOUNTAINS $5.50/6.99
_____	29014-2	SONG OF THE WOLF $4.99/5.99
_____	29015-0	THUNDER ON THE PLAINS $5.99/6.99
_____	29807-0	OUTLAW HEARTS $5.99/6.99

Iris Johansen

_____	28855-5	THE WIND DANCER $4.95/5.95
_____	29032-0	STORM WINDS $4.99/5.99
_____	29244-7	REAP THE WIND $4.99/5.99
_____	29604-3	THE GOLDEN BARBARIAN $4.99/5.99
_____	29944-1	THE MAGNIFICENT ROGUE $5.99/6.99
_____	29968-9	THE TIGER PRINCE $5.50/6.50
_____	29871-0	LAST BRIDGE HOME $4.50/5.50

Susan Johnson

_____	29125-4	FORBIDDEN $4.99/5.99
_____	29312-5	SINFUL $4.99/5.99
_____	29957-3	BLAZE..$5.50/6.50
_____	29959-X	SILVER FLAME $5.50/6.50
_____	29955-7	OUTLAW...$5.50/6.50

Teresa Medeiros

_____	29407-5	HEATHER AND VELVET $4.99/5.99
_____	29409-1	ONCE AN ANGEL................................$5.50/6.50
_____	29408-3	A WHISPER OF ROSES $5.50/6.50

Patricia Potter

_____	29070-3	LIGHTNING $4.99/5.99
_____	29071-1	LAWLESS $4.99/5.99
_____	29069-X	RAINBOW $5.50/6.50
_____	56199-5	RENEGADE $5.50/6.50
_____	56225-8	NOTORIOUS...$5.50/6.50

Deborah Smith

_____	28759-1	THE BELOVED WOMAN $4.50/5.50
_____	29092-4	FOLLOW THE SUN $4.99/5.99
_____	29107-6	MIRACLE $4.50/5.50
_____	29690-6	BLUE WILLOW $5.50/6.50

Ask for these titles at your bookstore or use this page to order.

Please send me the books I have checked above. I am enclosing $ _____ (add $2.50 to cover postage and handling). Send check or money order, no cash or C. O. D.'s please.

Mr./ Ms. _____

Address _____

City/ State/ Zip _____

Send order to: Bantam Books, Dept. FN 17, 2451 S. Wolf Road, Des Plaines, IL 60018
Please allow four to six weeks for delivery.
Prices and availability subject to change without notice.   FN 17 - 12/93